A TEXT BOOK OF
ENGINEERING METALLURGY

With Large Number of Multiple Choice Questions (MCQs)

For
Semester - II

I0681471

SECOND YEAR DEGREE COURSE IN MECHANICAL ENGINEERING AND AUTOMOBILE ENGINEERING (MECHANICAL GROUP)

As Per New Revised Syllabus of University of Pune, (Pattern 2012)

ADVAIT S. GHOLAP
M. Tech. (Mate. Tech.), I.I.T. Bombay,
Formerly, Lecturer in Metallurgy,
Maharashtra Institute of Technology,
PUNE - 411 038.

DR. MILIND S. KULKARNI
M. Tech. (Mate. Tech.), I.I.T. Bombay
Ph. D. (Texas A & M University, College Station U.S.A.)
Formerly, Lecturer in Metallurgy,
Maharashtra Institute of Technology,
PUNE - 411 038.

S. S. GHORPADE
B.E. (Mech.), M.E. (Mech.)
Assistant Professor,
Sinhgad Academy of Engineering
Kondhwa (Bk.), Pune.

NIRALI PRAKASHAN
Advancement of knowledge

N2852

ENGINEERING METALLURGY (SE MECH/AUTO)   ISBN 978-93-83750-93-3

First Edition : January 2014

© : **Authors**

Published By :
NIRALI PRAKASHAN
Abhyudaya Pragati, 1312, Shivaji Nagar,
Off J.M. Road, PUNE – 411005
Tel - (020) 25512336/37/39, Fax - (020) 25511379
Email : niralipune@pragationline.com

DISTRIBUTION CENTRES

PUNE

Nirali Prakashan
119, Budhwar Peth, Jogeshwari Mandir Lane
Pune 411002, Maharashtra
Tel : (020) 2445 2044, 66022708, Fax : (020) 2445 1538
Email : niralilocal@pragationline.com

Nirali Prakashan
S. No. 28/25, Dhyari,
Near Pari Company, Pune 411041
Tel : (020) 24690204Fax : (020) 24690316
Email : bookorder@pragationline.com

MUMBAI

Nirali Prakashan
385, S.V.P. Road, Rasdhara Co-op. Hsg. Society Ltd.,
Girgaum, Mumbai 400004, Maharashtra
Tel : (022) 2385 6339 / 2386 9976, Fax : (022) 2386 9976
Email : niralimumbai@pragationline.com

DISTRIBUTION BRANCHES

NAGPUR
Pratibha Book Distributors
Above Maratha Mandir, Shop No. 3, First Floor,
Rani Jhanshi Square, Sitabuldi, Nagpur 440012,
Maharashtra, Tel : (0712) 254 7129

BENGALURU
Pragati Book House
House No. 1, Sanjeevappa Lane, Avenue Road Cross,
Opp. Rice Church, Bengaluru – 560002.
Tel : (080) 64513344, 64513355,
Mob : 9880582331, 9845021552
Email:bharatsavla@yahoo.com

JALGAON
Nirali Prakashan
34, V. V. Golani Market, Navi Peth, Jalgaon 425001,
Maharashtra, Tel : (0257) 222 0395
Mob : 94234 91860

KOLHAPUR
Nirali Prakashan
New Mahadvar Road,
Kedar Plaza, 1st Floor Opp. IDBI Bank
Kolhapur 416 012, Maharashtra. Mob : 9850046155

CHENNAI
Pragati Books
9/1, Montieth Road, Behind Taas Mahal, Egmore,
Chennai 600008 Tamil Nadu, Tel : (044) 6518 3535,
Mob : 94440 01782 / 98450 21552 / 98805 82331, Email : bharatsavla@yahoo.com

RETAIL OUTLETS
PUNE

Pragati Book Centre
157, Budhwar Peth, Opp. Ratan Talkies,
Pune 411002, Maharashtra
Tel : (020) 2445 8887 / 6602 2707, Fax : (020) 2445 8887

Pragati Book Centre
Amber Chamber, 28/A, Budhwar Peth,
Appa Balwant Chowk, Pune : 411002, Maharashtra,
Tel : (020) 20240335 / 66281669
Email : pbcpune@pragationline.com

Pragati Book Centre
676/B, Budhwar Peth, Opp. Jogeshwari Mandir,
Pune 411002, Maharashtra
Tel : (020) 6601 7784 / 6602 0855

PBC Book Sellers & Stationers
152, Budhwar Peth, Pune 411002, Maharashtra
Tel : (020) 2445 2254 / 6609 2463

MUMBAI
Pragati Book Corner
Indira Niwas, 111 - A, Bhavani Shankar Road, Dadar (W), Mumbai 400028, Maharashtra
Tel : (022) 2422 3526 / 6662 5254, Email : pbcmumbai@pragationline.com

www.pragationline.com   info@pragationline.com

Preface ...

It gives us an immense pleasure to present this text Book of **"Engineering Metallurgy"** for Second Year Degree Course in Mechanical/Automobile, Engineering students. The object of this book is to present the subject matter in the most precise, compact and in a lucid manner.

As per the policy of University of Pune, Engineering Syllabi is revised every five years. Last revision was in the year 2009. New revision is coming little earlier, as university has introduced **Online System of Examination** from year 2012.

As per the new system, the **Online Examination** (separate Phase-I and Phase-II) will be conduced based on first, second and third and fourth units. The **Online Examinations** will have objective types of questions with multiple choices. End semester examination will be based on all the six units and that will be conducted in traditional way.

We hereby, welcome the positive changes made in this present revision of syllabus. Equilibrium Diagrams and Metallurgical Concepts, Classification of Steels and Alloy Steels. Heat Treatment of Steel and Non-Ferrous Metal, Corrosion and it's Prevention, Cast Irons, Non Ferrous Metals and Alloys.

Authors have tried to introduce the subject to the average students, with a large number of solved examples. The subject matter has been developed in a logical and coherent manner with neat illustrations along with a fairly large number of Multiple Choice Questions (MCQs) and Exercises.

The main objectives of this text are :

- **To cover the basic principles of metallurgy.**
- **To develop a very good understanding of the subject matter.**
- **To give practice to solve the multiple choice questions in the subject.**

We are very much thankful to Shri. Dineshbhai Furia and Shri. Jignesh Furia of M/s Nirali Prakashan, Pune for giving a platform to provide good inputs the students community. We are grateful to Mr. Mallikarjun Munde, a Senior Manager for his endless efforts to make this book as best as it can be. We are also thankful to Mrs. Prachi Sawant and Mrs. Prajakta Shrimandilkar for their co-operation throughout the work.

Although every care has been taken to check mistakes, and errors, yet it is difficult to claim perfection. Any errors, mistakes and suggestions for the improvement of this book, brought to our notice will be thankfully acknowledged and incorporated in the next edition.

January 2014
Pune.

Authors

Syllabus ...

Unit I: Type of Equilibrium Diagrams & Metallurgical Concepts.

Related terms and their definitions : System, Phase, Variable, Component, Alloy, Solid solution, Hume Ruther's rule of solid solubility, Allotropy and polymorphism, Concept of solidification of pure metals & alloys, Nucleation : homogeneous and heterogeneous, Dendritic growth, supercooling, equiaxed and columnar grains, grain & grain boundary effect. Cooling curves, Plotting of Equilibrium diagrams, Lever rule, Coring, Eutectic system, Partial eutectic and eutectoid system. Non Equilibrium cooling and it's effects. Microscopy, specimen preparation, specimen mounting, electrolytic polishing, etching procedure and reagents, electrolytic etching. Macroscopy : sulphur printing, flow line observations.

Unit II: Classification of Steels And Alloy Steels.

Iron-iron carbide equilibrium diagram, critical temperatures, solidification and microstructure of slowly cooled steels, non-equilibrium cooling of steels, widmanstaten structure, structure & property relationship, classification and application of steels & alloy steels, specification of steels. Classification & Effect of alloying elements, examples of alloy steels, stainless steels, sensitization & weld decay of stainless steel, tool steels, heat treatment of high speed steel, special purpose steels with applications, superalloys.

Unit III: Heat- treatment of Steels & Non-Ferrous Metals.

Transformation products of Austenite, Time Temperature Transformation diagrams, critical cooling rate, continuous cooling transformation diagrams. Heat treatment of steels : Annealing, Normalising, Hardening & Tempering, quenching media, other treatments such as Martempering, Austempering, Patenting, Ausforming. Retention of austenite, effects of retained austenite. Elimination of retained austenite (Sub zero treatment). Secondary hardening, temper embrittlement, quench cracks, Hardenability & hardenability testing, Defects due to heat treatment and remedial measures. Classification of surface hardening treatments, Carburising, heat treatment after Carburizing, Nitriding, Carbo-nitriding, Flame hardening, and Induction hardening. Heat treatment of Non ferrous metals: Precipitation/ Age Hardening, Homogenization. Strengthening mechanisms: Refinement of grain size, cold working/strain hardening, solid solution strengthening, dispersion strengthening.

Unit IV: Corrosion and Its Prevention.

Mechanism of Corrosion, Classification of Corrosion: General, Pitting, Crevice, Intergranular, Stress corrosion & cracking .Velocity related corrosion: Erosion, Impingement, and Cavitations corrosion. Corrosion fatigue, Hydrogen Blistering. High temperature corrosion. Corrosion prevention methods: Inhibitors, Internal & External coating, Cathodic & Anodic protection, Use of special alloys, Control over temperature & velocity, Dehydration, Improvement in design/changes in design to prevent or control corrosion.

Unit V: Cast Irons

Classification, Manufacturing, Composition , Properties & applications of white C.I., Grey cast iron, malleable C.I., S.G. cast iron, chilled and alloy cast iron, effect of various parameters on structure and properties of cast irons. Specific applications such as machine tools, automobiles, pumps, valves etc.

Unit VI: Non Ferrous Metals & Alloys

Classification, Composition, Properties & applications of: Copper and Its alloys, Nickel and Its alloys, Aluminum and Its alloys, Titanium and Its alloys. Specific alloys: soldering & brazing alloy, Precipitation hardening alloys. Bearing materials and their applications.

❖❖❖

Contents ...

2. Classification of Steels and Alloys Steels   2.1 – 2.76

Steels

4. Corrosion and its Prevention 4.1 – 4.74

Chapter 1

TYPES OF EQULIBRIUM DIAGRAMS AND METALLURGICAL CONCEPTS

1.1 METALLURGY

Metallurgy deals with extraction of metals form their ores and application of these metals and their alloys for various purposes –

Metallurgy has three branches :

    (a) Chemical metallurgy.

    (b) Physical metallurgy.

    (c) Mechanical metallurgy.

Chemical metallurgy deals with extraction of metal from their ore. Dressing, grinding, crushing, reduction, concentration are some alloys of the processes involved in extraction of metals.

The structure and properties of metals and alloys are studied in physical metallurgy. It also includes metallography, mechanical testing, and heat treatment.

In mechanical metallurgy working and shaping of metals and alloys is studied. Some of processes involved are casting, forging, rolling, extrusion, drawing and powder metallurgy.

1.2 RELATED TERMS

1.2.1 System

* It is any part of space or matter, which is under observation.
* It is specified within boundaries and has certain variables such as pressure, temperature, composition etc.

1.2.2 Component

* It is part of matter present in the system which has distinct or separate chemical formula.

- In a vessel ice and water are present. This system has only one component because both ice and water have same chemical formula H_2O.

- Consider Cu-Al system. It contains compounds as CuAl and $CuAl_2$. Therefore it is binary or two component system.

1.2.3 Phase

- A homogeneous, physically distinct and mechanically separable part of a system is known as phase.

- Two or more miscible fluids form one phase while immiscible fluids form more than 1 phases.

1.2.4 Variable

- It is any measurable characteristic of a system such as – pressure, temperature, composition etc.

- Due to change in any variable, properties of the system also change.

1.2.5 Variance or Degree of Freedom

- It is defined as the minimum number of independent properties required to define or describe the system completely.

- For example, at triple point, all 3 phases of water are in equilibrium with each other. This is maintained at fixed set of properties. Therefore value of any property is not required to be known at triple point to describe the system. Thus, this system has zero variance or degree of freedom and is also called as non-variant or invariant system.

- When water is in equilibrium with vapour, either pressure or temperature is sufficient to describe the system. Hence degree of freedom is 1 or system is univariant

1.2.6 Phase Rule

- It is stated by J. Willard Gibbs in 1876 as, in the absence of gravity, electrical or magnetic forces and surface action, the number of degrees of freedom (F) of the system at equilibrium at given pressure and temperature is related to the number of components (C) and of phases (P) by the phase rule equation as –

$$F = C - P + 2$$

where F = degrees of freedom, C = number of components, P = number of phases.

- Number 2 is for temperature and pressure which are variables. Generally, for the metallurgical processes that are taking place under atmospheric conditions, pressure is fixed and only temperature is a variable. Therefore for such systems, Gibbs' phase rule is given as

$$F = C - P + 1$$

1.2.7 Allotropy

- Existence of metal in more than 1 type of lattice structure at various temperatures is called as allotropy or polymorphism.

- For example, at room temperature pure iron has BCC structure. on heating, at 910°C, it is changed to FCC. On further heating, at 1400°C it again changes to BCC. These are called as allotropic forms of iron.

1.3 SOLID SOLUTION: ALLOY

- A homogeneous mixture of two or more metals in solid state is known as a solid solution.

- To form a solid solution, two metals must be completely soluble in liquid as well as solid state.

- In solid solutions, the metal available in larger quantity is called as solvent while metal available in less quantity is called as solute. For example in steels, iron is solvent and carbon is solute.

1.3.1 Types of Solid Solutions

- Solid solutions can be classified as follows –
  a) Substitutional solid solution
     (i) Ordered substitutional solid solution
     (ii) Disordered substitutional solid solution
  b) Interstitial solid solution

1.4   SUBSTITUTIONAL SOLID SOLUTIONS

- When the solute and solvent atoms have roughly same size, then the solute atoms will occupy the lattice positions in the crystal lattice of the solvent atoms and replace them. This type of alloy is called as **'substitution solid solution'** [Fig. 1.1 (a) & (b)].

- For example, Cu-Ni, Au-Ag etc. In Au-Ag (Gold-Silver) System, the silver atoms substitute for gold atoms without changing the FCC structure of gold, and similarly gold atoms substitute for silver atoms in the FCC structure of silver.

1.4.1 Hume-Rothery Rules for Substitutional Solid Solutions

The formation of substitutional solid solutions is influenced by certain factors. These are known as Hume-Rothery rules and are briefly discussed below.

(a) Relative size factor : The solid solution can be formed easily with greater solubility of solute if the relative size factor i.e. difference in size of atomic radii of solute and solvent is less than 15%. If the relative size factor is above 15%, solid solution formation is limited.

Examples : Silver and lead have the relative size factor of about 20%, and thus the solubility of lead in solid silver is only about 1.5%. On the other hand, antimony and bismuth with relative size factor of about 7% are completely soluble in each other in all proportions.

(b) Crystal structure : Basically, to form a substitutional solid solution both the elements should have the same crystal structure, otherwise it is not possible to form this type of solid solution.

Examples : Cu-Ni, Au-Ag, form this type of solid solution, all of these elements have FCC structure. On the other hand, though antimony (rhombohedral) and aluminium (FCC) have a highly favourable size factor ($\sim2^{0}$/o), they have an extremely low solubility ($\sim$0.1%), due to different crystal structures.

(c) Chemical Affinity : Metals which have a least chemical affinity for each other tend to form solid solutions, and metals with greater affinity tend to form inter-metallic compounds. The ions of all metals are electro positive, some are more electropositive than others. Higher the difference in electro-positivity higher will be the affinity.

Examples : Cu-Ni, Au-Ag systems which have the least difference in electro-positivity have very low affinity and form solid solution in all proportions.

(d) Relative Valance: A metal of lower valance tends to dissolve more of a metal of higher valence than vice versa, under other favourable conditions.

Examples : In the Al-Ni alloy system (both FCC; size factor about 14%), nickel has a lower valence than aluminium, solid nickel dissolves about 5% Al, on the other hand, higher valence aluminium dissolves only about 0.04% Ni.

The above four rules formulated by Hume-Rothery, give the idea of solid solubility of one metal in another. Basically, relative size factor affectsthe solid solubility to a greater extent. When the relative size factor is favourable, then the other three factors decide the extent of solid solubility. The other three factors are usually favourable when two metals are very close to each other in the periodic table – like side by side in the same period (Ni-Cu) or one above the other in the same group (Ag-Au).

1.4.2 Ordered and Disordered Substitutional Solid Solutions

- The substitutional solid solutions are of 2 types ordered or disordered.
- In the ordered type, the atoms of the solute metal occupy certain fixed positions in the solvent metal [Fig. 1.1 (a)].
- In the disordered type the solute atoms occupy random positions in the solvent lattice [Fig. 1.1 (b)].
- The ordered types, also called super lattices, are generally hard and brittle, while the disordered type are tough and ductile, and preferred in engineering applications. In practice, most of the substitutional solid solutions are disordered type.

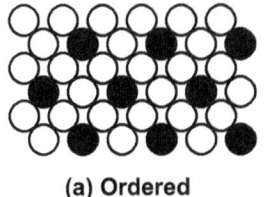 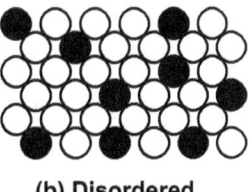

(a) Ordered   (b) Disordered

Fig. 1.1 : Substitutional solid solutions

- In certain alloys (like in Cu-Au, Fe-Al, Ni-Mn etc.) having disordered sequence, the atoms can be made to redistribute in a definite order at particular temperatures by slow cooling or heating. These effects are used wherever certain types of hard alloys are required.

1.5   INTERSTITIAL SOLID SOLUTIONS

- When atoms of small atomic radii occupy the spaces or interstices of the lattice structure of the larger solvent atoms, then they form **interstitial solid solutions (Fig. 1.2)**. Atoms with atomic radii less 1 Å (angstrom = 10^{-8} cm) tend to form this type of solid solutions. The elements like hydrogen, carbon, boron, nitrogen and oxygen are capable of forming interstitial solid solutions. The examples of this type of solid solutions are carbon in iron, nitrogen in iron etc.

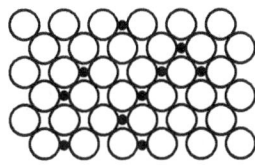

Fig. 1.2 : Interstitial solid solutions

- The solubility of interstitial solid solutions in limited and have less importance in engineering. However, carbon in iron and nitrogen in iron are exceptions, which contribute to heat treatment of steels and hardening effects. Thus, steel can be carburised or nitrided by diffusing carbon or nitrogen atoms into the interstices of iron atoms with FCC or BCC structure. The hydrogen embrittlerment phenomenon observed in many metals is a result of absorption of small hydrogen atoms into the interstices of the metals.

1.6 DIFFERENCE BETWEEN SUBSTITUTIONAL A INTERSTITIAL SOLID SOLUTIONS

- The important differences between substitutional and interstitial solid solutions are as follows :

(a) Atomic Position :

In substitutional solid solutions, the solvent atoms in the lattice are replaced by the solute atoms, while in interstitial solid solutions the solute atoms occupy the interstices (gaps between the atoms, i.e., inter-atomic spaces) in the lattice structure.

(b) Size of Atoms :

In substitutional solid solutions, the atoms of solvent and solute need to be of same size for the solid solubility to take place. The relative size factor of 7 to 15% is a favourable factor of good solid solubility. In interstitial types, the solute atoms must be very small (less than 1 Å), so that they can conveniently occupy the spaces between the solvent atoms. FCC structures have more spacious interstices as compared to BCC structures and hence solvent atoms with FCC structure have good solid solubility.

(c) Lattice Constant :

In forming a substitutional solid solution, the lattice constant can either increase or decrease depending upon the size of the solute atoms, while in an interstitial solid solution, the lattice constant of solvent always increases, since the solute atoms in between the solvent atoms contribute to the slight increase in the lattice constant.

(d) Solute location and stability :

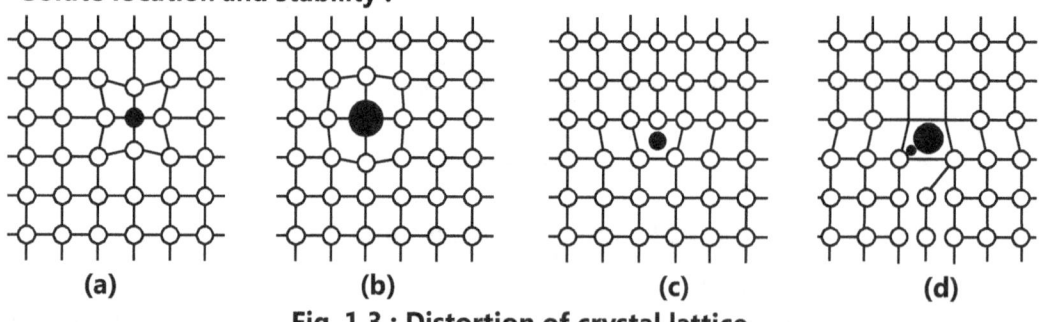

(a)   (b)   (c)   (d)

Fig. 1.3 : Distortion of crystal lattice

- In substitutional solid solutions, if solute atoms are smaller than solvent atoms, the lattice is compressed [Fig. 1.3 (a)]; and larger atoms occupy a place where the lattice is stretched [Fig. 1.3 (b)] In an interstitial solid solution, the solute atoms occupy positions in the stretched space under the edge of an extra plane [Fig. 1.3 (c)]. Also, interstitial atoms are more strongly held in the dislocations than the substitutional atoms [Fig. 1.3 (d)]. Thus, the lattice distortion with interstitial atoms is very less, which results in a stable solid solution as compared to substitutional solid solutions.

1.7 INTERMEDIATE PHASES OR COMPOUNDS

- Intermediate alloy phases are those phases, whose chemical compositions are intermediate between the two pure metals and generally have crystal structure different from those of base elements.

- These are formed in metals having widely divergent electrochemical properties, which are likely to combine to form a chemical compound, usually called as **intermetallic compound.**

- The phases formed between two extremes of substitutional solid solutions and intermetallic compound are collectively termed as **intermediate phases** and can also be termed as secondary solid solutions.

- The intermediate phases can be classified into three groups as below.

1.7.1 Intermetallic Compounds or Valency Compounds

- These are formed usually between chemically dissimilar metals based on the of chemical valence laws and hence the name valency compounds.

- These compounds have strong bonding (ionic or covalent), and show nonmetallic properties. They have poor ductility, poor electrical conductivity, with complex crystal structures.

- Fe_3C is an example of such an intermetallic compound. This forms a chemically complex orthorhombic lattice with Fe and C atoms in the ratio of 3:1. The lattice will not dissolve any excess iron or carbon. The lattice structure changes with the Fe-C ratio. The other examples of intermetallic compounds are Mg_2Sn, Mg_2Pb, $CaSe$, Cu_2Se and Mg_3Bi_2.

- Also, these compounds have a higher melting point than their parent metals. For example, Mg_2Sn has a melting point of 780°C, while the parent metals Mg and Sn melt at 650°C and 232°C respectively. This also indicates the high strength of chemical bond formed.

1.7.2 Electron Compounds

- Also called *Hume-Rothery compounds*, these are a class of intermediate phases. They exist at or near compositions in each system that have a definite ratio of electrons to atoms, and hence called **electron compounds.**

- In these, the normal valence laws are not obeyed in forming the compounds. There are three such ratios, and given in **Table 1.1**

Table 1.1 : Ratio of electrons to atoms

Ratio	Types of Structure	Phases
1. 3/2 (21/14)	BCC (β-brass types)	$CuZn$, Cu_5Sn, Cu_3Al, $CuBe$, $AgAl$
2. 21/13	Complex cubic (γ-brass type)	Cu_5Zn_8, $Cu_{31}Sn_8$, Cu_9Al_4, Ag_5Zn_8
3. 7/4 (21/22)	CPH(ϵ-brass type)	$CuZn_3$, Cu_3Sn, $CuBe_3$, Ag_5Al_3

- In the compound $CuZn$, the copper atom gives one valency electron while the zinc atom gives two, giving a total of three valency electrons for two atoms; and the valence electrons to atom ratio is 3:2. In the compound, Cu_9Al_4, each atom of copper has one valence electron, and each aluminium atom has three valence electrons thus making a total of 21 valence electrons for a total of 13 atoms, giving the valence electron to atoms ratio of 21:13.

- Usually, electron compounds have properties almost similar to those of solid solutions. They exist in wide range of compositions, have high ductility and low hardness.

1.7.3 Interstitial Compounds

- These compounds are formed between some transition metals and certain nonmetallic atoms. For example, scandium (Sc), titanium (Ti), tungsten (W) and iron (Fe) with hydrogen, oxygen, carbon, boron and nitrogen, form such compounds.

- These are formed when the solid solubility of interstitially dissolved element exceeds certain limit, precipitating *a* compound from the solid solution. As the name indicates in these compounds the small atoms occupy position between large atoms, but the overall crystal structure of the compound is different from that of the original interstitial solid solution.

- These compounds have metallic properties and comprise hydrides, nitrides, borides and carbides. The examples are TiC, TaC, Fe_4N, Fe_3C, TiB_2, W_2C, WC, CrN, and TiH. All of these compounds are extremely hard and brittle. These are used in tool steels and cemented carbide cutting materials. Fe_3C is the cementite phase of carbon steel. These compounds are also highly refractory having melting points above 3000°C.

1.8   SOLIDIFICATION

- Solidification or crystallization or freezing is the process of phase transformation of metals from liquid to solid state.

- In this process, an unstable system with high free energy (liquid metal) is converted into a more stable thermodynamic state with minimum free energy (solid metal).

- The process of solidification goes through different stages and understood by studying the solidification mechanism.

1.8.1 Importance of Solidification Mechanism

- Solidification is the primary process by which most metals and alloys melted and cast into a semi-finished or finished product.

- Also, we know that the mechanical properties of materials are directly related to their micro-structural features such as their basic crystal structure (like FCC, BCC, HCP, etc.), grain size, shape, orientation, impurities, etc. Though we have no control over the basic crystal structures (which is element/composition dependent), we can modify the grain size, shape, presence of impurities, etc., and control mechanical properties to a large extent.

- The formation of crystals or grains takes place during the solidification process, and the shape and size of grains in metals can be manipulated by controlling the solidification process. For this purpose, a thorough understanding of the solidification mechanism is essential, based on which we can obtain the desired properties in metals and alloys.

1.8.2 Solidification Process – A General View

- In general, a solidification process involves the following three aspects.

(a)   Growth of solid grains

Solidification takes place by the nucleation of minute grains or crystals, which grow to bigger grains under the prevailing crystallographic and thermal conditions. The size and characteristics, which contribute to the properties of the metals and alloys, are controlled by the composition and the rate of cooling. The grain growth stops after the complete solidification of the available liquid metal.

(b)   Heat evolution and transfer

For the solidification of liquid metal to take place the heat from the liquid metal has to be removed. This heat removal takes place in three stages.

- **In liquid stage:** In this stage the super heat of the liquid metal is removed, by way of transfer to the mould walls. This heat is removed till the beginning of the solidification processes.

- **During the solidification stage:** This is the latent heat of fusion. This heat is removed during the solidification process itself. Most of the heat transfer takes place to the mould walls and partly to the air in the exposed areas.

- **After the solidification:** In this stage, the heat is removed from the hot solid metal till it cools down to room temperature.

(c) Dimensional changes

- During the above three stages of cooling, i.e., liquid, liquid to solid, and solid stages, shrinkage of metal takes place. Thus, the metal contracts (looses its volume) as it loses superheat, as it transforms to the solid and as the solid cools room temperature.

1.9 MECHANISM OF SOLIDIFICATION

The mechanism of solidification always proceeds in two stages –

- The formation of stable nuclei in the liquid metal is called as **nucleation.**

- The growth of nuclei into solid crystals with the formation of grain structure is called as **crystal growth.**

Before we study these stages of mechanism of solidification, let us first understand really what happens when the liquid to solid phase transformation begins. This is discussed with respect to a pure metal for ease of understanding.

1.9.1 Solidification of Pure Metal

- The solidification of a pure metal in a mould takes place at a constant temperature which is called as freezing point. Consider the cooling of a pure metal, whose ideal cooling curve, which is the plot of temperature versus cooling time, is shown in Fig. 1.4.

- Generally in metals, nucleation is aided by the presence of impurity atoms, alloying elements, etc., and solidification starts at the freezing point.

- But, in the case of pure liquid metals, due to the absence of foreign elements, the formation of stable nuclei does not take place at the freezing point. In such cases, the instantaneous nucleation in the liquid metal can only start when the melt temperature drops much below the freezing point, and this is called **supercooling** or **undercooling** (shown by dotted line in Fig. 1.4).

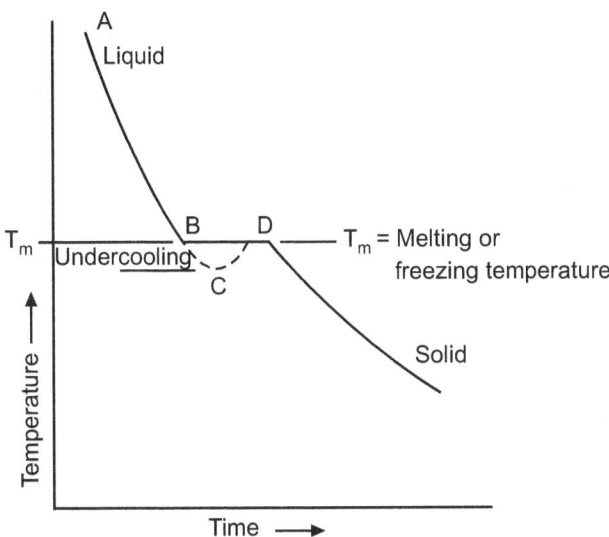

Fig. 1.4 : Cooling curve for a pure metal

- Once nucleation occurs, the temperature quickly reaches the equilibrium freezing point, as more and more atoms start joining the solid nuclei. Thus, solidification continues at the expense of liquid metal, with the growth of crystals. The solidification proceeds at a constant temperature with the release of latent heat of fusion.

- The degree of supercooling in metals is different for different metals and is of the order of few hundred degree Celsius. The freezing points and the degree of supercooling for some metals are listed in Table 1.2.

Table 1.2 : Freezing points and degree of supercooling

Metal	Freezing Point, °C	Degree of Super Cooling, °C
1. Aluminum	660	130
2. Copper	1083	236
3. Iron	1535	295
4. Lead	327	80
5. Nickel	1453	319
6. Platinum	1772	332
7. Silver	962	227

1.9.2 Solidification of Polycrystalline Materials

Most metallic materials used in engineering are polycrystalline in nature.

The stages in the solidification process in a polycrystalline material are schematically illustrated in Fig. 1.5. As discussed, the process involves nucleation and crystal growth.

The first stage is the formation of a number of stable nuclei. Fig. 1.5 (a) shows, the formation of a number stable nuclei at different points in the liquid phase. (Note that each square grid in the figure represents a unit cell, shown in the two' dimensions. Since the nucleation is spontaneous, they are randomly oriented.)

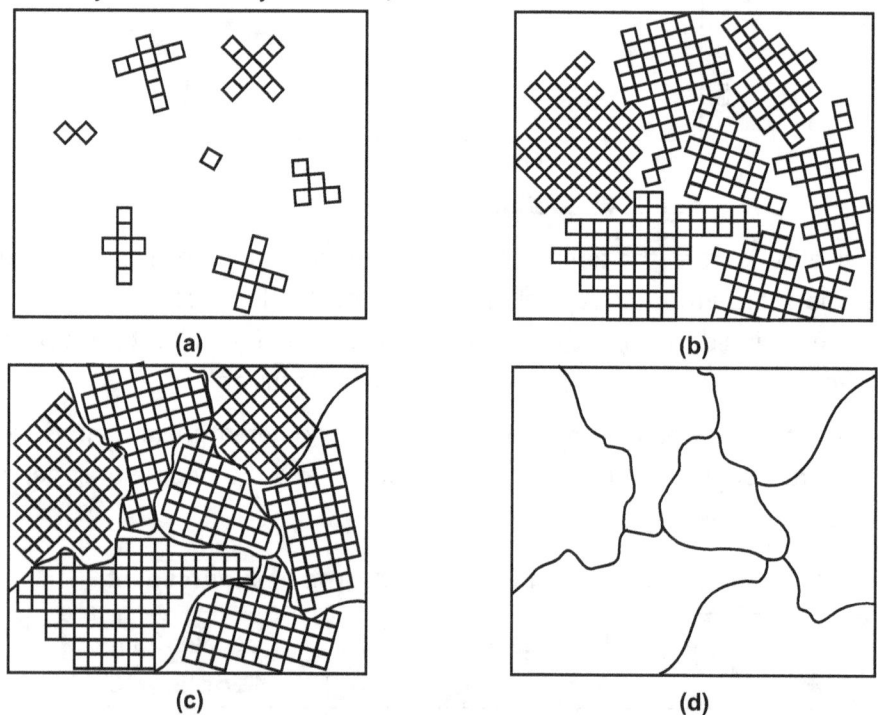

(a)　　　　　　　　　　　　　　(b)

(c)　　　　　　　　　　　　　　(d)

Fig. 1.5 : Stages in the solidification of a polycrystalline material

Gradually, more and more atoms are added from the adjacent melt to the nuclei and grow in the three dimensions (Fig. 1.5 (b)). With this, each nucleus grows and becomes a crystal or grain having its own crystal orientation and size. Finally, the crystal growth stops when each crystal is in contact with the surrounding crystals forming the grain boundary (Fig. 1.5 (c)).

It can be seen that, since the crystal orientations are different, there exists a mismatch at the area where two grains meet. This area where the crystals meet is termed as **grain boundary,** which is weaker than the normal crystals.

After solidification, the grain boundaries can be seen as dark areas in the polished and etched specimen under the microscope (Fig. 1.5(d)).

1.10 NUCLEATION – HOMOGENEOUS AND HETEROGENEOUS

1.10.1 Kinetics of Nucleation

The first stage in solidification is the formation a number of nuclei at a various points in the liquid phase.

Nuclei can be considered as a group or cluster of atoms or molecules to form the basic crystal structure (or one unit cell).

Thus, it involves the spontaneous formation of a new solid phase within the liquid phase, and this stage if termed as **nucleation** [Fig. 1.5 (a)].

At high temperatures, the atoms in a liquid phase have a high kinetic energy and are not stable. They keep colliding with each other. As the temperature drops down, their energy, hence the mobility reduces,; the atoms come together form a cluster and try to become a crystal. A stable nucleus (the basic unit cell) is formed only when the cluster reaches a critical size.

A cluster of atoms less than the critical size, called an **embryo,** will get dissolved back into the liquid phase due to the bombardment of vigorously moving neighbouring atoms.

Thus, nucleation involves the formation of stable nuclei, which can happen within the liquid phase by the parent atoms or due to the presence of foreign impurity atoms in the liquid metal. Based on this, nucleation is generally classified into two categories - homogeneous nucleation and heterogeneous nucleation.

1.10.2 Homogeneous Nucleation

The formation of spontaneous nuclei in liquid metal in a solidification process, without the aid of foreign particle is termed as **homogeneous** or **self nucleation.**

Such nucleation is based on the phase and energy fluctuation which can only take place in highly pure liquid metals. In homogeneous nucleation, the formation of a stable nucleus depends on the two main factors-

  a) The free-energy release during the liquid-solid phase transformation, called volume free-energy (G_v).

  b) The surface energy (G_s) required to form the new crystals.

When the melt is super cooled, the liquid-to,-solid transformation takes place due to the release of volume free-energy, i.e. due to the difference in volume free energy of liquid and solid.

The formation of a stable embryo (nucleus) is always retarded by the surface free-energy. The energy required to form surface, ΔG_s. If free energy of the system reduces, the formation of a stable nucleus starts.

1.10.3 Heterogeneous Nucleation

The formation of stable nuclei in a liquid metal in a solidification process with the help of foreign particles or the surface of the container (mould) or other structural particles, is called **heterogeneous nucleation.** The foreign particles or the mould surfaces help in reducing the critical free energy required to form stable nuclei.

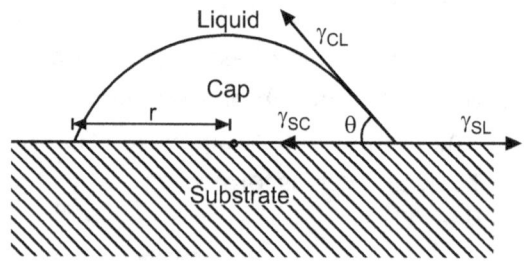

Fig. 1.6 : Heterogeneous nucleation

In practice, most metals solidify with heterogeneous nucleation. This is assisted by impurities of various kinds like, oxides, non-metallic inclusion, etc. For the heterogeneous nucleation to initiate, these impurity particles or surfaces should be wetted by the liquid metal, and the liquid should solidify easily on the nucleating particle. The wetting action of a liquid metal on the substrate of a foreign particle is illustrated in Fig. 1.6.

The solidifying nucleus can be considered as a spherical cap, on the flat substrate. The contact angle 0 at the nucleus-liquid-substrate (impurity) is lower for high wetting. With this, the surface energy required to form a stable nucleus is lower than with the formation of a nucleus within a liquid metal phase (like in homogeneous nucleation). As the surface energy is lower in this nucleation, the total free-energy change in the formation of stable nucleus is also lower, and hence the critical size *(r*)* of the nucleus is smaller. This situation necessitates, thus, a very small undercooling. In practical operations of castings, the undercooling requirement is usually less than 10 °C.

1.10.4   Rate of Nucleation

The rate of nucleation can be defined as the number of stable nuclei formed per unit volume of the liquid metal phase.

In homogeneous nucleation, the rate of nucleation (I) can be expressed by the Arrhenius-type equation,

$$I = A \exp\left(-\frac{\Delta G^*}{kT}\right)$$

where, I   =   rate of homogeneous nucleation

      A   =   a constant $\approx v \times N$

      v =   frequency of collisions of nucleus with atoms/second

      N   =   number of atoms per unit volume

      ΔG^* =   total free-energy change per nucleus

      k   =   Boltzmann constant = 1.38×10^{-23} J/K

      T   =   absolute temperature, K

Thus, the rate of nucleation increases with decreasing temperature. For most metals the homogeneous nucleation temperature is of the order of $0.8T_m$, where *T.* is the melting point of the metal.

1.11 CRYSTAL GROWTH

Once a stable nucleus is formed, either due to homogeneous or heterogeneous nucleation, it grows by acquiring more atoms from the liquid metal. The rate of crystal growth is influenced by the degree of undercooling. As already mentioned, the growth rate increases with the degree of undercooling, reaches maximum at a definite degree and then reduces.

Thus, it can be seen that the rate of nucleation and the rate of growth follow the same general trend with increasing amount of supercooling. However, the relative rates differ to the extent that nucleation is predominant in the early stages of freezing. As a result of this, the first layer of solid metal at the metal-mould interface consists of fine grained equi-axed crystals.

As solidification proceeds, the nuclei grow with the release of latent heat of fusion from the liquid metal. The crystals are arranged in a regular pattern, but each crystal will have its own orientation [Fig. 1.5 (b)]. Once the crystals grow fully, at the expense of liquid metal, they come in contact at their surfaces [Fig. 1.5 (c)]. But due to mismatch in their orientations, they will never unite, and form a weaker area called the **grain boundary** [Fig. 1.5 (d)]. Smaller the size of the grains, larger is the area of mismatch and larger is the grain boundaries.

1.11.1 Grain Size

The grain size is dependent on the cooling rate, nature of metal and its purity. The size of grains in a casting is determined by the relation between the rate of growth G and the rate of nucleation *I, i.e.,* -the size of grains S = f(G, I).

The factors that influence the grain size during solidification are as follows :

  a) The rate of nucleation,

  b) The rate of grain growth,

  c) Insoluble impurities in the melt and

  d) Stirring the melt during solidification.

If the number of nuclei formed is high, a fine-grained material will be, produced, and if only a few nuclei are formed a coarse-grained material will be produced.

The rate of cooling is most important factor in determining the rate of nucleation and therefore the grain size. Rapid cooling (chill cast) will result in a large number of nuclei formation and fine grain size, where as in slow cooling (sand cast or hot mold) only a few nuclei are formed, which lead to a coarse grained structure. Thus, the rate of grain growth depends only on the rate of cooling.

Insoluble impurities such as aluminium and titanium form insoluble oxides in steel. These impurities themselves act as nuclei at different parts of a mould and cause the grain growth. By stirring the melt during solidification, the crystals can be broken before they have got a chance to grow very large.

In general, the grain size, if it is fine, it exhibits better toughness or resistance to shock than coarse-grained material.

1.11.2 Effect of cooling Rate on the Grain Size

The rate at which a molten metal is cooled in solidification dification process affects the size of crystals (grains) formed.

A very slow rate of cooling leads to a small degree of undercooling and this promotes the formation of a smaller number of nuclei. This results in the growth of larger crystals.

On the other hand, rapid cooling brings in a high degree of under cooling, which promotes the formation of a larger number of nuclei. As a result, since each nuclei grows faster, a large number of small grains are formed. The formation of large number of nuclei and hence smaller grains is usually effected in solidification by chilling, i.e., rapid cooling which can be achieved by the use of metal moulds or water cooled copper moulds or by the use of external and internal chills. Since, pressure die-casting uses metal moulds, chilling takes place and the crystal size is very small as compared to that of sand-casting. In sand casting, heat loss is very slow, due to the insulating properties of the sand mould, and results in the formation of larger grains. Also, thin section both in sand and die-casting will have smaller grains because of faster rate of cooling.

1.12 CAST METAL STRUCTURES

The molten metal cast into a mould may form different structures with respect to the size and shape of the grains. With rapid cooling, a fine grained structure is obtained, which is preferable from the strength and performance point'of view. If the rate of nucleation is low, it may produce large grained structure.

In general, the factors which control the type of cast metal structure are,

- temperature of the melt and pouring temperature.
- melt composition, presence of impurities and alloying elements.
- the type of mould, like metal, sand, etc.
- cooling / solidification conditions.

Depending upon these factors, usually three types of cast metal structures are obtained, They include,

- equiaxed grains
- columnar grains
- combined equiaxed and columnar grains

1.12.1 Equi-axed Grained Structure

When a molten metal undergoes a large amount of supercooling, like in pure metals, the cast metal structure will have *equi-axed grains.*

This requires uniform rate of nucleation throughout the melt, and a uniform crystal growth condition.

That means the heat release rate should be uniform all around such that the crystals grow approximately equally in all directions. In the case of alloys undergoing heterogeneous nucleation, the presence of impurity/foreign atoms helps in the formation of stable nuclei uniformly throughout the melt and under controlled solidification conditions, equi-axed grains are formed.

The thermal gradient should be as small as possible, and the mould wall should not cause chilling action for this condition. A cast metal structure with equi-axed grains is schematically shown in Fig. 1.7 (a).

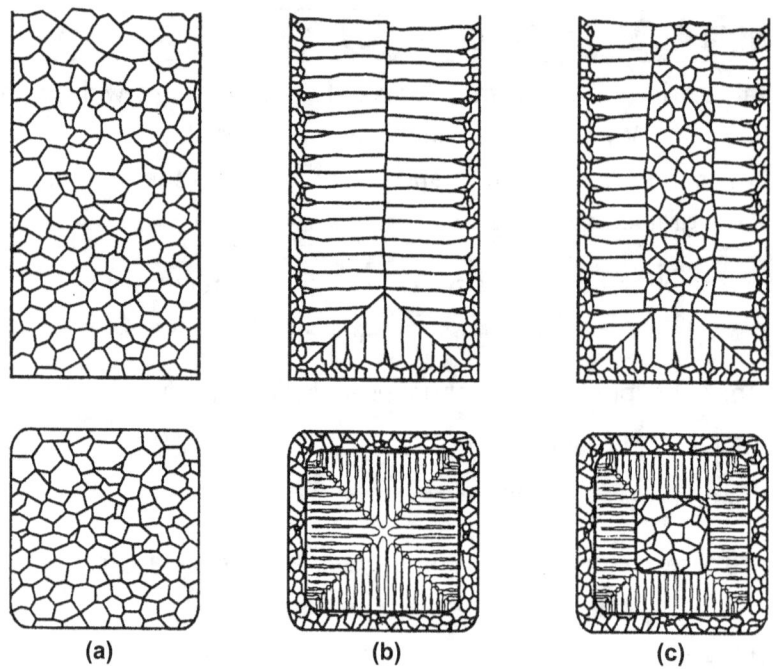

Fig. 1.7 : Cast metal structures

1.12.2 Columnar Grains

Columnar grains are long and coarse in sizes that grow perpendicular to the mould walls. Such grains are grown generally in metal moulds, and where the thermal gradients are very high. When a molten metal is poured into a metal mold, equi-axed fine grains are formed immediately by spontaneous nucleation and quick crystal growth due to chilling action of the mould wall leading to large undercooling.

The molten metal adjacent to the solidified skin with few nuclei will start solidifying and growing perpendicular to the mould wall as the heat is transferred from the melt to the mould wall in that direction. The columnar crystals, under these conditions, continue to grow and meet at the mould centre.

A typical cast metal structure with columnar crystals is shown in Fig. 1.7 (b). Such a grain structure is common in pure metals.

1.12.3 Combined Equi-axed and Columnar Crystals

Most industrial alloys cast in metal moulds will have both equi-axed grains and columnar grains. They also will exhibit fine grained crystals at the outer skins adjacent to the mould walls. .

In an alloy [Fig.1.7 (c)] the solidification initially occurs at the metal mould surface by chilling action, with fine grained structure. However, the presence of other metal (solid solution) at the centre also causes nucleation (heterogenous) leading to the grain formation and growth. The liquid metal in between the outer skin and the central metal (both equi-axed) starts receiving the latent heat of fusion and slows down the nucleation and growth process. This leads to the formation of columnar crystals as shown in figure 5.4 (b). The grains in the mould centre have slightly bigger sizes because of slow rate of heat dissipation as compared to the skin at the mould walls.

1.13 DENDRITIC GROWTH OR DENDRITIC SOLIDIFICATION

In most of the solidification processes crystals are grown by the formation of branched, tree-like structures called **dendrites.** This process is called **dendritic solidification.**

During crystal growth, they develop mainly in the directions perpendicular to the planes of maximum packing density of atoms.

This results in the formation of long branches first, and are called first-order (I) axes. As the first order axes grow in length, branches of the second order (II) start growing from their edges and grow in a perpendicular direction.

Next, the axes of third-order (III) evolve from the second order branches and grow further.

This growth continues as shown in Fig. 1.8 (a) land leads to the formation of dendritic crystals. Each crystal is made of such dendrites grown from a single nucleus and has a crystal lattice of single orientation.

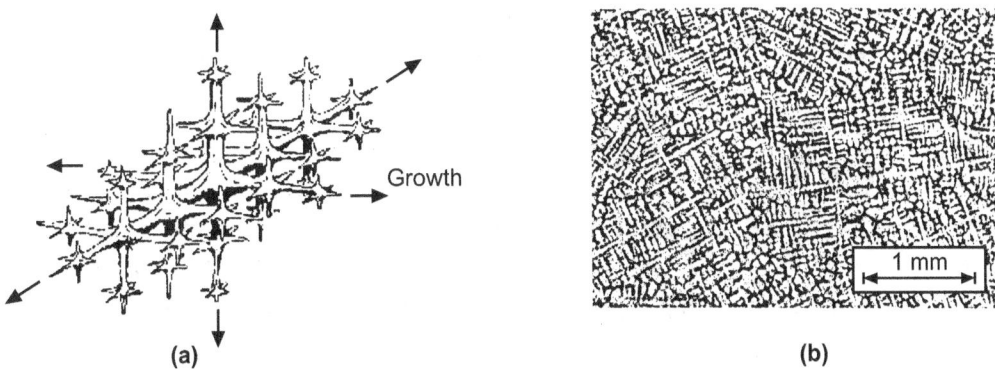

(a)   (b)

Fig. 1.8 : Dendritic growth solidification

Crystals of dendritic shape can be observed directly on the metal surface or on the surface of a pipe or shrinkage cavity. This is possible only after suitable etching of the sections of cast metals.

The regular shape of the dendrites is distorted due to the collision and the intergrowing of the particles in the solidification process. The branches of dendrites are separated from one another by very thin layers of impurities, that are insoluble in the liquid and especially in the solid state.

The separation may also include fine pores and cavities due to the liquid-solid shrinkage of the metal during solidification.

A typical dendritic, structure of 70Cu-30Ni cast alloy is shown in Fig. 1.8 (b).

1.14 COOLING CURVES

Cooling curve is a graphical representation of the falling temperature against time in the solidification process of a molten metal. The curves are different for different metal systems.

The cooling curves for a pure metal, for a binary solid solution and a multi-phase alloy (binary eutectic system) are shown in Fig. 1.9.

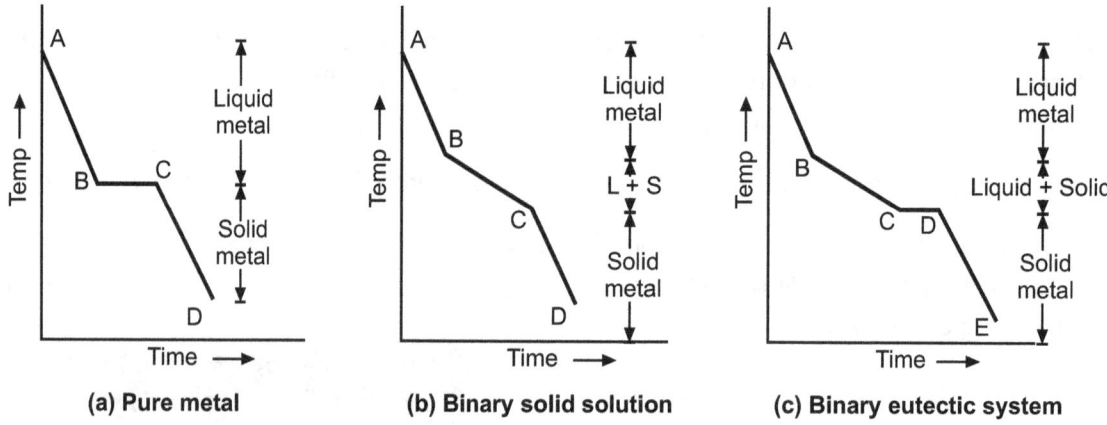

| (a) Pure metal | (b) Binary solid solution | (c) Binary eutectic system |

Fig. 1.9: Cooling curves

1.14.1 Cooling Curve for Pure Metal

For a pure metal, (Fig. 1.9 (a)), point *A* represents the highest temperature of the molten metal from where cooling starts. As the temperature drops to point *B*, the nucleation and crystal growth starts, and. this continues till point C. The curve *BC* is a straight horizontal line, which represents the beginning and end of the actual solidification (nucleation and grain growth) of the molten metal. This takes place at *constant temperature*, and at this the latent heat of fusion is liberated. Finally the solidified metal cools to room temperature, represented by curve *CD*. The slopes of curves *AB* and *CD*- depend upon the specific heats of the liquid metal and the solid metal respectively.

1.14.2 Cooling Curve for Binary Solid Solution

For a solid. solution (Fig. 1.9 (b)) consisting of two elements that are completely soluble in each. other in all proportions, the solidification starts at B, and completes at point C. It is seen that, the curve BC is not a straight horizontal line like for a pure metal. This indicates that the solidification of a solid solution takes place over a *temperature range*. The latent heat of fusion is liberated gradually a from B to C. Then solidified alloy cools down to room temperature, represented curve *CD*.

1.14.3 Cooling Curve for Binary Eutectic System

For an alloy (Fig. 1.9 (c)) consisting of two metals that are completely soluble in the liquid state but only partially soluble in the solid state (binary eutectic system) the solidification process takes place from B to D. From. to C, one of the metals which is excess in composition (to form the eutectic) crystallizes over a range of temperature. When the composition reaches the eutectic composition, at point C, the alloy crystallizes (solidifies) at a constant temperature like a pure metal. This is indicated. by line *CD*, which is a constant temperature. From D to E the solidified alloy cools down to room temperature.

1.15 PHASE DIAGRAMS

A temperature composition diagram which indicates the structural changes that take place during heating or cooling of an alloy system is known as phase diagram or equilibrium diagram or constitutional diagram.

- Normally it has temperature as ordinate and concentration or composition as absicca.

- These diagrams are obtained by extremely slow cooling or heating that gives sufficient time for phase change to take place.

- These diagrams are a very useful tool for the study of heat treatment and properties of alloys.

1.15.1 Construction of Phase Diagrams

A phase or equilibrium diagram for a solid solution can be constructed using a series of cooling curves obtained for different alloy compositions.

Consider for example, a binary alloy system comprising two metals X and Y. For simplicity, let us take six compositions – pure metal *X, 80X-20Y, 60X-40Y, 40X-60Y, 20X-80X* and pure metal Y. Now let us obtain the cooling curve for all these compositions and plot them on the same graph as shown in Fig. 1.10 (a).

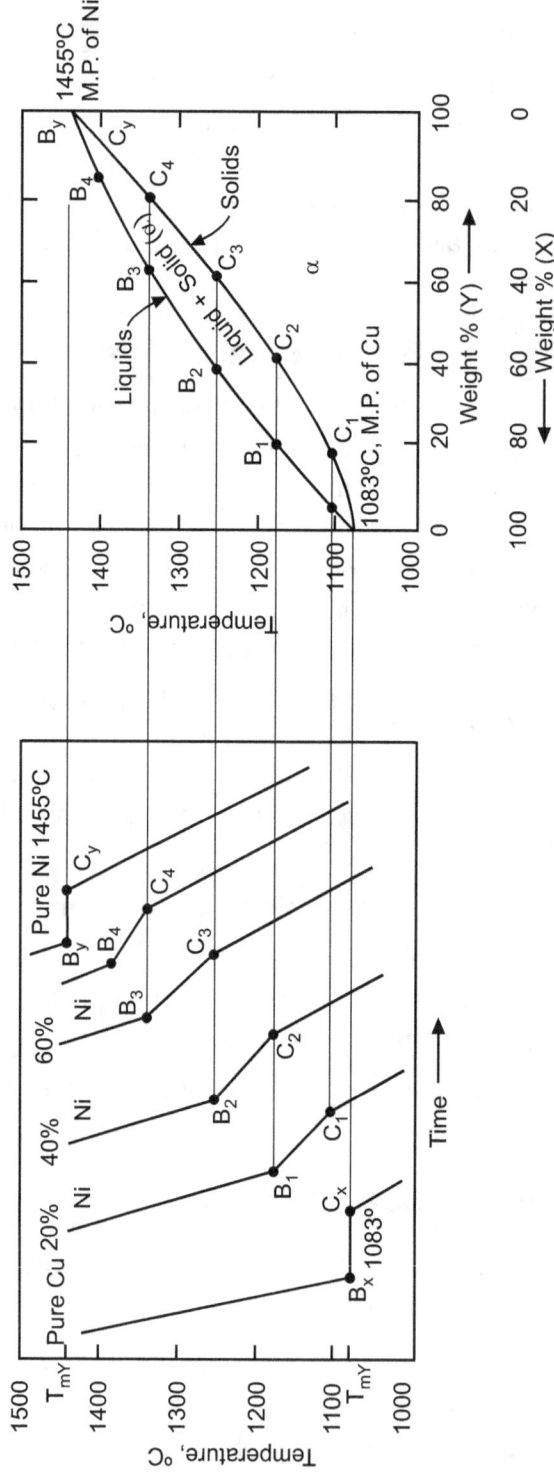

Fig. 1.10: Construction of phase diagram

From the figure, we can see that the pure metals X and Y have solidified at constant temperatures T_{mx} (curve B_xG_x) and T_{my} (curve B_yC_y) respectively, while the rest of the alloy compositions have solidified-over a range of temperature, like B, C, BA, etc. The upper points B_1, B_2, B_3 and B_4 indicate the melting points while the lower points C_1, C_2, C_3 and C_4 indicate the freezing points of the respective alloy compositions. Now, knowing the melting/freezing points for different compositions, we can construct the phase diagram (temperature versus alloy composition) as shown in Fig. 1.10 (b).

First, mark the alloy compositions *100X-0Y, 80X-20Y, 60X-40Y, 40X-60Y, 20X-80Y, OX-100Y* on the x-axis. Transfer the melting and- freezing points, B_x (C_x), B_1, B_2, B_3, B_4, C_1, C_2, C_3, C_4 and B_y (C_y) on to their respective compositions. When we join B_x (C_x), B_1, B_2, B_3, B_4, and B_y (C_y), we get the upper curve called the **liquidus**: Similarly by joining, B_x (C_x), C_1, C_2, C_3, C_4 and B_y (C_y) we get the lower curve called the **solidus.** This is the required *phase diagram* for the given alloy.

The liquidus line represents the freezing point of various compositions, whereas the solidus line represents the melting points of various compositions. The points, B_x and B_y correspond to the melting points of pure metals.

The region within the liquidus and solidus represents the two phase region, in which the solid crystals of homogeneous solid solutions are in equilibrium with the liquid of suitable composition (i.e., α + L).

Above the liquidus line, the system will have only a single liquid phase (L) and below the solidus line it will have a single solid phase (S)

1.15.2 Interpretation of Phase Diagrams

Phase or equilibrium diagram are quite useful in metallurgical studies.

After constructing a phase diagram, one should understand how the diagrams can be interpreted to obtain various information for a given temperature and equilibrium composition. They can be interpreted to obtain three types of important information.

   a) Type and number of phases

   b) Composition of phases

   c) Amount of phases - using the Lever rule

These are explained briefly with suitable illustrations. Let us use a Cu-Ni binary phase diagram to understand how the data can be obtained. The phase diagram of Cu-Ni system is shown in Fig. 1.11.

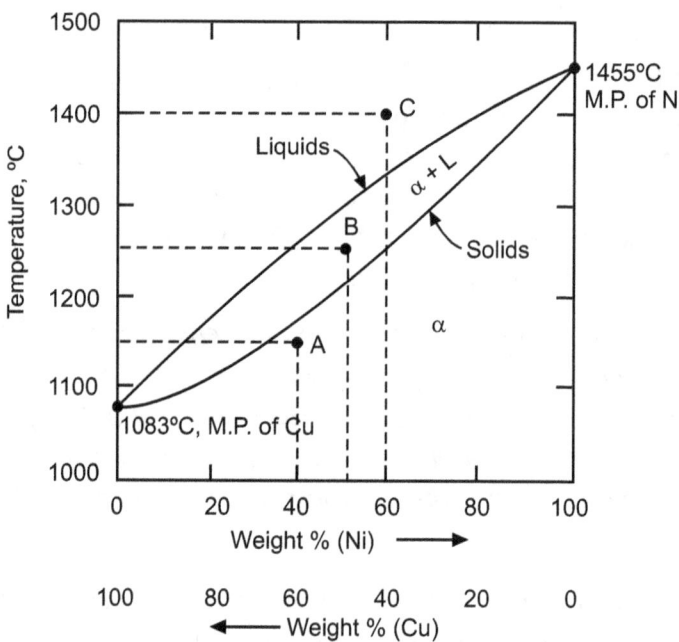

Fig. 1.11: Phase diagram of Cu-Ni system

a) Type and Number of Phases

Obtaining the information on the type and number of phases present in a phase diagram at a given temperatures and composition is quite simple.

For this, we have to locate the point corresponding to the temperature-composition on the phase diagram. By seeing the location of this point we can easily mention the type and number of phase. For example in Fig. 1.11, let us consider three points A, B and C.

Point A corresponds to an alloy composition of 60Cu-40Ni at 1150°C. Since this point is entirely below the solidus line, the complete phase is *solid* and only *one a phase* is present.

Point *B* corresponds to an alloy composition of 50Cu-5ONi at 1250°C. Since this point is located within the solidus-liquidus region it comprises *two phases,* one α (solid) and the other liquid phase, both in equilibrium.

Point C corresponds to an alloy composition 40Cu-6ONi at 1400°C. Since this point is entirely above the liquidus line, it has only one liquid phase.

Similarly, for any composition of the alloy, at required temperatures the type and number of phases can be determined.

b) Composition of Phases

Phase composition indicates the concentration of each component in the phase at a given temperature. The composition of the alloy in a *single phase* is same as overall composition of the solid solutions. For example, again consider the point A in Fig. 1.11 at temperature 1150°C and alloy composition of 40Cu- 60Ni. Here, the alloyVas a single phase a (solid), and thus the composition of the phase is same as that of the alloy considered, i.e., 40Cu-6ONi. In fact, the phase composition of this alloy remains same at different temperatures up to the solidus line.

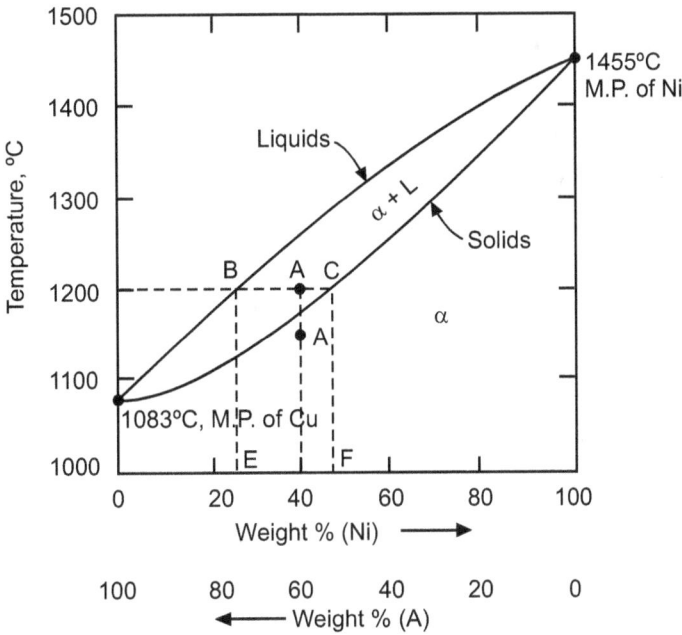

Fig. 1.12: Phase composition procedure

Determining the phase composition of the alloy in a two-phase region (between the liquidus-solidus region) i.e., α + L involves a bit complicated procedure. With reference to Fig. 1.12, the procedure is explained as follows.

- For the given temperature and alloy composition mark a point A, 1200°C and 60 Cu-40Ni in our case.

- Draw a horizontal line along point A so as to intersect the liquidus and solidus at point B and C respectively.

- Now drop perpendicular from points B and C to meet the composition axis at points E and F respectively.

The horizontal line *(BC)* is called a **tieline** or an **isotherm,** in phase diagram terminology. Now the composition of each of the phases (i.e., α and L) can be found as below.

- The point E, dropped from tie line intersection with the liquidus (B), represents the *composition of the liquid phase. In our case, it is 73.8Cu-26.2Ni.*

- The point *F*, dropped from tie line intersection with the solidus (C), represents the composition of the α phase. In our case it is 52ACu47.6Ni.

Note that the perpendicular dropped from the liquidus corresponds to the composition of the liquid phase and that dropped from the solidus corresponds to the composition of solid phase (A).

a) Amount of Phases – Lever Rule

The relative amounts of phases or the proportion of each phase (as a fraction or as percentage) at a given temperature and alloy composition can be determined using phase diagrams it is obtained by the **Lever rule.**

Lever rule which states that *for an alloy in a two phase system the proportionate amount of each phase is given by the ratio of difference between the gross alloy compositions of the two phases.*

This is illustrated with the help of a typical binary phase diagram, shown in Fig. 1.13, the procedure is as follows:

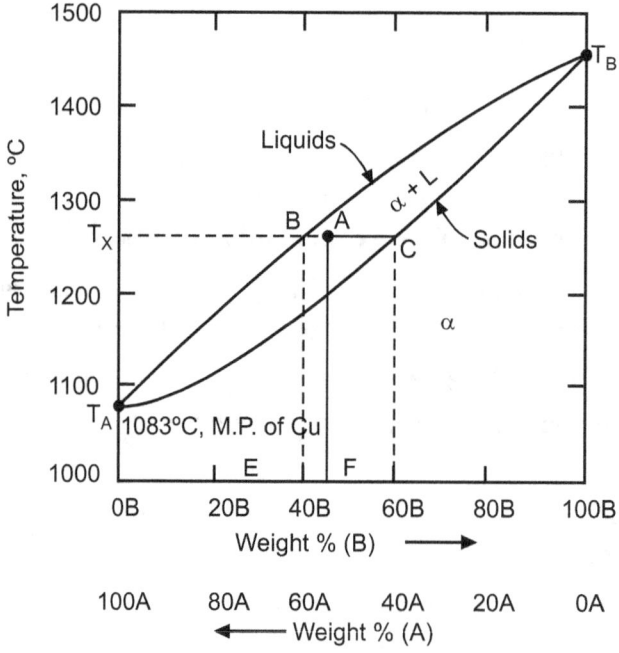

Fig. 1.13 : Use of lever rule

- For the given temperature *(Tx* in this case) and alloy composition (60A-40B in this case), mark point *A* as shown in Fig. 1.13.

- Along point *A*, draw the horizontal *BC* (the tieline or isotherm) so as to intersect the liquidus and solidus at points *B* and *C* respectively.

- The fraction of one phase is calculated as a ratio of length of the tie line from the overall alloy composition to the phase boundary for the other phase to the total length of the tie line.
- Similarly, the fraction of the other phase is also. calculated.

To find the weight fraction of the *liquid phase, we* can write that (refer to Fig. 1.13).

$$\% \ W_L \ = \ \frac{AC}{BC} \times 100$$

$$= \ \frac{15}{20} \times 100$$

$$= \ 75\%$$

Note that in determining the liquid phase proportion, we are using the part of the tie line towards the solid phase a (i.e., from over all composition point *A* to the point C on solidus).

Similarly, to find the weight fraction of the *solid phase,* we can write that,

$$\% \ W_\alpha \ = \ \frac{AC}{BC} \times 100$$

$$= \ \frac{5}{20} \times 100$$

$$= \ 25\%$$

or $\% \ W_\alpha \ = \ 100 - W_L$

Here, to determine the solid phase proportion, we are using the part of the tie line towards the liquid phase (i.e., from overall composition point A to the point *B* on the liquidus).

1.15.3 Classification of Equilibrium Diagrams

The equilibrium diagrams can be classified based on the relations of the components in the liquid and solid phases.

- Components-completely soluble in both-liquid and solid states.
- Components completely soluble in the liquid state and partly soluble in the solid state (eutectic reaction).
- Components completely soluble in the liquid state-and, nsoluble in the solid state (eutectic reaction).
- Components partly soluble in the liquid state (monotectic reaction).
- Components insoluble in both liquid and solid states.

The first three types of phase diagrams for binary alloys are discussed below.

1.16 EQUILIBRIUM DIAGRAMS FOR COMPLETE SOLUBILITY OR FOR TWO METALS COMPLETELY SOLUBLE IN LIQUID AND SOLID STATES

In this type, since both the metals are completely soluble in the solid state, only substitutional type of solid solution will be formed in the solid phase. These alloys generally will have metals of same type of crystal structure and one of the metals will have atomic radius less than 8% of the other element. The examples of this type alloys are Cu-Ni, Ag-Au, Cr-Mo, W-Mo, etc.

The phase diagram of Cu-Ni system is illustrated in Fig. 1.14 a. Pure copper and pure nickel solidify at 1083°C and 1453°C respectively. Cu-Ni alloys of various combinations solidify over a range of temperatures as shown in figure.

The phase diagram of this type of alloy is the most simple of all other systems. It consists of two lines only, the upper i.e., liquidus and the lower i.e., solidus. Any given point on the liquidus line represents the temperature and composition of an alloy, which is completely in liquid phase. Any point on the solidus gives the temperature and com position off the alloy in a solid phase. The phase between these two lines represents the region in which both liquid and solid phases co-exist.

Solidification of Alloy In the Cu-NI System

The solidification process and phase changes in an alloy of 70Ni-30Cu are illustrated in Fig. 1.14.

This composition is represented by vertical line XX and the lowest liquidus temperature of this composition is represented by line XYT. At temperatures above T the alloy exists as a homogeneous liquid and as a single phase. As the temperature drops to point T, the liquidus temperature of this alloy (70Ni-30Cu), solidification process starts. The horizontal line XYT cuts the solidus at Y, which represents the composition of the solid phase that can exist in equilibrium with the liquid phase of composition X at temperature T. Thus, at this point dendrites of composition Y begin to solidify. Since these dendrites are higher in nickel (about 91% Ni as seen from diagram) than the original liquid alloy, the rest of the liquid will be short of nickel, and correspondingly richer in copper. Thus, the composition of the remaining liquid moves to the left of the diagram, say to point X_1. No further solidification occurs until the temperature drops to T_1, and at this temperature, we can see that the solid phase which is in equilibrium with the liquid X_1, is now of composition Y_1, i.e., less rich in nickel than was the original dendrite. Solid of composition Y_1, therefore forms a coating over the original dendrite.

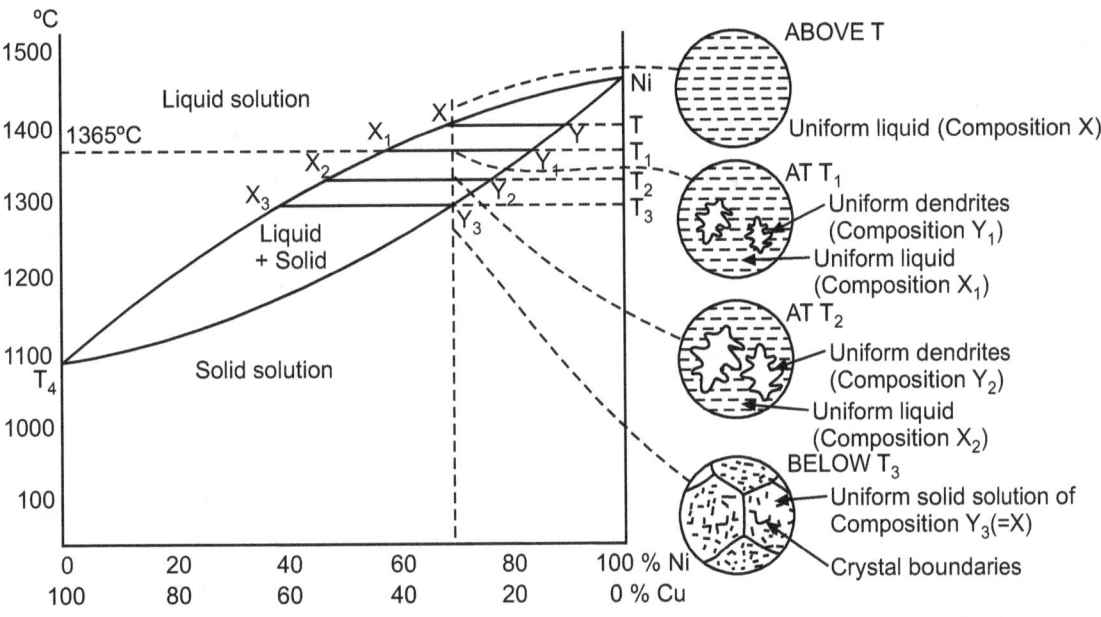

(a) Phase diagram for Cu-Ni system   (b) Microstructures during solidification

Fig. 1.14 : Solidification of 70Ni-30Cu alloy

By applying Lever rule to determine the composition and properties of each metal at temperature T, (i.e., 1365°C from diagram), we get the following-

$$\text{(Weight of liquid)} \times OX_1 = \text{(Weight of solid)} \times OY_1$$

$$\frac{\text{Weight of liquid}}{\text{Weight of solid}} = \frac{OY_1}{OX_1}$$

From Fig. 1.14

$$\frac{\text{Weight of liquid (59\% Ni)}}{\text{Weight of solid (85\%Ni)}} = \frac{85-70}{70-59} = \frac{15}{11}$$

Hence, the liquid to solid proportion is 15 to 11, and the liquid has 59% Ni and 41% Cu and the solid has 85% Ni and 15% Cu.

As the temperature falls, solidification continues and the composition of the alloy keeps changing along X_1, X_2, X_3 (due to mixing caused by convection) and the composition of the solid changes along Y_1, Y_2, Y_3 (due to diffusion). At T_2, the composition of the growing dendrites will have changed to Y_2 while the composition of the uniform liquid in equilibrium with them will be X_2. At the same time, the proportion of liquid to solid will be $\frac{OY_2}{OX_2}$.

Finally, at temperature T_3 the last trace of liquid of composition X_3 solidifies at the crystal boundaries and absorbed by diffusion. This makes the solid of uniform composition Y_3, which will be equivalent to that of the original liquid X.

1.17 PHASE DIAGRAMS FOR PARTIAL SOLUBILITY

1.17.1 Eutectic System or Two Metals Completely Soluble in Liquid State and Totally Insoluble in Solid State

In practice, the existence of such a system is really doubtful, since most solid metals appear to dissolve at least some quantity of other metals. However, in the case of bismuth and cadmium, the mutual solid solubility is so small that it can be considered that both metals are completely insoluble in the solid state.

The phase diagram of a Bi-Cd alloy is shown in Fig. 1.15. Pure bismuth solidifies at 271°C and pure cadmium solidifies at 321°C. Though alloys of Bi and Cd solidify at various temperature ranges only the alloy of 40Cd and 60Bi solidifies at a fixed temperature of 144°C. This 60Bi-40Cd alloy solidifies like a pure metal, and is called as an eutectic alloy; the temperature at which it solidifies is called the *eutectic temperature*, and the composition as the *eutectic composition*. The alloys to the left of eutectic composition are called *hypoeutectic* alloys and to the right as *hypereutectic* alloys.

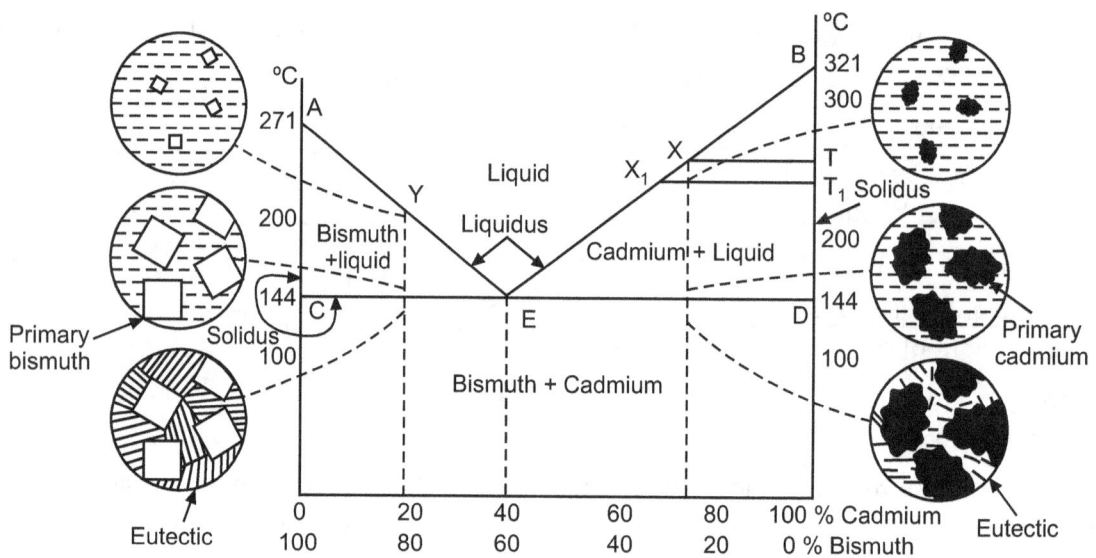

Fig. 1.15: Phase diagram of Bi-Cd system

The phase diagram consists of two sloping *liquidus* lines *AE* and *BE* both meeting at the eutectic point. The solidus line is always a continuous line connecting the melting points of the pure metals and the eutectic alloy, that is the line *ACEDB*. The phase diagram consists of four areas. The area above the liquidus is a single homogeneous liquid solution, since the two metals are completely miscible in the liquid state. The remaining three areas are two-phase areas as shown in figure.

a) Solidification of an Hypereutectic Alloy

Now consider the solidification of a 25Bi and 75Cd alloy, indicated by line XX in Fig. 1.15. The crystallisation is schematically represented on the right side of the phase cnagram. Any point above the liquidus *AEB* is a homogeneous liquid and solidification will start once the temperature drops to *T.*

At this temperature, the solid in equilibrium with the liquid *X* is pure cadmium since the relevant solids phase boundary is the 100% cadmium ordinate, *BD.* Hence, dendrites of pure cadmium begin to form and the rest of the liquid becomes correspondingly richer in bismuth, hence its composition moves down along *BE,* say to *X,.* With further fall in temperature to *T,* more pure cadmium will crystallise. This crystallisation continues till the temperature reaches *144°C,* at which the remaining liquid contains 60% Bi and *40%* Cd, the eutectic composition.

By applying Lever rule,

$$\text{Weight of liquid (composition E)} \times EP = \text{Weight of pure Cd} \times DP$$

or $\quad \dfrac{\text{Weight of liquid (composition E)}}{\text{Weight of pure cadmium}} = \dfrac{DP}{EP}$

From Fig. 1.15

$$\frac{DP}{EP} = \frac{100 - 75}{75 - 40}$$

$$= \frac{25}{35} = \frac{5}{7}$$

Thus there are *7* parts by mass of cadmium to *5* parts by mass of liquid.

At this stage two metals are in equilibrium with each other in the liquid. However, due to the momentum of crystallisation of the primary cadmium, a little extra cadmium deposits, moving the composition of the liquid slightly to the left of *E.* Equilibrium is immediately restored as a film of bismuth deposits and in this fashion the remaining liquid solidifies by depositing alternate layers of cadmium and bismuth as the liquid composition swings to the left and right of E. The temperature remains at 144°C until the complete solidification takes place.

The final structure is thus made of primary crystals of cadmium in a matrix of eutectic, consisting of alternate layers of pure cadmium and pure bismuth in a laminated structure which is typical of metallic eutectics.

b) Solidification of an Hypoeutectic Alloy

Now consider the solidification of an alloy of 80Bi and 20Cd shown by line YY in Fig. 1.15 The schematic representation of the crystallisation process of this type of alloy is shown to the left of the phase diagram. Initially the process starts with the formation of primary dendrites of bismuth below the point Y. These do not resemble the dendrites of other metals but are roughly cubic in shape. Since, bismuth has been rejected from solution the alloy becomes correspondingly richer in cadmium so that the composition moves down along the liquidus AE, and towards the eutectic E. Finally, the liquid will contain 60% Bi and 40% Cd at the eutectic temperature of 144°C and solidifies as an eutectic alloy.

Hence in these systems, any solution of composition on either side of the eutectic point will first deposit the metal which ever is in excess of the eutectic composition in the form of primary crystals until the liquid reaches the eutectic composition at 144°C. Also, in the eutectic portion of these alloys the alternate layers of pure metals can be readily seen by even a low power microscope, thus indicating the complete insolubility in the solid state.

At the eutectic point, three phases i.e., liquid, solid cadmium and solid bismuth co-exist in equilibrium. Hence, there are two components and three phases.

Since the degree of freedom is zero, the system is *invariant,* which means, if either the composition or temperature are altered, at least one of the phases will disappear.

1.17.2 Partial Eutectic System or Two Metals Completely Soluble in Liquid State and Partially soluble in Solid State

This is an intermediate system of the above two systems discussed. The silver-copper alloy system is an example a partial solid solubility. The phase diagram of this system is shown in Fig. 1.16. Pure copper melts at 1083°C and pure silver melts at 960°C. The line AEB indicates the liquidus, and ACEDB the liquids. The lines CF and DG are termed as **solvus,** which indicates a change in solubility of one metal in another in solid phase.

As can be seen from the Fig. 1.16 it consists of an eutectic point E. The special feature of this system is that the phase boundaries are below the *solidus,* which indicate that phase changes taking place in the solid phase (i.e., the *solvus* lines CF and DG).

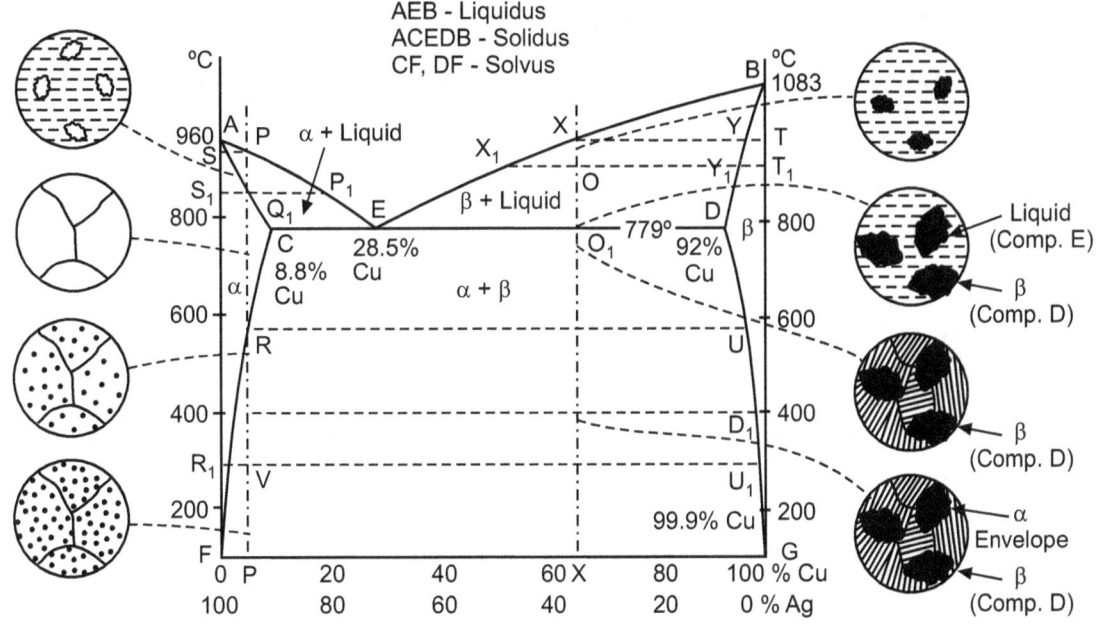

Fig. 1.16: Phase diagram of Ag-Cu system

From the figure, it can be seen that there are two solid solutions a and 0 respectively, since-

a) Silver will dissolve a maximum of 8.8% Cu at the eutectic temperature and forms the solid solution α;

b) Copper will dissolve a maximum of 8.0% Ag at the eutectic temperature and forms the solid solution β.

The slopes of *solvus* lines *CF* and *DG* indicate that both the solubility of copper in silver (α) and the solubility of silver in copper (β) decrease with fall in temperature. This phenomenon called *coherent precipitation* is a common feature in partial solubility systems.

a) Solidification of an Hypereutectic Alloy

Consider the solidification of a hypereutectic alloy of composition 35% Ag and 65% Cu. It is represented by line *XX* on the phase diagram (Fig. 1.16). The dendrite formation and precipitation of α phase (eutectic (α) are schematically shown on the right of the phase diagram. The crystal formation starts as soon as the temperature *T* is reached, where dendrites of the solid solution of β (primary (β) of composition Y will commence. Since, the β dendrites are relatively rich in copper, the remaining liquid will become correspondingly richer in silver and the composition will move to the left along *EB*, say to X_1. Further deposition of β of composition Y_1 takes place as the temperature drops to T_1.

By applying Lever rule, at temperature T_1 we have-

Weight of liquid (composition X_1) X_1O = Weight of solid solution β (composition Y_1) OY_1

As the temperature drops continuously, β continues to deposit and composition charges along Y_1D and the rest of the liquid changes in composition along X_1E. At 779°C, the eutectic temperature, the liquid will have composition E, and solid solution β of composition D. This ratio is given by-

Weight of liquid (composition E). EO_1 = Weight of solid solution β (composition D). O_1D

Further, as the temperature falls below 779°C, the remaining liquid solidifies as a eutectic by depositing alternate layers of α (composition C) and β (composition D), until the complete liquid solidifies. The ratio,

$$\frac{\text{Weight of primary } \beta}{\text{Weight of eutectic}}, \text{ will be the same as above, i.e. } \frac{EO_1}{O_1D}$$

Assuming a very slow rate of cooling, further changes will occur in the structure of the solid alloy. As the temperature falls, the solid solubility of each metal in the other decrease along CF and DG respectively. Thus copper will be rejected from the α layers of the eutectic in the form of particles of the other solid solution β. These particles will join the layers of β adjacent to those of α. Similarly silver will be precipitated from the β layers in the form of small amounts of α which will join the α layers.

The crystals of primary β will also reject some silver in the form of α and this is seen as a film surrounding the primary β crystals. At, say, 400°C, the composition of a will be given by C, and the composition of P (both eutectic and primary) by D_1. Because of the extremely slow rate of ionic diffusion at low temperature, little change in structure occurs below 300°C.

b) Solidification of an Hypoeutectic Alloy

Now consider the solidification of an hypoeutectic alloy of composition 95% Ag and 5%Cu. This can be represented by vertical line PP as shown in Fig. 1.16. The schematic of dendrite formation and precipitation of β phase (eutectic (β) are shown on the left of phase diagram. Crystal formation starts at temperature S, by the deposition of dendrites of α (Primary α) at S_1, at which the remaining liquid will become richer in copper and the composition moves to P_1. Under slow cooling conditions, so as to maintain equilibrium, the liquid P_1 will be absorbed by diffusion and the overall composition of the solid solution α will be Q_1 i.e., same as the original liquid P.

Further, as the temperature falls, no change take place in the uniform a crystals, and they cool towards R. At R, the solid solution a becomes fully saturated with copper, and as the temperature drops below R, copper will be rejected from the solution in the form of solid solution β (eutectic β) of composition U, which is the phase in equilibrium with a at that temperature. With further fall in temperature, β continues to precipitate from α and both solid solutions change in compositions along RF and UG respectively. Below this temperature, say at 300°C, α contains about 0.5% Cu (R,) and β about 0.2% Ag (U$_1$). By Lever rule, the relative amounts of α and β at this temperature are given as-

Weight of α (composition Rd. R$_1$V = Weight of β (Composition Ud. VU$_1$

1.18 TYPES OF REACTIONS BETWEEN PHASES

1.18.1 Eutectic Reaction

In the previous two systems explained, it can be observed that for a particular composition (40Cd-60Bi and 28.5Cu-61.5Ag), the freezing point of the alloys is minimum. This composition is called *eutectic composition,* and this mixture always freezes at a temperature below the melting points of either of the metals. An eutectic mixture always solidifies at a constant temperature like a pure metal. At the eutectic temperature, the liquid of two metals changes into two solids and this process is known as **eutectic reaction.** A eutectic reaction can be written as-

$$\text{Liquid} \xleftarrow[\text{Heating}]{\text{Cooling}} \text{(solid A + solid B) (eutectic mixture)}$$

The degree of freedom is zero. This indicates that the system is *invariant,* which means, if either the composition or temperature are altered, at least one of the phases will disappear.

The general characteristics of eutectic mixtures can be summarised as follows:

- In a binary system it is made of a heterogeneous mixture of two phases, i.e., it must not be considered as a Angle phase.

- It solidifies at a constant temperature - the lowest temperature in the series. It solidifies at temperature lower than either of the metals forming the eutectic mixture.

- It will have a fixed composition, whatever may be the overall composition of the alloy system, in which it exists.

- It solidifies in a typical lamellar fashion. In some cases, the lamellae of one of the phases may get converted into globular form due to surface-tension effects. This structure can be seen even in a low-power microscope.

1.18.2 Eutectoid Reaction

In an eutectoid reaction, a solid solution decomposes into two other solid phases, to forma eutectic structure. This solid-solid transformation is called an **eutectoid reaction.** It can be written as-

$$Solid_1\ (\gamma) \xrightleftharpoons[\text{Heating}]{\text{Cooling}} [solid_2\ (\alpha) + solid_3\ (\beta)]\ (eutectoid\ mixture)$$

The example of this reaction in steel is the formation of *pearlite* from solid *solution austenite (y)*. Pearlite Js an intimate mixture of ferrite ((x-iron) and cementite (iron-carbide).

$$Austenite\ (\gamma) \xrightleftharpoons[\text{Heating}]{\text{Cooling}} Ferrite\ (\alpha) + cementite\ (Fe_3C)$$

This reaction forms the basis of heat treatment of steel to change the structure to obtain various properties. The eutectoid reaction also takes place in other systems like Cu-Al, *Cu-Zn,.Cu-Be, Al-Mn,* etc.

Difference between Eutectic and Eutectoid Reactions

*   Basically, an eutectic reaction is a liquid to solid transformation, while eutectoid involves solid to solid transformation.

*   Since, an eutectoid reaction occurs in a solid state, the eutectoid temperature is always lower than the eutectic temperature which is a liquid to solid transformation.

*   An eutectoid reaction forms the basis for heat treatment of alloys, while an eutectic reaction has no such relevance.

1.18.3 Peritecdc Reaction (Transformation)

In a **peritectic reaction,** a liquid and 4 solid phase react isothermally to form new solid phase on cooling. This reaction takes place at a fixed temperature. This word is derived from Greek *peri,* which means *around,* since during the transformation process, the original solid phase becomes surrounded or coated by the transformation product. The reaction is expressed as-

$$Liquid + solid_1 \xrightleftharpoons[\text{Heating}]{\text{Cooling}} solid2$$

For example, transformation of δ-iron into γ-iron, in iron-carbon system-

$$Liquid + \delta \xrightleftharpoons[\text{Heating}]{\text{Cooling}} \gamma\ (austenite)$$

1.18.4 Peritectoid Reaction

This is similar to a peritectic reaction which produces a new solid solution. However, in this case two solids react together to forma third solid. This is given by the reaction-

$$Solid_1 + Solid_2 \xrightleftharpoons[Heating]{Cooling} Solid_3$$

An example of this reaction is the silver-aluminium (Ag-Al) alloy system.

The new phase is usually an intermediate alloy, but can also be a solid solution. The peritectoid reaction has the same relationship to the peritectic reaction as the eutectoid has to the eutectic. Mainly, it is the replacement of a liquid by a solid, as indicated in the above reaction.

1.19 CORING

During solidification of an alloy, variation in composition is observed from one point to another. This variation in composition is called as coring.

We have studied solidification and nucleation of binary alloy system. It is seen that when all alloy is being cooled element having higher melting or freezing point, solidifies firstly and thus forms nucleus or centre of grains.

Obliviously the outer region becomes richer with the element having low melting point. When cooling continues and the grains are thus formed, we can observe, the metal with high melting point at core or centre and metal with low melting point at the grain boundaries. This variation in composition of alloys from core to surface of grains is called as coring.

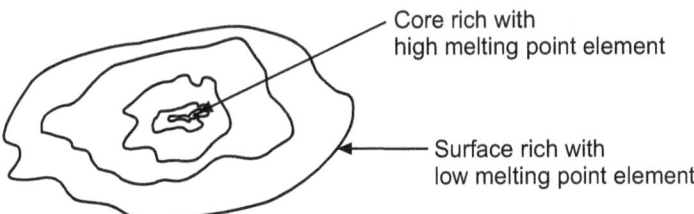

Fig. 1.17 : Coring

The magnitude of coring increases as the distance between solidus and liquidus curve increases.

Under microscopy, coring can be revealed by different colours developed due to varied responses of the regions having different composition to the etchant.

Coring is more common in castings of brasses, bronzes, steels.

1.19.1 Effects of Coring

Coring is not desirable as it –

  a) increases brittleness

  b) gives non-uniform mechanical and physical properties.

  c) decreases corrosion resistance.

1.19.2 Elimination of Coring

Due to above ill effects, coring must be eliminated from the structure. This methods used for this are –

a) Slow cooling rates during solidification:

Slow cooling rates provides scope for adjustment of compositions. But it will lead to coarse grain structure resulting in inferior mechanical property.

b) Homogenization:

This is a heat treatment in which alloy is heated to a temperature just below the solidus temperature and held there for sufficient time. Due to this diffusion takes place and castings get homogeneous structure.

The holding time is inversely proportional to the process temperature which must not be greater than solidus temperature.

1.20 NON-EQUILIBRIUM COOLING

It means cooling which will not take the alloy through equilibrium conditions. When cooling of alloys takes place at faster rates structures obtained are different than structures obtained as per equilibrium diagram.

Due to rapid cooling both liquidus and solidus lines shifts below i.e. solidification starts and completes at lower temperatures as shown in Fig. 1.18.

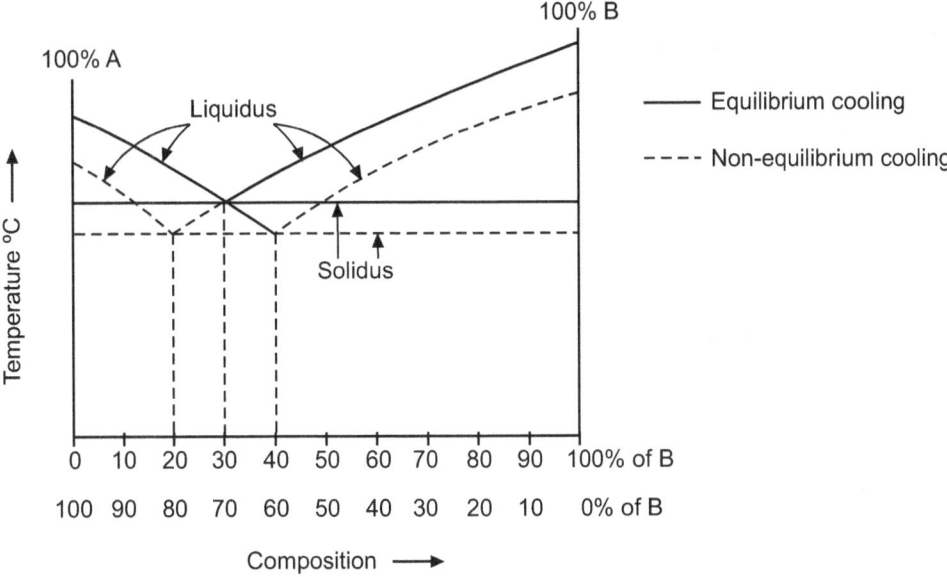

Fig. 1.18: Effect of Non-equilibrium cooling on Phase Diagram

Generally higher cooling rates during solidification of alloys give cored and in homogeneous structures.

1.21 METALLOGRAPHY

It is the study of structural characteristics of metals and their alloys w.r.t. their physical and mechanical properties.

There are two approaches of this study

- Microscopy
- Macroscopy

1.22 MICROSCOPY

In microscopy study of metal surfaces is done by using higher magnification (greater than 60X)

Higher magnification reveals large number of details about the metals and alloys under study.

1.23 SPECIMEN PREPARATION

For microscopic study, the specimen must be prepared properly. This involves sampling, polishing, mounting, electrolyte polishing and etching.

1.24 SAMPLING

The part of the object must be carefully selected so that the purpose of study is fulfilled. e.g. if nitriding is to be studies, edges and outer surfaces should be selected.

1.25 POLISHING

Polishing of samples is done in 2 steps i) rough polishing, ii) Fine.

1.25.1 Rough Polishing

Top and bottom surfaces are made flat and parallel to each other by using motor driven emery belt.

During polishing, pressure on specimen should be adequate as more pressure will given scratches on specimen.

The temperature due to friction should not rise above critical temperature otherwise, the microstructure may get changed. For this purpose, specimen is cooled by dipping in cold water during polishing.

After polishing on belt grinder, further grinding is done by using emery papers by either dry or wet method.

In dry method, emery papers of grade numbers 0,00,000 and 0000 are used in this sequence only. Between switching from one paper to another, sample is washed to remove traces of previous emery particles.

In wet method, water proof emery papers of grade numbers 200, 300, 400, 500 and 600 are used in succession. During polishing, water is flowing continuously on papers.

The emery papers use abrasive particles like alumina, chromium oxide, brasso, diamond dust and magnesium oxide.

1.25.2 Fine Polishing

During fine polishing, scratches made during rough polishing by emery papers are completely removed.

This is done on polishing wheels or laps which are made up of brass, bronze, or stainless steel covered with polishing cloth.

The laps are rotated by means of motors. Polishing of soft metals is carried out at low rpm. The clothes are made up of selvyt, velvyt, mocrocloth or miracloth.

1.25.3 Electrolytic Polishing

a) **Principle:** Whenever a direct current is passed through two electrodes viz. cathode and anode separated by an electrolyte, the material is removed from anode.

b) **Procedure:** In electrolyte polishing, the specimen whose polishing is to be cone, is made anode i.e. it is connected to +ve of direct current source as shown in Fig. 1.19.

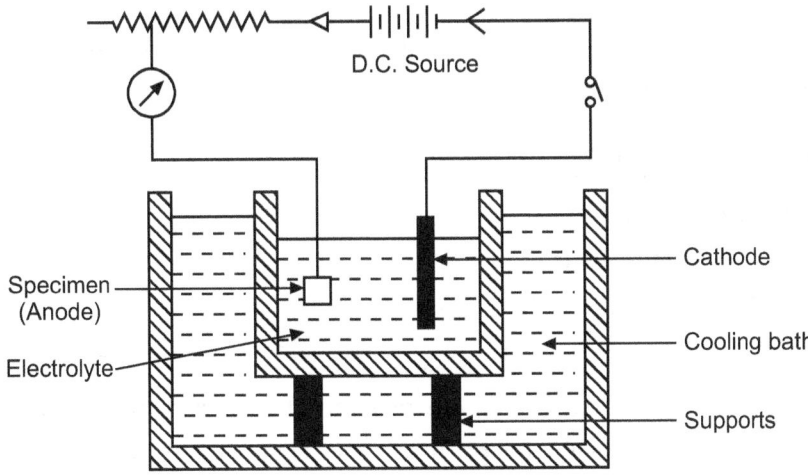

Fig. 1.19: Electrolytic polishing

When d.c. is passed by means of external source, reduction of anode takes place. As a result material is removed from it.

Now the specimen surface is rough. Therefore there are ups and downs on the surface. However material is removed only from ups or peaks whereas downs or valleys remain as it is.

After some time, all the peaks or ups will come at the level of down or valleys and the specimen gets polished.

This method is suitable for soft metals, single phase alloys and alloys.

1.26 MOUNTING

The specimens that are too small or have awkward shapes are not easy to handle. Therefore for their convenient handling during polishing, these are mounted on embedded in suitable plastic.

Mounting is done in mounting press.

The plastics used are thermosetting or thermoplastics. Bakelite moulding powder is the most commonly used material.

1.27 ETCHING

Microscopic examination of polished surface reveals non-metallic inclusions, cracks, defects. However this does not reveal structural details like grain size, presence of second phase etc. In order to reveal such structural details specimen is etched.

1.27.1 Principle

Some of the micro areas dissolve or dis-coloured to a large extent than other micro areas when specimen is subjected to a specific reagent.

1.27.2 Mechanism of Etching

a) For single alloys and pure metals:

In these difference in energy levels or potentials between grains and grain boundaries in not large. Therefore rate of reaction of etching reagent depends mainly on orientation of grains w.r.t. polished surface.

Due to extensive etching, sharp valleys are developed near the grain boundaries. These valleys appear dark than the adjacent areas as shown in Fig. 1.20 under microscope.

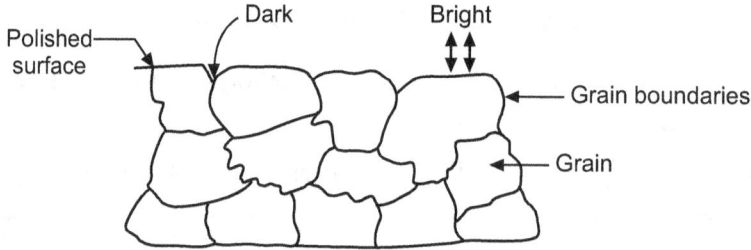

Fig. 1.20 : Microscopic appearance of single phase alloys and pure metals after etching

b) For two phase alloys

The potential of the two phases in these alloys is different. Whenever these alloys are etched the phase having lower potential or anodic phase gets depleted whereas high potential or cathoic phase gets protected.

Due to this, his lower potential phase appears darker than higher potential phase under microscope. This is shown in Fig. 1.21. e.g. pearlite is two phase mixture of ferrite and cementite. Ferrite has lower potential hence it appears dark whereas cementite as bright under microscope after etching.

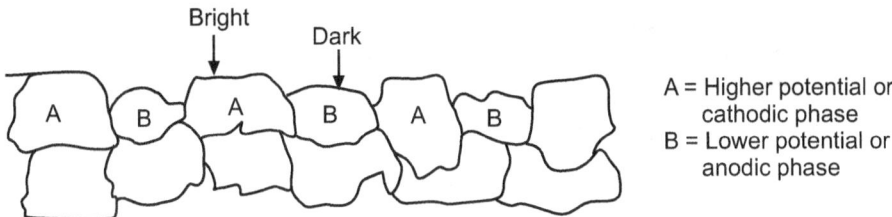

Fig. 1.21 : Microscopic appears of two phase alloy after etching

1.27.3 Etching Reagents

Some of the commonly used etching reagents are –

a) **For iron and steel:**

- Nital – Nitric acid (2 to 5 ml) + ethyl or methyl alcohol (100 ml)

- Picral – Picric acid (4 gm) + ethyl or methyl alcohol (100 ml)

- Alkaline sodium picrate – Picric acid (2 gm) + sodium hydroxide (25 gm) + distilled water (100 ml)

- Stead's reagent – $CuCl_2$ (5 gm) + $MgCl_2$ (4 gm) + HCl (1 ml) + distilled water (20 ml) + C_2H_5OH (100 ml)

b) **For stainless steel:**

- Murakami's reagent – Potassium ferricyanide (10 gm) + Potassium hydroxide (10 gm) + distilled water (100 ml.)

- Marbles reagent : CuSO4 (4 gm) + HCl (20 ml) + distilled water (100 ml)

- Aqua regia : Mixture of conc. HNO_3 and conc. HCl in proportion 1:3.

c) **For Al and its alloys:**

- Vilella's reagent: Hydrofluoric acid (20 ml) + HNO_3 (10 ml) + Glycerine (50 ml)

- Keller's etch: Hydrofluoric acid (1 ml) + HCl (1.5 ml) + HNO_3 (2.5 ml)

1.27.4 Electrolytic Etching

It is just similar to electrolytic polishing.

This method is most suitable for chemically less active metals and alloys e.g. Al and its alloys, Eight cromium steels, stainless steels.

1.27.5 Etching Procedure

For etching, the specimen is simple dipped in the etchant by means of tongs or with hand without touching its polished surface.

The specimen is held in the etchant for suitable time which depends upon type of etchant, type of material to examined and magnification required.

1.28 MACROSCOPY

Macroscopy means study of metals and alloys either by unaided eyes or with the help of low power microscope with magnification less than 10X.

It involves various methods such as sulphur prineing, phosphorus priting, oxide printing, flow line observation etc.

Macroscopy technique is used to get information about –

- Nature and structure of solidification pattern
- Flow lines in forged, extruded or drawn parts.
- Segregation of sulphide, phosphide or oxide inclusions
- Fabrication defects
- Fractures
- Presence of detects
- Size, shape and distribution of inclusions
- Porosity

1.28.1 Sulphur Printing

It is used to detect sulphur in steel. Sulphur exists in steel in the form of FeS or MnS.

The process of sulphur printing in carried out in day light and involves following steps:

a) **Cleaning:** The surface of component to be tested is firstly cleaned and grease, dirt or scale is removed.

b) **Polishing:** The cleaned surface is then hand polished with 0 or 00 number emery paper.

c) **Washing:** The surface is washed in order to remove the traces of abrasive particles of polish paper.

d) **Soaking:** A photographic bromide paper is soaked for 3 to 4 minutes in a 2% aqueous solution of sulphuric acid.

e) **Reaction:** The emulsion side of paper is held on the surface of specimen for 2 to 3 minutes with moderate pressure. Due to this, H_2SO_4 from paper comes in contact with FeS or MnS from steel and the following reactions take place –

$$FeS + H_2SO_4 \longrightarrow FeSO_4 + H_2S$$

$$MnS + H_2SO_4 \longrightarrow MnSO_4 + H_2S$$

f) **Development:** The photographic paper is then removed and washed in water. Then photographic fixer solution of silver bromide is applied fro about 15 min.

$$H_2S + 2AgBr \longrightarrow Ag_2S + 2HBr$$

This Ag_2S is brown in colour.

g) **Observation:** Thus presence of sulphur is revealed from the dark brown colour of silver sulphide.

1.28.2 Flow Observation

During manufacturing of various components, material undergoes several processes. Under the influence of various deformation forces during the manufacturing processes, material flows in a particular direction in specific pattern. These flow lines can be observed so that characteristics of material and the processes can be analysed.

For flow line observation, the surface of material is firstly cleaned and then polished by emery paper. It is then etched in a 50% aqueous solution of HCl at temperature of 50 to 60°C for about 5 to 10 min.

Due to this etching, the flow lines are emerged on the surface. By observing these flow lines, indication of mechanical processes can be obtained.

MULTIPLE CHOICE QUESTIONS (MCQ's)

1.   For a solid solution

   (a) Two metals must be completely soluble in solid state.

   (b) Two metals must be completely soluble in liquid state.

   (c) Two metals must be completely soluble in liquid and solid state.

   (d) Two metals must be completely soluble in solid and partially soluble in liquid state.

2.   A solid solution is formed between

   (a) Two metals only   (b) Two non-metals only

   (c) One metal and one non-metal   (d) One metal and one liquid

3. A solid solution is –

    (a) Homogeneous mixture

    (b) Heterogeneous mixture

    (c) Either homogenous or heterogeneous mixture

    (d) Either homogenous or heterogeneous compound

4. In brass copper is about 60% and zinc is about 40%. Here copper and brass are referred as ---- and ----- respectively.

    (a) Solution, solute   (b) Solvent, solute

    (c) Solute, solvent   (d) Solute, solution

5. In solid solutions, proportions of constituents are measured on ----- basis.

    (a) Volume   (b) Density

    (c) Valency   (d) Mass

6. The atomic number of Al and Cu are and respectively. In Duralumin, Al is about 95% and Cu is about 5%. Then Al and Cu are referred as ------ and ------ respectively.

    (a) Solvent, solution   (b) Solution, solvent

    (c) Solute, solvent   (d) Solvent, solute

7. Hume Ruther's rule is applicable to ----

    (a) Any solution   (b) Solid solution

    (c) Intermetallic compound   (d) Mixtures

8. Hume Ruther's rule govern ----

    (a) Formation of interstitial solid solutions.

    (b) Formation of substitutional solid solutions.

    (c) Formation of both interstitial and substational solid solution

    (d) Formation of intermatallic compounds

9. According to Hume Ruther which factor does not govern solid solubility ?

    (a) Crystal structure   (b) Relative size

    (c) Relative density   (d) Relative valency

10. Which of the following includes all the factors governing solid solubility according to Ruther ?

    (a) Crystal structure, relative size, chemical affinity, relative valency.

    (b) Crystal structure, relative size, specific gravity, relative valency.

    (c) Crystal structure, relative size, specific volume, atomic number.

    (d) Crystal structure, relative size, chemical affinity, atomic weight.

11.   Which of the following will have complete solid solubility?

(a) Ni (FCC structure) and Cr (BCC structure)

(b) Mg (HCP structure) and Cr (BCC structure)

(c) Cu (FCC structure) and Ni (FCC structure)

(d) Cu (FCC structure) and Mg (HCP structure)

12.   Substitutional solid solution can be easily formed with more solubility if ---

(a) Solute atom radius is more than solvent atom radius by about 20%.

(b) Solvent atom radius is more than solute atom radius by about 20%.

(c) Solvent atom radius is nearly same as solute atom radius.

(d) Solubility is independent of atomic size.

13.   If in the periodic table; two metals are separated widely then their solid solubility is

(a) Less   (b) More

(c) Unity   (d) Independent of separation

14.   Al and Ag have valencies 3 and 1 respectively. Then in solid solution.

(a) Al will dissolve more percentage of Ag.

(b) Ag will dissolve more percentage of Al.

(c) Both will dissolve each other by same percentage.

(d) Percentage dissolution is independent of valency.

15.   Interstitial solid solutions are formed by –

(a) Atoms having larger size

(b) Atoms having larger atomic mass.

(c) Atoms having less atomic mass.

(d) Atoms having less size.

16.   Iron-carbon is –

(a) Substitutional solid solution

(b) Interstitial solid solution

(c) Intermetallic compound

(d) Intermetallic mixture

17.   Intermetallic compounds are formed when

(a) 1 metal has strongly metallic and 1 metal has weakly metallic properties.

(b) 1 metal has strongly metallic and 1 metal has strongly non-metallic properties.

(c) Both have strongly metallic properties.

(d) Both have strongly non-metallic properties.

18. Mg_2Sn will have melting point.

(a) Less than Mg but higher than Sn.

(b) Less than Sn.

(c) Less than both Mg and Sn

(d) Higher than both Mg and Sn

19. Intermetallic compounds have melting point

(a) Higher than parent metal due to weak chemical bond.

(b) Less than parent metal due to weak chemical bond.

(c) Higher parent metal due to strong chemical bond.

(d) Less parent metal due to strong chemical bond.

20. If the difference in atomic size of 1 metals is more they will more likely form –

(a) Substitutional solid solution   (b) Intermetallic compound

(c) Metallic compound   (d) Interstitial solid solution

21. Phase is

(a) Homogeneous, physically distinct, and mechanically separable portion

(b) Homogeneous, physically distinct, but mechanically insepearble portion

(c) Homogeneous, physically same and mechanically separable portion

(d) Heterogeneous, physically distinct and mechanically separable portion

22. Water is poured in a vessel containing petrol then resulting system will have –

(a) One phase   (b) Two phases

(c) Three phases   (d) Zero phases

23. Petrol is poured in a vessel half filled with diesel. Then resulting system will have ----
     phases.

(a) One phase   (b) Two phases

(c) Three phases   (d) Zero phases

24. In duralumin, copper atoms concentration vary from place to place this is called as ---

(a) Disordered solid solution   (b) Ordered solid solution

(c) Interstitional solid solution   (d) Intemetallic compound

25. In duralumin, copper percentage vary from place to place, then duralumin has ---
    (a) Zero phases   (b) One phase
    (c) Two phases   (d) Many phases

26. A binary system has ---
    (a) 2 independent variables   (b) 2 dependant variable
    (c) 2 molecular species   (d) 2 independent invariables

27. Gibbs phase rule is applicable under the influence of ---
    (a) Gravity   (b) Electrical forces
    (c) Surface action   (d) Concentration

28. Gibbs phase rule is applicable in the absence of ----
    (a) Gravity   (b) Magnetic forces
    (c) Surface action   (d) Pressure

29. According to Gibbs, equilibrium is not affected by ---
    (a) Degree of freedom   (b) Pressure
    (c) Temperature   (d) Concentration

30. An invariant system requires ---- parameters to define itself
    (a) 0   (b) 1
    (c) 2   (d) Infinity

31. A system which is in equilibrium only at a definite temperature and a definite pressure is ----
    (a) Zero variant   (b) Univariant
    (c) bivariant   (d) Multivariant

32. Water, water vapour and ice are in equilibrium with each other. This system has how many degrees of freedom?
    (a) Infinity   (b) 3
    (c) 1   (d) 0

33. Water and ice are in equilibrium with each other. This system has how many degrees of freedom?
    (a) 0   (b) 1
    (c) 2   (d) Can't determine

34. A system consists of water. This system is ----
    (a) Zero variant   (b) Invariant
    (c) Bivariant   (d) Non-variant

35. A system consists of only vapour to definte this system, number of parameters required are ----

(a) 0   (b) 1

(c) 2   (d) infinity

36. Gibbs phase rule is applicalbe to systems that are at ----- state.

(a) Equilibrium   (b) Non-equilibrium

(c) Tending to equilibrium   (d) Any

37. Phase diagram shows relationship between ---- of an alloy system

(a) Temperature, phase, and structure

(b) Temperature, composition and structure

(c) Pressure, composition and structure

(d) Pressure, temperature and composition.

38. Constitutional diagrams shows –

(a) Structural changes during slow cooling and slow heating.

(b) Structural changes during fast cooling and fast heating.

(c) Chemical changes during fast cooling and fast heating.

(d) Chemical changes during slow cooling and slow heating.

39. Phase diagram is obtained by

(a) Very fast cooling   (b) Very fast heating

(c) Very slow cooling   (d) Initially cooling and then heating

40.

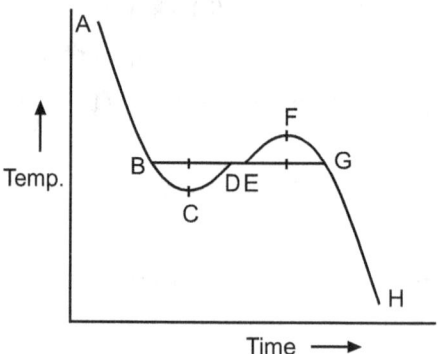

Fig. 1.22

In the cooling curve pure liquid phase is observed during

(a) A – B   (b) G – H

(c) A – B – D – E – G   (d) B – D – E – G – H

41. Cooling of pure metal without any foreign particles is shown by
    (a) A – B – 1 – D – E – 2 – G – H   (b) A – B – C – 1 – D – E – 2 – G – H
    (c) A – B – 1 – D – E – F – G – H   (d) A – B – C – D – E – F – G – H

42. In above diagram undercooling is shown by –
    (a) B – C – D   (b) E – F – G
    (c) G – H   (d) D – G

43. Undercooling is observed during cooling of –
    (a) Molten alloy
    (b) Molten metal with foreign particles
    (c) Molten metal without any foreign particles
    (d) Metallic compound

44. In above Fig. two phases are observed during –
    (a) A – B   (b) B – D
    (c) G – H   (d) B – G

45. In above figure freezing point is shown by –
    (a) Point D   (b) Point F
    (c) Point D   (d) Point B

46. In above figure solidification ends at point
    (a) H   (b) G
    (c) B   (d) C

47. The above Figure shows :
    (a) Cooling of an alloy   (b) Cooling of a metal
    (c) Heating of an alloy   (d) Heating of a metal

48.

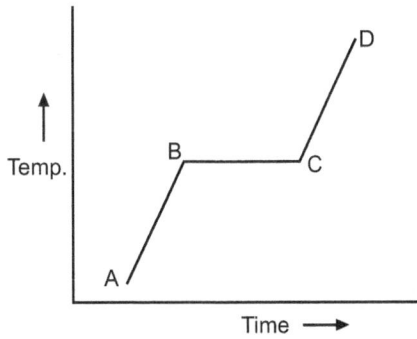

Fig. 1.23

Above figure shows –
    (a) Cooling of an alloy   (b) Cooling of a metal
    (c) Heating of an alloy   (d) Heating of a metal

49. In above figure point B shows –

(a) Starting of solidification   (b) Starting of liquid phase

(c) Completion of solidification   (d) Completion of liquid phase

50. In above figure commencement of liquidification is shown by ---

(a) Point A   (b) Point B

(c) Point C   (d) Point D

51. During solidification of metals, the crystals grow in the direction if ---

(a) in which free liquid is present   (b) Opposite to direction of free liquid

(c) in which crystals are present   (c) from centre of surface

52.

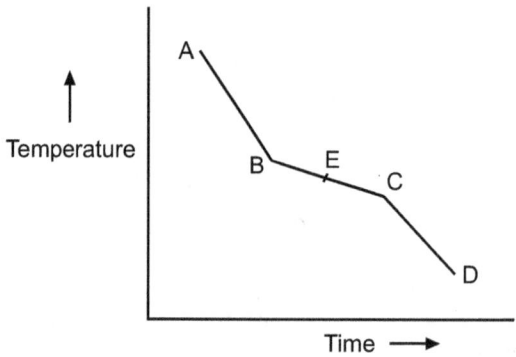

Fig. 1.24

The above figure shows –

(a) Cooling of pure metal   (b) Heating of pure metal

(c) Cooling of binary alloy   (d) Heating of binary alloy

53. In above figure solidification starts at point

(a) Point A   (b) Point B

(c) Point C   (d) Point E

54. In cooling of an alloy during solidification –

(a) Temperature is constant

(b) Temperature increases

(c) Temperature increases and then decreases

(d) Temperature decreases

55. During allotropic change in metal, the change is observed in its –

   (a) Density   (b) Mass

   (c) Temperature   (d) Valency

56. Which is not true about an allotropic change of any metal ?

   (a) It takes place at constant temperature while heating.

   (b) It takes place at constant temperature while cooling.

   (c) When it takes place heat is either evolved or absorbed.

   (d) Due to this change, physical properties do not change.

57. Which is not true about allotropic changes of any metal?

   (a) All allotropic changes are exothermic when metal is cooled.

   (b) All allotropic changes are exothermic when metal is heated.

   (c) All allotropic changes are take place at constant temperature.

   (d) Chemical properties do not vary during allotropic changes.

58. All allotropic changes are exothermic when a metal is cooled. Therefore temperature of metal will ---- during an allotropic change.

   (a) increase   (b) decrease

   (c) remains same   (d) Unpredictable

59. All allotropic change gives heat when the metal is being cooled. These changes on temperature time diagram are shown by ---

   (a) Horizontal line   (b) Vertical line

   (c) Parabola   (d) Slanting line

60. Allotropic changes takes place under the influence of ---

   (a) Density and pressure   (b) Pressure and temperature

   (c) Density and mass   (d) Density and temperature

61. Equiaxed crystals can be obtained by cooling in ---

   (a) Furnace   (b) air

   (c) oil   (d) water

62. The direction of crystal growth mainly depends upon

   (a) Density   (b) Cooling rate

   (c) Allotropic form   (d) Mass

63. Large metallic casting show ---- grain at the surface and ---- grains at the centre.

(a) Fine, coarse   (b) Coarse, fine

(c) Fine, fine   (d) Coarse, coarse

64. Coarse grain structures have mechanical qualities ----- as compared to fine grain structure.

(a) Superior   (b) Equal

(c) Inferior   (d) Unknown

65. Coarse grain structures shows corrosion resistance ----- as compared to fine

(a) more   (b) less

(c) equal   (d) unpredictable

66. Particles having radius larger than critical radius are called as

(a) embryos   (b) Nuclei

(c) Dendrites   (d) Critical particles

67. Particles smaller than critical, size are called as ---

(a) Embryos   (b) Nuclei

(c) Dendrites   (d) Critical particles

68. Dendritic structures are shown by the components that are ----

(a) Forged   (b) Rolled

(c) Spun   (d) Casted

69. Dendritic structure is formed when the further solidification takes place in the ------ direction to original direction.

(a) Parallel   (b) Same

(c) perpendicular   (d) Opposite

70. During solidification of a binary alloy forming solid solution, as time increases, the temperature.

(a) increases   (b) decreases

(c) remains same   (d) firstly decreases then remain same

71. During solidification of eutectic type alloy as time lapses the temperature ----

(a) Increases   (b) Decreases

(c) remains same   (d) Firstly decreases then remain same

72. The information that can be obtained from phase diagram is ----

(a) Phases that are present   (b) Chemical composition of each phase

(c) Structure of phase   (d) Relative amount of each phase

73.

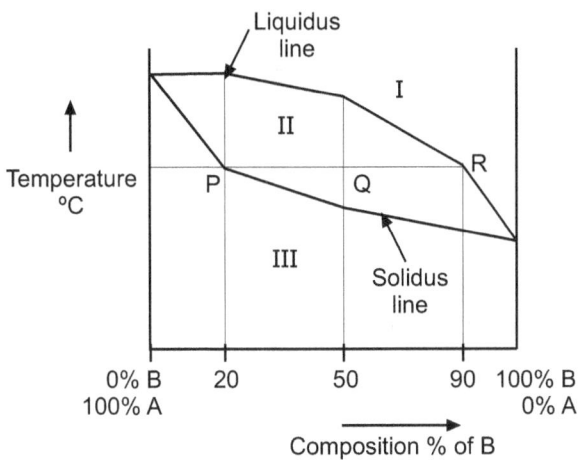

Fig. 1.25

In above diagram, number of phases present in region III ----

(a) 0   (b) 1

(c) 2   (d) 3

74. In above diagram, number of phases present in the region II ----

(a) 0   (b) 1

(c) 2   (d) 3

75. In above diagram, amount of element B present at point P is ----

(a) 20%   (b) 100%

(c) 43%   (d) 57%

76. In above diagram, amount of solid phase present at point R is ----

(a) 0%   (b) 100%

(c) 43%   (d) 57%

77. Ina above diagram, phases present in the region I ---

(a) only solid   (b) Only liquid

(c) Solid and liquid   (d) Liquid and solid

78. In above diagram, amount of element B present at point Q is ----

(a) 20%   (b) 50%

(c) 43%   (d) 57%

79. In above diagram, amount of solid phase present at point Q is ----

(a) 50%   (b) 43%

(c) 57%   (d) 100%

80. In above diagram, amount of liquid phase present at point Q is ----

(a) 50%   (b) 43%

(c) 57%   (d) 100%

81. Eutectic reaction can be given as ---

(a) Liquid + solid$_1$ $\xrightarrow{\text{Cooling}}$ solid$_2$

(b) Liquid $\xrightarrow{\text{Cooling}}$ solid$_1$ + solid$_2$

(c) Solid$_1$ $\xrightarrow{\text{Cooling}}$ liquid + solid$_2$

(d) Liquid $\xrightarrow{\text{Heating}}$ solid$_1$ + solid$_2$

82. During eutectic reaction, the temperature of the system ----

(a) Increases   (b) Decreases

(c) Remains same   (d) Initially increases then remains same

83. Peritectic reaction can be given as ----

(a) Solid$_1$ $\xrightarrow{\text{Heating}}$ liquid + solid$_2$

(b) Liquid $\xrightarrow{\text{Heating}}$ solid$_1$ + solid$_2$

(c) Solid$_1$ $\xrightarrow{\text{Cooling}}$ liquid + solid$_2$

(d) Liquid $\xrightarrow{\text{Cooling}}$ solid$_1$ + solid$_2$

84. Eutectic reaction is ----

(a) invariant   (b) univariant

(c) bivariant   (d) trivariant

85. In eutectic system, two solids are ----

(a) Completely soluble in solid state but completely insoluble in liquid state

(b) Completely soluble in liquid state but completely insoluble in solid state

(c) Completely soluble in liquid and solid state

(d) Completely insoluble in liquid and solid state

86. If a system is invariant, its phase is changed by changing ----

(a) Composition

(b) Temperature

(c) Both composition and temperature only simultaneously.

(d) Either composition or temperature

87.

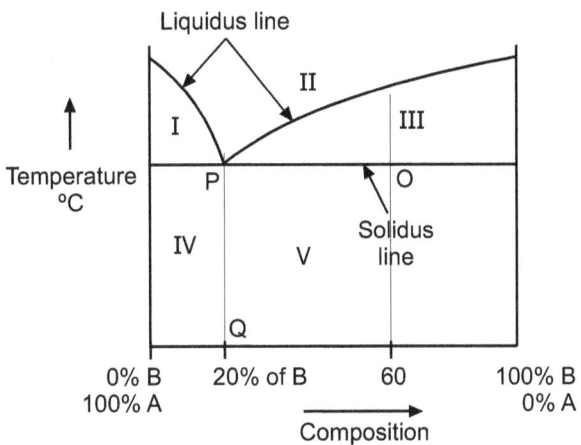

Fig. 1.26

In above figure, the reaction taking place at point P is ----

(a) Eutectic   (b) Eutectoid

(c) Peritectic   (d) Peritectoid

88. In above figure, the phases observed in the region I ----

(a) Liquid   (b) Liquid + A

(c) Liquid + B   (d) Solid

89. In above diagram, phases observed along line PQ are ----

(a) Solid A   (b) Solid A + liquid B

(c) Eutectic (A + B)   (d) Liquid A + solid B

90. In above diagram, phases observed in the region V are ----

(a) Solid A + eutectic

(b) Eutectic,

(c) Solid B + eutectic

(d) Solid A + Solid B + eutectic

91. In above diagram, composition at point O will be ----

(a) 60% B and 40% eutectic

(b) 40% eutectic and 60% B

(c) 50% A and 50% eutectic

(d) 50% B and 50% eutectic

92.

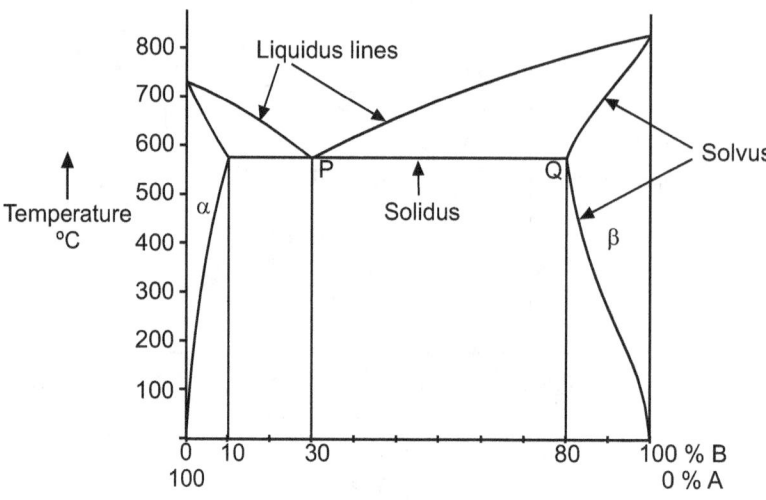

Fig. 1.26

In above figure the reaction taking place is -----

(a) Peritectic   (b) peritectoid

(c) Eutectoid   (d) Eutectic

93. Considering above Figure solubility of B in A at 500 °C is ----

(a) 10%   (b) 20%

(c) 90%   (d) 80%

94. Considering above figure maximum solubility of A in B is ----

(a) 10%   (b) 20%

(c) 90%   (d) 80%

95. In above figure along line QR, the phase observed are ----

(a) Eutectic ($\alpha + \beta$)   (b) Eutectic + β

(c) Eutectic + α (d) $\alpha + \beta$

96. Considering above figure at 500°C composition at point QR is ----

(a) 20% of eutectic + 80% β (b) 80% β + 20% eutectic

(c) 43% eutectic + 57% β (d) 57% eutectic + 43% β

97. Considering above figure composition at point Q is ----

(a) 43% β + 57% eutectic   (b) 57% β + 43% eutectic

(c) 80% eutectic + 20% β (d) 100% β

98. The eutectoid reaction in general is given by ----

(a) Liquid $\xrightarrow{\text{Cooling}}$ solid$_1$ + solid$_2$ (b) Solid $\xrightarrow{\text{Cooling}}$ solid$_1$ + solid$_2$

(c) Liquid $\xrightarrow{\text{Heating}}$ solid$_1$ + solid$_2$ (d) Solid $\xrightarrow{\text{Heating}}$ solid$_1$ + solid$_2$

99. Coring is common in parts that are ----

(a) Casted   (b) Forged

(c) Rolled   (d) Spun

100. Which of the following is not an effect of coring?

(a) Non-uniform mechanical properties (b) Increase in brittleness

(c) Non-uniform physical properties   (d) Decrease in corrosion resistance

101. Homogenization is done by ----

(a) Mechanical working   (b) Applying slow cooling

(c) Using large parts   (d) Heating and holding at high temperature

102. Homogenization is called out to ----

(a) Increase brittleness

(b) Decrease corrosion resistance

(c) Decrease coring

(d) Get different properties at different locations

103. Due to coring, the dendritic surface gets richer with element having

(a) Lower melting point   (b) Higher melting point

(c) Lower density   (d) Higher density

104. The magnitude of coring depends upon ----

(a) Melting points of elements   (b) Separation of liquidus and solidus curves

(c) Densities of elements

105. Homogenization is done at temperature ---- solidius temperature.

(a) Below   (b) Above

(c) Equal to   (d) Above or equal to

106. During non-equilibrium cooling, eutectic reaction takes place at temperature ---- than that of equilibrium cooling.

(a) More   (b) Less

(c) More or less depending upon composition

(d) Same or more

107. From microscopic observations, we can not find ----

   (a) Grain size   (b) Distribution of secondary phase

   (c) Number of phases   (d) Composition of alloy

108. From macroscopic study on can reveal

   (a) History of mechanical processes   (b) Composition of alloy

   (c) Number of phases   (d) Grain size and shape

109. Water proof emery papers are used for ----

   (a) Dry polishing   (b) Wet polishing

   (c) Fine polishing   (d) Electrolytic polishing

110. Emery papers of grade numbers 0,00,000 and 000 are used in ----

   (a) Dry polishing   (b) Wet polishing

   (c) Fine polishing   (d) Electrolytic polishing

111. Emery papers of grade numbers 200, 300, 400, 500 and 600 are used in ----

   (a) Dry polishing   (b) Wet polishing

   (c) Fine polishing   (d) Electrolytic polishing

112. In which polishing method, specimen is washed by water while switching from one emery paper to another?

   (a) Dry   (b) Wet

   (c) Fine   (d) Electrolytic

113. Clothes of selvyt or velvyt are used in which type of polishing?

   (a) Dry   (b) Wet

   (c) Fine   (d) Electrolytic

114. For polishing of very soft metals or alloy, the most suitable polishing method is ---

   (a) Dry   (b) Wet

   (c) Fine   (d) Electrolytic

115. In electrolytic polishing, the anode is made up of ----

   (a) Cu   (b) Al

   (c) Carbon   (d) Specimen to be polished

116. For mounting of specimen, the most commonly used materials is ----

   (a) Mica   (b) Bakelite

   (c) Rubber   (d) Asbestos

117. Microscopic inspection of polished surface that is not etched will reveal –

    (a) Grain size   (b) Presence of second phase

    (c) Non-metallic inclusions   (d) Composition

118. Microscopic inspection of polished surface that is not etched will not reveal ----

    (a) Non-metallic inclusions   (b) Cracks

    (c) Grain size   (d) Defects

119. For electrolytic etching, anode is made up of ----

    (a) Cu   (b) Carbon

    (c) Fe   (d) Specimen itself

120. For single phase alloys etching is mainly governed by ----

    (a) Chemical properties of material

    (b) Difference in potentials between grain and grain boundaries

    (c) Orientation of grains

    (d) Non-metallic inclusions

121. In two phase alloys etching is mainly governed by ----

    (a) Orientation of grains

    (b) Difference in potentials of two phases

    (c) Shape and sizes of grain

    (d) Non-metallic inclusions

122. During etching, anodic phase has ---- potential hence it gets ---- depleted that cathodic phase.

    (a) Lower, less   (b) Lower, more

    (c) Higher, less   (d) Higher, more

123. Which of the following etchant is not suitable for stainless steel?

    (a) Nital   (b) Murakami's reagent

    (c) Marble's reagent   (d) Aqua regia

124. Vilella's reagent is most suitable for etching of ----

    (a) Iron and steel   (b) Stainless steel

    (c) Al and its alloys   (d) Carbon

125. Stead's reagent is most suitable for etching of ----

    (a) Iron and steel   (b) Stainless steel

    (c) Al and its alloys   (d) Cu alloys

126. Electrolytic etching is most suitable for ----

    (a) Soft metals

    (b) Thin metals

    (c) Chemically less active metals and alloys

    (d) Chemically more active metals and alloys

127. Ething of high cromium steels can be effectively done by ----

    (a) Keller's etch   (b) Vilella's reagent

    (c) Nital   (d) Electrolytic etching

128. Which of the following is not true about sulphur printing?

    (a) It is used to detect sulphur in stainless steel.

    (b) It uses photographic bromide paper for printing.

    (c) It uses sulphuric acid for reaction.

    (d) The process is carried out in day light.

129. In sulphur printing, presence of sulphur is revealed from colour of ----

    (a) FeS   (b) MnS

    (c) Ag_2S (d) AgBr

130. From flow line observations, we can find ----

    (a) Mechanic processes carried out   (b) Composition

    (c) Number of phases present   (d) Solubility of phases

ANSWER KEY

1. (c)	2. (a)	3. (a)	4. (b)	5. (d)	6. (d)
7. (b)	8. (b)	9. (c)	10. (a)	11. (c)	12. (c)
13. (a)	14. (b)	15. (d)	16. (b)	17. (a)	18. (d)
19. (c)	20. (d)	21. (a)	22. (b)	23. (a)	24. (a)
25. (b)	26. (c)	27. (d)	28. (d)	29. (a)	30. (a)
31. (a)	32. (d)	33. (b)	34. (c)	35. (c)	36. (a)
37. (b)	38. (a)	39. (c)	40. (a)	41. (b)	42. (a)
43. (c)	44. (d)	45. (d)	46. (b)	47. (b)	48. (d)

49. (b)	50. (b)	51. (a)	52. (c)	53. (b)	54. (d)
55. (a)	56. (d)	57. (b)	58. (c)	59. (a)	60. (b)
61. (a)	62. (b)	63. (a)	64. (c)	65. (a)	66. (b)
67. (b)	68. (d)	69. (c)	70. (b)	71. (d)	72. (c)
73. (b)	74. (c)	75. (a)	76. (a)	77. (b)	78. (d)
79. (c)	80. (b)	81. (b)	82. (c)	83. (a)	84. (a)
85. (b)	86. (d)	87. (a)	88. (b)	89. (c)	90. (c)
91. (d)	92. (d)	93. (a)	94. (b)	95. (b)	96. (c)
97. (d)	98. (b)	99. (a)	100. (c)	101. (d)	102. (c)
103. (a)	104. (b)	105. (b)	106. (b)	107. (d)	108. (a)
109. (a)	110. (a)	111. (b)	112. (a)	113. (c)	114. (d)
115. (d)	116. (b)	117. (c)	118. (c)	119. (d)	120. (c)
121. (b)	122. (b)	123. (a)	124. (c)	125. (a)	126. (c)
127. (d)	128. (a)	129. (c)	130. (a)		

QUESTIONS

1. State whether the following statements are true or false. Justify your answers.

    1. Just after sectioning, the specimen shows micro-structure.
    2. A forged component of size 45 mm · · 60 mm height requires mounting.
    3. Lead samples are easily hot mounted.
    4. Rough polishing uses polish papers with various grades of coarseness and fineness.
    5. Lapping is necessary to all metallographic samples.
    6. Graphite may be observed without etching.
    7. Single phase and two phase alloys show same etching mechanism.
    8. Usually etchant for microscopy contains alcohol as base solvent and not water.
    9. Electrolytic polishing and etching is not recommended for gray cast iron.
    10. Macroscopy and microscopy do not differ principally.
    11. Silver utensils turn black, if kept open in air.
    12. Forged components show flowlines.

13. Fractures are observed without polishing and etching.

Ans. Q. 1

1.	False	2.	False	3.	False	4.	True	5.	True	6.	True
7.	False	8.	True	9.	True	10.	False	11.	True	12.	True

13. True

2. What is the importance of sampling ?

3. What are wet polishing and dry polishing processes ?

4. Explain etching mechanism.

5. Give any four etching reagents used for microscopy.

6. What are the various properties of lenses ?

7. Give any five applications of macroscopy.

8. Differentiate microscopy from macroscopy in respect of the following points :

    (a) Sample preparation

    (b) Etching

    (c) Result interpretation and

    (d) Applications

9. Write short notes on :

    (a) Mounting of samples.

    (b) Electro-polishing and Electro-etching.

    (c) Bright and dark field illumination.

10. Draw neat figures for :

    (a) A typical sulphur print

    (b) Flowlines in a forged sample

11. Suggest with justification a suitable test for

    (a) Segregation of tool steel from gray cast iron

    (b) Segregation of a forged shaft from a machined shaft of same material and identical dimensions.

    (c) Analysis of hot shortness in a hot rolled channel.

    (d) Observation of ferrite and pearlite.

❑❑❑

Chapter 2

CLASSIFICATION OF STEELS AND ALLOY STEELS

2.1 INTRODUCTION

Steels are known as alloys of iron and carbon containing upto 2.0 per cent carbon. Steels are principal alloys used for engineering applications. Pure iron shows higher ductility and less hardness and strength. With addition of carbon as an alloying element, the strength and the hardness of pure iron increases. The steels not containing other alloying elements are called as plain carbon steels. According to carbon content, the plain carbon steels are grouped as -

 (a)   Low carbon steels
 (b)   Medium carbon steels
 (c)   High carbon steels.

The binary system of iron and carbon is known as *Iron-Iron carbide diagram*. This diagram shows various phases present at different carbon percentages and temperatures. The properties of steel depend on the amount of these phases. The phases observed are ferrite, pearlite, austenite, cementite, ledeburite etc. The micro-structures of various plain carbon steels may be related to their engineering properties.

Finally, on commercial basis, the steels may be classified as per their alloy content, method of manufacture etc.

2.2 PURE IRON

Iron is a principal element in all engineering steels. In pure form it is termed as *Ingot iron*. Pig iron is manufactured in a 'Blast Furnace' by reduction of iron ore. For reduction and slag formation purpose, various elements such as coke, carbonates are added. Pure iron always contains some other elements, may be in traces. A typical chemical composition of pig iron (Ingot iron) is:

Carbon	:	0.012%
Manganese	:	0.017%
Phosphorus	:	0.005%
Sulphur	:	0.025%
Silicon	:	< 0.01%

Pure iron shows highest ductility in the range of various plain carbon steels. It shows almost 30 to 40% elongation in tensile testing. At the same time, it shows poor hardness as low as RB 15 to 30. However, due to higher ductility and malleability, it is mostly used in wire and sheet form. On the other hand, the corrosion resistance of ingot iron is poor. It is used, where applications and working conditions are not too critical.

Considering the physical and structural properties of iron, it shows allotropic forms. *'Allotropy' is the existence of metal in more than one type of lattice structure at various levels of temperature.*

Allotropic forms of iron on its cooling curve are shown in Fig. 2.1.

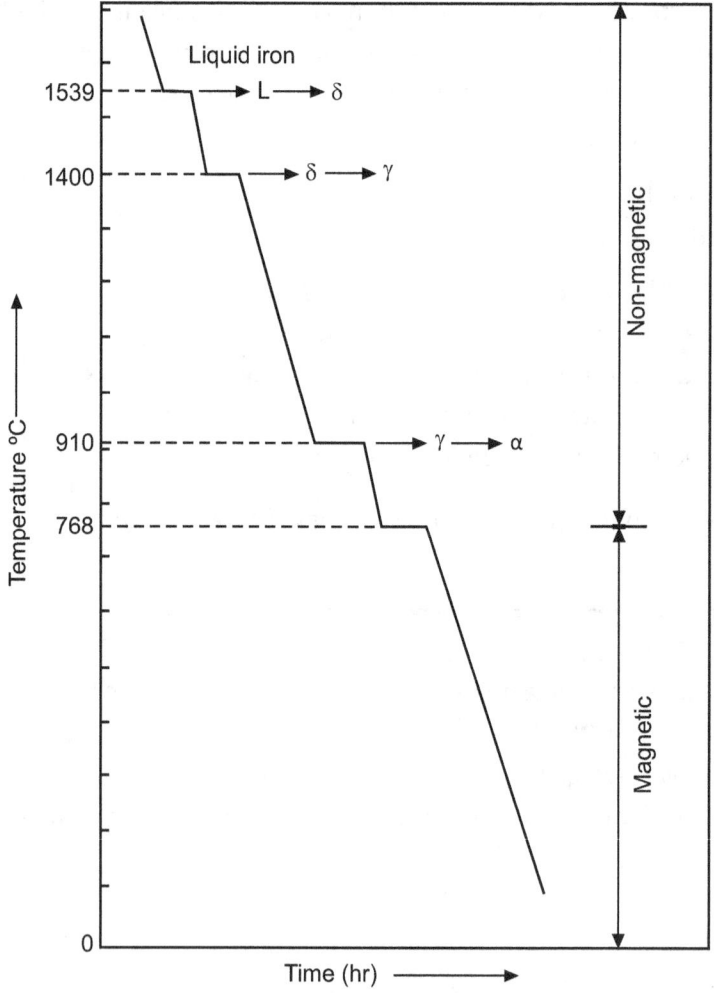

Fig. 2.1: Cooling curve of pure iron showing allotropic transformations

The melting point of iron is as high as 1539°C. It starts solidifying with formation of delta iron having B.C.C. structure, which is stable upto 1400°C. From the temperature 1400°C to 910°C, it shows gamma iron having F.C.C. crystal structure. From 910°C to room temperature, alpha iron having B.C.C. crystal structure is observed. It may be summarized as follows:

Table 2.1: Allotropic Forms of Iron

Temperature	Form and Crystal Structure
1539°C	Solidification Temperature
1539°C to 1400°C	Delta iron B.C.C.
1400°C to 910°C	Gamma iron F.C.C.
910°C to room temperature	Alpha iron B.C.C.

Within the range of temperature 910°C to room temperature, the magnetic property of iron changes. From 910 to 768°C, it is non-magnetic, while from 768°C to room temperature it is magnetic. The temperature at which its magnetic property changes is called as 'curie temperature'. It is 768°C for iron.

Volume change occurs during solidification of pure iron, which is due to its structural changes (allotropy). These are observed during heating or cooling of iron. This may be explained on the basis of closely packed property of a crystal structure. Face-centered cubic crystal structure contains more number of atoms compared to the body-centered cubic crystal structure. F.C.C. is more dense than B.C.C. When iron changes from B.C.C. to F.C.C., the density increases by 8.9%. The density of material is inversely proportional to the volume, if its mass is constant. Due to this, specific volume decreases.

All the allotropic changes give off heat (i.e. exothermic reaction), when iron is cooled and absorbs heat (i.e. endothermic reaction), when iron is heated.

Allotropy of iron is also termed as polymorphism of iron.

2.3 WROUGHT IRON

This type of iron is usually mechanically worked (and not used in as cast condition) hence, called as *wrought iron*. It consists high purity iron and slag. The slag does not have any chemical relationship with iron. It is very fine and uniformly distributed. Production of wrought iron consists of the following steps:

(a) Melting of iron,

(b) Production of iron silicate as slag, and

(c) Mechanically mixing of slag in iron.

A typical chemical analysis of wrought iron is as follows:

Carbon	:	0.06%	Phosphorus	:	0.068%
Manganese	:	0.045%	Sulphur	:	0.009%
Silicon	:	0.101%	Slag by wt.	:	2.00%

Wrought iron shows a fibrous fracture as it is similar to a composite material. The microstructure shows a uniform distribution of slag in ferrite matrix. Wrought iron shows higher ductility and strength in rolling direction. It shows better mechanical properties, if alloyed with nickel. It gives better corrosion resistance as slag fibres resist rusting.

Wrought iron is used for pipes, nails, wires, rivets etc. It is used in rail, road, oil industries etc.

Following are the distinct properties of wrought and cast irons.

Table 2.2: Comparison between Wrought Iron and Cast Iron

Sr. No.	Wrought Iron	Cast Iron
1.	It is very malleable and ductile and can readily forged when heated. It can not be cast.	It has to be melt and cast in final shapes and cannot be mechanically deformed.
2.	It has very high melting point.	It has relatively lower melting point.
3.	It cannot be hardened due to lack of carbon.	A variety of hardening processes can be used due to wide range of carbon percentage.
4.	It has fibrous fracture due to slag contents.	It has a typical dendrite structure and colour of fracture determines its type.
5.	Commercially its pure iron.	Cast iron are alloys.
6.	The most suitable processing is by mechanical deformation and welding.	The most suitable processing is by casting and machining.
7.	Typical applications include - rivets, nut bolts, structural parts, boiler plates, railway couplings, chains water and steam pipes etc.	Typical applications include - IC engine cylinder heads, blocks and gear box cases, machine and automobile parts, machine housing etc.

(May 07, 08, 13; Dec. 08, 10, 13)

2.4 IRON-IRON CARBIDE EQUILIBRIUM DIAGRAM   (Dec. 09, 10)

Earlier discussion was related to allotropic transformation of pure iron. Naturally, when carbon is added as an alloying element to iron, a change in temperature for allotropic transformation is observed.

As iron carbon alloys start with carbon percent from 0 to 6.67, the iron carbon system is limited upto 6.67% carbon. This is called as *iron-iron carbide diagram* as it starts with pure iron and ends with iron carbide. Iron carbide is chemical compound of iron and carbon called as *cementite*.

Iron-Iron carbide equilibrium diagram is plotted as temperature on Y-axis versus weight percent carbon on X-axis (Fig. 3.2). This diagram shows following phases:

(a) Ferrite (b) Austenite (c) Pearlite (d) Cementite (e) Ledeburite

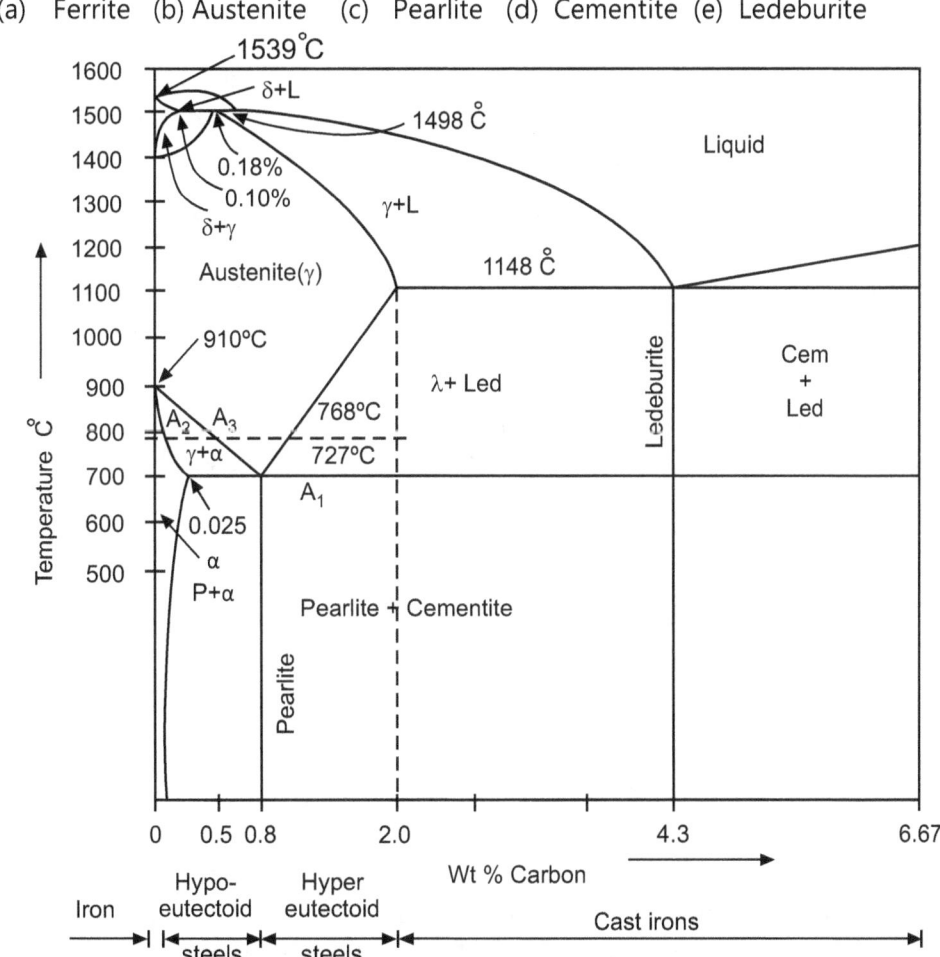

Fig. 2.2: Iron-carbon equilibrium phase diagram   (May 09, May 11)

These phases occur by slow cooling and can be explained as follows: (May 09, May 10)

(a) Ferrite:

In iron-iron carbide system, ferrite exists in two forms as delta and alpha ferrite. Delta (δ) ferrite (B.C.C.) is defined as an *interstitial solid solution of carbon in delta iron*. Delta iron exists at high temperature. Alpha (α) ferrite is defined as an *interstitial solid solution of carbon in alpha iron* (B.C.C.). It exists at room temperature. The solubility of carbon in α iron is 0.008 per cent at room temperature.

Under microscope, ferrite is seen as homogeneous polyhedral grains. It is a soft and ductile phase. It cannot be hardened by heat treatment. However, it can be hardened by cold working. It is magnetic upto 768°C and then it becomes non-magnetic.

(b) Austenite:

It is an interstitial solid solution of carbon in gamma (γ) iron (F.C.C.). It is very weak in magnetic property. The maximum solubility of carbon in austenite is 2.0% at 1148°C. This phase is stable only upto 727°C during cooling. Below 727°C, it decomposes to ferrite and cementite. It is ductile and soft phase.

Usually, steels are hot worked in austenite region. The grain size of steel at room temperature is determined by austenite grain size. Austenite transforms to various phases as pearlite, bainite and martensite. These newly formed phases show properties, which are not present in austenite e.g. Martensite is formed from austenite, showing higher hardness than austenite.

Austenite phase is observed at room temperature only in special steels such as austenitic stainless steels. For almost all heat treatments, the steels are initially heated to austenite region.

(c) Pearlite:

The alternate layers of ferrite and cementite form pearlite. It shows better strength and hardness. 100% pearlite is observed in 0.8% carbon steels.

(d) Cementite:

Cementite is an inter-metallic compound of iron and carbon. It has a fixed chemical formula as Fe_3C. Cementite has carbon content of 6.67 per cent. It is the hardest (700 BHN) and most brittle phase. It is found with ferrite in pearlite. Usually, it appears at grain boundaries in high carbon steels. Its crystal structure is orthorhombic. It is also termed as carbide, iron carbide or combined carbon. It dissolves only at high temperature. It has melting point around 1550°C. Under certain conditions, cementite decomposes to form free carbon called as graphite.

(e) Ledeburite:

It is an eutectic, consisting of pearlite and cementite. It is observed in cast irons containing 4.3% carbon. As this is found in cast irons and not in steels, it is not discussed in detail here.

2.5 VARIOUS REACTIONS OBSERVED IN IRON-IRON CARBIDE DIAGRAM   (May 09, 11; Dec. 09, 10)

This diagram consists of transformations such as liquid to solid and solid to solid. The following reactions are observed during solidification of steel:

(1) Peritectic reaction   (2) Eutectoid reaction and (3) Eutectic reaction

2.5.1 Peritectic Reaction

This is a high temperature reaction observed at 1498°C. It occurs in 0.18% carbon steel. The reaction is as follows:

$$\delta + L \underset{\text{Heating}}{\overset{\text{Cooling}}{\rightleftarrows}} \gamma$$

where, δ = Delta iron (Ferrite),

L = Liquid steel (Molten steel),

γ = Gamma iron (Austenite).

The carbon contents of these constituents are:

δ = 0.1%,

L = 0.5% and

γ = 0.18%.

In general, the reaction is given as:

$$\text{Solid}_1 + \text{Liquid} \underset{\text{Heating}}{\overset{\text{Cooling}}{\rightleftarrows}} \text{Solid}_2$$

By using lever rule, the amount of δ and L can be calculated as:

$$\text{Amount of } \delta = \frac{0.5 - 0.18}{0.5 - 0.1} \times 100 = 82.2\%$$

$$\text{Amount of liquid} = \frac{0.18 - 0.1}{0.5 - 0.1} \times 100 = 17.8\%$$

The steels having carbon less than 0.18 may be termed as *hypoperitectic steels,* while those containing more than 0.18% are termed as *hyperperitectic steels.* All steels containing carbon in the range of 0.10% to 0.45% show peritectic reaction (Fig. 2.3 a).

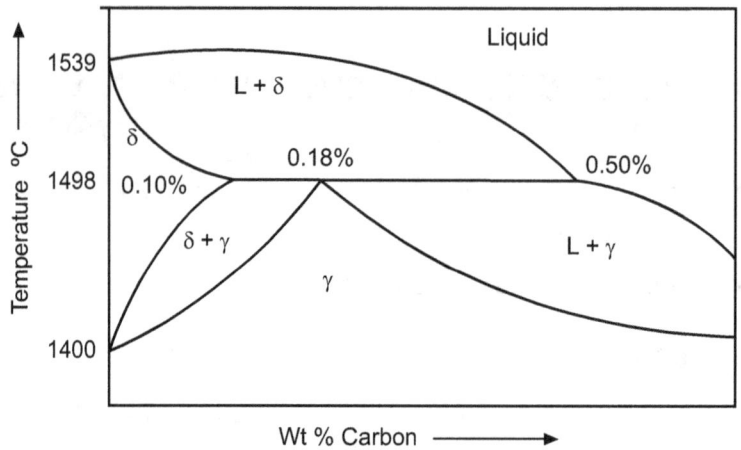

Fig. 2.3 (a): Peritectic reaction in iron-carbon system

However, commercial heat treatment is not done in delta region; we will not refer this portion again during study of steels.

2.5.2 Eutectoid Reaction   (Dec. 09)

This is a low temperature reaction observed at 727°C. It occurs in 0.8% carbon steel. The reaction is as follows:

$$\gamma \underset{\text{Heating}}{\overset{\text{Cooling}}{\rightleftharpoons}} \alpha + Fe_3C$$

where, γ = Austenite,

α = α iron (Ferrite),

Fe_3C = Combined carbon (cementite).

The carbon contents of these constituents are:

$$\gamma = 0.8\%,$$

$$\alpha = 0.025\% \text{ and}$$

$$Fe_3C = 6.67\%.$$

In general, the reaction is given as,

$$Solid_1 \underset{\text{Heating}}{\overset{\text{Cooling}}{\rightleftharpoons}} Solid_2 + Solid_3$$

The characteristic of this reaction is that, it is a solid to solid transformation. By using lever rule, the amount of phases at room temperature can be calculated as:

$$\text{Amount of ferrite} \quad = \quad \frac{6.67 - 0.8}{6.67 - 0.008} = 88.1\%$$

$$\text{Amount of cementite} \quad = \quad \frac{0.8 - 0.008}{6.67 - 0.008} = 11.9\%$$

The ratio of ferrite to cementite in pearlite is 7 : 1.

The steels having carbon less than 0.8% are called as *hypoeutectoid steels*, while the steels having more than 0.8% and less than 2.0% carbon are called *hypereutectoid steels*. The steels containing carbon in the range 0.008 to 2.0% show eutectoid reaction (Fig. 3.3 b).

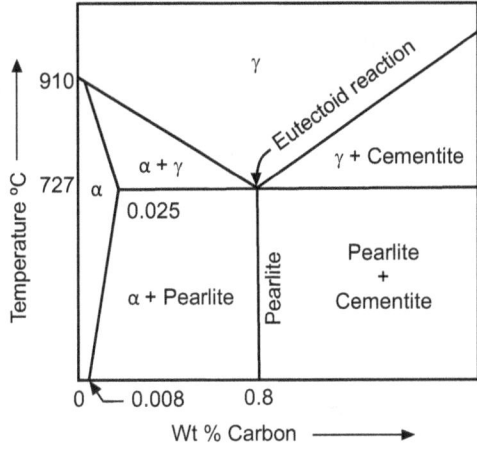

Fig. 2.3 (b): Eutectoid reaction in iron-carbon system

Since, steels are defined as iron-carbon alloys having carbon content upto 2.0% and eutectoid products are also found upto 2.0% carbon steels, this reaction is very important.

2.5.3 Eutectic Reaction

This is a medium temperature reaction observed at 1148°C. It occurs at 4.3% C alloys. It is observed only in cast irons. The reaction is as follows: (Fig. 3.3 c).

$$L \rightarrow \gamma + Fe_3C$$

where,
$$L = \text{Liquid (molten) cast iron,}$$

$$\gamma = \text{Austenite,}$$

$$Fe_3C = \text{Combined carbon or cementite.}$$

The carbon contents of these constituents are –

$$L = 4.3\% \text{ C,}$$

$$\gamma = 2.0\% \text{ C and}$$

$$Fe_3C = 6.67\% \text{ C.}$$

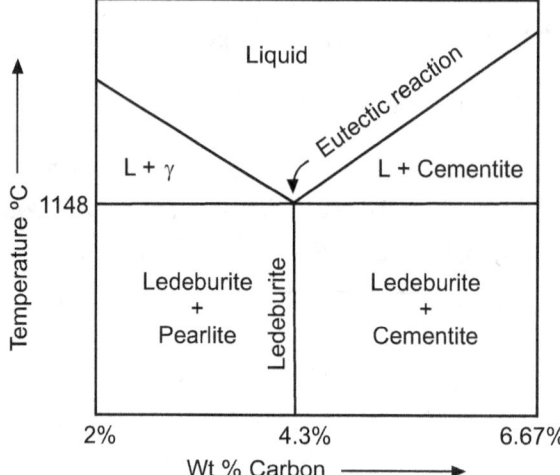

Fig. 2.3 (c): Eutectic reaction in iron - carbon system

In general, the reaction is given as

$$\text{Liquid} \underset{\text{Heating}}{\overset{\text{Cooling}}{\rightleftharpoons}} \text{Solid}_1 + \text{Solid}_2$$

By using lever rule, the amount of phases can be calculated as –

$$\text{Amount of pearlite} = \frac{6.67 - 4.3}{6.67 - 0.8} = 40.4\%$$

$$\text{Amount of cementite} = \frac{4.3 - 0.8}{6.67 - 0.8} = 59.6\%$$

The cast irons having carbon less than 4.3% are called hypoeutectic cast irons, while those containing more than 4.3% carbon are hypereutectic cast irons. The cast irons containing carbon in the range of 2 to 6.67% undergo eutectic reaction. As ledeburite contains pearlite and cementite, which are hard phases, resultant eutectic is also hard. However, cast iron usually shows graphite (free carbon) instead of cementite due to high carbon content, show cooling rates of graphitizing agents.

2.6 SOLUBILITY OF CARBON IN IRON

At a higher temperature, the allotropic form of iron is austenite. It is F.C.C. It is a dense structure having four atoms per unit cell. The low temperature allotropic form of iron is ferrite. It is B.C.C. It is a less dense structure having two atoms per unit cell. So, expansion takes place during formation of ferrite from austenite. The voids (interstices) available in austenite are 25 per cent, while in ferrite 32 per cent. When carbon forms an interstitial solid solution with iron, it occupies voids or interstices. So above numbers may show that carbon has more solubility in ferrite than in austenite. But practically, carbon has more solubility in austenite.

This may be explained as the largest interstitial atom that would just fit in a B.C.C. and has a radius of 0.36×10^{-8} cm. While the largest interstitial atom that would just fit in a F.C.C. has a radius of 0.52×10^{-8} cm. Since, the carbon atom has a radius of 0.7×10^{-8} cm, it can fit into interstices of F.C.C. easily than in B.C.C. Also, the solubility of carbon atoms in B.C.C. gets restricted as lattice distortion in B.C.C. is more than that in F.C.C. Therefore, carbon shows maximum 2 per cent solubility in austenite.

2.7 CRITICAL TEMPERATURES   (Dec. 09, May 06, 10, 13)

These are defined as the *temperatures at which a phase change occurs during heating or cooling.* Various critical temperatures are given as follows:

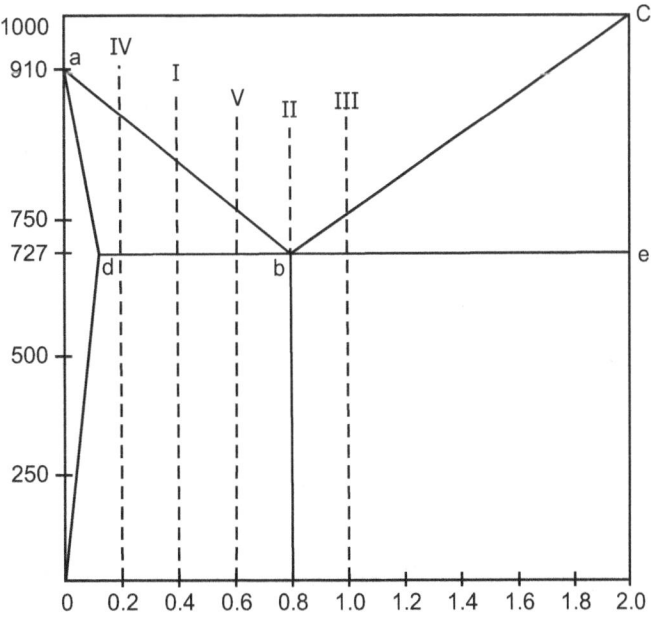

Fig. 2.4: Critical temperature lines of Fe-C system

1. **A_1:** During heating, at this temperature, pearlite transforms to austenite. This transformation occurs at a constant temperature of 727°C called as eutectoid temperature. It has importance in various annealing processes. It is called as lower critical temperature line. It denoted by AC_1 and Ar_1 during heating and cooling respectively.

2. **A_2:** This line indicates curie temperature 768°C. During heating, the ferrite which is magnetic becomes non-magnetic above this line.

3. **A_3:** This line, in hypoeutectoid steels, shows the completion of ferrite to austenite transformation during heating. The line declines from temperature axis with increasing carbon content. It starts at 910°C with 0% carbon and comes to 727°C with 0.8% carbon. Hereafter, A_3 line goes parallel to x-axis, at 727°C, till 2.0% carbon. For various heat treatment, the hypoeutectoid steels should be heated above this line. This line represents upper critical temperature for ferrite. It is denoted by AC_3 and AC_2 during heating and cooling respectively.

4. **AC_m:** At this line, in hypereutectoid steels, the cementite to austenite transformation is completed during heating. The line shows increasing slope from 727°C to 1148°C. It starts at 727°C with 0.8% carbon and ends at 1148°C with 2% carbon. For certain heat treatment, which involves dissolution of cementite, hypereutectoid steels are heated above this line. This line represents upper critical temperature for cementite.

During heating or cooling with faster rates, the transformations occur at higher or lower temperatures respectively. This shifts the equilibrium of critical temperature lines. These lines are denoted by letter C (from the French word Chauffage - means heating) and by a letter r (from the French word refroidissement means cooling), e.g. AC_1, AC_3, – During heating, and Ar_1, Ar_3 – During cooling.

2.8 SLOW COOLING OF STEEL

During solidification of steels, various phase transformations occur. Here, slow cooling of different carbon steels from austenite region is considered.

(a) Slow cooling of hypoeutectoid steels (Alloy a):

These steels are having carbon less than 0.8 per cent. Consider the slow cooling of alloy (a) (Fig. 2.5) having 0.4% carbon. A part of iron-carbon diagram is used to explain this slow cooling.

In austenite region, the alloy contains only single phase austenite. Each grain contains carbon in dissolved state. During slow cooling, the alloy crosses A_3 line. At this line, allotropic changes take place and F.C.C. starts changing to B.C.C. Therefore, ferrite starts forming at the austenite grain boundaries. Formation of ferrite proceeds with rejection of carbon, which

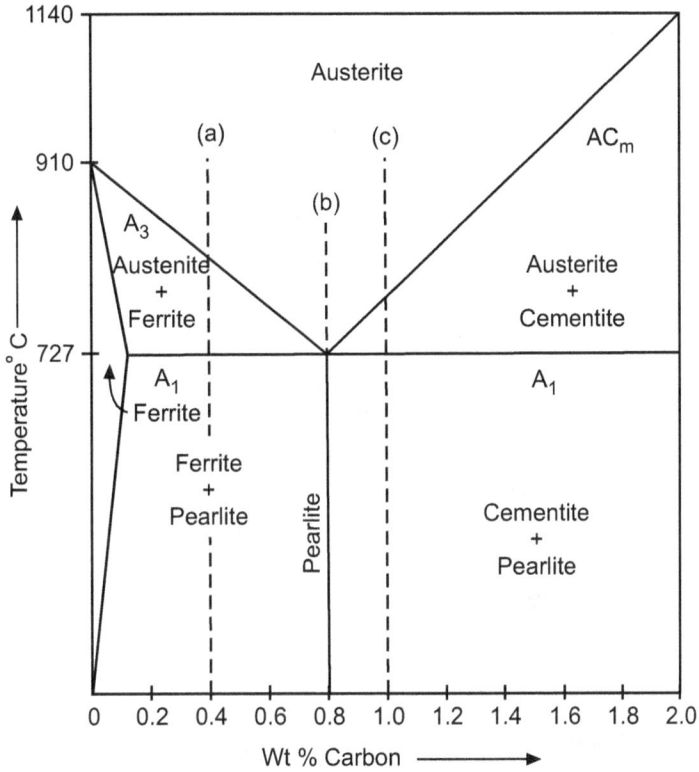

(a) 0.4% carbon steel, (b) 0.8% carbon steel, (c) 1.0% carbon steel

Fig. 2.5: Slow cooling of steel from austenite region

dissolves in austenite. So austenite becomes rich in carbon. Upto A_1 line, the steel contains ferrite and carbon rich austenite . As this steel crosses A_1 i.e. eutectoid transformation line, the austenite undergoes eutectoid transformation and forms pearlite. These combinations of ferrite and pearlite remain unchanged upto room temperature. The percentage of phases may be calculated as per lever rule as -

$$\text{Amount of ferrite} = \frac{0.8 - 0.4}{0.8 - 0.008} \times 100 = 50\%$$

$$\text{Amount of pearlite} = \frac{0.4 - 0.008}{0.8 - 0.008} \times 100 = 50\%$$

Similarly, the slow cooling of 0.2 and 0.6% carbon steel may be explained.

(b) **Slow cooling of eutectoid steel (alloy b):**

The 0.8% carbon steel is known as eutectoid steel. Consider the transformations of 0.8% C steel from austenite region. Alloy b shows a homogeneous austenite. When cooling proceeds due to eutectoid reaction, the total austenite transforms at 727°C to 100% pearlite. The details of eutectoid reactions are explained earlier. At room temperature, the micro-structure shows lameller pearlite.

(c) Slow cooling of hypereutectoid steels (Alloy c):

The steels having more than 0.8 and upto 2.0% carbon are known as *hypereutectoid steels*.

Consider the slow cooling of 1.0% carbon steel. In the austenite region, the alloy consists of a uniform austenite phase. During slow cooling, no appreciable change is observed upto AC_m line. As the temperature decreases, the solubility of carbon in austenite decreases along AC_m line towards eutectoid point. Due to decrease in carbon solubility, excess carbon comes out. This gets precipitated along the grain boundaries of austenite. Upto A_1 line, the micro-structure consists of proeutectoid cementite and austenite. The excess cementite forms a network along austenite grains. As soon as the A_1 line is crossed, the austenite gets transformed to pearlite, while cementite remains unchanged. Therefore, the micro-structure of hypereutectoid steel at room temperature consists of pearlite grains surrounded by cementite network. The amount of phases may be calculated as per lever rule as -

$$\text{Amount of cementite} = \frac{1.0 - 0.8}{6.67 - 0.8} \times 100 = 3\%$$

$$\text{Amount of pearlite} = \frac{6.67 - 1.0}{6.67 - 0.8} \times 100 = 97\%$$

Similarly, slow cooling of any steel ranging from 0.8 to 2.0% carbon may be studied.

Table 2.3 shows amount of ferrite, pearlite and cementite with carbon content of steel. This also helps to estimate the carbon from micro-structure.

Table 2.3: Amount of phases present in various carbon steels

Specimen	% Carbon	Approximate percentage of phases		
Number		Ferrite	Cementite	Pearlite
a	0.008	100	–	–
b	0.2	75	–	25
c	0.4	50	–	50
d	0.6	25	–	75
e	0.8	–	–	100
f	1.0	–	3	97

The micro-structures of carbon steels listed in Table 2.3 are shown in Fig. 2.6.

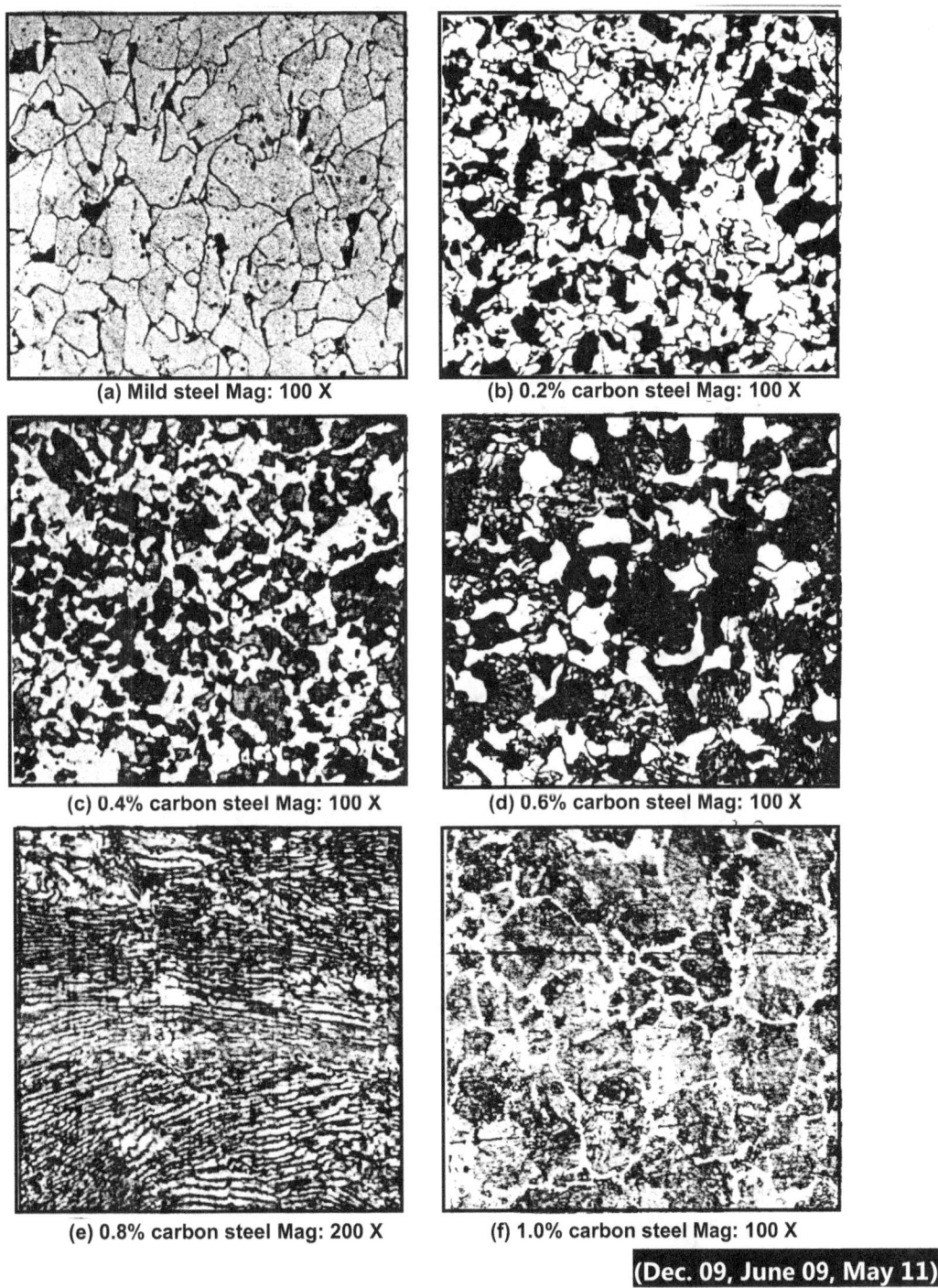

(a) Mild steel Mag: 100 X   (b) 0.2% carbon steel Mag: 100 X

(c) 0.4% carbon steel Mag: 100 X   (d) 0.6% carbon steel Mag: 100 X

(e) 0.8% carbon steel Mag: 200 X   (f) 1.0% carbon steel Mag: 100 X

(Dec. 09, June 09, May 11)

Fig. 2.6: Micro-structures of slow cooled steels

2.9 ETCHING OF VARIOUS PHASES

After etching with Nital, various phases may be distinguished by their appearance. e.g.

- Very low carbon steels having 100% ferrite show dark grain boundaries with bright ferrite grains.
- Hypoeutectoid steels show bright ferrite grains and pearlite dark.
- A typical eutectoid structure shows thumb print type appearance.
- A hypereutectoid steel shows bright network of cementite surrounding to dark grains of pearlite.

In pearlite, cementite phase appears dark, when etched with nital. In fact, the boundary between ferrite and cementite gets etched. Since, the cementite is thin, both edges are closer and many times are not resolved. Therefore, it appears as a one line, showing presence of cementite.

Both cementite and ferrite phase appear bright under microscope, when etched with nital. However, the ferrite phase shows polyhedral and massive grain shape and cementite shows sharp boundaries with tendency of grain boundary network formation. To distinguish them, some special etchant like picral is used. It darkens the cementite and leaves ferrite as bright.

2.10 NON-EQUILIBRIUM COOLING OF STEELS   (Dec. 09)

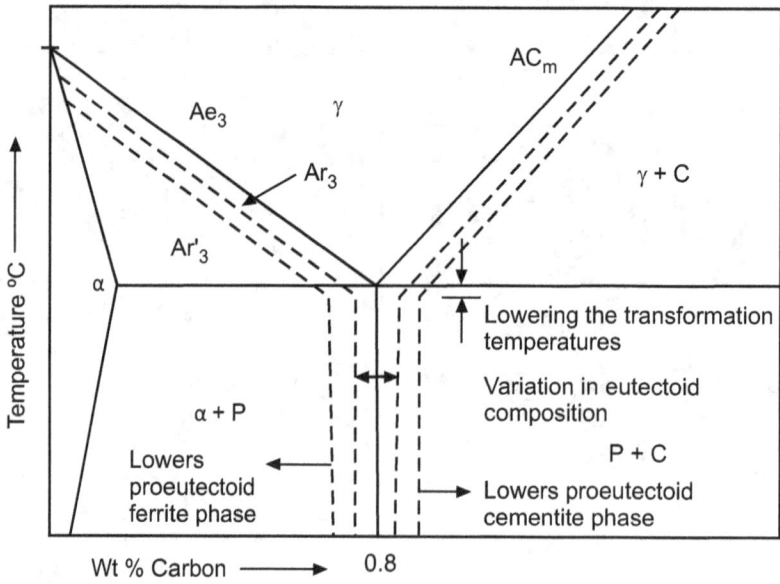

Fig. 2.7: Effect of faster cooling rates on iron-carbon diagram

The iron-iron carbide equilibrium diagram is based on slow cooling of austenite. This results in the combination of cementite and ferrite. Non-equilibrium cooling refers to fast cooling of steel. Naturally, fast cooling results in different transformation. If steel is heated in austenite region and rapidly cooled, martensite will be formed instead of pearlite. Interrupted cooling gives bainite.

Due to change in micro-structure, the mechanical properties of steel change. Eutectoid temperature lowers due to fast cooling. This decreases amount of proeutectoid phase and increases amount of eutectoid phase (Fig. 2.7). Slightly fast cooling results in fine pearlite due to decrease in inter-lameller spacing.

2.11 WIDMANSTATTEN STRUCTURES

Usually, during cooling of steel from austenite region, the proeutectoid phase separates along grain boundary. However, the phase sometimes separates not only along the grain boundaries, but also in the grain interiors. It separates out in a definite orientation. These types of structures are called as Widmanstatten structures (Fig. 2.8).

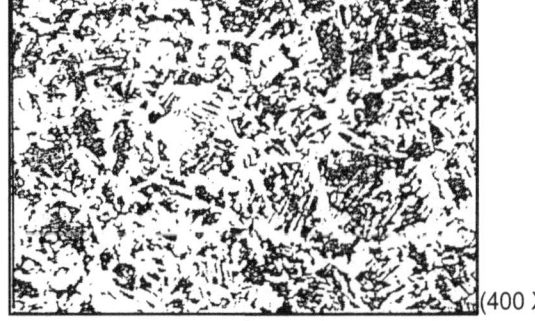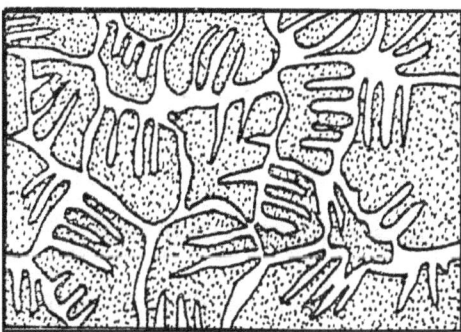

(400 X)

Fig. 2.8: Widmanstatten structures

(Photograph and Schematic)

The formation of Widmanstatten structure is higher, if the steel has a composition deviating from the eutectoid point. This is for the reason that the formation of proeutectoid phase increases, if steel is not eutectoid. The proeutectoid phase cannot reach to grain boundary, if the grain size is more. So the chances of formation of this structure are more, if grain size is coarse. Similarly, non-equilibrium cooling does not permit diffusion of proeutectoid phases towards boundary and increases possibility of Widmanstatten structure. These structures are observed in steels having carbon percentage upto 0.7 and above 0.9.

In hypereutectoid steels, the Widmanstatten structure is desirable. It is because the hard and brittle cementite phase does not appear in the form of continuous network along grain boundary. This improves the strength. Whereas in hypoeutectoid steels, Widmanstatten structure reduces ductility by breaking the continuity of ferrite. And, therefore, it is not desirable in hypoeutectoid steels.

2.12 STRUCTURE-PROPERTY RELATIONSHIP

Basically, steel is an alloy of iron and carbon. With increasing carbon percentage, steel shows phases like ferrite, pearlite and cementite. Ferrite is a very soft and ductile phase, pearlite shows better strength and cementite is the hardest of the phases. Therefore, the properties of steel depend upon the proportion of these phases.

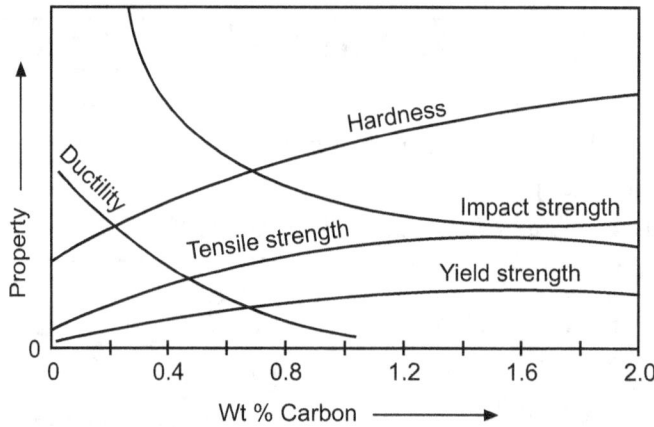

Fig. 2.9: Effect of carbon content on various properties of plain carbon steels

In general, the hardness increases as the carbon content increases upto about 2.0% (Fig. 2.9). The tensile strength and yield strength also increases up to about 0.8% carbon. The percentage of elongation and reduction in area drops sharply with increase in carbon percentage. The impact strength also decreases very sharply after 0.8% carbon.

Ferrite shows tensile strength of about 40,000 psi and cementite shows about 40,000 to 60,000 psi. Pearlite, which is combination of ferrite and cementite shows higher tensile strength as 100,000 psi. It shows hardness inbetween ferrite and cementite.

Usually, for a two phase material having phases as x and y, average property may be given as follows:

Average property = (Amount of x × property of x) + (Amount of y × Property of y)

For hypereutectoid steels (V.P.N.)

= 10 [(90 × Amount of cementite) + (24 × Amount of pearlite)]

Similarly, the hardness is expressed as for hypoeutectoid steel (B.H.N.)

$$= [(8 \text{ times ferrite}) + (23 \text{ times pearlite})]$$

Hypoeutectoid steel shows less hardness so they may be measured in B.H.N., while due to higher hardness, normally hypereutectoid steels are given in V.P.N.

Similarly, the tensile strength may be given as:

$$\text{T.S. kg/mm}^2 = 4 [(7 \times \text{Amount of ferrite}) + (21 \times \text{Amount of pearlite})]$$

Tensile strength is also expressed in terms of hardness as: For stress relieved and soft plain carbon steels U.T.S. $(\text{kg/mm}^2) = 0.36 \times \text{B.H.N.}$

For hardened and tempered plain carbon steels, U.T.S. $(\text{kg/mm}^2) = 0.32 \text{ BHN}$.

Micro-hardness may be used for finding hardness of individual phases.

As austenite is not a stable phase and it is not observed at room temperature, mechanical properties of steels are usually independent of austenite. However, the final grain size of steel depends upon initial grain size of austenite. The structure-property relationship for austenite phase may be considered in austenitic stainless steel.

2.13 CLASSIFICATION AND APPLICATIONS OF STEELS

The steels are classified on the basis of various factors like:

(1) Carbon content,

(2) Amount of alloy additions,

(3) Deoxidation method used,

(4) Manufacturing method and

(5) Applications.

2.13.1 Classification Based on Carbon Content

Plain carbon steels are classified as per its carbon content as follows:

- Low carbon steels (carbon content upto 0.3%)
- Medium carbon steels (carbon content from 0.3 - 0.7%)
- High carbon steels (carbon content more than 0.7%)

(A) Low carbon steels:

These steels show good ductility and formability. They exhibit better fabrication properties. Mild steel is widely used (< 0.2% C). They can be easily cold worked as rolling, forging, pressing, drawing etc. Depending upon their carbon content, they are used for the following purposes:

0.02 to 0.10% C → Nails, stampings, rivets.

0.10 to 0.20% C → Free cutting steels, carburising steels, bolts and structural steels.

0.20 to 0.30% C → Carburising steels, cams, camshafts, gears, cranks and levers.

(B) Medium carbon steels:

They show high hardness than low carbon steel. They are not so ductile and malleable. They are usually hot worked. They are mostly recommended for applications requiring a combination of strength and hardness. As per carbon content, they may be used for the following purposes:

0.30 to 0.40% C → Heat treated bolts, screws, nuts, axles, cold heading machine parts.

0.40 to 0.50% C → Axles, bolts, camshafts, forgings, studs etc.

0.50 to 0.60% C→ Oil hardening gears.

0.60 to 0.70% C → Washers, dies, screw drivers, socket screws, less load tools.

(C) High carbon steels:

They are hard due to higher carbon percentages. They show good wear and abrasion resistance. High carbon steels are characterised by poor machinability and weldability. They are mostly suitable for tools. As per carbon content they are grouped as follows for applications:

0.70 to 0.80% C → Wrenches, band saw, medium load tools.

0.80 to 0.90% C → Agricultural applications, knives, springs, chisels, punches, shear blade, music wires, various blades.

0.90 to 1.00% C → Various dies and cutting blades.

1.00 to 1.10% C → Ball bearings, drill bits, tool bits, milling cutters, taps.

1.10 to 1.20% C → Various cutting tools.

1.20 to 1.30% C → Various grades of files, heavy cutting tools.

1.30 to 1.40% C → Boring tools, mining tools, stone crushing plates.

2.13.2 Classification Based on the Amount of Alloy Additions

Various alloying elements are added to improve mechanical properties of steels. Some of the alloying elements get dissolved in ferrite and improve its strength, while others form carbides and increase hardness, wear and abrasion resistance. These are basically low alloy steels (alloying elements < 10%) and high alloy steels (alloying elements > 10%). With carbon content, they may be further grouped as:

- Low carbon low alloy steels,
- Low carbon high alloy steels,
- Medium carbon low alloy steels,
- Medium carbon high alloy steels,
- High carbon low alloy steels and
- High carbon high alloy steels.

2.13.3 Classification as per Deoxidation Method Used

(May 07, 09, 10, 11, 13; Dec. 07)

Molten steel contains dissolved oxygen in large amount. This oxygen gives rise to blowholes, gas porosity, macro-segregation etc. Deoxidation, therefore, becomes necessary. Depending upon the deoxidation method used, steels are classified as:

- Rimmed steels,
- Semi-killed steels and
- Killed steels.

Rimmed steels are not deoxidised. Oxygen combines with carbon to form CO. During solidification, it gets entrapped in the ingot. After cooling, a thin outer layer (rim) gets solidified and does not contain blowholes or segregation. The entrapped gases form blowholes and macro-segregation at the centre. These can be eliminated by mechanical working. However, these steels are not used for forging operations.

In semi-killed steels, part of dissolved oxygen is removed by using deoxidisers. Less blowholes are observed. They are used for structural parts.

In killed steels, the dissolved oxygen is completely removed by using strong deoxidisers as Aluminium and Silicon. These deoxidisers remove oxygen, but form oxide inclusions. They do not show blowholes. They are usually forged, rolled etc. and they are used in making machine parts subjected to dynamic load.

2.13.4 Classification based on manufacturing process

According to manufacturing methods, the steels are classified as:

- Basic open hearth process.
- Electric furnace process.

- Basic oxygen process.
- Acid Bessemer process.
- Acid open hearth process.

The description of these processes is a part of extractive metallurgy and iron and steel productions, so it is not explained in detail here.

2.13.5 Classification based on applications

As per applications, the steels are classified as follows:

- Boiler steels
- Magnetic steels
- Spring steels
- Machinery steels
- Bearing steels

- Electrical steels
- Corrosion resistant steels
- Structural steels
- Tool steels
- Die steels

2.14 SPECIFICATIONS OF STEELS

The steels are specified as follows:

- Indian standards - IS
- American standards - AISI

    (American Iron and Steels Institute) or

    SAE - (Society of Automotive Engineers)
- British Standards: En, BS.

2.14.1 Specifications as per Indian standards

This is covered in two parts:

- Designation of steels based on letter symbols (part I).
- Designation of steels based on numerals (part II).

Usually, steels are classified on the basis of chemical composition or mechanical properties.

Following are the considerations used in IS -

- Symbol Fe denotes minimum tensile strength (N/mm^2) e.g. Fe 200 means steel with min. T.S. = 200 N/mm^2.

- Symbol FeE denotes minimum yield strength (N/mm^2) e.g. FeE 225 means steel with min Y.S. = 225 N/mm^2.

- The letter given next to Fe symbol denotes characteristics as deoxidation, weldability etc. e.g. Fe 200 K means killed steel with min T.S. = 200 N/mm^2.

- Plain carbon steels are designated by letter C and tool steel by T.

- Actual carbon content is given by a number indicating 100 times the average percentage of carbon, e.g. 0.2% C plain carbon steel is designated as C 20.

- In free cutting steels, symbols such as S, Pb or P are followed by a number indicating 100 times the percentage content of that element. Carbon content is followed by a number indicating 10 times Manganese content e.g. 35 C 10 S 14 means 0.35% C, 1.0% Mn and 0.14% S.

- In alloy steels, designation carries alloying element along with a number. When element is < 10% then this number is a product of element content and a multiplication factor given in Table 2.4.

Table 2.4: Element and multiplying factor

Element	Multiplying factor
(1) Cr, Co, Ni, Mn, Si and W	4
(2) Al, Be, V, Pb, Cu, Nb, Ti, Ta, Zr, and Mo	10
(3) P, S and N	100

e.g. 40 Ni 8Cr 8V2 means 0.4% C, 2% Ni, 2% Cr and 0.2% V.

- High alloy steels containing > 10% alloy content are indexed by X (alloy steel other than tool steels) and XT (alloy tool steels), e.g.

    - X15 Cr 25 Ni 12 means high alloy steels with 0.15% C, 25% Cr, 12% Ni.

    - XT 75 W 18 Cr 4 V1 means high alloy tool steels with 0.75% C, 18% W, 4% Cr and 1% V.

Some typical examples of steels specified by IS are given in Table 2.5.

Table 2.5: Typical is specifications of steel

	Designation	Details
1.	14 C 6	0.14% C, 0.6% Mn
2.	113 C 6	1.13% C, 0.6% Mn
3.	10 C 8 S 10	0.1% C, 0.08% S, 1% Mn
4.	15 Cr 65	0.15% C, 0.65% Cr
5.	20 Mn Cr 1	0.2% Cr, 1% Mn, 1% Cr
6.	13 N; 3Cr 80	0.13%C, 3%Ni, 0.8% Cr
7.	15 Ni Cr 1 Mo 12	0.15% C, 1% Ni, 1% Cr, 0.12% Mo
8.	40 Cr 3 Mo 1 V 20	0.40% C, 3% Cr, 1% Mo, 0.2% V
9.	55 Cr 70	0.55% C, 0.7% Cr
10.	04 Cr 17 Ni 12 Mo 2 Ti 20	0.04% C, 17% Cr, 12% Ni, 2% Mo, 0.2% Ti
11.	T 70	0.70% C tool steel
12.	T 80 V 23	0.80% C tool steel
13.	T 83 Mo W 6 Cr 4 V 2	0.8% C Tool steel, 6% Mo, 6% W, 4% Cr, 2% V.

2.14.2 Specifications as per American Standards (AISI or SAE)

This system uses 4 to 5 numbers for designation of steels. First number indicates the type of steel; second indicates alloy per cent and last two or three numbers give carbon content divided by 100.

The first number indicates the steel as follows:

Table 2.6: Meaning of First Digit as per AIST

Number	Designation
1	Carbon steels
2	Nickel steels
3	Nickel - Chromium steels
4	Molybdenum steels
5	Chromium steels
6	Chromium - Vanadium steels
7	Tungsten steels
8	Nickel - Chromium Molybdenum steels
9	Silicon-Manganese steels

Consider some examples of AISI steel as follows:

    1040 - Plain carbon steels with 0.4% carbon.

    2440 - Nickel steels 4% Ni and 0.4% carbon.

These are average percentages, practically, a range of metal content is given as:

AISI 2330 means 0.28 - 0.33% C, 3.25 - 3.75% Ni and called as 3% Nickel steels.

Some AISI steel specifications are given in Table 2.7.

Table 2.7: AISI specification of steels

Sr. No.	AISI No.	Composition percentage
1.	1010	0.1% Plain carbon steel
2.	1035	0.35% Plain carbon steel
3.	1095	0.95% Plain carbon steel
4.	1112	0.12% Carbon free machining steel
5.	12L14	0.12% Carbon, 0.14% Lead, free machining steel
6.	1330	0.3% Carbon, Manganese steel
7.	2317	0.17% Carbon, 3% Ni
8.	2512	0.12% Carbon, 5% Ni
9.	3115	0.15% Carbon, 1% Ni, 1% Cr
10.	4419	0.19% C, 0.4% Mo
11.	5130	0.30% C, 1% Cr
12.	6118	0.18% C, 1% Cr, 0.1% V
13.	8620	0.20% C, 0.6% Ni, 0.6% Cr, 0.2% Mo
14.	9260	0.6% C, 2% Si, 1% Mn
15.	94B30	0.3% C, 1% Ni, 1% Cr, 0.2% Mo, Boron steel

2.14.3 Specifications as per British standards

These are also widely used. As per these specifications, the steels are not related with any typical mechanical property or manufacturing process. They are expressed as En numbers.

    e.g. En 8 means 0.4% C, 0.8% Mn carbon steel.

Table 2.8 gives some En numbers with compositions of steels.

Table 2.8: In number and composition of steels

En. No.	Composition percentage
En 1	0.09% C, 0.1% Si, 1% Mn, 0.2% S
	Plain Carbon free cutting steel
En 8	0.4% C, 0.8% Mn
En 42	0.8% C, 0.8% Mn
En 15	0.4% C, 0.3% Si, 1.0% Mn
En 18	0.4%C, 0.3% Si, 0.7% Mn, 1% Cr
En 24	0.4% C, 0.3% Si, 0.6% Mn, 1.7% Ni
	1% Cr, 0.25% Mo
En 59	0.8% C, 2% Si, 0.5% Mn, 1.5% Ni, 18% Cr.

Other than these specifications following standards are also used as:

(1) DIN - German Standard

(2) GOST - Russian standard

Equivalence between various standards may be obtained as follows:

Table 2.9: Equivalence between various standards

Sr. No.	IS No.	AISI / SAE No.	En No.
1.	30 C 8	1030	5
2.	55 C 4	1055	9
3.	80 C 6	1080	42
4.	20 Mn Cr 1	5120	207
5.	37 Mn 2	1036	15
6.	40 Ni Cr 1 Mo 15	4340	110
7.	55 Si 2 Mn 90	9255	45
8.	04 Cr 18 Ni 11	304	58E
9.	04 Cr 17 Ni 12 Mo 2	316	58J
10.	T 90	W1	–
11.	105 Cr 1 Mn 60	52100	31
12.	35 Ni 1 Cr 60	3140	111

2.15 LIMITATIONS OF PLAIN CARBON STEELS

Plain carbon steels are suitable at ordinary temperature and atmosphere. They are not recommended for use in critical applications. Following are some of the limitations of plain carbon steels:

(a) Low hardenability,

(b) Less strength at elevated temperature,

(c) Low wear and abrasion resistance and

(d) Low corrosion and oxidation resistance.

Therefore, a range of plain carbon steels cannot cover all engineering applications.

Steel is essentially an alloy of iron and carbon with the presence of other elements in the form given below:

1. Manganese, silicon, aluminium, phosphorus, sulphur etc. are present as permanent or common impurities,

2. Oxygen, nitrogen and hydrogen as latent impurities,

3. Some elemental traces as occasional impurities, and

4. Intentionally added elements as molybdenum, chromium, nickel etc. for making alloy steels.

2.16 ALLOY STEELS   (Dec. 13)

Alloy steel may be defined as the type of steel, whose properties are superior to plain carbon steels due to the presence of some elements; other than carbon and iron.

These elements are intentionally added-

Due to the presence of alloying elements, the alloy steels possess the following properties:

(Dec. 09, May 10)

• Desired strength, hardness and toughness at very low or elevated temperatures,

• Higher wear and abrasion resistance,

• More hardenability,

• Improved mechanical properties at the various temperatures,

• Improved corrosion resistance,

• Higher resistance to grain coarsening,

• Higher oxidation and scaling resistance,

- Easily heat treatable,
- Improved electrical and magnetic properties and
- Uniform properties throughout the cross-section.

Except the cost, the alloy steels are superior to plain carbon steels.

2.17 EFFECT OF ALLOYING ELEMENTS   (Dec. 09, May 10)

Alloying elements show a considerable effect on:

- Ferrite matrix,
- Carbide formation,
- Iron-iron carbide diagram,
- Tempering,
- Formation of intermetallic compounds and
- Critical cooling rate etc.

2.17.1 Effect of Alloying Elements on Ferrite

Many of the alloying elements are soluble in ferrite and form solid solutions. Nickel, aluminium, silicon, cobalt get dissolved largely into ferrite. Solid solutions are always stronger and harder than pure metals.

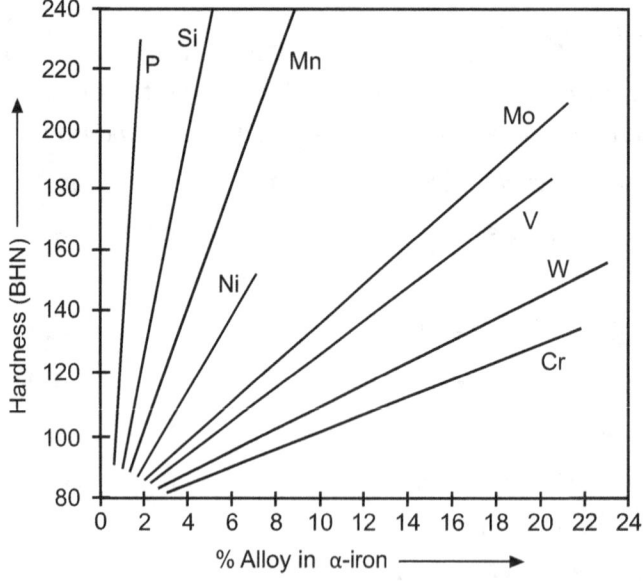

Fig. 2.10: Effect of various alloying elements dissolved in ferrite on hardness value

Any element dissolved in ferrite increases its hardness and strength. The hardening effect of various elements, when dissolved in alpha iron, is shown in Fig. 2.10.

2.17.2 Effect of Alloying Elements on Carbide

Some of the alloying elements, when combined with carbon, form carbides. Any alloy carbide possesses higher hardness and brittleness. They improve wear and abrasion resistance of steels. Complex carbides are sluggish to dissolve and tend to remain out of solution in austenite. Undissolved carbides reduce grain growth. Chromium and vanadium carbides have an outstanding hardness and wear resistance.

2.17.3 Effect of Alloying Elements on the Iron-iron Carbide Diagram

Iron-Iron carbide is a binary equilibrium diagram. When a third element is added to steel, the binary diagram no longer represents equilibrium conditions. The presence of alloying elements changes the following:

- (a)   critical range,
- (b)   position of eutectoid point and
- (c)   location of alpha and gamma regions.

Nickel and manganese tend to lower the critical temperatures during heating, while molybdenum, aluminium, silicon, tungsten and vanadium tend to increase it.

Higher nickel and manganese content tend to lower the critical temperature, so that austenitic transformation gets prevented. Therefore, austenite will be retained at the room temperature.

Most of the alloying elements shift the eutectoid carbon to lower values.

2.17.4 Effect of Alloying Elements on Tempering

Hardened plain carbon steels are softened by reheating. With increase in tempering temperature, hardness drops continuously. Alloying elements retard this softening rate. The alloying elements, which are complex carbide formers, raise the tempering temperature and increase the hardness. This is called *secondary hardness* obtained due to precipitation of fine alloy carbides in tempering.

2.17.5 Formation of Intermetallic Compounds

Some of the elements like Ni, Si, Cr, Zr etc. form intermetallic phases like $Fe_x Cr_y$ compounds (sigma) in stainless steel. These compounds are hard and brittle. Hence, they are not desirable.

2.17.6 Effect of Alloying Element Critical Cooling Rate

Most of the alloying elements except cobalt, shift the T.T.T. diagram to the right side. This decreases the critical cooling rate. At the lower cooling rate, martensite can be formed. This increases hardenability of steel.

2.18 CLASSIFICATION OF ALLOYING ELEMENTS

The alloying elements are classified as follows:

a. **Carbide forming elements:** Cr, Mn, Mo, V, Zr etc. form carbides, when added to steels.

b. **Neutral elements:** e.g. cobalt. It has no effect on carbide formation or graphitization.

c. **Graphitizing elements:** Ni, Cu, Al, Si etc. decompose the carbides into graphite.

d. **Austenite stabilizers:** The elements like Ni, Mn, Cu increase stability of austenite, so that austenite is observed at the room temperature.

e. **Ferrite stabilizers:** The elements like Cr, W, Mo, Si, Al etc. increase stability of ferrite. The ferrite exists from the room temperature to the melting point without the austenite phase.

2.19 PROPERTIES AND USES OF ALLOYING ELEMENTS

The influence of alloying elements on micro-structural and mechanical properties can be discussed as follows:

a) **Sulphur:**

- Sulphur easily dissolves in ferrite and austenite. It is always present in the steel in the form of non-metallic inclusion as FeS.

- Iron sulphide is a hard and brittle phase. It has a strong tendency to form films and small particles at the grain boundary. It has a low melting point.

- During hot rolling or forging operations, FeS inclusion softens and may melt at working temperatures. This causes disintegration of metal by cracking. It is called as **hot-shortness**. This problem can be reduced by lowering sulphur content below 0.05% and adding manganese to the extent more than 4 to 5 times the amount of sulphur. This forms MnS instead of FeS. However, the sulphur content is increased with manganese upto 0.33% for better machinability. These steels are called as *free cutting steels*.

b) **Phosphorus:**

- Phosphorus dissolves in ferrite. It increases strength, hardness and resistance to corrosion. So, it is added to low carbon steels upto 0.12 per cent.

- In certain grades of free cutting steels, it is added upto 0.12% to improve machinability.

- It is undesirable to have phosphorus in high carbon steels. It has a tendency to segregate in steels.

- If it is added in excess of its solubility limit, it separates as iron phosphide (Fe_3P). This is a hard and brittle phase. This introduces **cold-shortness** in steels.

- With higher phosphorus content, it reduces solubility of carbon in ferrite. It leads to the rejection of carbon into the adjacent areas. This forms a banded structure in low carbon steels. It consists of alternate layers of ferrite and pearlite. The interface area of ferrite and pearlite is weak and hence, this structure is not desirable.

c) **Silicon:**

- Silicon dissolves in ferrite, increasing strength and hardness without reducing ductility. It is added as a deoxidiser during casting of ingots. It combines with oxygen forming SiO_2. It is added between 0.1 and 0.3 per cent.

- To improve strength and soundness of casting, 0.3 to 0.5 percent silicon is added.

- Silicon upto 5 percent is added to produce magnetic steels used in transformers, motors and generators. It improves permeability and reduces iron losses.

- It is one of the important alloying elements added in electrical steels. It is intentionally added in spring steels, chisels and punches to improve toughness.

- It is a strong graphitizer. It tends to decompose carbides into graphite and ferrite. Therefore, its amount is always kept below 0.2 per cent in tool steels.

d) **Manganese:**

- It dissolves in ferrite and increases strength, toughness and hardness. It increases hardenability, but tends to make the steel temper embrittle with carbon more than 0.6%. So Mn content in water hardening high carbon steel is kept at less than 0.5%.

- It takes care of sulphur forming MnS. It reduces the possibility of hot-shortness of steel.

- Higher amount of manganese (12 to 14%) with high carbon steels (1 to 1.2% C) produces extremely tough wear resistant and non-magnetic steel called *Hadfield steel*.

- Manganese acts as an austenite stabilizer (Fig. 2.11), so austenitic structure can be obtained in Hadfield steels.

- The surface of such steel can be work hardened by cold working, while the core remains tough. This steel finds its use as frog and switches in railroad trackwork, jaw plates for crushers and power shovels.

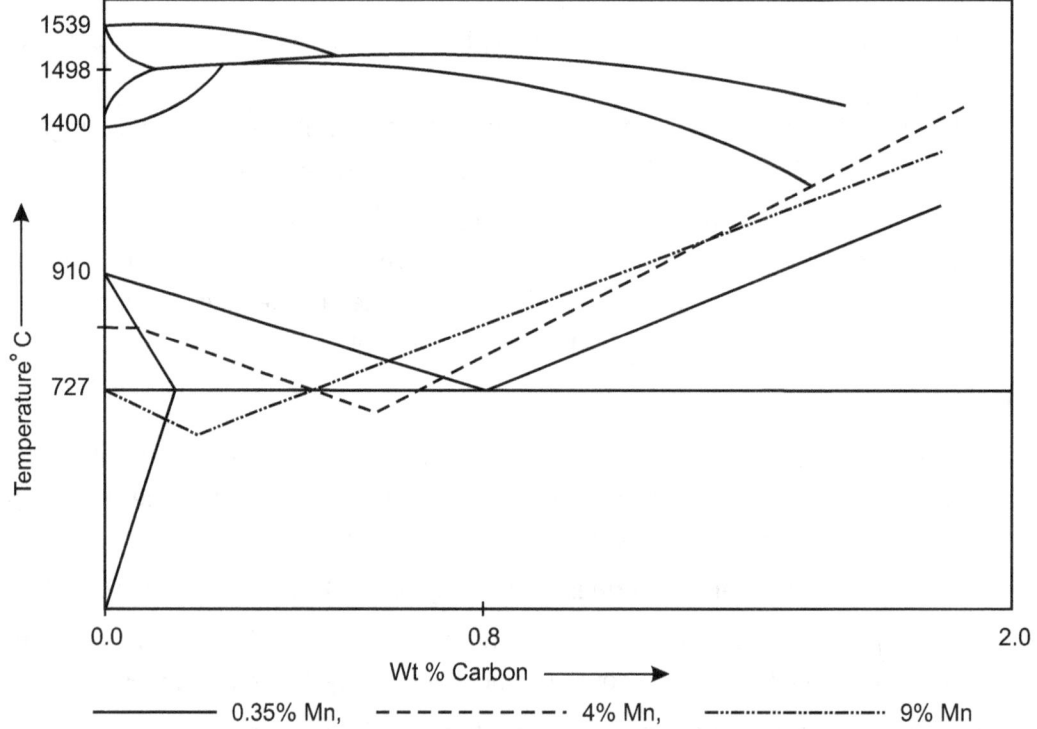

Fig. 2.11: Effect of manganese on iron-carbon diagram

e) Nickel:

- It dissolves in ferrite, increasing hardness, strength and toughness without lowering ductility. It is added upto 5% for the parts subjected to high static and impact stresses.

- It improves impact resistance of steel at very low levels of temperature, hence, it is added to low temperature steels.

- It is an austenite stabilizer. High addition of Ni gives austenitic structure at the room temperature. It is soft and non-magnetic and increases corrosion resistance of high chromium steels.

- It gives low thermal expansion, so it can be used in measuring instruments because of the dimensional stability of steel.

- It improves hardenability of steel. It gives higher mechanical properties after annealing and normalising. So these steels are used for large forgings and castings. It is used in carburising and stainless steels.

f) Chromium: (June 09)

- It is a carbide former. It forms chromium carbides, which are very hard.

- Chromium improves wear and abrasion resistance. It gives strength at elevated temperature.

- Higher amount of chromium is added to increase corrosion resistance. It forms chromium oxide film, which is adherent and non-porous, stopping further corrosion.

- It is used as a principal alloying element in stainless steels and heat resisting steels. It is also used as an alloying element in bearing steels.

g) Tungsten: (June 09)

- It is an expensive alloying element. It increases hardenability.

- It is a strong carbide former. It increases wear and abrasion resistance.

- The hardness can be retained at higher temperature, so tungsten becomes an important alloying element of tool steel.

- It refines grain size and inhibits grain coarsening.

- About 2 to 3% of tungsten can be added to replace 1% molybdenum.

h) Molybdenum:

- It performs functions similar to those of tungsten. Molybdenum to the extent 0.15 to 0.30% is added to improve the effects of other alloying elements.

- It reduces temper brittleness. It is used in high strength structural steels. It increases resistance to grain coarsening.

i) Vanadium:

- It inhibits grain growth, when the steel is heated at high temperature. It is a strong carbide former.

- It gives an excellent hardness, wear and abrasion resistance. It improves fatigue resistance.

- It is generally found in tool steels. It acts as a strong deoxidiser.

j) **Titanium:**

- It is a strong carbide former.

- It is used to fix carbon in stainless steels. It, thus, prevents precipitation of chromium carbide and sensitisation.

- It acts as a stabilizing agent for austenitic stainless steels.

k) **Cobalt:**

- This element has no effect on graphitizing or carbide forming process.

- It becomes an important addition for magnetic materials. It is used as a binder for cemented carbide tip tools.

l) **Aluminium:**

- About 0.01 to 0.06% Al is added during solidification of castings to obtain fine grained steels.

- In nitriding grade of steels, aluminium upto 3% may be added. This forms aluminium nitride, which gives higher hardness to steels after nitriding.

m) **Boron:**

- It increases hardenability, even if added in a small quantity (0.001 to 0.003%). It is used as an inoculator to obtain a fine grain size.

- It is added to steels which are used for boriding heat treatment.

2.20 VARIOUS ALLOY STEELS   (Dec. 06, 13)

The alloying elements, when added to steels give certain specific properties. This enables the particular application of steel. Some of the important alloy steels are discussed below:

a) **Free-cutting steels:**

These are also known as *free machining* steels. Due to their high machinability, they can be machined very easily. They give a high quality surface finish after machining. Two types of free cutting steels, namely high sulphur steels and leaded steels are used. Higher sulphur content (upto 0.33%) and phosphorus (upto 0.12%) are added to improve machinability. The sulphur exists in the form of MnS inclusions. These inclusions promote the formation of small brittle chips and reduce the friction on the surface being machined. Phosphorus gets dissolved in the ferrite and increases its hardness and brittleness. This makes chip more brittle.

Lead may be added upto 0.35%. It forms very small submicroscopic globules, which break the structure to produce brittle chips. It improves machinability without disturbing ductility, toughness etc.

These steels have lower dynamic strength and corrosion properties. These steels are used for machine parts, subject to comparatively light loads as bolts, nuts, screws etc.

b) Structural steels:

These steels are used for bridges, buildings, railroad cars etc. The components including valve, pins, studs, gears, clutches, shafts etc. are also made from these steels. These steels must have high strength, toughness, resistance to softening at high temperature and corrosion resistance. They should also possess good weldability and workability.

0.25 to 0.45% carbon steels with addition of alloying elements as manganese (0.4 to 1.7%), nickel (0.3 to 1.6%), chromium (1.5%) and molybdenum (0.3%), possess UTS more than 100 kg/mm^2.

c) Rail steels:

These steels show a good combination of strength, ductility, high impact resistance and fatigue resistance. Medium carbon steel having carbon in the range of 0.4 to 0.6% with small additions of manganese and chromium upto 1% are used for making rails.

d) Spring steels:

These are used under various loads as compression, tension and torsion. These steels have high elastic limit, better elongation and high fatigue resistance.

A typical spring steel shows 0.6% carbon, 0.85% Mn and 2.0% silicon. Cr, Ni, Mo, V may be added to replace silicon.

Austempering heat treatment can be given to these steels effectively. These steels are used for coil and leaf springs.

e) Tor steels:

Reinforcing bars are often required to be bent into shapes; so they must possess adequate formability. These are medium carbon steels (0.3 to 0.6% C) with 0.5 to 1% Mn. The deformed reinforcing bars are known as tor steels. Due to the twisted and ribbed pattern, this steel possesses higher yield strength and greater surface area for bonding.

f) Creep resisting steels:

In thermal or hydropower plants, various components are used at high temperature and pressure. Therefore, the steels used in such application must have higher creep resistance, oxidation resistance and corrosion resistance. The creep resistance is increased by adding

Mo (0.4 - 0.6%), V (0.2 to 1.0%) and Cr (upto 6%) to low carbon steel. These elements form hard carbides, which increase the resistance to softening at high temperature.

g) High temperature alloys or superalloys:

These are used at high temperatures, where strength, hardness, wear resistance and oxidation resistance is required. In low alloy steels, containing less than 10% alloy, molybdenum and vanadium are most effective in raising the creep resistance. The carbon is less than 0.15%. 0.5% molybdenum steel is used for piping and superheater tubes.

Chromium - molybdenum - vanadium steels containing upto 0.50% carbon are used for bolts, steam turbine rotors etc.

Straight chromium stainless steels are used for steam valves and pump shafts.

Nickel based alloys containing 50 to 70% nickel with Co, Ti and Al are used for manifolds, collector rings and exhaust valves.

Refractory metals and their alloys are used for high temperature applications.

The above alloys are also referred as 'superalloys'.

h) Ball bearing steels:

These are also called as antifriction bearing steels. They show good wear and abrasion resistance, corrosion resistance and sustain high alternating loads.

They have hardness upto 60 RC. High carbon steels (upto 1.0% C) with 0.5 to 1.5% Cr and 0.2 to 0.45% Mn are used as bearing steels. These are used for rings, balls and rollers.

i) Low expansion steels: (Dec. 06, 08, May 10, 13)

These are the alloys of nickel and iron containing 36% Ni, 0.2% C, 0.5% Mn and balance iron. This is called Invar.

Elinvar contains 36% Ni, 12% Cr, and W with balance iron.

These steels have a very low coefficient of expansion and are used for gauges, rules, tapes and micrometers. These components require dimensional stability.

j) High strength low alloy steels (HSLA):

The strength of steel increases with increase in carbon content.

Low carbon steels show good ductility, formability, weldability and low strength. However, the strength can be improved by addition of small quantities of alloying elements.

These are called as High Strength Low Alloy (HSLA) steels. This is also known as microalloyed steels. Conventional plain carbon steels can be replaced by HSLA steels due to its high strength to weight ratio.

HSLA steel contains less than 0.5% alloying elements with carbon percentage 0.07 to 0.13.

HSLA steel shows superior mechanical properties due to ultrafine grain size, solid solution strengthening of ferrite and precipitation of carbides and nitrides.

These are used in automotive industries.

k) Maraging steels: (Dec. 11)

These are low carbon steels containing C < 0.03%, 18 to 25% Ni, 3 to 5% Mo, 3 to 7% Co and 0.2 to 1.6% Ti.

The martensitic structure in these steels is possible to be obtained by air hardening. It can be precipitation hardened by ageing and hence, the name maraging steels.

The martensite formed after hardening is soft due to low carbon content, which can be cold worked and aged.

These show superior fracture toughness compared with quenched and tempered medium carbon steels. Since, these steels are extremely low in carbon, decarburisation cannot occur during heating. Besides, low ageing temperatures also reduce the distortion. These steels have good weldability and machinability.

The microstructure of maraging steel consists of fine precipitates (e.g. Ni_3TiAl, Ni_3Mo) in martensitic matrix.

These steels find application as hulls for hydrospace vehicles, motor cases for missiles, hot extrusion dies, cold headed bolts, mortar and rifle tubing etc.

l) Dual phase steels: (May 10, 13)

Those are low carbon steels with or without addition of alloying elements. These are obtained by heat treatment.

The steel is heated just above A_1 temperature and rapidly cooled to the room temperature. Due to this treatment, the ferrite-pearlite microstructure is changed to a mixture of martensite pools dispersed in a ferrite matrix.

The amount of martensite varies from 15% to 30%. This microstructure is called as dual phase structure.

These steels are characterized by low yield strength to tensile strength ratio, high work hardening rate and high tensile strength.

These are used for bumpers, wheels, discs, door panels etc. because of better formability.

2.21 STAINLESS STEELS   (Dec. 09, May 11)

These are one of the most important group of alloy steels. The alloying elements used in stainless steels are mainly chromium, nickel and molybdenum. Due to their high corrosion resistance, they are called as stainless steels. This group possesses a combination of the following properties:

1. Wide range of strength and hardness.

2. High ductility and formability.

3. Higher corrosion resistance.

4. Good creep resistance.

5. Oxidation and scaling resistance.

6. Good machinability.

7. Easy cold working property.

8. Better surface finish.

9. Non-reactive in usual environment.

10. Non-reactive with highly acidic and corrosive gases.

The high corrosion resistance of these steels is due to its principal alloying element i.e. chromium. When these steels are exposed to oxidising medium, chromium gets rapidly oxidised. It forms a very thin and stable oxide film. It is adherent and non-porous. So further oxidation stops. If the oxide film gets damaged through abrasion, it gets immediately repaired. This self-healing nature of the film makes steel highly corrosion resistant.

Chromium gives passivity to these steels, if it is adequately added i.e. more than 12 per cent.

Addition of nickel to iron-chromium alloys improves ductility and impact strength. This is because of stability of austenite. Nickel improves the corrosion resistance, particularly in chloride solution. It is added upto 20 per cent.

Molybdenum improves corrosion resistance of steel in sulphuric acid. It also increases corrosion resistance in halogen salts. Mo stainless steels give better properties than do the Cr-Ni steels.

Carbon in stainless steel is always kept low (less than 0.2%) to avoid carbide forming.

Due to large content of chromium, the iron-chromium-carbon alloys, belong to a ternary system (Refer Fig. 2.12).

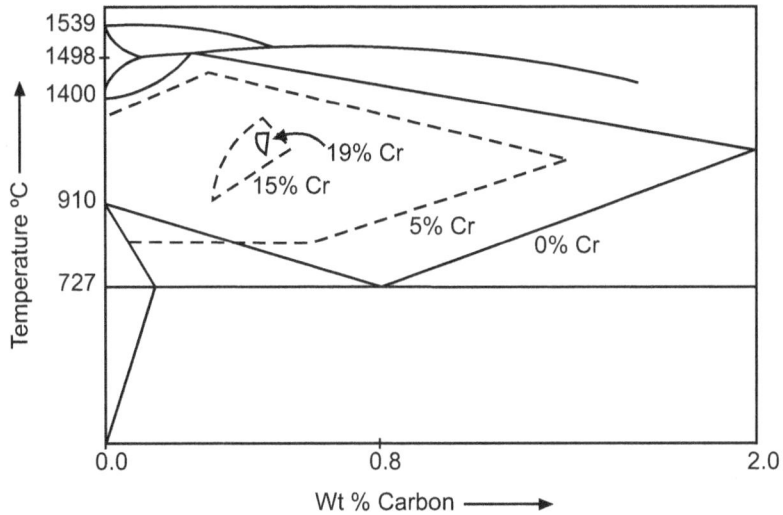

Fig. 2.12: Effect of chromium on iron-carbon diagram

2.21.1 Classification of Stainless Steels   (May 06, 11, 12; Dec. 07, 08)

The stainless steels are classified as follows:

(A) Martensitic stainless steels:

These are basically straight chromium steels. They contain chromium between 11.5 and 18 per cent. These are specified as AISI 403, 410, 416, 420, 501 and 502. These are magnetic and can be cold worked easily. They have good machinability, toughness and hardness. These steels show austenite phase at a high temperature and hence can be hardened by martensitic transformation. The high alloy content of this steel causes the transformation so sluggish that maximum hardness can be produced by air cooling.

These steels contain carbon from 0.15 to 1.2 per cent.

The microstructure shows a hard martensite phase.

These steels are used for razors, razor blades, surgical instruments, cutlery items, steam turbine blades, pump shafts, paper machinery parts etc.

(B) Ferritic stainless steels:

These are straight chromium stainless steels having 14 to 27 per cent chromium and 0.08 to 0.2 per cent carbon. These include types as AISI 405, 430 and 446. These steels cannot be hardened by heat treatment as ferrite is the non-hardenable phase. They can be moderately hardened by cold working. They are magnetic and can be cold worked or hot worked. They show maximum softness, ductility and corrosion resistance in the annealed condition.

Since, the ferritic steels can be cold formed easily, they are extensively used for deep drawn parts.

The only heat treatment given to ferritic steels is annealing.

Modification of AISI 430 with addition of sulphur gives free machining properties and is used for heavy cuts and screw machined parts.

High chromium content steels are used for furnace parts, nozzles, combustion chambers etc.

(C) Austenitic stainless steels:

These are the chromium-nickel (Fig. 2.13) and chromium-nickel-manganese stainless steels. These are non-magnetic in annealed condition. They cannot be hardened by heat treatment. The chromium and nickel content together is at least 23 per cent. They can be hot worked or cold worked. In cold worked condition, they become slightly magnetic.

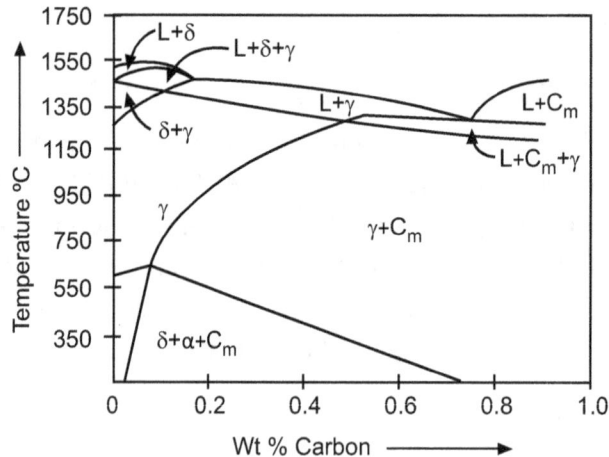

Fig. 2.13: Phase diagram for typical austenitic stainless steel

A typical microstructure of austenitic stainless steel is as shown in Fig. 2.14.

(400 X)

Fig. 2.14: Photomicrograph of an austenitic stainless steel

The machinability of these steels can be improved by sulphur and selenium additions. These steels show good shock resistance. The corrosion resistance of these steels is better than that of ferritic or martensitic stainless steels.

These steels are specified as AISI 202, 302, 304, 316, 321 etc. A low carbon grade is specified as 304 L.

These steels become more expensive due to high cost of nickel.

These are used in food handling equipments, chemical industries, aircraft heaters, aircraft exhaust manifold, boiler shell, photographic equipments, domestic and industrial utensils etc.

(D) Precipitation hardening stainless steels:

These steels contain carbon around 0.07%, Mn 0.7%, Cr 17% and Ni 7%. These steels are usually solution annealed and after forming they are aged to increase hardness and strength. Higher strength is developed due to precipitation of certain compounds. The strength can be retained upto 540°C. These steels find applications in air craft and missile industries as materials for skins, nibs, bulkheads and other structural components.

(E) Duplex stainless steels:

These are chromium-molybdenum ferritic stainless steels to which sufficient amount of austenite stabilizers are added. At the room temperature, a balanced structure of austenite and ferrite is present. These steels show excellent toughness.

2.21.2 Sensitisation and Weld Decay   (May 10)

a) Sensitisation

This problem is observed in austenitic stainless steel. If such steel is heated slowly in the temperature range of 500 to 800°C, chromium gets precipitated as chromium carbides (Fig. 2.14 a, b). These complex carbides are observed at grain boundaries. Chromium, which is intentionally added to improve corrosion resistance, gets consumed with carbon. This sharply reduces the corrosion resistance of steel. The steel is said to be sensitised to corrosion environment. Such sensitised steel shows intergranular corrosion in corrosive media.

This depletion of chromium and precipitation of carbides also affects other mechanical properties. These precipitated carbides are very stable and can be dissolved only at higher temperature (e.g. 1000°C).

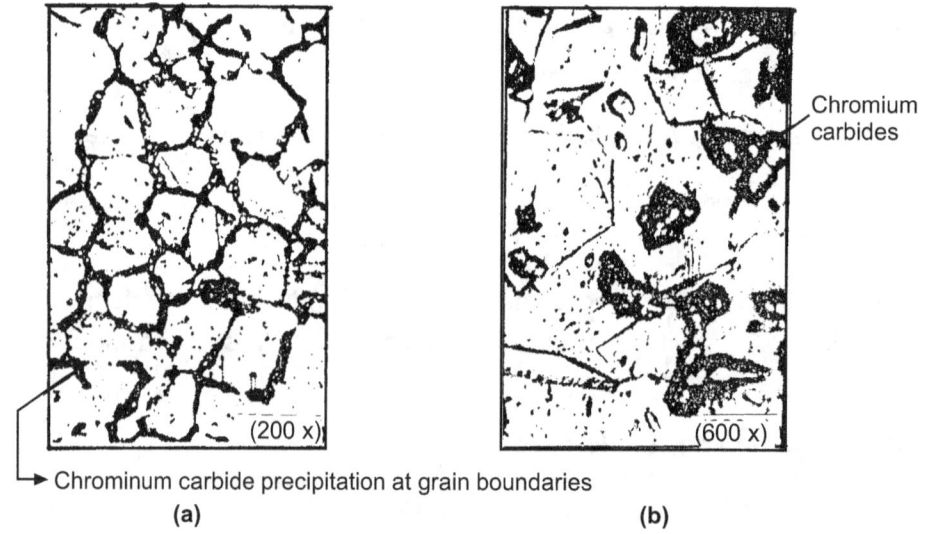

Chromium carbides

(200 x)   (600 x)

Chrominum carbide precipitation at grain boundaries

(a)   (b)

Fig. 2.15: Sensitisation of austenitic stainless steel by chromium-carbide precipitation

b) Weld Decay: (Dec. 07)

During welding of austenitic stainless steels, chromium carbide precipitation occurs. The steel undergoes a temperature range of 500 to 800°C. This precipitation is observed at the area near weldment. Due to poor thermal conductivity of these steels, the heat remains in HAZ portion for certain time. This accelerates sensitisation. The sensitisation occurred due to welding is referred as weld decay.

Weld decay may be avoided by following ways:

i) Solutionising and Quenching:

The steels with chromium carbide precipitation are heated at 1050°C for few minutes. This dissolves the carbides completely in austenite. Then the steels are rapidly cooled to avoid reprecipitation of carbides.

ii) Use of Stabilizing Elements:

Titanium is added to these steels. It has greater affinity towards carbon than chromium. So, chromium carbides are not formed.

iii) Use of L-grade Steels:

Steels with very less carbon percentage (about 0.03) overall reduce amount of carbides. These are specified as L grade steels, e.g. 304 L will have better resistance to carbide precipitation than simply 304 type.

Fine grained steel can be used to reduce intensity of precipitation by increasing total grain boundary area.

Various welding factors such as current, heat input will govern the sensitisation.

2.21.3 Heat Treatment of Stainless Steels

Similar to other carbon steels, various heat treatments as stated below can be given to stainless steels also.

(a) Stress relief treatment:

Internal stresses are produced in stainless steel due to:

1. mechanical deformation or
2. thermal process.

The stress relief treatment is carried out by heating steel below 370°C followed by slow cooling. This improves elastic properties of cold drawn materials.

The steel may be heated to a temperature above 700° C and slowly cooled to avoid its possibility of stress corrosion cracking.

(b) Annealing:

Annealing heat treatment is given to ferritic stainless steels to relieve welding or cold working stresses. It is carried out by heating the stainless steel above 800°C and then cooling either in furnace, air or water by avoiding precipitation of carbides.

(c) Solution annealing:

The solutionising treatment consists of healing the austenitic steel to a temperature of 1050° C and soaking for some time. This helps to dissolve the formed carbides. After homogenising, the steel is rapidly cooled to avoid reprecipitation of carbides. The choice of quenchant depends on the section thickness. Small sections may be air quenched.

This eliminates the effect of sensitising in austenitic stainless steel.

(d) Hardening and tempering:

This treatment is used for martensitic stainless steels. The treatment is similar to plain carbon and alloy steels. The steels are heated to a temperature of 950 to 1100°C and then quenched in air or oil. This forms hard martensite phase. Maximum hardness and strength depends on the percentage of carbon. After hardening, the tempering is carried out depending upon requirement of hardness.

(e) Stabilizing treatment:

This treatment is given to stabilized grades of austenitic stainless steels. Stabilized grades are used to avoid sensitisation and weld decay problems. It consists of holding the steel at 850 to 900°C for 2 to 4 hours. It is followed by rapid cooling in air or water.

It precipitates all carbon as carbides of titanium or columbium, which prevents chromium carbide precipitation.

(f) Post-weld heat treatment:

The heat treatment like stress relief annealing or solution annealing are given after welding. This improves mechanical and corrosion resistance properties.

2.22 TOOL STEELS   (Dec. 10, 13, May 11, 12, 13)

These are special quality steels used for cutting or forming operations. Various grades of steels with special heat treatments are used as tool steels.

There are several methods of classifying tool steels. These may be classified as per -

- quenching media used,
- alloy content and
- applications.

AISI (American Iron and Steel Institute) has classified tool steels as per the method of quenching, applications, special properties and steels for special industries.

The commonly used tool steels have been grouped as follows:

Table 2.10: Commonly used tool steels

Group	Type and symbol	
Water hardening	W	High carbon with Cr, V
Shock resisting	S	Medium C with Mn, Si, Cr, W, Mo
Cold work	O	Oil hardening
	A	Air hardening
	D	High C, High Cr
Hot work	H	Chromium base, Tungsten base
High speed	T	Tungsten base
	M	Molybdenum base
Mould	P	Mould steels
Special purpose	L	Low alloy
	F	Carbon tungsten

2.22.1 Selection of Tool Steels

During selection of tool steels for a particular application, its metallurgical properties are correlated with the requirements. Most of the tool steel operations are classified as cutting, shearing, forming, drawing, extrusion and rolling. Hence, as per the operation, the tool steel must fulfil necessary requirements. For example, when cutting is chief function of tool, it should have high hardness and good heat and wear resistance; shearing tools must have high toughness; forming tool must have higher strength and non-deforming properties.

2.22.2 Properties of Tool Steels

The most common tool steels should possess one or more of the following properties:

- Non-deforming properties,
- Depth of hardening,
- Toughness,
- Wear resistance,
- Red hardness,
- Machinability and
- Resistance to decarburisation.

(a) Non deforming properties:

Steels expand and contract during heating and quenching. This alters the dimensions of tool. Intricately designed tools and dies must maintain their dimensions after hardening.

The steels having better non-deforming properties can be machined very close to size before heat treatment.

Air hardening gives least distortion, oil show moderate and water hardening gives higher distortion.

(b) Depth of hardening:

This depends on hardenability of steel. The hardenability increases with increasing alloy content.

Shallow hardening steels are quenched in water. High-alloy steels are used to develop high strength throughout a large section.

(c) Toughness:

For plain carbon and alloy steels, toughness is considered as the ability to adsorb energy during deformation. However, it may be taken as the ability to resist breaking during operation. The tool must be rigid enough. The tool may become useless even if a small degree of plastic deformation of tool occurs.

The cold work tool steels show brittleness and low toughness due to high carbon content.

(d) Wear resistance:

Normally, tool steels show good wear resistance. It is the resistance to abrasion or resistance to loss of dimensional tolerances. Hard and undissolved particles improve wear resistance.

(e) Red-hardness (hot hardness):

It is resistance of the steel to the softening effect of heat. It is an important property for high speed and hot work tools. Alloying elements, which form hard and stable carbides, improve the red hardness.

(f) Machinability:

This is the ability of the material to be cut freely and produce a good surface finish after machining.

The hardness in the annealed condition, the microstructure of the steel and the quantity of carbides, affect the machinability. Tool steels are difficult to machine. The machinability decreases with increasing carbon and alloy content.

(g) Resistance to decarburisation:

Decarburisation usually occurs, when steels are heated above 700°C. The loss of surface carbon occurs, if protecting atmosphere is not used. It results in a soft surface instead of a hard one, after hardening.

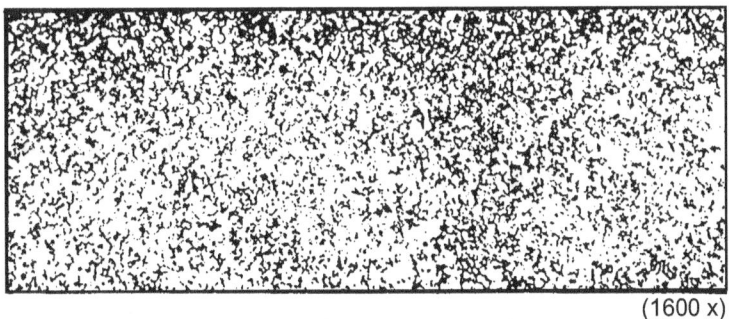

(1600 x)

Fig. 2.16: A typical microstructure of tool steel

showing spheroidal pearlite and alloy carbides

The straight carbon tool steels are subject to the least decarburisation. The shock resisting tool steels are poor in this property. A majority of tool steels have good resistance to decarburisation. A typical structure of tool steel is as shown in Fig. 2.16.

2.22.3 Types/Classification of Tool Steels   (May 11)

(A) Water Hardening Tool Steels (W):

These are plain carbon tool steels with high carbon content. Small amounts of chromium and vanadium are added to improve hardenability.

Steels, with 0.60 to 0.75% carbon are used, where the toughness of the tools such as hammers, concrete breakers, rivet sets and heading dies, is of prime importance.

Steels, with 0.75 to 0.95% carbon, give better toughness as well as hardness. These are used for manufacture of the tools like punches, chisels and shear blades.

Steels, with 0.95 to 1.40% carbon, give increased wear resistance and retention of cutting edge. These are used for wood working tools, drills, taps, reamers and turning tools.

A proper heat treatment gives a hard martensitic surface with tough core. These are water quenched to achieve higher hardness.

They have low red hardness. A typical microstructure of hardened and tempered water quenching tool steel shows undissolved carbides in matrix of tempered martensite.

(B) Shock Resisting Tool Steels:

The steel must show good toughness and the ability to withstand repeated shocks.

They have carbon in the range 0.45 to 0.65 per cent. The alloying elements as silicon, chromium, tungsten and molybdenum are added. Silicon strengthens the ferrite, while chromium improves hardenability. Most of these steels are oil hardening. These steels are used in the manufacture of forming tools, punches, chisels, pneumatic tools and shear blades.

A typical shock resisting steel is austenitised at 940°C, oil quenched and tempered at 420°C. It shows spheroidal carbide particles in tempered martensite.

(C) Cold-work Tool Steels:

A majority of tool steels are grouped under this category. This type is further sub-divided as:

- Oil hardening steels,
- Air hardening steels and
- High carbon high chromium tool steels.

The oil hardening low alloy tool steels contain manganese, chromium and tungsten. They exhibit very good non-deforming properties. These steels are austenitised at 800°C and oil quenched. The tempering is carried out at 200°C. It shows the microstructure consisting of spheroidal carbide particles in tempered matrix of martensite.

They are used for taps, solid threading dies, form tools and expansion reamers.

The air hardening steels contain carbon 1.0%, manganese 3%, chromium 5% and molybdenum upto 1%. This medium alloy content makes the steel air hardenable. These steels are austenitised at 970°C, air cooled and tempered at 160°C. The microstructure shows small white spots of alloy carbides in matrix of tempered martensite. This group of steels shows excellent non-deforming properties, good wear resistance and resistance to decarburisation.

These steels are used for blanking, forming, trimming and thread rolling dies.

The high carbon high chromium (HCHCr) type steel contains upto 2.25 per cent carbon and 12 per cent chromium. They may also be alloyed with molybdenum, vanadium and cobalt. They show excellent wear resistance, non-deforming properties, good abrasion resistance and dimensional stability in hardening. These steels are used for preparing blanking and piercing dies, drawing dies, thread rolling dies and master gauges.

(D) Hot-work Tool Steels:

These steels are used for working at high temperature. These steels should have good red hardness, which is achieved by adding chromium, molybdenum and tungsten upto 5%. These steels are used mostly for extrusion, hot forging, die casting and plastic moulding.

These are further subdivided as:

(i) Chromium base:

These contain upto 3.25 per cent chromium with small amounts of vanadium, tungsten and molybdenum. The low carbon and low alloy content imparts good red hardness and toughness. These steels can be deep hardened by air cooling. It avoids distortion in hardening.

These steels are austenitised at 1080°C, oil quenched and double tempered at 580°C. The microstructure shows a few rounded carbides in matrix of coarse tempered martensite.

These steels are used for the manufacture of extrusion dies, diecasting dies, forging dies, mandrels, hot shears and in highly stressed structural parts for supersonic aircraft.

(ii) Tungsten base:

This contains at least 9% tungsten and 2 to 12% chromium. This higher alloy content improves resistance to high temperature softening. They can be air hardened for low distortion. They can also be quenched in oil or hot salt to minimize scaling. They are used for making of mandrels and extrusion dies for brass, nickel alloys and steels.

(iii) Molybdenum base:

These steels contain 8% molybdenum, 4% chromium and small amounts of tungsten and vanadium. They are used in place of tungsten steels due to low cost and identical properties.

These steels show more resistance to heat cracking, but they may get decarburised during heat treatment.

All hot-work tool steels are designated by H series.

(E) High Speed Tool Steels   (Dec. 13)

These are highly alloyed tool steels. These steels contain large amounts of tungsten or molybdenum along with chromium, vanadium and cobalt. They have carbon content of 0.70 to 1.3%.

High speed tool steels are used to cut the material at higher speed. A high speed steel gives excellent red hardness and shock resistance. They show good non-deforming properties, deep hardenability, wear resistance and poor resistance to decarburisation.

These are subdivided as:

1. Molybdenum based and

2. Tungsten base.

The widely used tungsten base steel is known as 18 - 4 - 1 (i.e. 18% W, 4% Cr and 1% V). Compared to tungsten steels, the molybdenum steels are low in price.

For obtaining higher red hardness, cobalt is added. For cutting of abrasive material, the steel is alloyed with vanadium. These steels are austenitised at 1270°C, salt quenched to 600°C, air cooled and double tempered at 525°C.

W, Mo, Cr and V are carbide formers. Hence, the microstructure consists of carbides in the matrix of tempered martensite. This gives a combination of wear resistant carbides in heat resisting matrix.

These tools are used as cutting tools as tool bits, drills, reamers, broaches, taps, milling cutter, saws etc.

(F) Mold Steels:

The main alloying elements in these steels are chromium and nickel with molybdenum and aluminium. These steels show a very low hardness in annealed condition and resistance to work hardening.

These steels are used for manufacture of low temperature diecasting dies and moulds for injection or compression moulding of plastics.

(G) Special Purpose Tool Steels:

The low alloy type (group L) contains chromium, vanadium, molybdenum and nickel. Molybdenum increases hardenability. High chromium content increases wear resistance due to formation of hard complex iron chromium carbides.

Nickel improves toughness, while vanadium refines the grains.

These steels show dimensional stability during hardening as they are oil hardened.

These steels are used in bearings, rollers, clutch plates, cams, collets and wrenches. The steels with higher carbon content are suitable for dies, drills, taps, knurls and gauges.

The carbon-tungsten type (group F) steels contain higher percentage of carbon and tungsten. These are water quenched due to their shallow hardening nature. They are brittle. They show excellent wear resistance. They are used for paper cutting knives, wire drawing dies, plug gauges and forming and finishing tools.

2.22.4 Heat Treatment of Tool Steels

Tool steels are always used after heat treatments. Following are the various heat treatments carried out for tool steels.

- Normalizing and annealing
- Preheating
- Austenitising and quenching
- Martempering and austempering
- Tempering and stabilization.

These heat treatments are discussed in detail in chapter 3. However, they can be summarized for steel as follows:

(a) Normalizing and Annealing:

Most of the tool steels are initially forged and then machined to final dimensions. Forging is carried out at a higher temperature, which produces non-uniform structures, residual stresses and coarse grain size. So, tool steels must be normalized. High alloy steels may be annealed instead of normalizing.

At certain stages, the tool steels are given heavy machining. It produces strain hardening effects due to cold working. So, intermediate or process annealing is recommended.

(b) Preheating:

Tool steels, in general, exhibit lower thermal conductivity. So, tool steels must be preheated at about 600 to 800°C, before actual heat treatment. It avoids cracking and distortion. The more holding time at this temperature makes the steel thermally stable and reduces thermal stresses.

(c) Austenitising and Quenching:

Most of the alloying elements added in tool steels are carbide formers. Austenitising dissolves these carbides and produces fine grained austenite. Then the steel is rapidly cooled from austenitising temperature. It produces fine martensite. The quenching may be done in brine, water, oil, air or molten salt both depending upon the hardenability of steel.

(d) Martempering and Austempering:

These treatments minimize distortion and impart certain properties to tool steels. These treatments are carried out by quenching the steel from austenitising temperature into a salt bath maintained at a constant temperature.

(e) Tempering and Stabilization:

After hardening, the microstructure of steel consists of retained austenite, untempered martensite and alloy carbides. This structure is undesirable and unstable.

During high temperature tempering, the hardness of steel increases. This is known as *secondary hardness*. The increase in hardness is due to transformation of retained austenite into martensite and precipitation of carbides. The high hardness obtained by tempering in the range of 550°C to 570°C is retained, when the steel is subsequently heated to 600°C. This gives the high red hardness to high speed tool steels.

Stabilization of tool steel is achieved by cooling the steel after hardening to subzero temperature (– 75°C or – 195°C); which may be obtained in solid carbon dioxide or liquid nitrogen. This reduces the retained austenite. It gives maximum hardness, wear resistance and dimensional stability.

2.22.5 Heat Treatment Cycle for High Speed Tool Steel

This heat treatment is discussed for 18–4–1 high speed tool steel.   **(May 06, Dec. 11)**

The heat treatment consists of hardening and tempering cycles as shown in Fig. 3.16.

It consists of heating the steel initially about 800°C and holding it for few minutes. This helps to avoid thermal shocking and micro cracking of steel. Then the steel is transferred to a salt bath maintained at the temperature of 1250 to 1300°C. Salt bath is recommended to avoid oxidation and decarburisation in the heating process. The steel is then soaked for few minutes. The less soaking time helps to avoid grain coarsening. At this temperature, almost all alloy carbides dissolve in austenite, except the vanadium carbides, which are most stable. The steel is then oil quenched to the room temperature. This transforms austenite to martensite. As the martensite finish (M_f) temperature is below the room temperature, a part of austenite remains untransformed, which is called as retained austenite. After quenching, the microstructural phases are martensite and retained austenite. The distortion during quenching is not observed because of soft phase i.e. retained austenite, which gives cushioning effect for the hard martensite phase.

The temperature from which the steel is quenched has also its effect on hardness. If the steel is quenched from a lower temperature, less carbon is dissolved in austenite. After quenching, this results in lower hardness. If the steel is quenched from higher temperature, carbides get dissolved and grain coarsening occurs with higher amount of retained austenite. The retained austenite lowers the cutting properties, so, a sub-zero treatment is applied. This treatment is used directly after hardening.

The sub-zero treatment is carried out at a temperature of 70 to 80°C below 0°C. This treatment should be immediately followed by several (three to five) tempering operations at 550°C.

The martensite formed during quenching gets tempered and gives rise to fine complex alloy carbides. Also, a large part of retained austenite gets transformed to martensite.

The first tempering produces stresses due to this newly formed martensite. Hence, second tempering cycle is used. After second tempering, already formed martensite will get tempered; some part of retained austenite will be transformed to martensite and some more alloy carbides will be formed. At the end of tempering cycles, the retained austenitising sets reduced below 5%.

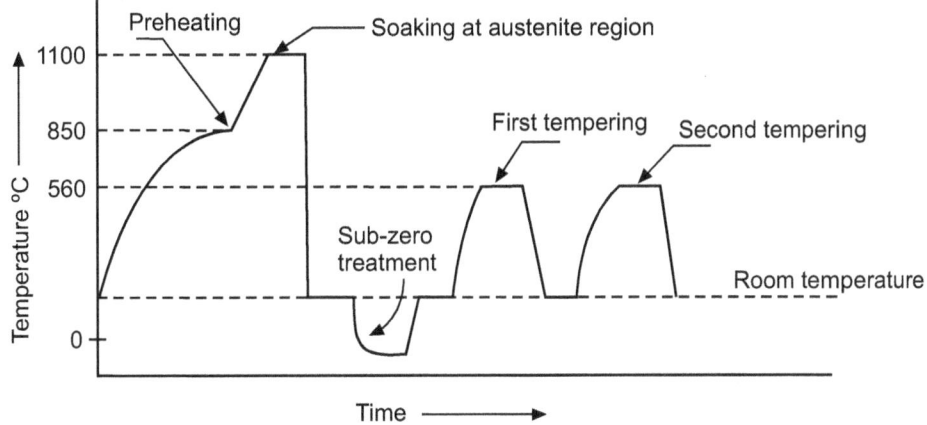

Fig. 2.17: Heat treatment of H.S.S. tool steel

Some of other steels from this group have a similar heat treatment cycle. Only austenitising and tempering temperature differ; but slightly.

2.23 SPECIAL CUTTING MATERIALS

In addition to the various tool steels, some other alloys are also used as cutting materials. These include:

    (A) Stellites

    (B) Cemented carbides and cermets

    (C) Ceramic tools.

(A) Stellites:

These are cobalt-chromium-tungsten alloys. They contain 1 to 3% carbon, 25 to 35% chromium, 4 to 25% tungsten and remainder cobalt. The hardness of stellite varies from RC

40 to RC 60. The microstructure consists of tungstides and carbides. They have high hardness, high wear and corrosion resistance and excellent red hardness.

They are used for machining steel, cast iron, cast steel, stainless steel etc. They can be operated at higher speeds than H.S.S. They are not so tough because they are manufactured by casting.

These tools are used as single point lathe tools, milling cutter blades, spot facers, reamers, form tools etc.

(B) Cemented carbides and cermets:

Cemented carbides are produced by using very finely divided carbide particles of the refractory metals. These particles are cemented together by a metal. They have very high hardness and compressive strength. They are manufactured in the following steps:

- Mixing of powder carbides of tungsten, titanium with cobalt.
- Compaction and
- Sintering.

Cemented carbides have low toughness and tensile strength. So, they are brazed or mechanically fastened to a steel shank.

They are also used for cutting abrasive materials, white cast irons etc. Their applications include drills, reamers, boring and facing tools and saws.

They are widely used for earth drilling and mining operations, sandblast nozzles, ring and plug gauges, drawing dies.

Cermets contain the carbides of titanium and chromium with nickel or nickel base alloy as the binder. They have high hardness, high oxidation resistance, thermal shock resistance and low toughness.

It is used, where high temperature abrasion resistance is required

(C) Ceramic tools:

Most of the ceramic tools are made from alumina i.e. aluminium oxide. Bauxite which is a hydroxide of aluminium is chemically processed and converted into a denser crystalline form, called as alpha alumina. Fine grains are obtained from the precipitation of the alumina.

Ceramic tools are produced by cold or hot pressing. A small amount of TiO_2 or MgO_2 is added to achieve better sintering properties.

They are used as disposable inserts. They have high hardness, chemical inertness and wear resistance.

They are used for machining of cast iron and hardened steel at high cutting speeds. They have higher work life than that of cemented carbides. They are more brittle and costlier than the carbide tools.

MULTIPLE CHOICE QUESTIONS (MCQ's)

1. At room temperature pure iron is obtained in the structure of -
    (a) B.C.C. non-magnetic
    (b) B.C.C. Magnetic
    (c) F.C.C non-magnetic
    (d) F.C.C Magnetic

2. Melting point of pure iron is ----
    (a) 1539°C   (b) 768°C
    (c) 1401°C   (d) 1600°C

3. Curie temperature is the temperature at which –
    (a) δ-iron changes into γ-iron
    (b) γ-iron changes into α-iron
    (c) α-iron (non-magnetic) changes into α-iron (magnetic)
    (d) α-iron (non-magnetic) changes into γ-iron (magnetic)

4. Curie temperature for iron is –
    (a) 768°C   (b) 910°C
    (c) 1400°C   (d) 1539°C

5. At which state iron will have magnetic and properties?
    (a) α iron at 700°C   (b) α-iron at 850°C
    (c) γ-iron at 1100°C   (d) γ-iron at 1250°C

6. While cooling of pure iron, what happens at 1539°C?
    (a) Liquid iron gets solidify to α-iron (magnetic)
    (b) Liquid iron gets solidify to α-iron (non-magnetic)
    (c) Liquid iron gets solidify to γ-iron
    (d) Liquid iron gets solidify to δ-iron

7. Which of the following state of pure iron has F.C.C. structure.
    (a) α-iron (magnetic)   (b) γ-iron
    (c) δ-iron   (d) α-iron (non-magnetic)

8.

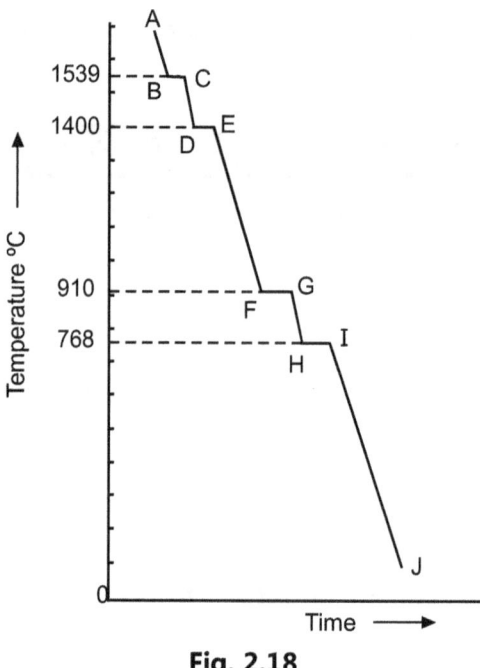

Fig. 2.18

The above figure shows:

(a) Cooling curve of pure iron and chemical transformation.

(b) Cooling curve of pure iron and allotropic transformation

(c) Heating curve of pure iron and allotropic transformation

(d) Heating curve of pure iron and chemical transformation.

9.   In above diagram what happens between D and E?

(a) Liquid gets solidify   (b) α-iron transforms to δ-iron

(c) δ iron transforms to γ-iron   (d) γ-iron transforms to δ-iron

10.   In above diagram what happens during F to G?

(a) α-iron transforms into δ-iron   (b) γ-iron transforms into δ-iron

(c) δ iron transforms into α-iron   (d) γ-iron transforms into α-iron

11.   In above figure the state of iron at point B is-

(a) δ-iron   (b) γ-iron

(c) α-iron   (d) liquid

12.   In above figure the state of iron at point G is –

(a) liquid.   (b) δ-iron

(c) α-iron   (d) γ-iron

13. Considering above figure the process taking place during E to F is –

(a) Transformation of δ-iron into γ-iron.

(b) Transformation of γ-iron into δ-iron.

(c) Cooling of γ-iron

(d) Cooling of δ-iron

14. When structure of iron changes from BCC to FCC its

(a) density increases   (b) mass increases

(c) volume increases   (d) temperature increases

15. Which is not true about the allotropic changes of iron?

(a) These take place at constant temperature during heating

(b) These take place at constant temperature during cooling

(c) When these take place heat is either evolved or absorbed

(d) Due to these changes, physical properties do not change

16. Which is not true about the allotropic change of iron?

(a) All allotropic changes are exothermic when iron is cooled

(b) All allotropic changes are exothermic when iron is heated

(c) All allotropic change take place of constant temperature

(d) Chemical properties do not change during allotropic changes

17. All allotropic changes are exothermic when iron is cooled. Therefore temperature of iron will -------- during an allotropic change.

(a) increase   (b) decrease

(c) remain constant   (d) unpredictable

18. All allotropic changes give heat when iron is cooled. These changes on temperature time cooling curve are shown by –

(a) horizontal line   (b) vertical line

(c) slanting line   (d) parabolic curve

19. Steel is ------- of carbon and iron.

(a) Disordered substitutional solid solution

(b) Ordered

(c) Interstitial solid solution

(d) Intermetallic compound

20. Interstitial solid solution of carbon in γ-iron is called as –

(a) Austenite   (b) Ferrite

(c) Cementite   (d) Pearlite

21. Interstitial solid solution of carbon in α-iron is called as –
    (a) Austenite   (b) Ferrite
    (c) Cementite   (d) Pearlite

22. Chemical compound of carbon and iron is called as
    (a) Austenite   (b) Ferrite
    (c) Cementite   (d) Pearlite

23. Pearlite is ------
    (a) Interstitial solid solution
    (b) Substitutional solid solution
    (c) Chemical compound
    (d) Mixture of solid solution and chemical compound

24. Ledeburite is –
    (a) Interstitial solid solution
    (b) Substitutional solid solution
    (c) Chemical compound
    (d) Mixture of solid solution and chemical compound

25. Which phase is not observed in steels?
    (a) ledeburite   (b) Ferrite
    (c) Pearlite   (d) Austenite

26. The solubility of carbon in α-iron at room temperature is –
    (a) 0.008%   (b) 0.025%
    (c) 0.8%   (d) 2%

27. The maximum solubility of carbon in α-iron is –
    (a) 0.008%   (b) 0.025%
    (c) 0.8%   (d) 2%

28. The maximum solubility of carbon in α-iron is observed at temperature of-
    (a) 727°C   (b) 910°C
    (c) 1148°C   (d) 1498°C

29. The maximum solubility of carbon in γ-iron is-
    (a) 0.008%   (b) 0.025%
    (c) 0.8%   (d) 2%

30. The maximum solubility of carbon in γ-iron is observed at temperature of-
    (a) 727°C   (b) 910°C
    (c) 1148°C   (d) 1498°C

31. Steels are hot worked in which phase?

    (a) Austnite   (b) Ferrite

    (c) Pearlite   (d) Eutectoid

32. Which phase of steels can not be hardened by heat treatment?

    (a) Austenite   (b) Ferrite

    (c) Pearlite   (d) Eutectoid

33. Which phase is not generally observed at room temperature?

    (a) Ferrite   (b) Pearlite

    (c) Austenite   (d) Cementite

34. The phases of iron-carbon alloy system can be arranged in the ascending order of hardness as –

    (a) Cementite, pearlite, austenite, ferrite

    (b) Pearlite, austenite, ferrite, cementite

    (c) Ferrite, cementite. austenite, pearlite

    (d) Ferrite, austenite, pearlite, cementite

35. Alternate layers of ferrite and cementite are observed in

    (a) Austenite   (b) Ledeburite

    (c) Pearlite   (d) Martensite

36. Alternate layers of austenite and cementite are observed in –

    (a) Ferrite,   (b) Ledeburite

    (c) Pearlite   (d) Mastensite

37. Which phase shows maximum ductility?

    (a) Ferrite   (b) Austenite

    (c) Pearlite   (d) Cementite

38. which structure is seen as homogeneous polyhedral grains?

    (a) Austenite   (b) Pearlite

    (c) Cementite   (d) Ferrite

39. The reactions observed in Fe-Fe$_3$C diagram can be arranged in descending order of temperatures at which these take place as –

    (a) Peritectic, eutectic, eutectoid

    (b) Peritectic, eutectoid, eutectic

    (c) Eutectoid, peritectic, eutectic

    (d) Eutectoid, eutectic, peritectic

40. Peritectic reaction is shown by
     (a) All steels   (b) Steel with carbon less than 0.1%
     (c) Steel with carbon more than 0.45%   (d) Steel with carbon between 0.1% to 0.45%

41. Peritectic reaction can be given as -
     (a) $Solid_1 + Liquid \xrightarrow{Cooling} Solid_2$ (b) $Solid_1 + Liquid \xrightarrow{Heating} Solid_2$
     (c) $Solid_1 + Solid_2 \xrightarrow{Heating} Liquid$ (d) $Solid_1 + Solid_2 \xrightarrow{Cooling} Liquid$

42. δ-iron, austenite and molten steel are involved in --- reaction
     (a) Eutectic   (b) Peritectic
     (c) Eutectoid   (d) Ledibutite

43. Pericectic reaction for steel is given as -
     (a) $δ + γ \xrightarrow{Cooling} Liquid$ (b) $δ + α \xrightarrow{Cooling} γ$
     (c) $δ + Liquid \xrightarrow{Cooling} γ$ (d) $δ + liquid \xrightarrow{Heating} γ$

44. Peritectic reaction takes place at temperature of –
     (a) 1539°C   (b) 1498°C
     (c) 1148°C   (d) 727°C

45. Peritectic reaction occurs at carbon percentage
     (a) 0.8   (b) 0.1
     (c) 0.45   (d) 0.18

46. Amount of d phase in steel taking part in peritectic reaction is –
     (a) 82.2%   (b) 17.8%
     (c) 88.1%   (d) 11.9%

47. In steels undergoing peritectic reaction, amount of liquid is –
     (a) 82.2%   (b) 17.8%
     (c) 88.1%   (d) 11.9%

48. What is the transformation product of peritectic reaction taking place on Fe-Fe₃C cooling curve?
     (a) 0.18% austenite   (b) 82.2% δ and 17.8% liquid
     (c) 82.2% liquid and 17.8% δ   (d) 100% austenite

49. In general, eutectoid reaction can be given as –
     (a) $Solid_1 + Solid_2 \xrightarrow{Cooling} Solid_3$ (b) $Solid_1 \xrightarrow{Cooling} Solid_1 + Solid_2$
     (c) $Liquid \xrightarrow{Cooling} Solid_1 + Solid_2$ (d) $Liquid + Solid_1 \longrightarrow Solid_2$

50. For steels, eutectoid reaction takes place as –

(a) $\gamma \xrightarrow{\text{Heating}} \alpha$ + cementite

(b) $\gamma + \alpha \xrightarrow{\text{Cooling}}$ + cementite

(c) $\gamma \xrightarrow{\text{Cooling}} \alpha$ + cementite

(d) Cementite $\xrightarrow{\text{Cooling}} \gamma + \alpha$

51. Eutectoid reaction for $Fe-Fe_3C$ takes place at –

(a) 727°C

(b) 768°C

(c) 910°C

(d) 1148°C

52. Eutectoid reaction in steels takes place at carbon content

(a) 0.008%

(b) 0.18%

(c) 4.3%

(d) 0.8%

53. Eutectoid reaction is shown by steels with carbon content

(a) Less than 0.008%

(b) Between 2% to 4.3%

(c) Between 0.008% to 2%

(d) Between 0.008% to 4.3%

54. Eutectoid mixture of ferrite and cememtite is called as –

(a) Pearlite

(b) Ledeburite

(c) Austenite

(d) δ-ferrite

55. In pearlite at room temperature amount of ferrite is –

(a) 11.9%

(b) 88.1%

(c) 40.4%

(d) 59.6%

56. In pearlite at room temperature amount of cementite is

(a) 11.9%

(b) 88.1%

(c) 40.4%

(d) 59.6%

57. Steels with carbon less than 0.8% are called as ------ steels

(a) Hypercutectoid

(b) Cufectoid

(c) Hypoeutectoid

(d) Eutectic

58. Hypereutectoid steels contain carbon

(a) Less than 0.8%

(b) Between 0.8% to 2%

(c) Between 0.8% to 4.3%

(d) More than 4.3%

59. In general, eutectic reaction can be shown as –

(a) $Solid_1 \xrightarrow{\text{Cooling}} Solid_2 + Liquid$

(b) $Solid_1 \xrightarrow{\text{Cooling}} Solid_1 + Solid_2$

(c) $Liquid + Solid_1 \xrightarrow{\text{Cooling}} Solid_2$

(d) $Liquid \xrightarrow{\text{Cooling}} Solid_1 + Solid_2$

60. For Fe-Fe$_3$C system, eutectic reaction takes place as –

    (a) L $\longrightarrow$ Fe$_3$C + γ   (b) L $\longrightarrow$ δ + γ

    (c) L $\longrightarrow$ δ + α   (d) L $\longrightarrow$ Fe$_3$C + δ

61. Eutectic reaction for Fe-Fe$_3$C takes place at –

    (a) 727°C   (b) 768°C

    (c) 1498°C   (d) 1148°C

62. Eutectic reaction for Fe-Fe$_3$C takes place at carbon content –

    (a) 0.8%   (b) 0.18%

    (c) 2%   (d) 4.3%

63. Eutectic reaction for Fe-Fe$_3$C system can be seen with carbon content -

    (a) Between 2% to 6.67%   (b) 2% to 4.3%

    (c) 0.008% to 2%   (c) 0.8%

64. Eutectic mixture of austenite and cementite is called as –

    (a) Ledeburite   (b) pearlite

    (c) δ-ferrite   (d) α-ferrite

65. In ledeburite, amount of pearlite is –

    (a) 11.9%   (b) 88.1%

    (c) 40.4%   (d) 59.6%

66. In ledeburite amount of cementite as compared to pearlite is –

    (a) 11.9%   (b) 88.1%

    (c) 40.4%   (d) 59.6%

67. In ledeburite, at room temperature amount of ferrite is about –

    (a) 40.4%   (b) 35.5%

    (c) 59.6%   (d) 64.5%

68. In ledeburite, at room temperature amount of cementite as compared to ferrite

    (a) 40.4%   (b) 35.5%

    (c) 59.6%   (d) 64.5%

69. During heating with faster rates the transformations takes place at temperature

    (a) Higher   (b) Lower

    (c) Constant   (d) Same

70. During cooling with higher rates, the transformations take place a t ------ temperature

    (a) Higher   (b) Lower

    (c) Constant   (d) Same

71. During annealing steel is heated –
    (a) Above higher critical temperature   (b) Above lower critical temperature
    (c) Above curie temperature   (d) Above A_3

72. At lower critical temperature –
    (a) During heating pearlite transforms to austenite
    (b) During cooling pearlite transforms to austenite
    (c) During cooling pearlite transforms to cementite
    (d) During heating pearlite transforms to cementite

73. At A1 temperature during cooling –
    (a) Transformation of pearlite into austenite starts
    (b) Transformation of pearlite into austenite complete
    (c) Transformation of austenit into pearlite starts
    (d) Transformation of austenit into pearlite completes

74. Upper critical temperature for ferrite is shown by line –
    (a) A_1 (b) A_2
    (c) A_3 (d) A_{Cm}

75. For various heat treatments, hypoeutectoid steels must be heated above line –
    (a) A_1 (b) A_2
    (c) A_3 (d) A_{Cm}

76. Along A_3 line during heating of hypoeutectoid steels –
    (a) Transformation of austenite into ferrite starts
    (b) Transformation of austenite into ferrite complete
    (c) Transformation of ferrite into austenite starts
    (d) Transformation of ferrite into austenite complete

77. Along A_1 line during heating of hypoeutectoid steels –
    (a) Transformation of pearlite into austenite starts
    (b) Transformation of pearlite into austenite complete
    (c) Transformation of austenite into pearlite starts
    (d) Transformation of austenite into pearlite complete

78. Along A_3 line during cooling –
    (a) Transformation of austenite into ferrite starts
    (b) Transformation of austenite into ferrite complete
    (c) Transformation of ferrite into austenite complete
    (d) Transformation of ferrite into austenite starts

79. Upper critical temperature for ferrite hypoeutectoid steels is given by line –

   (a) A_1 (b) A_2

   (c) A_3 (d) A_{cm}

80. Upper critical temperature for cementite is given by –

   (a) A_1 (b) A_2

   (c) A_3 (d) A_{cm}

81. During heating, along A_{cm} line –

   (a) Transformation of austenite into cementite starts

   (b) Transformation of austenite into cementite complete

   (c) Transformation of cementite into cementite starts

   (d) Transformation of cementite into cementite complete

82. During cooling, along A_{cm} line –

   (a) Transformation of austenite into cementite starts

   (b) Transformation of austenite into cementite complete

   (c) Transformation of cementite into austenite starts

   (d) Transformation of cementite into austenite complete

83.

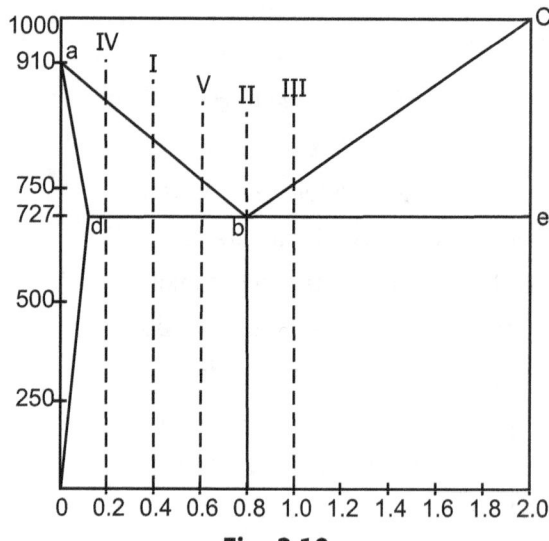

Fig. 2.19

   In above figure steel shown by state 1 is –

   (a) hypoeutectic   (b) hypereutectic

   (c) hypoeutectoid   (d) hypereutectoid

84. At room temperature considering above figure steel I will have about –
    (a) 50% ferrite and 50% pearlite   (b) 50% ferrite and 50% cementite
    (c) 50% pearlite and 50% cementite   (d) 50% ferrite and 50% ledeburite
85. In above figure steel shount by III is –
    (a) Hypoeutectoid   (b) Hypereutectoid
    (c) Hypoeutectic   (d) Hypereutectic
86. At room temperature considering above figure steel at III will have –
    (a) 3% cementite and 97% pearlite   (b) 3% cementite and 97% ferrite
    (c) 97% cementite and 3% pearlite   (d) 97% cementite and 3% ferrite
87. At room temperature steel at III will have about –
    (a) 14% ferrite   (b) 97% ferrite
    (c) 86% ferrite   (d) 3% ferrite
88. At room temperature, steel at 1 will have about –
    (a) 6% cementite   (b) 50% cementite
    (c) 94% cementite   (d) 12% cementite
89. In above figure states having can be arranged in ascending order of their pearlite content as –
    (a) IV, I, V, II, III   (b) IV, I, III, V, II
    (c) III, IV, I, V, II   (d) IV, I, V, III, II
90. In above figure upper critical temperature for ferrite is shown by line
    (a) ad   (b) ab
    (c) db   (d) bc
91. In above figure lower critical temperature line is -----
    (a) ad   (b) ab
    (c) db   (d) de
92. In above figure higher critical temperature for cementite is shown by line
    (a) ab   (b) bc
    (c) ce   (d) be
93. In above figure A_{cm} temperature line is shown by ----
    (a) ab   (b) de
    (c) bc   (d) be
94. Due to fast cooling, eutectoid temperature ---
    (a) increases   (b) decreases
    (c) remains constants   (d) is not affected

95.   Widemanstatten structure is formed when proeutectoid phase seperates –

(a) Only along grain boundary

(b) Only inside the grains

(c) Both along grain boundary and inside

(d)   Neither along the boundary nor inside the grains

96.   Formation of widmanstaften structure is higher in ----

(a) eutectoid steels   (b) pro eutectoid steel

(c) eutectic   (d) pro eutectic

97.   Widmanstatten structure is more desirable in –

(a) eutectoid steel   (b) Proeutectoid steel

(c) Hypoeutectoid steel   (d) hypereutectoid steel

98.   Widemanstatten structure is observed in steels with carbon percentage

(a) 0.8   (b) upto 0.7

(c) above 0.9   (d) upto 0.7 and above 0.9

99.   In hypoeutectoid steels, effect of widmanstatten structure is –

(a) Reduction in ductility   (b) reduction in strength

(c) reduction in hardness   (d) no effect

100. Maximum solubility of carbon in δ-ferrite is –

(a) 0.008%   (b) 0.025%

(c) 0.8%   (d) 0.1%

101. Maximum solubility of carbon in austenite is –

(a) 0.008%   (b) 4.3%

(c) 0.8%   (d) 2%

102. Considering carbon percentage, steels can be arranged in ascending order as –

(a) ferrite, pearlite, cementite   (b) ferrite, cementite, pearlite

(c) pearlite, ferrite, cementite   (d) pearlite, cementite, ferrite

103. -------- has highest tensile strengh

(a) α-ferrite   (b) Pearlite

(c) Cementite   (d) δ-ferrite

104. The phase with highest hardness is ----

(a) α-ferrite   (b) Pearlite

(c) Cementite   (d) δ-ferrite

105. The phase with highest impact strength is ---

    (a) α-ferrite   (b) Pearlite

    (c) Cementite   (d) δ-ferrite

106. The property of steel that depend upon austenite is ----

    (a) hardness   (b) tensiel strength

    (c) ductility   (d) Grain size fabrication

107. Steels with highest ductility, formability and brication properties are

    (a) Low carbon steels   (b) High carbon steels

    (c) Medium carbon steels   (d) Stainless steels

108. Steels with good wear and abrasion resistance are –

    (a) Low carbon steels   (b) High carbon steels

    (c) Medium carbon steels   (d) Mild steels

109. Steels with poor machinability and weldability are

    (a) Low carbon steels   (b) Medium carbon steels

    (c) High carbon steels   (d) Mild steels

110. For applications requiring both strength and hardness steel used are ---

    (a) Low carbon steels   (b) Medium carbon steels

    (c) High carbon steels   (d) Mild steels

111. If dissolved oxygen is completely removed, steels are called as –

    (a) Killed steels   (b) Semi-killed steels

    (c) Rimmed steels   (d) Live steels

112. If dissolved oxygen is remaining as it is steels are called as –

    (a) Killed steels   (b) Semi-killed steels

    (c) Rimmed steels   (d) Live steels

113. For machine parts subjected to dynamic loading, suitable steel is ---

    (a) Rimmed   (b) Semi-rimmed

    (c) Semi-killed   (d) Killed

114. Steel Fe200 will have –

    (a) Minimum tensile strength of 200 N/mm^2

    (b) Minimum hardness of 200 BHN

    (c) Maximum tensile strength of 200 N/mm^2

    (d) Maximum hardness of 200 BHN

115. Steel FeE200 will have –
    (a) Minimum tensile strength of 200 N/mm^2
    (b) Minimum yield strength of 200 N/mm^2
    (c) Maximum tensile strength of 200 N/mm^2
    (d) Maximum yield strength of 200 N/mm^2

116. The steel 10C851D has composition as –
    (a) 10% carbon, 8% S and 10% Mn
    (b) 0.1% C, 0.8% S, 0.1% Mn
    (c) 1% C, 0.08% S, 0.01% Mn
    (d) 0.1% C, 0.08% S, 1% Mn

117. The steel 13Ni3Cr4D has composition as –
    (a) 13% C, 3% Ni, 40% Cr
    (b) 0.13% C, 0.3% Ni, 0.4% Cr
    (c) 1.3% C, 0.3 % Ni, 4% Cr
    (d) 0.15 % C, 3% Ni, 0.4% Cr

118. The steel X15Cr25Ni12 has composition of –
    (a) 15% C, 25% Cr, 12% Ni
    (b) 1.5% C, 2.5% Cr, 1.2% Ni
    (c) 0.15% C, 25% Cr, 12% Ni
    (d) 0.15% C, 0.25% Cr, 0.12% Ni

119. According to AISI, steel designated as 1010 is –
    (a) 10% carbon 10% Mn, plain carbon steel
    (b) 1% C plain carbon steel
    (c) 0.1% plain carbon steel
    (d) 0.1% free cutting steel

120. Steels are designated by En numbers as per which standards?
    (a) British
    (b) Indian
    (c) SAE
    (d) AISI

121. Which of the following is intentional impurity in steels?
    (a) Mn
    (b) Oxygen
    (c) S
    (d) Ni

122. Whenever an element is dissolved in ferrite, changes in properties of ferrite are –
    (a) Hardness increases, strength decreases
    (b) Both hardness and strength decreases
    (c) Hardness decreases strength increases
    (d) Both hardness and strength increases

123. Due to alloying elements, in the Fe-Fe$_3$C diagram eutectoid points –
    (a) Shifts towards left
    (b) Shift towards righ
    (c) Shifts up
    (d) Remains as it is

123. In order to retain austenite at room temperature, one has to –
    (a) Increase lower critical temperature (b) Decrease lower critical temperature
    (c) Increase higher critical temperature (d) It is independent of critical temperature

124. The alloying elements which forms carbide will –
    (a) Raise tempering temperature   (b) Lower tempering temperature
    (c) Raise annealing temperature   (d) Lower annealing temperature

125. Due to precipitation of alloy carbides in tempering steels become hard this is called –
    (a) Secondary hardness   (b) Primary hardness
    (c) Secondary tempering   (d) Primary tempering

126. Effect of most of the alloying elements is ---
    (a) Shifting of TTT diagram to right   (b) Shifting of TTT diagram to left
    (c) Shifting of TTT diagram to up   (d) No effect

127. Effect of most of the alloyine elements on steel is –
    (a) Increase in hardenability   (b) Decrease in hardenability
    (c) No effect on hardenability   (d) Unpredictable

128. Due to ferrite stabilizers ferrite
    (a) is observed at room temperature
    (b) is formed quickly
    (c) is observed at melting point without austenite
    (d) Only austenite is forms

129. Hot shortness in steels is due to –
    (a) Mn   (b) S
    (c) P   (d) Al

130. Element added to reduce hot shortness is steels
    (a) Mn   (b) S
    (c) Si   (d) Al

131. Free cutting steels have –
    (a) Higher Mn content with S upto 0.33%
    (b) Lower S content with Mn upto 0.3%
    (c) Higher S content with Mn upto 0.33%
    (d) Lower Mn content with S upto 0.33%

132. The element that causes cold shortness is –
    (a) Mn   (b) S
    (c) P   (d) Al

133. To increase permeability and to reduce iron losses, element added to steel is –
   (a) Mn   (b) Si
   (c) S   (d) P

134. Hadfield steels are –
   (a) Wear resistant and magnetic   (b) Soft and non-magnetic
   (c) Wear resistant and non-magnetic   (s) Soft and magnetic

135. The element added to steels used in measuring instruments is ---
   (a) Mn   (b) S
   (c) Si   (d) Ni

136. Excellent corrosion resistance of stainless steels is due to –
   (a) Mn   (b) S
   (c) Cr   (d) Si

137. Which steels are non-magnetic?
   (a) Martensitic stainless steel   (b) Ferritic stainless steel
   (c) Austenitic stainless steel   (d) All type of stainless steel

138. Which steels can be hardened by heat treatment?
   (a) Martensitic stainless steel   (b) Austenic stainless steel
   (c) Ferritic stainless steel   (d) All types of stainless steel

139. Steels most suitable for food handling equipment are –
   (a) Martensitic stainless steel   (b) Ferritic stainless steel
   (c) Austenitic stainless steel   (d) Hadfield steel

140. Sensitisation is observed in –
   (a) Austenitic stainless steel   (b) Martensitic stainless steel
   (c) Martensitic stainless steel   (d) Duplex stainless steel

141. Sensitisation means –
   (a) Increase in corrosion resistance   (b) Decrease in corrosion resistance
   (c) Increase in hardness resistance   (d) Decrease in hardness resistance

142. Sensitisation takes place when
   (a) Cr gens consumed with C   (b) Cr is added in excess
   (c) Mn gens consumed with C   (d) Mn is added in excess

143. L-grade steels have low percentage of –
   (a) Mn   (b) S
   (c) P   (d) C

144. The tool steel designated by 18-4-1 has composition as –

    (a) 18% Mn, 4% Ni, 1% U   (b) 18% Cr, 4% Ni, 1% Mn

    (c) 18% W, 4% Cr, 1% U   (d) 18% Ni, 4% Cr, 1% W

145. The steels designated by H series are

    (a) High speed steels   (b) High alloy steels

    (c) Hot work tool steels   (d) High strength stees

147. The element added to low temperature steels is –

    (a) Mn   (b) S

    (c) Si   (d) Ni

148. Due to addition of Silicon in steels

    (a) Strength, hardness increase with decrease in ductility

    (b) Strength, hardness increase without decrease in ductility

    (c) Strength, hardness decrease without increase in ductility

    (d) Strength, hardness increase with increase in ductility

149. The element that increases temper embrittlement in steels is –

    (a) Mn   (b) S

    (c) Si   (d) Ni

150. The element added in steels for electric and magnetic applications is ---

    (a) Mn   (b) S

    (c) Si   (d) Ni

151. In stainless steel, to improve ductility and impact strength element added is

    (a) Cr   (b) V

    (c) Mo   (d) Ni

152. Stainless steels more suitable for razors and surgical instruments –

    (a) martensitic stainless steel (b) Austenific stainless steel

    (c) Ferritic stainless steel   (d) Duplex stainless steel

153. The only heat treatment given to ferritic stainless steels is –

    (a) Tempering   (b) Normalizing

    (c) annealing   (d) Hardening

154. Steels used for high temperature applications have –

    (a) High Cr content   (b) High Mg content

    (c) High Mn content   (d) High S contents

ANSWER KEY

1. (b)	2. (a)	3. (c)	4. (a)	5. (a)	6. (d)
7. (b)	8. (b)	9. (c)	10. (d)	11. (d)	12. (c)
13. (c)	14. (a)	15. (d)	16. (b)	17. (c)	18. (a)
19. (c)	20. (a)	21. (b)	22. (c)	23. (d)	24. (d)
25. (a)	26. (a)	27. (b)	28. (a)	29. (d)	30. (c)
31. (b)	32. (b)	33. (c)	34. (d)	35. (c)	36. (b)
37. (a)	38. (d)	39. (a)	40. (d)	41. (a)	42. (b)
43. (c)	44. (b)	45. (d)	46. (a)	47. (b)	48. (d)
49. (b)	50. (c)	51. (a)	52. (d)	53. (c)	54. (a)
55. (b)	56. (a)	57. (c)	58. (b)	59. (d)	60. (a)
61. (d)	62. (d)	63. (a)	64. (a)	65. (c)	66. (d)
67. (b)	68. (d)	69. (a)	70. (b)	71. (b)	72. (b)
73. (d)	74. (c)	75. (c)	76. (d)	77. (a)	78. (a)
79. (c)	80. (d)	81. (d)	82. (a)	83. (c)	84. (a)
85. (b)	86. (a)	87. (c)	88. (a)	89. (d)	90. (b)
91. (d)	92. (b)	93. (c)	94. (b)	95. (c)	96. (b)
97. (d)	98. (d)	99. (a)	100. (d)	101. (d)	102. (a)
103. (b)	104. (c)	105. (b)	106. (d)	107. (a)	108. (b)
109. (c)	110. (b)	111. (a)	112. (c)	113. (d)	114. (a)
115. (b)	116. (d)	117. (d)	118. (d)	119. (c)	120. (a)
121. (d)	122. (d)	123. (a)	124. (b)	125. (a)	126. (a)
127. (a)	128. (a)	129. (c)	130. (b)	131. (a)	132. (c)
133. (c)	134. (b)	135. (c)	136. (d)	137. (c)	138. (c)
139. (a)	140. (c)	141. (a)	142. (b)	143. (a)	144. (d)
145. (c)	146. (c)	147. (d)	148. (b)	149. (a)	150. (c)
151. (d)	152. (a)	153. (c)	154. (a)		

QUESTIONS

STEELS

1. State whether the following statements are True or False. Justify your answers.
   1. Iron shows allotropic changes.
   2. Wrought iron contains slag.
   3. Austenite is observed at room temperature in plain carbon steels.
   4. Ferrite has higher hardness.
   5. Peritectic reaction is useful for hot working of steels.
   6. Carbon has more solubility in ferrite than in austenite.
   7. Slow cooling of steel is usually studied from austenite region.
   8. Martensite is not shown in iron-iron carbide equilibrium diagram.
   9. High carbon steels are recommended for tools.
   10. Iron-Iron carbide equilibrium diagram is called as an equilibrium diagram.

   Ans.

1.	True	2.	True	3.	False	4.	False	5.	False
6.	False	7.	True	8.	True	9.	True	10.	True

2. Explain the allotropic changes in iron.
3. With respect to Fe-C diagram, explain:
   (a) slow cooling of 0.35% carbon steel and
   (b) slow cooling of 1.6% carbon steel. What are the amount of phases that are present at room temperature for above steels ?
4. 'The mechanical properties of steels are structure dependent'. Comment.
5. Is there any relation of percentage of carbon in steel and its application ? Give some examples.
6. What is the importance of deoxidation of steel ?
7. What are the different specifications used for steels ?
8. How will you find the chemical composition of following steels:
   (a) C 20   (b) 40 C 10 S 14
   (c) 30 Ni 8 Cr V 3 and   (d) AISI 2440

VARIOUS ALLOY STEELS

1. State whether the following statements are True or False and justify your answers.
   (i) Nickel is added to improve toughness, while vanadium is added to increase wear resistance.

(ii)   Manganese is always added in steel, if it contains sulphur.

(iii) Steadite is not desirable.

(iv)   Creep resisting steel contains Mo, V and Cr.

(v)   Dual phase steels have better formability.

(vi)   Sensitization is observed in ferritic stainless steel.

(vii) Tool steel requires high red hardness.

(viii) High carbon high chromium tool steel is used for drawing dies.

(ix)   Multiple tempering is used for H.S.S.

(x)   Tool steels are preheated before austenitising.

Ans.:

(i) True	(ii) True	(iii) True	(iv) True	(v) True
(vi) False	(vii) True	(viii) True	(ix) True	(x) True

2. Why is nickel added to austenitic stainless steel ?

3. Why high sulphur or leaded steels are called as free cutting steels ?

4. What are the high temperature metals ? What are their applications ?

5. What are the microalloyed steels ? Explain their properties.

6. Explain maraging steels.

7. What are the various heat treatments used for stainless steels ?

8. Explain any three outstanding properties of tool steels.

9. Write short notes on:

    (i)   Water hardening tool steels.

    (ii)   Steels used for pneumatic tools.

    (iii) High carbon high chromium steels.

    (iv)   Steels used for hot extrusion dies.

10. Compare the hardening and tempering treatments for

    (i)   A plain carbon steel (e.g. 0.4% C) and

    (ii)   A high speed tool steel (e.g. 181411).

11. What are the special purpose steels ? What are their applications ?

12. Explain the following terms with reference to alloy content, properties and applications.

    (a)   Stellites

    (b)   Cemented carbides and

    (c)   Ceramic tools.

UNIVERSITY QUESTIONS

STEELS

1. Define and explain the following terms: **(May 08)**
   (a) Ferrite,
   (b) Austenite,
   (c) Cementite.

2. What is the importance of reactions observed in Fe-C diagram ? Explain the reactions in detail. Draw the diagram.   **(May 08, 09, 10, 11; Dec. 10)**

3. Draw typical micro-structures of 0.2, 0.4, 0.6 and 0.8% carbon steel. Comment on the amount of phases present.   **(May 09, Dec. 09)**

4. What are critical temperatures ? Explain its significance.   **(May 09, 10)**

5. Explain the classification of steels.   **(Dec. 08)**

6. Write short notes on:
   (a) Wrought iron
   (b) Widmanstatten structures.   **(Dec. 08)**

7. Compare steel and cast iron on basis of composition properties and application.
                                                                      (May 11)

VARIOUS ALLOY STEELS

1. Explain the limitations of plain carbon steels. How can they be overcome ?
                                                                (May 09, Dec. 09)

2. Explain the effect of various elements on the properties of steel.   **(May 09, May 10)**

3. What are the outstanding properties of stainless steel ?   **(June 09)**

4. What are the factors that differentiate ferritic, austenitic and martensitic stainless steels from each other ?   **(May 09, May 11)**

5. Why should the austenitic stainless steel be stabilized ? What is the importance of using L-grade stainless steel ?   **(May 10)**

6. How are the tool steels classified ?   **(May 11)**

7. Classify stainless steels. Give typical composition, properties and application of each class of stainless steel.   **(May 11)**

8. State requirement of steels used for various tools. Explain the significance of Cr and V in tool steel.   **(Dec. 10)**

9. Suggest suitable steel for the following and justify your choice.   **(May 08)**
   (a) Sitar wires

(b) Nut and bolts

(c) RCC bar

(d) Wood working tool

(e) Connecting rod

(f) Gears

(g) Sanitary fitting

(h) Trying pans

(i) Forging die

(j) Die casting die

(k) Milling cutter   **(May 09)**

(l) Fan blades   **(May 09)**

(m) Taps   **(May 09)**

(n) Surgical instrument   **(May 09)**

10. Compare gray cast iron of SG iron on basis of manufacturing method, micro structure, properties of applications.   **(May 11)**

11. Note – classification of steels on basis of degree of deoxidation.   **(May 11)**

12. Explain free cutting steel w.r.t. composition and machinabillity.   **(Dec. 10)**

❑❑❑

Chapter 3

HEAT TREATMENT OF STEELS AND NON-FERROUS METALS

3.1 INTRODUCTION

Heat treatment is a very important process in metallurgy. It can alter the properties of metals. Usually, it consists of heating and controlled cooling. Heat treatment is a very essential step for many alloy steels and tool steels. Heat treatment can alter the following properties of steel:

- Hardness
- Ductility
- Machinability
- Grain structure
- Modification of dendritic structure
- Formation of stable phases
- Toughness

- Internal stress level
- Cold working
- Segregation
- High impact strength and increased notch toughness
- Reduction in embrittlement after cold working

Considering all the above points, it can be concluded that heat treatment is a very necessary treatment for steel.

Following are the various heat treatments carried out to improve properties of steel:

- Annealing
- Hardening
- Tempering
- Austempering
- Patenting

- Normalizing
- Sub-zero treatment
- Martempering
- Ausforming

After heat treatment, some new phases may be introduced. This phase transformation alters properties of steel. Martensite, bainite, tempered martensite spheroidal pearlite, various precipitates etc. improve mechanical properties of steel.

3.2 TRANSFORMATION PRODUCTS OF AUSTENITE

(May 06, 07, 10, 11; Dec. 08, 13)

From iron-iron carbide diagram, it can be observed that austenite is not a stable phase. Normally, in plain carbon steel, austenite does not exist at room temperature. On cooling from high temperature, it always gets transformed into different phases. Following transformations are observed, when steel is heated and cooled with controlled cooling rate.

(A)   Austenite to Pearlite,

(B)   Austenite to Bainite and

(C)   Austenite to Martensite.

3.3 TRANSFORMATION OF AUSTENITE TO PEARLITE

It is also termed as Isothermal decomposition of austenite. Austenite is unstable below 727°C. Cementite gets nucleated at the grain boundaries of austenite during cooling. Carbon diffuses from the adjacent austenite to cementite. Due to this, cementite growth starts. This carbon diffusion depletes the adjacent austenite in carbon and ferrite is formed.

Carbon has less solubility in ferrite. So, growth of ferrite rejects carbon in excess of its solubility limit to the adjacent austenite. This gives rise to the formation of more nuclei of cementite. These nuclei are formed and grow at two sides of ferrite (Fig. 3.1).

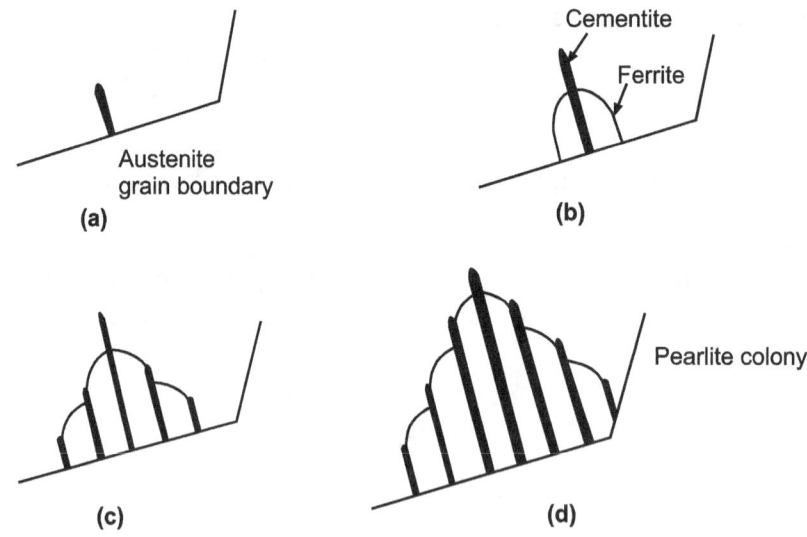

(a) Nucleation of cementite plate at austenite grain boundary,

(b) Formation of ferrite plate on sides of cementite plate,

(c) and (d) Pearlite formation proceeds

Fig. 3.1: Austenite to Pearlite transformation

Nucleation and growth of alternate plates of cementite and ferrite are observed at the various areas of austenite. These alternate layers of ferrite and cementite are called as "*Pearlite*".

Several colonies of pearlite are formed within the austenite grain. The process of diffusion and pearlite formation continues until all austenite gets transformed to pearlite. Inter-lamellar spacing of pearlite is termed as the distance between the two consecutive cementite plates.

Fine pearlite is formed at lower transformation temperature. At this temperature, the rate of nucleation and number of nuclei are more; while the rate of growth is less. This reduces the inter-lamellar distance and tends to the formation of fine pearlite. The fine pearlite has more hardness (RC 40) and better strength.

At higher transformation/temperature and with the lowest cooling rate, coarse pearlite is formed. In this condition, the rate of nucleation and number of nuclei is less, while the rate of growth is high. This increases the inter-lamellar distance and tends to the formation of coarse pearlite. The coarse pearlite has less hardness (RC 15) and strength compared to fine pearlite.

3.4 TRANSFORMATION OF AUSTENITE TO BAINITE

If austenite is rapidly cooled below 550°C and held isothermally, "Bainite" is formed (Fig. 3.2). This is a fine mixture of ferrite and cementite. This transformation starts with nucleation of ferrite and not with cementite as in pearlite transformation.

In pearlite, the cementite plates appear to be embedded in ferrite matrix; while in bainite, the cementite appears as small spheroids in ferrite.

The bainitic transformation occurs at a very low temperature, when compared with the temperature required for pearlitic transformation.

At this temperature, the rate and number of nuclei formation is very high compared to its rate of growth. This results in very fine bainite. Due to this, bainite usually gets resolved at very high magnifications as 500X, 1000X etc. At upper temperature range of bainite transformation, upper or feathery bainite is formed. At low temperatures, lower or an accicular bainite is formed. The upper bainite looks like a pearlite, while lower bainite as martensite.

A typical upper bainitic micro-structure shows tiny carbide platelets, oriented parallel with a long ferrite needle.

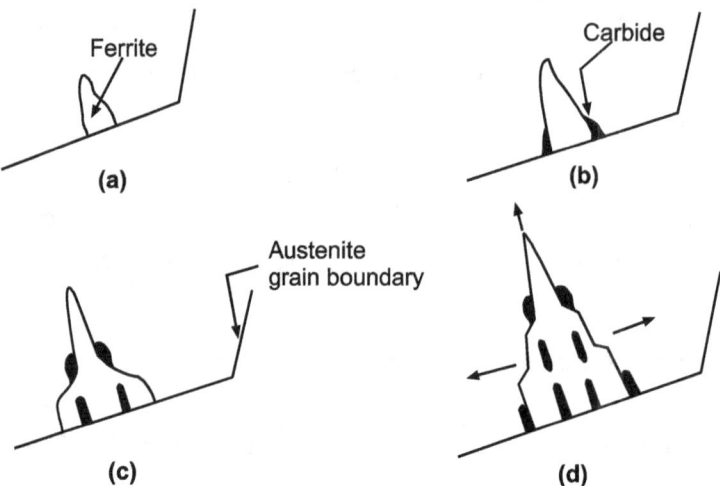

(a) Nucleation of ferrite at austenite grain boundary,

(b) Formation of carbide particles on sides of ferrite plate,

(c) and (d) Bainite formation proceeds

Fig. 3.2: Austenite to Bainite transformation

Carbide platelets are oriented at an angle of about 60° to the long axis of the ferrite needle in lower bainite. Pearlite is nucleated by carbide, while bainite is nucleated by ferrite. The upper bainite shows less hardness (RC 40) than lower bainite (RC 60) (Figures in bracket indicate the hardness for 0.8% carbon steel.) However, the hardness of bainite is higher than that of pearlite. This is because of decrease in spacing of carbide plates and low temperature transformation. Austempering heat treatment gives a fully bainitic structure.

3.5 TRANSFORMATION OF AUSTENITE TO MARTENSITE

(Dec. 09, 11, 13)

The transformation of austenite at a low temperature and very fast cooling rate produces martensite. It forms at a temperature below the bainitic region. Carbon atoms are able to diffuse out, of the austenite structure, under very slow cooling rates. This changes the gamma iron (F.C.C.) to alpha iron (B.C.C.). This transformation is possible by nucleation and growth process. This process is time dependent.

With increasing cooling rate, enough time is not allowed for the carbon to diffuse out of solution. The structure cannot get converted to alpha iron (B.C.C.). Due to fast cooling, the carbon gets trapped in solution. The structure produced due to entrapping of carbon is called Martensite.

It may be defined as a *super saturated solid solution of carbon in alpha iron with B.C.T. (Body centred tetragonal) structure* (Fig. 3.3).

This transformation takes place without diffusion and involves no change in composition.

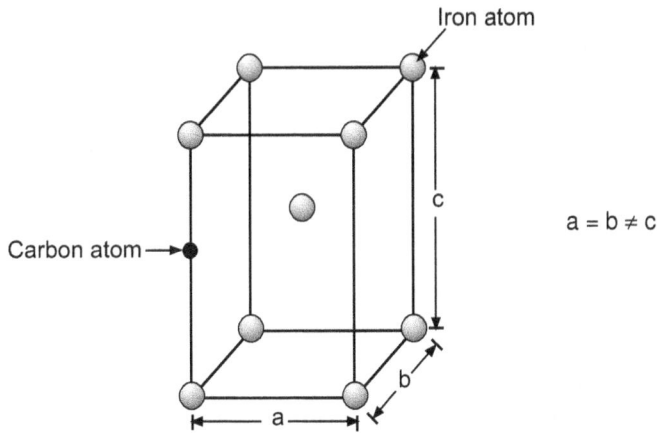

Fig. 3.3: B.C.T. structure of martensite

In a standard B.C.C. structure, the lattice parameters are equal (i.e. a = b = c). But in B.C.T. structure, two dimensions of the unit cell are equal and the third is expanded because of trapped carbon (a = b ≠ c). So, the axial ratio c/a increases. The c/a ratio increases with increase in carbon content of the martensite.

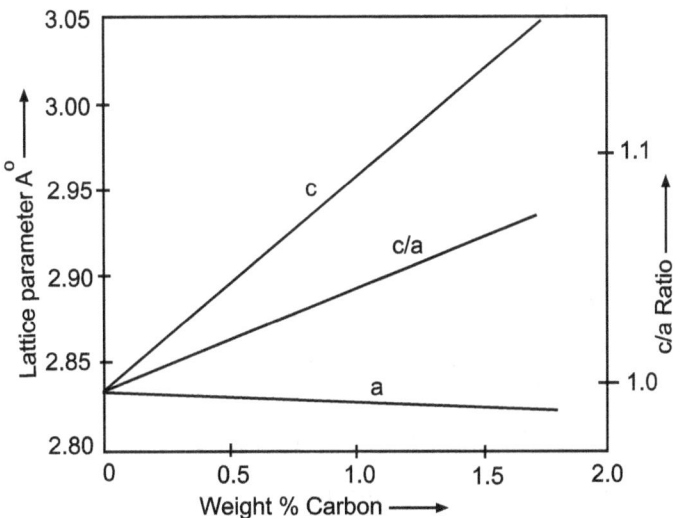

Fig. 3.4: Unit cell dimensions of martensite as a function of carbon content in steel

Martensite has a characteristic needle like structure formed as a result of intersection with the surface of the micro-section of martensite plates.

These plates are flat discs, thicker in the centre than at the edges. The increase in c/a ratio (Fig. 3.4) is responsible for structure distortion. This highly distorted lattice structure gives high hardness to martensite (Fig. 3.5).

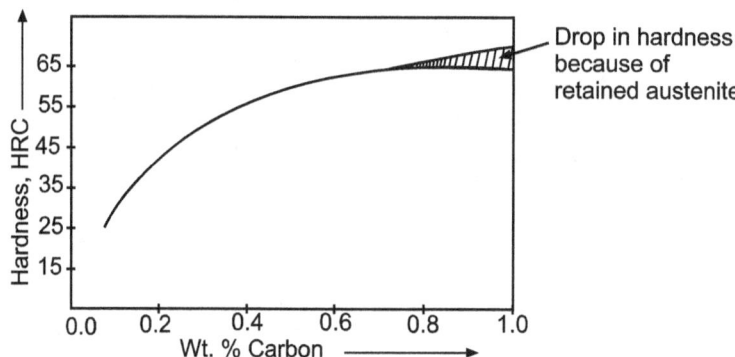

Fig. 3.5: Variation in hardness of martensite with increase in carbon content

Microscopically, martensite appears as a white needle like structure. In most steels, it is unresolved. High carbon alloy steels show martensite with small percentage of retained austenite.

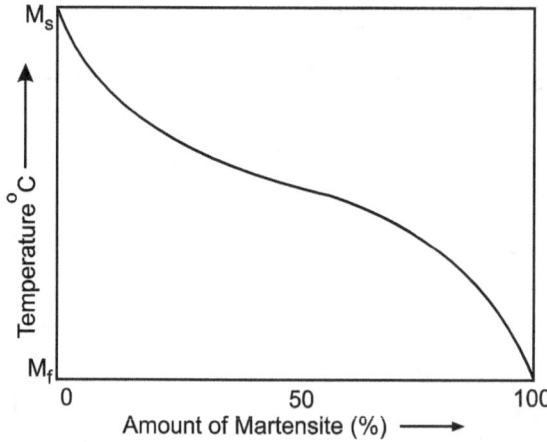

Fig. 3.6: Effect of temperature on martensitic transformation

Following are the characteristics of martensite transformation:

- Chemical composition does not change during the transformation.
- Due to fast cooling, diffusionless transformation occurs.

- It is a thermal transformation. If cooling is interrupted, transformation ceases.

- It is temperature dependent and independent of time (Fig. 3.6).

- Initially, the number of martensite needles formed is small; then it increases and finally, at the end of transformation again decreases. So the amount of martensite formed with decreasing temperature is not linear.

- Martensite transformation temperature (M_s) is a function of chemical composition (Fig. 3.7).

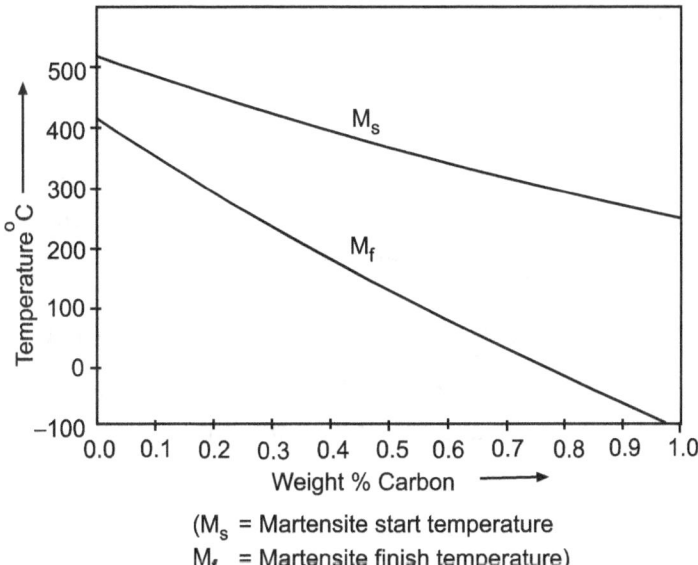

(M$_s$ = Martensite start temperature
M$_f$ = Martensite finish temperature)

Fig. 3.7: Austenite to Martensite transformation temperatures for different carbon steels

- Martensite is unstable phase.

- It shows high hardness.

- Martensite is formed at a cooling rate higher than critical cooling rate and

- Practically, this transformation is never completed.

3.5.1 Micro-Structure of Martensite

Two principal morphological types of martensite are,

- Lamellar Martensite

- Lath Martensite

(A) Lamellar Martensite:

It is also called as accicular or low temperature martensite. This is one of the most typical types in which martensite crystals are in the form of thin plates. Adjacent platelets are not parallel to each other and often form a truss shape. The initial plates formed penetrate the austenite grain completely and separate it into two portions.

The maximum size of platelet is determined by the size of austenite grain. As the transformation proceeds, austenite grain breaks down in smaller portions and very small plates are formed. A fine austenitic grain structure gives very fine platelets. It is not possible to reveal as it is a needle like structure. This is most desirable type in steel.

(B) Lath Martensite:

It is also called as massive or high temperature martensite. Crystals of lath martensite are observed to be parallel to each other and form a dense structure. The size of all laths is roughly the same. It is very difficult to see lath structure under optical microscope as it reveals beyond the resolution limit of optical microscope.

3.5.2 Effect of carbon content on hardness of martensite

The lattice distortion and c/a ratio increases with increase in carbon content. With very low carbon, the c/a ratio approaches to one and ferrite structure is observed.

The hardness of martensite increases upto 1.0% carbon. This can give hardness as high as RC 50 to RC 60. Martensite is always harder than the austenite from which it is formed. Upto 0.4% carbon in steel, the hardness of martensite rapidly increases. It remains almost constant upto 0.8% C steel. This is because the amount of retained austenite increases with increase in carbon percentage (Fig. 4.5).

3.6 TIME-TEMPERATURE TRANSFORMATION (T-T-T) CURVES

Austenite is not stable below lower critical temperature (A_1). If the steel is cooled below this temperature, austenite transforms to various phases as pearlite, bainite or martensite.

These transformations are time and/or temperature dependent. They are explained by T-T-T curves.

This also describes the cooling rates necessary for phase transformations, e.g.

- Very slow cooling gives pearlite,
- Very fast cooling gives martensite and
- Interrupted cooling gives bainite.

3.6.1 Plotting of T-T-T Curves

Following steps are followed for plotting T-T-T curves:

- A large number of samples from a steel bar are heated to austenitizing temperature.

- The samples are held at this temperature for sufficient time. This helps to homogenise austenite.

- The samples are then transferred to a salt bath kept at a constant temperature between A_1 and M_S temperature lines.

- The samples are removed one by one at a fixed interval of time.

- The samples are then quenched in water immediately.

- Finally, samples are prepared for metallographic study.

- The procedure is repeated by gradually changing the temperature of salt bath in step No. 3.

After the above treatments, an eutectoid steel shows the following observations:

- First few samples, which were held for less time and then quenched, show martensite.

- Next, few samples show pearlite and martensite.

- The rest of the samples show pearlite only.

In hypoeutectoid steels, initially proeutectoid ferrite is observed, while hypereutectoid steel shows proeutectoid cementite separating at early stages.

With the obtained data, a smooth curve is drawn as temperature (°C) Vs time (log sec). As the curves are drawn from the data of transformation products at a constant temperature, these are also called as Isothermal Transformations (I.T.). Typical T-T-T curves for hypoeutectoid, eutectoid and hypereutectoid steels are shown in Fig. 3.8.

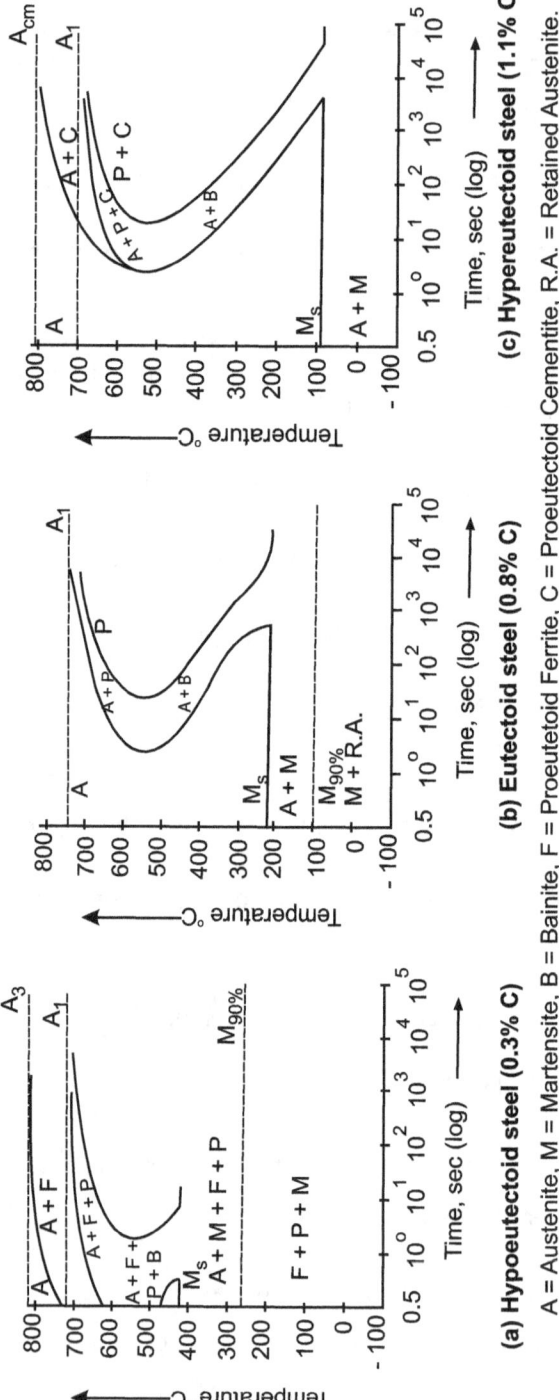

Fig. 3.8: Time-Temperature-Transformation diagrams of different steels (Dec. 10)

Usually, a T-T-T curve is explained as follows:

The dotted line at a temperature 727°C shows a line, upto which the austenite is stable. The initial C curve near the temperature axis gives a start of transformation, while another adjacent C curve denotes end of transformation. The intermediate dotted line gives 50% transformation of the phase.

The important part of this curve is its nose. The upper region of nose gives austenite to pearlite transformation. The lower region of nose (above M_s line) indicates austenite to bainite transformation. The lowest part of the curve gives an idea about the austenite to martensite transformation.

P_s, B_s and M_s indicate the start of pearlite, bainite and martensite transformations respectively. Similarly, P_f, B_f and M_f denote the end of transformations of pearlite, bainite and martensite respectively.

For hypoeutectoid and hypereutectoid steels, the T-T-T curve shows an additional line indicating initial transformation of austenite to proeutectoid ferrite or cementite.

Hypoeutectoid steel shows M_f above room temperature, while hypereutectoid shows M_f below room temperature. The nose of the T-T-T curve for hypoeutectoid is to the extreme left (sometimes may not be visible) than for a hypereutectoid steel.

3.6.2 Factors Affecting Position of T-T-T Curve

- With increase in carbon percentage, the most of the T-T-T curve shifts to the right and again to the left. So, for martensite formation, hypoeutectoid and hypereutectoid steel requires higher cooling rate than eutectoid steels.
- M_s and M_f temperatures decrease with increase in carbon content.
- Alloy additions shift the nose of the T-T-T curve to the right. Thus, they retard the start of the transformation.
- Increase in austenite grain size shifts the curve to the right. The shifting of the nose to the right is beneficial in the formation of martensite at slow cooling rate.
- Alloy additions are preferred for this purpose as increased austenite grain size may decrease toughness.

3.6.3 Critical Cooling Rate (CCR)

It is the minimum cooling rate by which full martensite structure is formed. CCR is tangent to the most of the T-T-T curve. It decreases with higher carbon and alloy content. Except cobalt, all alloying elements shift the T-T-T curve to the right.

Low CCR shows more hardenability of the steel. As the martensite is obtained at a slower cooling rate, usually alloy steels show less cracking and distortion in hardening. Very low carbon steel does not show CCR as the nose of the T-T-T curve is invisible. So, they are called as non-hardenable steels.

3.6.4 Relation of Various Cooling Curves with Transformation Product

This is obtained by superimposition of cooling curves on T-T-T curve as both are having the same axes (Fig. 3.9).

The slowest cooling curve (1) is obtained by the process of annealing. It gives less hard and coarse pearlite. A typical normalizing (air cooling) may be given by curve (2). Compared to above curve (1), it gives hard and fine pearlite.

Oil quenching gives cooling curve (3).

A cooling curve (4) gives combination of two phases as pearlite and martensite. This is due to passing the curve near 50% transformation line. Some of the austenite transforms to pearlite and remaining to martensite.

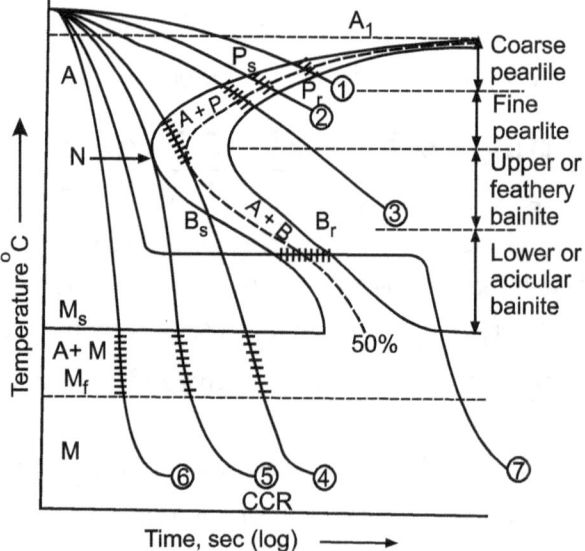

Fig. 3.9: Cooling curves superimposed on T-T-T curve

CCR is shown by cooling curve (5). Fully martensite structure is obtained by cooling curve (6) in water quenching. This continuous cooling gives pearlite and martensite and not bainite.

For bainitic transformation, the steel should be cooled rapidly and held at a temperature just below the nose, until it crosses B_s and then B_f. This is termed as interrupted quenching cooling curve (7).

3.7 CONTINUOUS COOLING TRANSFORMATION (CCT) CURVES

(May 09)

The validity of a T-T-T curve remains, if the transformations of austenite take place isothermally. When the steel is cooled continuously at a constant cooling rate, the T-T-T curve moves down and to the right. This increases the time allowed to austenite-pearlite transformation (Fig. 3.10).

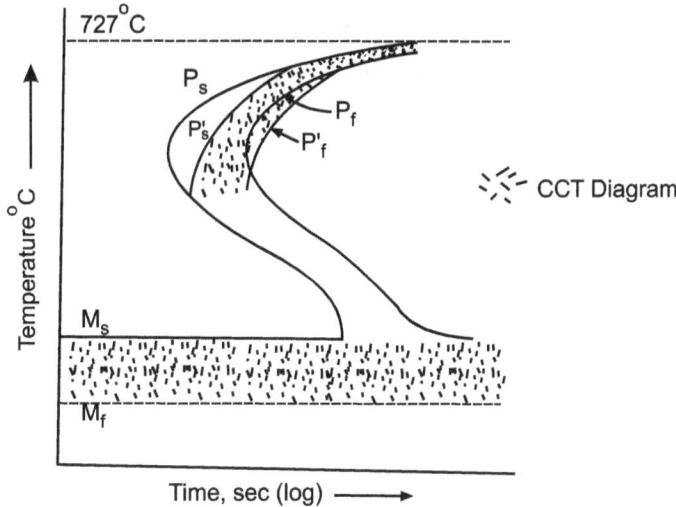

Fig. 3.10: Continuous cooling transformation (CCT) diagram superimposed on isothermal transformation diagram

These curves are plotted by similar method used for T-T-T curves. Steel samples are heated to austenitising temperatures and cooled with a constant cooling rate to some temperature. Then these are rapidly cooled in water. The start and finish of the various transformations are noted and a curve is plotted. Various terms in these curves may be explained in the manner similar to those in the T-T-T curves.

3.8 HEAT TREATMENT OF STEELS

Basically, all heat treatments consist of heating and cooling of steels. The variation in cooling rate decides the nature of heat treatment. The heating may be carried out in air or fused salt bath depending upon the requirement.

Cooling is carried out using following mediums:

(a) Furnace
(b) Air
(c) Oil
(d) Liquid/Fused salts
(e) Water and
(f) Brine (water + salt as NaCl)

3.9 ANNEALING   (Dec. 10, May 11, 12)

Annealing is defined as *heating the steel to austenite region and then cooling slowly in transformation range.* Slow cooling is carried out in the furnace (by switching off the supply of furnace) or in any good heat insulating materials.

Following are the purposes of annealing:

1. To relieve the internal stresses induced in fabrication processes,

2. To reduce strain hardening effect of cold working. This increases ductility,

3. To improve machinability,

4. To make the steel suitable for further cold working,

5. To alter the micro-structure to improve properties of steel,

6. To improve homogeneity of the material,

7. To make the steel suitable for further heat treatment and

8. To improve electrical and magnetic properties.

Annealing Temperatures and Soaking Time:

Annealing temperature (Fig. 3.11) generally depends upon carbon content of steel.

Steel	Annealing Temperature
Hypoeutectoid	$AC_3 + 50°C$
Hypereutectoid	$AC_1 + 50°C$

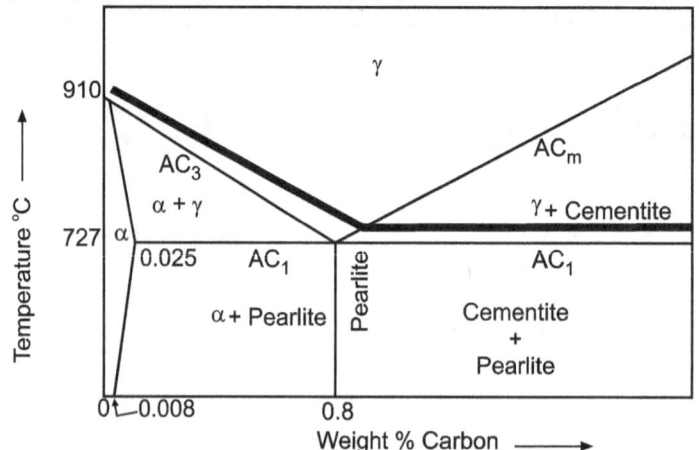

Fig. 3.11: Heating temperature band for full annealing

Usually, the sections upto 25 mm thick are soaked for one hour. For heavy sections, the time is increased at a rate of 30 - 40 minutes/additional 25 mm of thickness. Longer holding time generally reduces the hardness of steel.

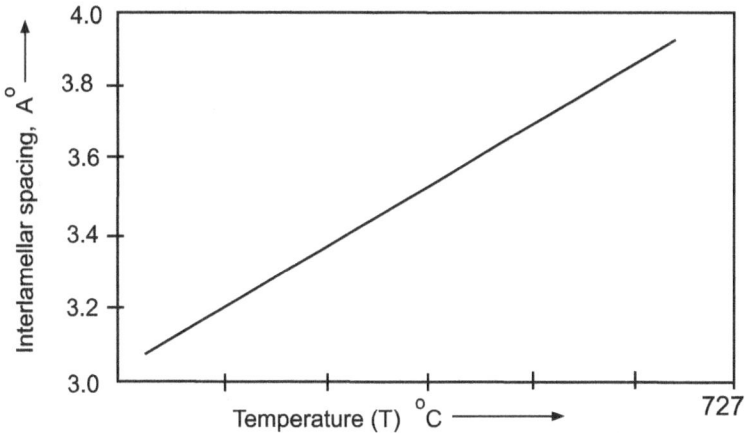

Fig. 3.12 (A): Inter-lamellar spacing in cementite plates in pearlite

(T = Austenite to Pearlite transformation temperature, °C)

Hypereutectoid steels are never annealed from the above AC_m line because -

1.   Slow cooling from AC_m develops undesirable micro-structure as a network of cementite along pearlite grain boundaries and

2.   Grain coarsening, oxidation and decarburization may occur.

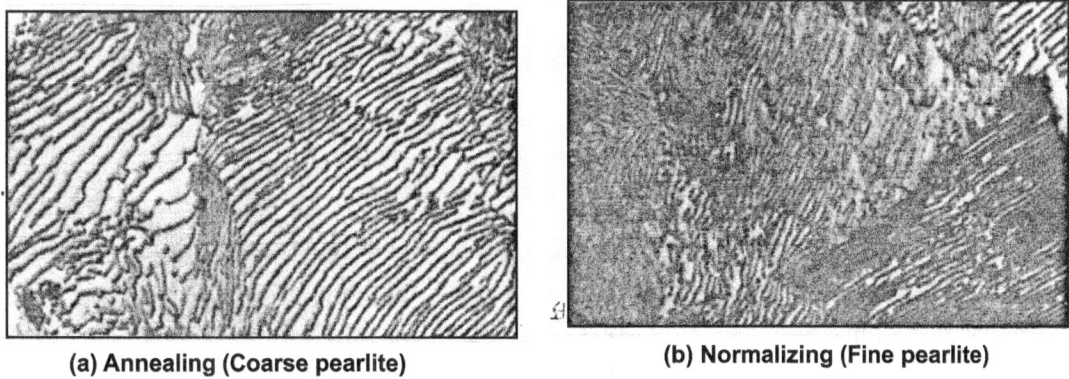

|(a) Annealing (Coarse pearlite)|(b) Normalizing (Fine pearlite)|

Fig. 3.12 (B): Schematic representation of pearlite after annealing and normalizing

As annealed, a hypoeutectoid steel shows small grains of proeutectoid ferrite and coarse lamellar pearlite [Fig. 3.12 (B)].

Annealing should never be a final heat treatment for hypereutectoid steel as it gives thick, hard and brittle grain boundary (of cementite network), which results in less machinability.

3.9.1 Types of Annealing   (Dec. 10)

(a) Full annealing: It consists of heating the steel to austenite region and then cooling it very slowly (The details are explained under Annealing).

(b) Bright annealing: This is an annealing process carried out in a protective atmosphere. It prevents discolouration of steel. It gives a bright surface and hence, termed as bright annealing. Argon, nitrogen or reducing atmospheres are used. Usually, a reducing gas contains 15% H_2, 10% CO, 5% CO_2, 1.5% CH_4 and balance N_2.

(c) Box annealing: For this type of annealing, the components are packed in sealed container using charcoal or cast iron chips. This reduces oxidation. The annealing procedure is similar to full annealing. It is also known as black annealing.

(d) Stress relieving: This is used mainly for cold worked steels. It is a low temperature (about 500 °C) annealing. This process is sometimes called as sub-critical annealing. It does not affect the strength and hardness of steel. This heat treatment is more useful for low carbon steels, which are often cold worked.   (May 10)

(e) Spheroidizing: This heat treatment is used for hypereutectoid steels. This improves machinability of steel. When the coarse pearlite is too hard and the carbon content is high, this long time process spheroidizes the microstructure. It gives globules of cementite in ferrite matrix.

Spheroidizing is carried out by,

(a) hardening followed with high temperature tempering,

(b) holding the steel just below the lower critical temperature for long time and

(c) cyclic heating and cooling around A_1 temperature.

(f) Process or Intermediate annealing: During cold working, steel gets work hardened and further plastic deformation is not possible. So, the material is intermediately annealed in the process. This helps to increase the ductility of steel. The cold worked steel is heated above its recrystallization temperature. This produces stress free equiaxed grains. This treatment is useful for wire drawing, tube drawing and rolling operations.   (May 06, 11)

(g) Recrystallization annealing: It consists of heating a steel below AC_1. Re-crystallization of ferrite and spheroidization of cementite occurs. This process eliminates internal stresses and improves ductility.

(h) Isothermal or Cycle annealing: The process consists of fast cooling a steel from austenitising temperature to a constant temperature just below A_1. The steel is held at this temperature until the transformation is completed. Then it is cooled to room temperature. This is used for medium and high carbon steel as conventional annealing cycles are longer for these steels. This treatment produces coarse pearlite.

In general, annealing is recommended for various steel castings, forgings and rolled products.

3.10 NORMALIZING   (May 06, 11, Dec. 06, 10, 13)

It can be defined as heating the steel to austenite region followed by air cooling.

Following are the purposes of normalizing:

- To eliminate coarse grained structure,
- To modify dendritic structure,
- To reduce segregation,
- To obtain required mechanical properties,
- To improve machinability,
- To produce harder and stronger steel than annealing and
- To refine grain structure.

Normalizing Temperatures and Soaking Time:

Normalizing temperature (Fig. 3.13) depends on carbon content and soaking time depends on the mass of the component.

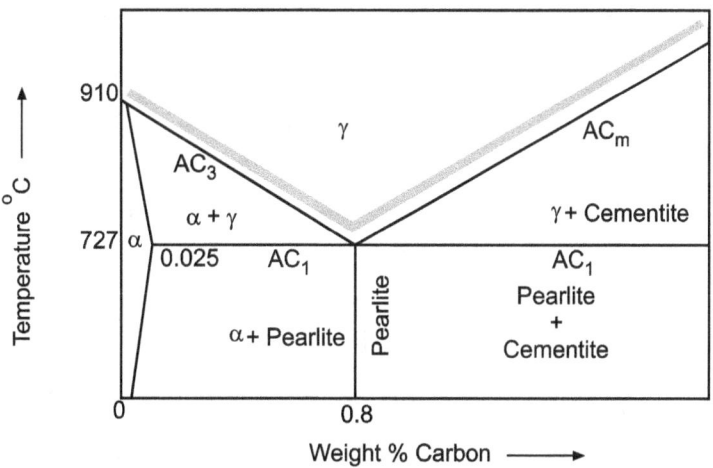

Fig. 3.13: Heating temperature band for normalizing   (Dec. 10)

Steel	Normalizing Temperature
Hypoeutectoid steel	AC_3 + 50°C
Hypereutectoid steel	AC_m + 50°C

Soaking time may be given as 1 hr/25 mm thickness. Normalizing produces fine pearlite due to higher cooling rate and the transformation occurs at lower temperature. The inter-lamellar spacing of pearlite is much smaller than the pearlite produced by annealing.

3.11 HARDENING   (May 09, 12; Dec. 07, 10, 11, 12)

It may be defined as *heating the steel to austenite region and quenching it into suitable medium as water, oil etc.* Basically, hardening is carried out to increase hardness, wear resistance and abrasion resistance.

Rapid cooling or quenching gives martensite (BCT) structure. This highly stressed structure increases hardness of steel.

Hardening Temperatures and Soaking Time:

Hardening temperatures (Fig. 3.14) depend upon carbon content, while soaking time depends upon section thickness.

Steels	Hardening Temperature
Hypoeutectoid steels	AC_3 + 50°C
Hypereutectoid steels	AC_1 + 50°C

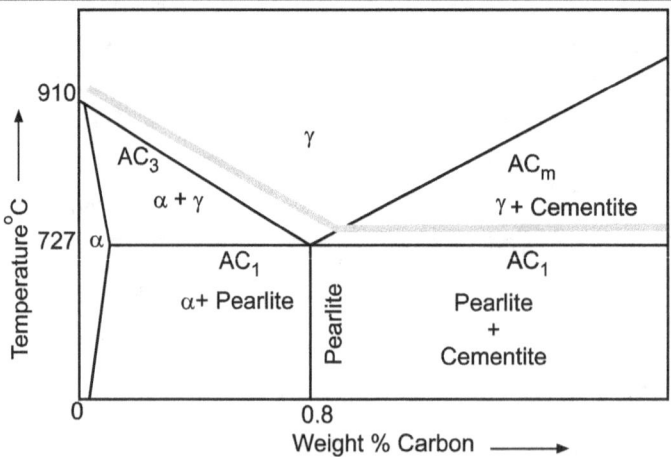

Fig. 3.14: Heating temperature band for hardening

Recommended soaking time for hardening is 1 hour/25 mm section thickness.

Hypoeutectoid steels are not hardened from $AC_1 + 50°C$ as hypereutectoid steel, for the reason that proeutectoid ferrite and austenite are present at this temperature. After quenching, only austenite transforms to martensite, while ferrite (soft phase) remains untransformed. This results in lower hardness.

Similarly, hypereutectoid steels are quenched from the region between AC_1 and AC_m. In this region, austenite and proeutectoid cementite are present. After quenching, austenite transforms to martensite and hard cementite remains unchanged, which does not lower the hardness. On the other hand, if hypereutectoid steels are quenched from above AC_m temperature, following points are observed:

- Grain coarsening occurs at high temperatures.

- Oxidation/decarburization may occur.

- Tendency of cracking increases.

The hardness of steel after quenching depends upon the hardness of martensite, which is the function of carbon content.

Factors Affecting Hardening:

- Lower austenitising temperature results in incomplete transformation and gives less hardness.

- Higher austenitising temperature gives rise to grain coarsening.

- The soaking time should be enough to homogenize austenite.

- Quenching should be carried out immediately after heating. If it is delayed, other phases may form.

- Type, agitation, contamination and temperature of quenching medium play an important role as wrong selection of any of these factors may give distortion to steel. Alloying elements lower the CCR by retarding the transformation. So, oil quenching or air cooling may, therefore, give martensite structure.

3.11.1 Heat Removal During Quenching

When heated, steel is quenched in a suitable medium, it shows temperature gradient between the surface and the core of steel. The surface cools down more rapidly than does the core. As a result of this, the following stages are observed:

(a) Vapour blanket stage: Due to high temperature of steel, the quenching medium gets vaporised at the surface of metal and forms a thin vapour film (blanket). Further cooling occurs by conduction and radiation. The cooling rate is slow because the vapour film is a poor thermal conductor.

(b) Vapour transport or boiling stage: The vapour film is stable upto 400°C. When the temperature falls below this, the vapour film breaks away and the quenching medium comes in contact with the hot metal. This gives rise to a vigorous boiling and rapid cooling of steel. Bubbles are formed continuously. Martensite formation occurs at this stage.

(c) Liquid cooling stage: In this stage, the surface temperature of the metal reaches the boiling point of the liquid. Vapour formation stops. The cooling continues by conduction and convection. It gives slow cooling rate.

3.11.2 Quenching Mediums   Dec. 13

The quenching medium must show effective heat removal during quenching. It should possess the following characteristics:

- High initial cooling rate to avoid transformations at nose region and
- Slow cooling rate below nose to minimize cracking and distortion.

The various quenching mediums used are as follows:

- Furnace
- Air
- Water and

- Oil
- Liquid or fused salts
- Brine (i.e. water + salt as NaCl)

These are given in the order of increasing severity of quenching.

Alloy steels have less CCR and hence, they can be hardened by air cooling. Oil quenching is used for high carbon steels as they show more CCR. Medium carbon steels have very high CCR so water or brine quenching is required. Very low carbon steels cannot be hardened as CCR is not achieved even by water or brine cooling.

3.12 HARDENABILITY   (Dec. 10; May 09, 10, 11)

Hardening is carried out to increase the hardness of steel. Properly quenched steel should give hardness of about 60 RC. The hardness of hardened steel is measured on its surface. The surface shows higher hardness, which decreases towards the centre of steel. This variation in hardness along its cross-section may be termed as hardenability.

Hardenability is the case with which a steel piece can be hardened. It is defined as the *depth upto which 50% martensite or hardness RC 50 is observed.*

Hardenability is a very important property in heat treatment of steels. It gives following information in heat treatment:

- required cooling rate or quenching medium,
- maximum hardness that can be obtained,
- distribution and depth of hardness,
- stress level on the surface etc.

Hardenability is measured by one of the following tests:

- Jominy - End Quench Test and
- Grossman's method.

3.12.1 The Jominy-End Quench Test   (Dec. 09, 10; May 11)

This method uses a standard specimen. It is cylindrical in shape with a collar on one end. It is shown in Fig. 3.15 with standard dimensions. This specimen is austenitised and soaked for some time.

Austenitising temperature and soaking time depend upon carbon content of steel. It is then immediately transferred to a fixture.

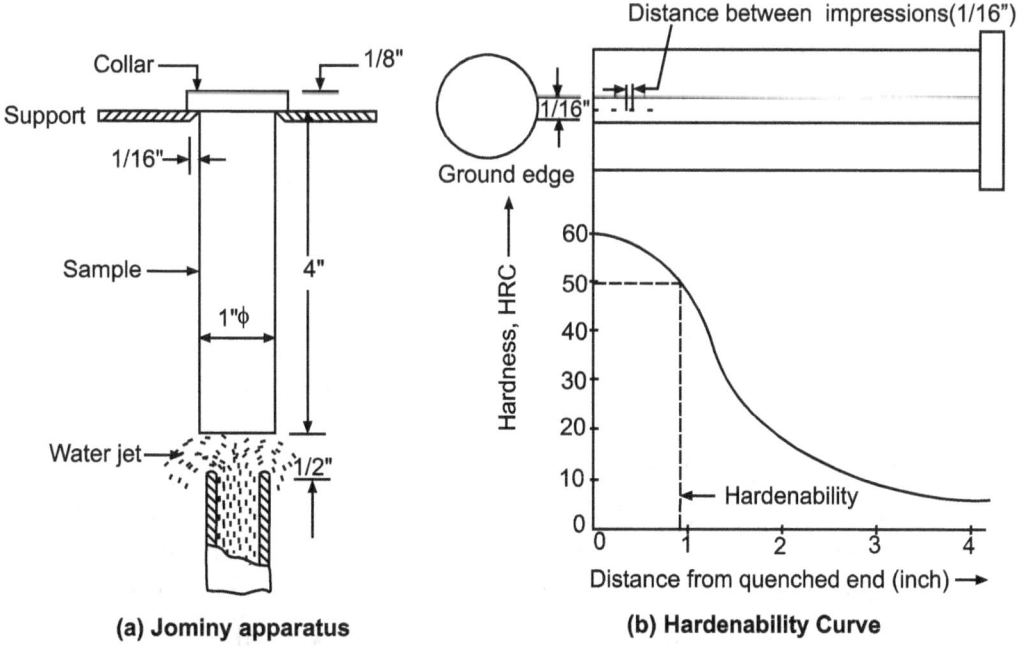

| (a) Jominy apparatus   (b) Hardenability Curve |

Fig. 3.15: Jominy-End quench test for hardenability

Water is sprayed on the bottom end of the heated sample. The rate of water flow diameter of the nozzle and distance between nozzle and bottom end of the sample is as per ASTM A 255 – 48T. The flow of the water should be such that it forms an umbrella shape as shown in Fig. 3.15 and cool the test piece only from the lower end and not from the sides.

The cooling rate is therefore, the highest at the bottom. This gives maximum hardening. This cooling rate decreases towards the collar of the specimen. Therefore, water cooling occurs at the bottom end of the sample, while air cooling occurs at the collar.

After 10 minutes, the specimen is removed from the fixture. Two flat surfaces are ground longitudinally to a depth of 0.015 in (3 mm). On this flat surface, the hardness is measured (in Rockwell C) at 1/16 – inch intervals from the quenched end.

The hardness values are plotted against the distance from quenched end. The curve so plotted is called as Hardenability curve (Fig. 3.16).

The test is carried out for hundreds of samples of each grade of steel. The minimum and maximum hardenability curves have been established by AISI and are known as hardenability bands.

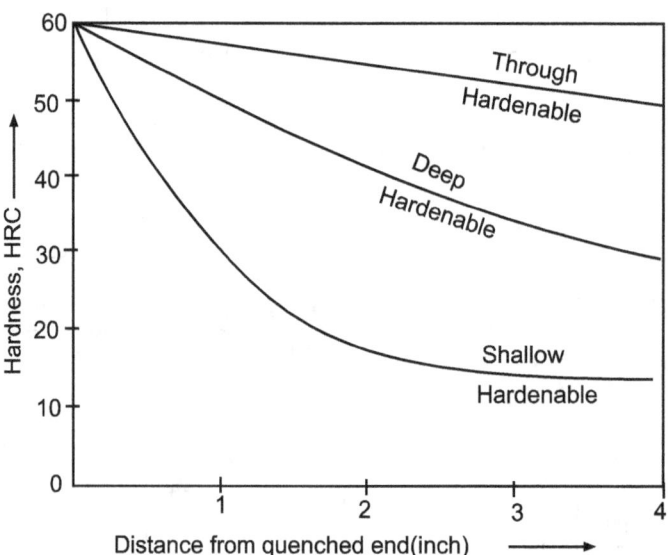

Fig. 3.16: Hardenability curves for different steels

3.12.2 Grossman's Method

This method consists of heating a number of cylindrical pieces of different diameters of the same steel to austenitising temperature and quenching. The samples are cut in the centre of the length and on that cross-section, hardness measured from surface towards the centre.

The samples with smaller diameter get through hardened, while the samples with larger diameter are not fully hardened (Fig. 3.17).

The maximum diameter of sample which shows 50% martensite or RC 50 at the centre is called as critical diameter and is taken as a measure of hardenability.

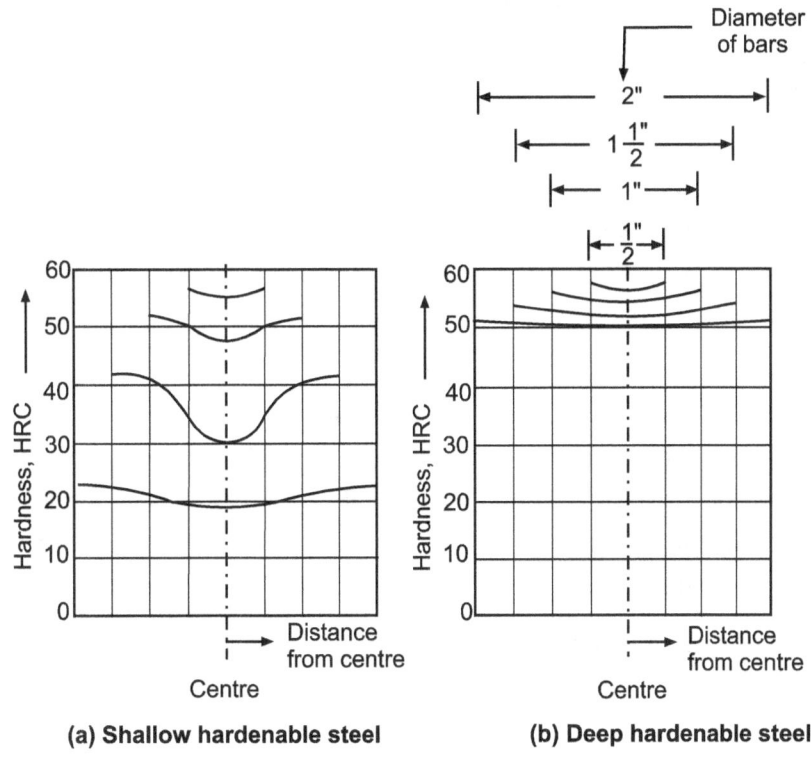

(a) Shallow hardenable steel   (b) Deep hardenable steel

Fig. 3.17: Grossman's method for hardenability

3.12.3 Factors Affecting Hardenability and Interpretation of Hardenability   (May 11)

Hardenability depends on the following factors:

(a) Composition of steel.

(b) Homogeneity of austenite.

(c) Austenite grain size.

(d) Non-metallic inclusions in the austenite.

(e) Undissolved carbides in the austenite.

(a) **Chemical composition of steel:** An increase in carbon content shifts the T-T-T curve to right decreasing the critical cooling rate. This increases the hardenability. Except cobalt, all alloying elements increase hardenability. When the alloying elements are dissolved in austenite, hardenability greatly increases. This is achieved, when manganese, molybdenum, chromium, silicon and nickel are dissolved in austenite. So, the hardenability may be controlled by controlling alloying element additions.

(b) **Homogeneity of austenite:** Non-uniformity of austenite tends to reduce hardenability of steel. Non-homogeneous austenite arises from incomplete dissolution of carbides in austenite. Moreover, segregation may also lead to inhomogeneity of austenite.

(c) **Austenite grain size:** With increasing grain size of austenite, hardenability of steel increases. The depth of hardening is greater in coarse grained steel than in fine grained steel. This may be explained on the basis of the promotion of nucleation of pearlite in fine grain size. Though hardenability increases with grain coarsening, it results in lower toughness. Grain boundaries also reduce cooling rate and fine grain steel has more grain boundaries.

(d) **Non-metallic inclusions in the austenite:** The non-metallic inclusions reduce hardenability as they increase inhomogeneity of austenite. Moreover, these inclusions may become nuclei for pearlite formation.

(e) **Undissolved carbides in the austenite:** Iron carbides and alloy carbides are present in austenite. Once, the carbides are formed, alloy content and carbon content gets reduced, decreasing the hardenability. Some of the carbide forming elements tend to reduce gain size and lower hardenability. Higher temperatures for hardening dissolve carbides and coarsen austenite grains.

Some of the hardenability curves are shown in Fig. 3.16.

Various Hardening Methods:

Depending upon heating temperature, cooling medium and style of cooling, the hardening methods may be explained as follows.

3.13 CONVENTIONAL HARDENING

Conventional Hardening consists of quenching in a single medium such as water, oil or air. It is widely used in industries. The details regarding hardening process, temperatures, quenching etc., explained earlier are for conventional hardening.

A typical heat treatment cycle for conventional hardening is shown in Fig. 3.18.

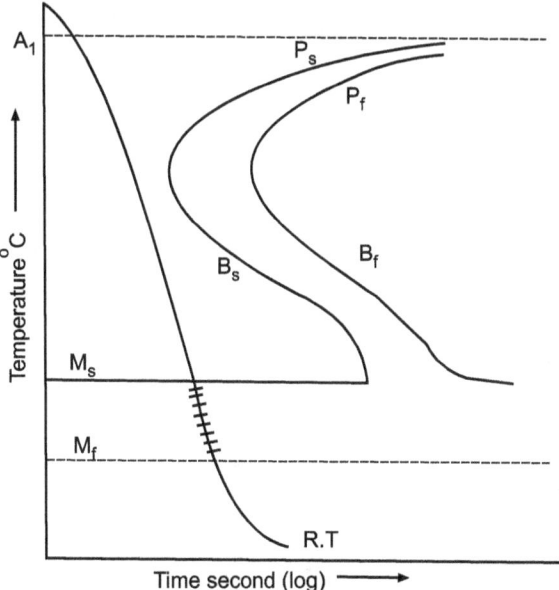

Fig. 3.18 : Conventional hardening

3.14 TWO-MEDIA QUENCHING

Quenching in water or brine gives higher cooling rates and high degree of distortion. To minimize distortion, warping and cracks, two media quenching is used (Fig. 3.19).

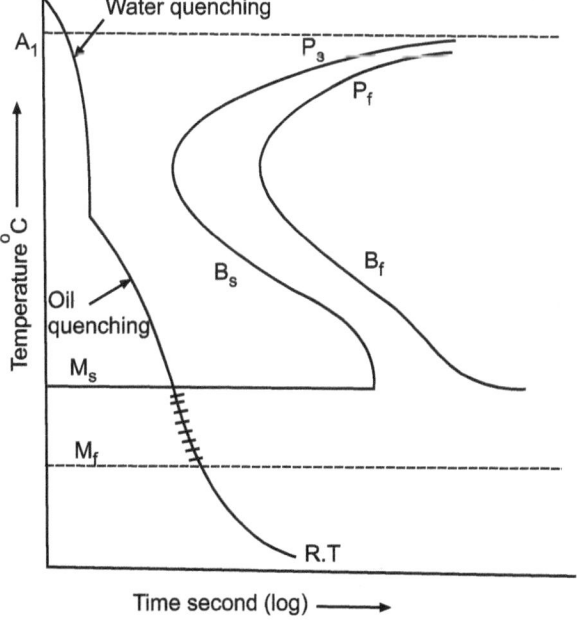

Fig. 3.19: Two-media quenching

Plain carbon steels with low and medium carbon content show very high critical cooling rates. To prevent pearlite or bainite formation, these steels should be rapidly cooled in water till the nose of T-T-T curve is avoided. This is carried out in water.

Once the nose is avoided, the steel may be oil cooled between M_s and M_f range. As the cooling rates are reduced during martensite formation, less distortion and cracking is observed.

Similarly, for alloy steels and high carbon steels, which show lower critical cooling rate, two-media quenching is used. These steels are initially quenched in oil to avoid the nose of the curve and may be air cooled from M_s temperature. This also avoids distortion and quench cracks.

3.15 OTHER HEAT TREATMENTS OF STEELS

3.15.1 Martempering or Marquenching

(May 07, 08, 10, 13; Dec. 08, 09, 11, 12)

The term martempering is little misguiding as that makes one feel that it is a type of tempering. But practically, it is a type of hardening process. (Fig. 3.20).

In this method, steels are initially heated to austenitising temperature. The steels are rapidly cooled and held in a salt bath kept at a temperature just above M_s.

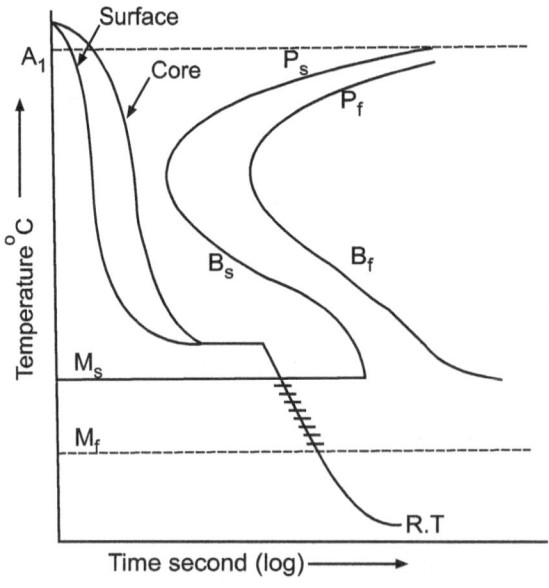

Fig. 3.20: Martempering

The holding time at this temperature should be such that it does not enter in the bainite transformation region. After holding steel at this temperature sufficiently, it is cooled to room temperature in oil or air. This transforms austenite to martensite.

Holding the heated steel above M_S for some time equalizes the surface and core temperature of the steel. This minimises warping and distortion. There is less danger of quenching cracks. This method is mostly used for high carbon and alloy steels having higher hardenability. In this method, due to less temperature gradient at the surface and at core, the martensite is formed nearly at the same time throughout the component.

3.15.2 Austempering or Isothermal Quenching

(May 08, 12, 13; Dec. 09, 12)

In this process, steel is heated initially to austenitising temperature. It is then rapidly cooled to a temperature between the nose of T-T-T curve and M_S temperature. The steel is held at this temperature for sufficient time so that it enters into bainite transformation region. When the austenite gets completely transformed to bainite, it is slowly cooled in air (Fig. 3.21).

The steel may be held isothermally in a suitable salt bath kept in the temperature range of 260 - 400°C. After austempering, the micro-structure obtained is fully bainite without traces of pearlite or martensite.

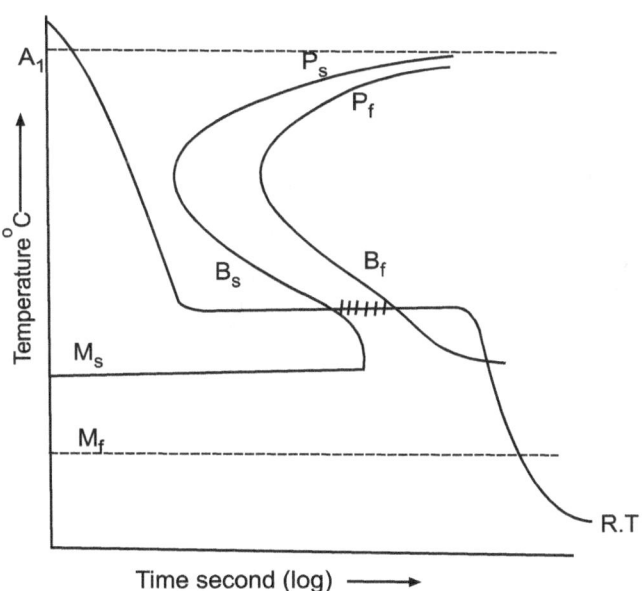

Fig. 3.21: Austempering

This structure shows intermediate properties of pearlite and martensite. Austempering gives high impact strength and increases notch toughness at high hardness. The process is suitable for high hardenable steels.

Austempering has nothing to do with the term tempering as it does not involve tempering.

Austempering shows superior properties, better elongation and hardness. It shows less distortion and danger of quenching cracks as the quench is not so drastic as that of the conventional method.

The basic limitation of this process is the effect of mass on the part being heat treated. The sections, which can be cooled fast enough to avoid transformation to pearlite, are suitable. The sections less than 1/2 inch thick should be used.

3.15.3 Patenting   (May 08, 12, 13; Dec. 07, 09)

This heat treatment is similar to austempering. Plain carbon steel (with 0.3 to 0.6% C) and some of the alloy steels are heated to austenitising temperature. They are then quenched in a molten bath.

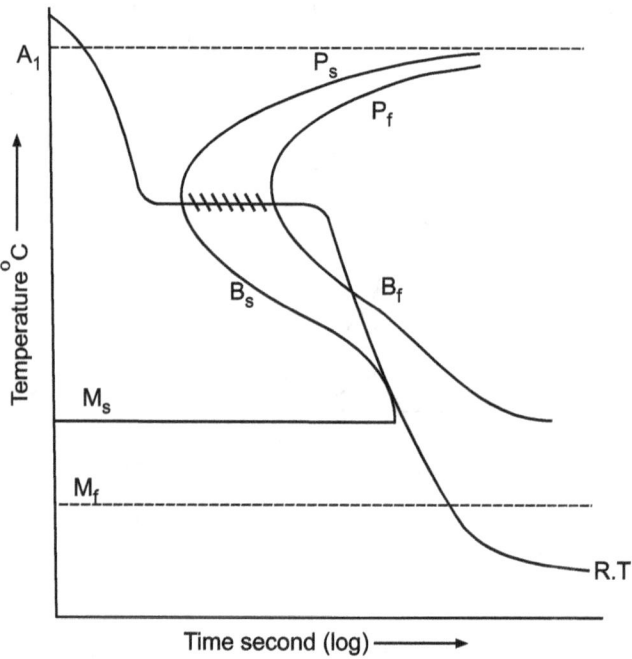

Fig. 3.22: Patenting

The bath is maintained at a temperature just above or below the nose temperature of T-T-T curve.

The steel may be held at this temperature until the transformation is completed. The steel may be slowly cooled to room temperature (Fig. 3.22). The micro-structure may be fine pearlite or upper bainite. Patenting is used in wire drawing as it improves toughness. Higher reductions in area of wire are possible, which may not be obtained in the annealing process.

During wire drawing, patenting may be used as a subsequent treatment. The drawn wire goes slowly and directly in a salt bath maintained at required temperature and may be redrawn again. Patenting also provides good surface finish and lubricating surface.

3.15.4 Ausforming or Austenite Forming or Isoforming

(May 07, 13; Dec. 07)

By ausforming treatment, extremely high strength steels are obtained. It consists of mechanical working (rolling, forging etc.) of austenitised steel in the regions of existence of pearlitic and bainitic reactions. It is immediately followed by oil quenching to prevent formation of non-martensitic transformation products. Very fine martensitic plates are formed after this treatment (Fig. 3.23).

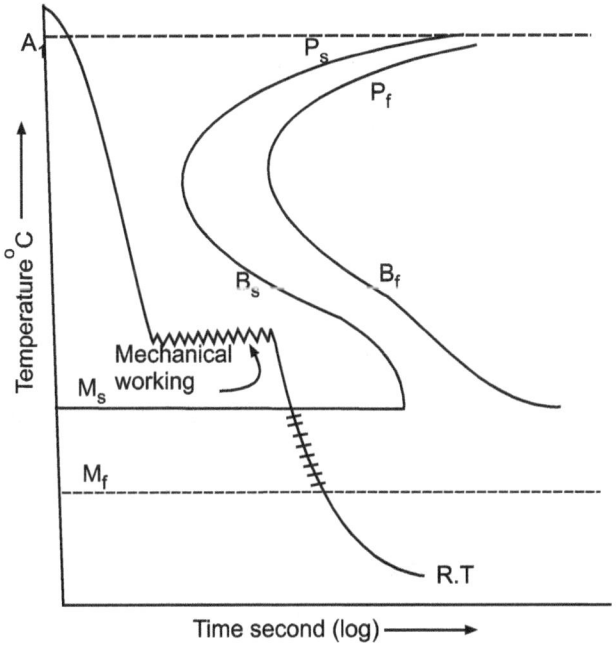

Fig. 3.23: Ausforming

This is mostly used for AISI 4340 and hot work tool steels. AISI 4340 shows a tensile strength of 300,000 PSI by conventional heat treatment and 400,000 PSI by ausforming.

Highly stressed structural parts for aircraft and automotive leaf springs are usually ausformed.

3.16 QUENCH CRACKS   (May 06)

The quench cracks arise due to residual stresses. In the various heat treatment, due to temperature variation (gradient), non-uniform plastic deformation occurs, which increases internal stresses. These stresses are the main reasons for distortion or cracking.

During quenching, the surface gets cooled very fast than does the centre (or core). This results in temperature gradient. Due to this, the surface contracts, while core expands. The core tries to prevent the contraction of surface giving tension. So, the outer surface is in tension and inside will be at compression. If this stress exceeds the ultimate strength of the material, cracking occurs. These are called as quench cracks.

Austenite (FCC) is a close packed dense structure than ferrite (BCC) or martensite (BCT). When austenite changes to other phases, an expansion occurs. This increase in volume is also responsible for quench cracks.

Usually, surface cracks are observed in a thorough hardened steel, while internal cracks are observed in shallow hardened steels.

Other parameters responsible for the quench cracks are:

- Large amount of non-metallic inclusions.
- Wrong quenching medium.
- Higher hardening temperature.
- Improper designing of component.
- Improper insertion of heated components in quenching medium.

Usually, alloy steels due to their less CCR show no quench cracks and minimum distortion.

3.17 RETENTION OF AUSTENITE   (May 06; Dec. 09)

When steel is heated to austenitising temperature and quenched, austenite transforms to martensite. For martensite transformation, cooling rates higher than critical cooling rates are required. In many cases, M_s (i.e. temperature at which martensite transformation starts) is in the range 200 to 375°C, while M_f (i.e. temperature at which martensite transformation ends) may be below room temperature or even below 0°C.

This shows that martensite transformation is never a complete process. All austenite cannot get transformed to martensite.

Fig. 3.24: Retained austenite in hardened structure

The untransformed austenite observed at room temperature is called as retained austenite (Fig. 3.24). Retained austenite is always present in steel in a small percentage (about 5%). The amount of retained austenite is less at the surface. Its percentage increases towards centre. Higher quenching temperature increases the amount of retained austenite.

3.17.1 Effects of Retained Austenite   (May 06)

About 8-10 per cent retained austenite is desirable as it reduces the tendency to cracking. Cold working is also possible with higher (about 35%) retained austenite.

The hardness of hardened steel gets reduced as austenite is comparatively soft phase. If retained austenite gets transformed to martensite by plastic deformation, strain hardening occurs; which increases brittleness of the steel.

The transformation of retained austenite to bainite at room temperature results in the linear expansion, which creates problems in measuring instruments as scales, gauges etc. It affects the dimensional stability of hardened parts.

3.17.2 Elimination of Retained Austenite   (May 13)

Usually, retained austenite is observed in steels having M_f below room temperature. This creates incomplete transformation. This problem can be eliminated by cooling the steels below 0°C using a suitable quenching medium as:

    (a)   Ice + Salt   = − 23 °C

    (b)   Acetone + dry ice   = − 76 °C

    (c)   Liquid air   = − 182 °C

    (d)   Liquid N_2 = − 190 °C etc.

Quenching in these media converts the retained austenite to martensite. This is called as subzero treatment.

Mechanical working of austenite just above M_s can accelerate martensite transformation. This is used for steels having higher retained austenite. For steels having less retained austenite, tempering may be carried out for martensitic transformation.

3.18 TEMPERING   (June 09, Dec. 09, May 10)

Hardened steel is not suitable for engineering applications because of the following reasons:

- Hardening produces martensite, which is extremely hard and brittle.
- During martensite formation, higher internal stresses are produced and
- After hardening, the structure consists of martensite and retained austenite. Both these phases are unstable. Subsequent transformation of these phases may alter the properties of steel.

Tempering is carried out for the following purposes:

- To relieve the internal stresses produced in hardening,
- To reduce hardness,
- To improve ductility and toughness,
- To reduce retained austenite and
- To obtain spheroidal structure, which improves machinability.

Tempering Temperatures and Soaking Time:

Tempering temperature varies from 100°C to 700°C. Tool steels are tempered at low temperature. High alloy tool steels are tempered at a higher tempering temperature. Low alloy steels are tempered above 350°C. Tempering time varies from 1 to 2 hours.

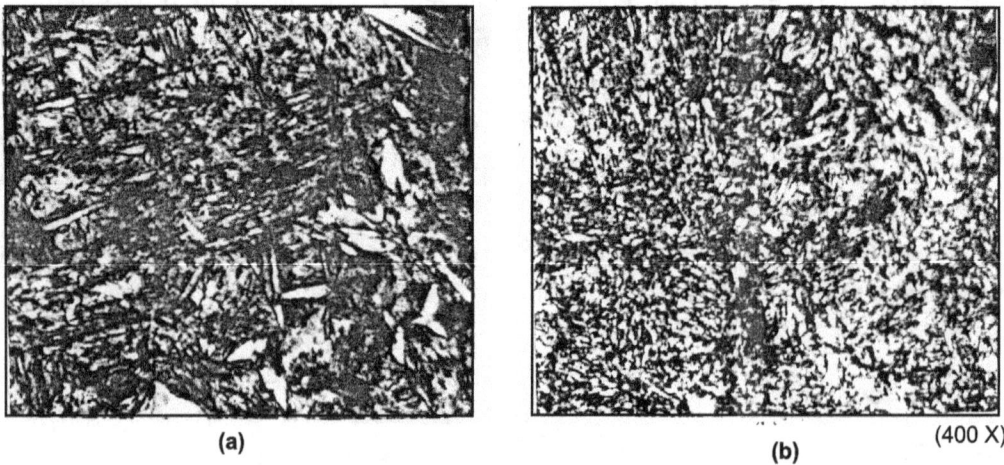

(a)   (b)   (400 X)

Fig. 3.25: Photomicrograph of hardened (a) and tempered (b) steel

The Treatment:

Tempering, in general, consists of heating hardened steel to a temperature below A_1 and cooling in air (Fig. 3.25). Depending upon temperature, tempering is classified as:

 (a) Low temperature tempering (100 - 200°C)

 (b) Medium temperature tempering (200 - 500°C)

 (c) High temperature tempering (500 - 700°C)

(a) Low temperature tempering: This type of tempering reduces internal stresses. Martensite decomposes as low carbon martensite and epsilon carbides. The brittleness of hardened steel decreases. No appreciable change is observed in properties related to micro-structure.

(b) Medium temperature tempering: During this tempering, the retained austenite may be transformed to bainite or decompose to form carbides and martensite. The low carbon martensite and epsilon carbides transform to ferrite and cementite. The hardness drastically decreases with improvement in toughness and ductility.

(c) High temperature tempering: This produces spheroidal cementite in ferrite matrix. This is also known as spheroidizing. In some cases, coarse cementite is observed. This micro-structure gives high machinability.

3.18.1 Secondary Hardness During Tempering

This is especially observed in alloy steels. Hardened plain carbon steels are softened by tempering. As the tempering temperature increases, the hardness is reduced continuously. Usually, alloying elements retard this softening rate and require high temperature tempering to lower hardness. The alloying elements, which have a tendency to dissolve in ferrite do not affect the hardness of tempered steel, e.g. nickel, silicon and manganese.

On the other hand, the complex carbide forming elements have a very noticeable effect on retardation of softening, e.g. chromium, tungsten, molybdenum and vanadium. During tempering of such alloy steel, it is observed that instead of softening, the hardness of steel increases. This increase in hardness during tempering is called as secondary hardness. This arises due to delayed precipitation of fine alloy carbides.

3.18.2 Temper Embrittlement   (Dec. 09)

Certain alloy steels show temper embrittlement. It is a loss of notched bar toughness (Fig. 3.26), when tempered in the range of 350 - 550°C followed by relatively slow cooling. This may be due to precipitations of some hard and brittle phases along the grain boundaries during slow cooling. However, the toughness may be maintained, if the part is quenched in water from the tempering temperature. Higher content of manganese, phosphorus and chromium promotes susceptibility, while molybdenum retards the effect.

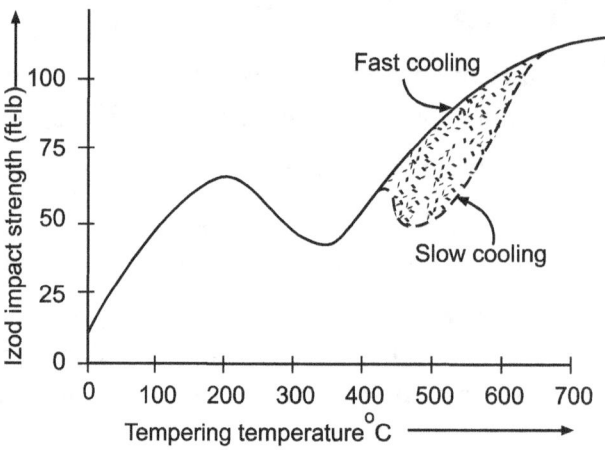

Fig. 3.26: Temper embrittlement

3.19 GRAIN SIZE IN STEEL

Whenever the grain size of steel is to be mentioned, it always refers to the austenite grain size. The transformation product of austenite depends upon its size, e.g. the length of martensite needle depends upon the austenite grain size; from which it is formed. Austenite grain size is greatly controlled by carbide forming elements. The grain growth at high temperature occurs by coarsening the grains at the cost of some smaller grains. Rapid grain growth occurs, when coarse grained steels are heated above 850°C. The steels which do not show an appreciable grain coarsening, are called as fine grained steels.

Grain size of steel shows a considerable effect on mechanical properties of steel.

A coarse grained steel shows the following properties:

- they tend to coarsen, if heated above critical range.
- they possess more tendency to warping, distortion and cracking.
- less toughness, more temper embrittlement and more retained austenite is observed for coarse grained steels and
- they show better hardenability and deep carburized case.

A fine grained steel shows the following characteristics:

- The heating above critical range does not affect its size.
- Lower stresses and distortion are observed during hardening.
- Better toughness.
- Less embrittlement and retained austenite is obtained and
- It gives shallow hardenability and less case depth.

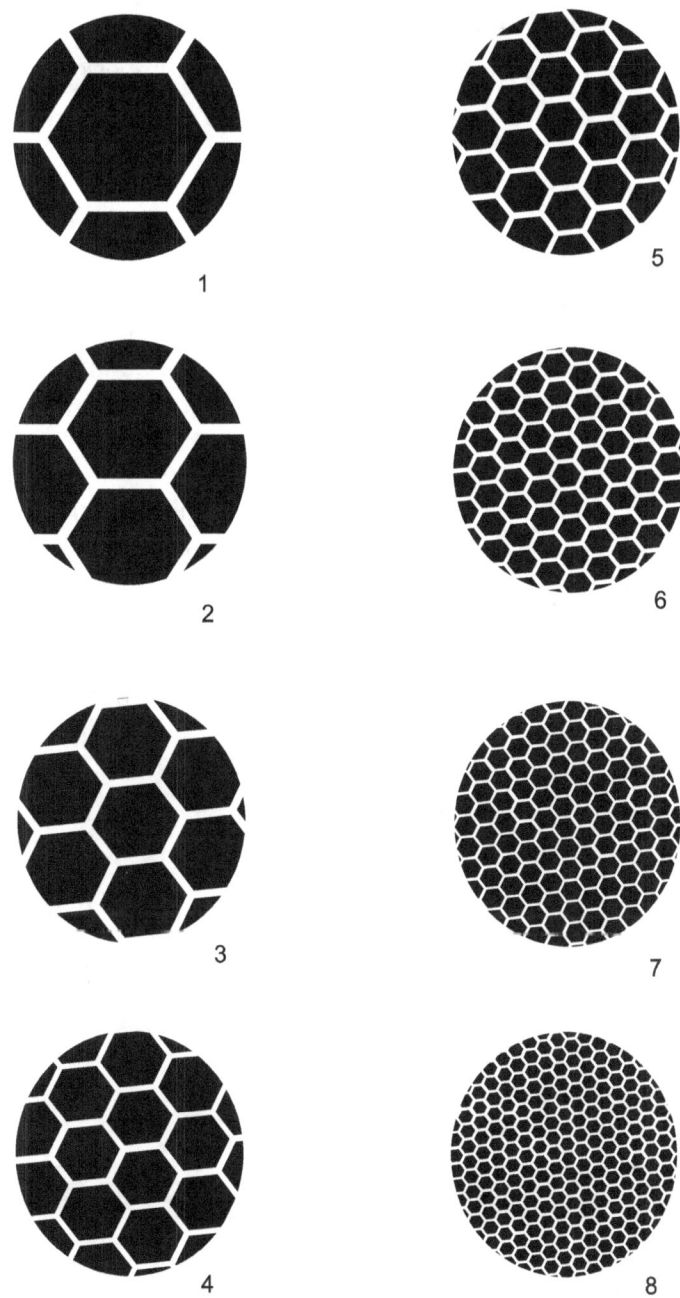

Fig. 3.27: Grain size number chart for comparison

Grain size is measured by one of the following methods:

- Comparison method
- Heyn's intercept method and
- Jefferies planimetric method

Comparison method is used for equiaxed grains. The grain size is reported by ASTM grain size number. This number can be found out by measuring number of grains (N) per square inch at 100X and given by the following relation:

$$N = 2^{n-1}$$

where, n = ASTM grain size number.

Standard charts are also used for comparison of grain size (Fig. 3.27).

Heyn's intercept method is used for non-equiaxed grains. The number of grains intercepted by a line of fixed length are measured. The grains touched by the lines are counted as half grains.

$$\text{Grain diameter} = \frac{\text{The length of the line (mm)}}{\text{Average number of grains intercepted}}$$

Jefferies planimetric method is supposed to be superior method than comparison method. In this method, a circle of known area is drawn on the photograph of grain structure. The total number of grains inside the circle are counted. The grains cut by periphery of the circle are considered as half grains. The number of grains per mm² is determined by multiplying the total number of grains by Jefferies multiplier (f), e.g.

Magnification	f
10	0.02
50	0.50
100	2.00
200	8.00

3.20 SURFACE HARDENING TREATMENTS OF STEELS

Basic heat treatment processes give properties, which are constant throughout the section of steel component. Rotating components like shafts have maximum stress at the surface than core. They require hard surface and soft core. This combination is obtained by surface or case hardening. The hardened surface is known as case and interior part is known as core.

Non-hardenable low carbon steel is tough, while very hard high carbon steel is brittle. So these materials are not useful for components requiring hard surface and tough core. For this purpose, it is necessary to use case hardening treatments.

Surface hardening can be achieved by following types:

- Without altering the chemical composition at the surface of steel.

- By changing the chemical composition at the surface of steel.

There are five principal methods of case hardening. They are: **(Dec. 09)**

- Carburising,

- Nitriding,

- Cyaniding and carbunitriding,

- Flame hardening and

- Induction hardening.

In the last two methods, the hardening is carried out without altering the chemical composition at the surface.

3.21 CARBURISING   **(May 09; Dec. 07, 09, 10)**

In carburising, the surface of steel is enriched with carbon. Carburising occurs due to diffusion of carbon at the surface of steel. This diffusion gets accelerated at higher temperature. Carbon has less solid solubility in ferrite at room temperature. Carbon can dissolve maximum upto 0.008% at room temperature and 0.025% at 727°C. So ferrite phase cannot be carburised. Austenite can dissolve upto 2.0% carbon at 1148°C. This higher solid solubility of carbon in austenite and higher temperature are main driving forces for diffusion of carbon in steel. Therefore for carburising, the steel should be heated upto austenite region.

Following are the two types of carburising processes:

(a) Pack carburising, (b) Liquid carburising, (c) Gas carburising and (d) Selective carburising.

3.21.1 Pack Carburising   **(Dec. 11)**

This is also called as box carburising. The components are placed in steel box and surrounded with carbonaceous material. After sealing, the box is heated to austenite region (Fig. 3.28).

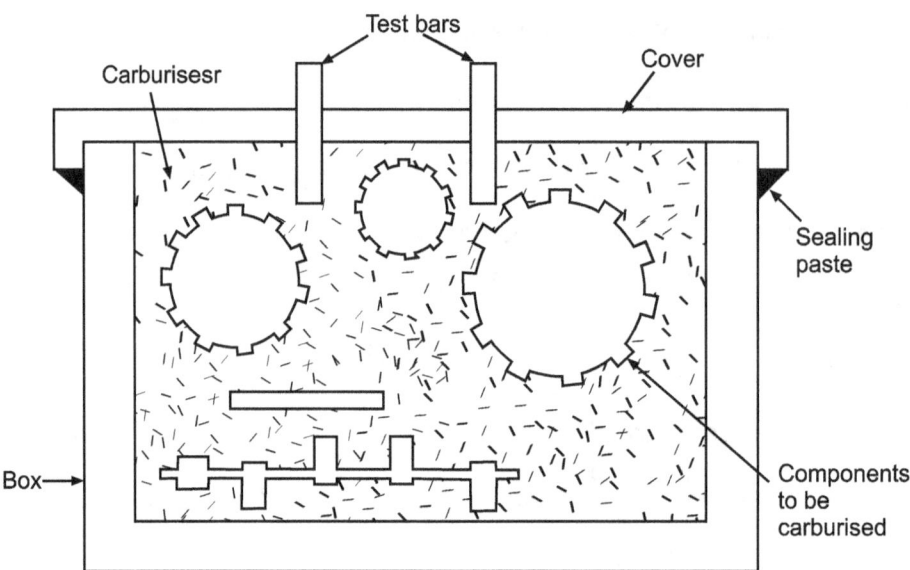

Fig. 3.28: Arrangements in pack carburising process

After the desired carburising time, the boxes are cooled in air and the carburised parts are heat treated for the required properties.

The carbonaceous materials for pack carburising are activated charcoal, coal, semi coke and peat coke. Barium carbonate ($BaCO_3$) and soda ash (Na_2CO_3) are added to the extent from 10 to 40 per cent of the weight of the charcoal to accelerate the process.

Table 3.1 gives the compositions of carburisers that are used for pack carburising.

Table 3.1: Composition of Solid carburiser

% $BaCO_3$	% Na_2CO_3	Charcoal
20 to 25	5 to 10	Balance
35 to 40	Upto 5 %	Balance

Usually, about 70% used carbonaceous material is recycled with fresh packing material. Oil may be added to improve the mixing of coal and carbonates. The components, which are to be carburised, are first cleaned; then placed in a box. The components are covered with a carburiser from all sides. The box is then sealed carefully to avoid the contamination with air. The sealing may be done by using clay material.

The carburising temperature ranges from 900 to 950°C. The carburising time depends upon the required depth of the carburised case. For deeper case, longer holding time is required (Fig. 3.29).

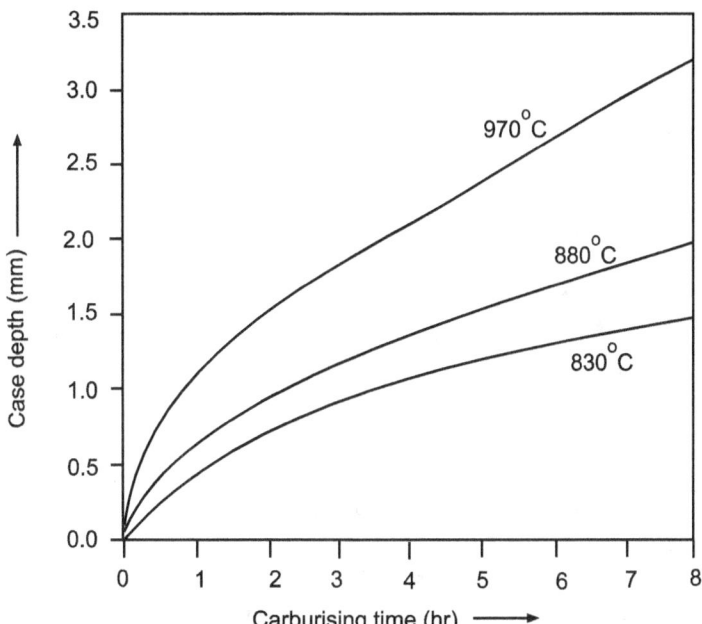

Fig. 3.29: Increase in case depth with time at various temperatures for pack carburising

Table 3.2: Relation between Case depth and Holding time

Case depth (mm)	Holding time (hrs)
0.4 to 0.7	4.5 to 5.5
1.7 to 1.2	6 to 10
1.2 to 1.8	11.5 to 16
1.8 to 2.2	16 to 22

Carburising occurs by the following reactions:

1. $2\,C$ + $O_2 \rightarrow$ $2\,CO$

      (Charcoal)   (air)

      $2\,CO \rightarrow$ C + CO_2

        (Active carbon)

      CO_2 + $C \rightarrow$ $2CO$

        (Charcoal)

2. $BaCO_3 \rightarrow BaO + CO_2$

      CO_2 + $C \rightarrow$ $2\,CO$

        (Charcoal)

      $2\,CO \rightarrow$ $C + CO_2$

        (Active carbon)

      CO_2 + $C \rightarrow$ $2\,CO$

        (Charcoal)

The rate of diffusion of carbon at a given temperature depends upon diffusion coefficient and the carbon-concentration gradiant.

A typical carburised structure is as shown in Fig. 3.30. It shows a typical hypereutectoid steel structure at surface, supported by a eutectoid, hypoeutectoid and parent metal structure.

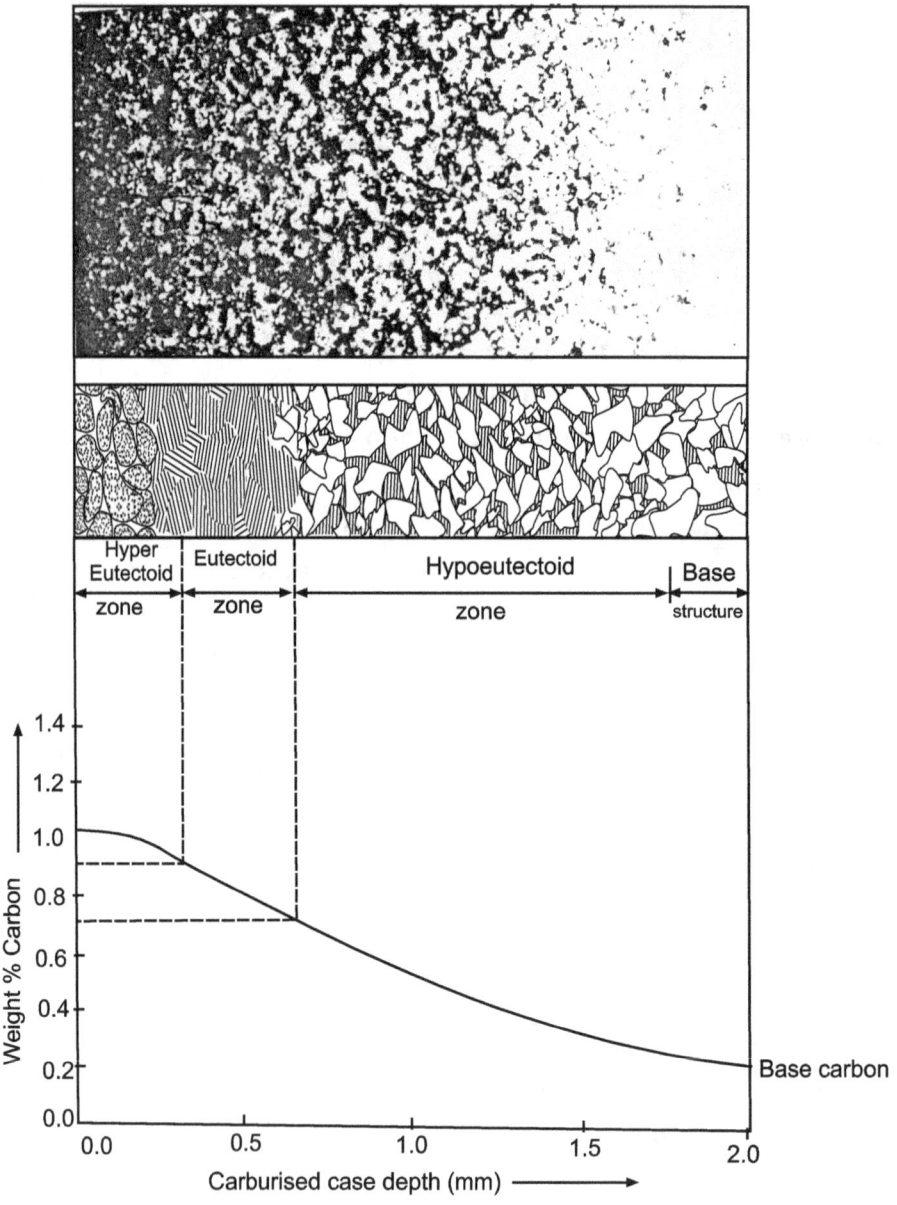

Fig. 3.30: Variation of carbon composition and microstructure from surface to core of a carburised component

The main advantage of peak carburising process is that, it does not require controlled atmosphere. It is used for small lots. It is a batch type process.

However, it becomes disadvantageous as:

- It is not suitable to produce thin and uniform carburised cases.

- Close tolerances for case depth are not possible.

- Direct quenching is not possible as the parts are embedded in solid carburiser.

- More energy gets consumed for heating the charge.

- More time is required for heating and cooling the charge.

3.21.2 Liquid Carburising

This process consists of carburising steel in baths of molten salts having a composition as follows:

Sodium carbonate	75 to 85 per cent
Sodium chloride	10 to 15 per cent
Silicon carbide	6 to 10 per cent
Sodium cyanide	5 to 10 per cent

These baths may be operated either at low temperature (840 – 900°C) or at high temperature (900 - 950°C) depending upon their composition.

Following reactions occur during carburising:

(1) $2 NaCN + O_2 \rightarrow 2 NaCNO$

$3 NaCNO \rightarrow NaCN + Na_2CO_3 + C + 2N$

(2) $2 NaCN + 2O_2 \rightarrow Na_2CO_3 + CO + 2N$

$2 CO \rightarrow C + CO_2$

Time of immersion in this process varies from 30 min. to 15 hours. Case depths obtained are in the range of 0.07 to 3.0 mm. The depth depends upon composition and temperature of bath and the composition of steel. Plain low carbon steels and low alloy steels are used for this process. The carbon in steels is not more than 0.2 per cent.

Liquid carburising extending the following advantages, is suitable for small and medium sized parts.

Advantages:

- No oxidation and sooting problems.
- Uniform case depth.
- Rapid process compared to pack carburising.
- Less heating time.

Disadvantages:

- Post treatment as washing is a must.
- Adjustment of bath composition is necessary.
- Some shapes cannot be carburised as they may float on liquid salt.
- Cyanide salts are poisonous and require careful handling, during storage and drainage.
- Large sized components cannot be liquid carburised.

3.21.3 Gas Carburising

It may be either batch or continuous type. The steel is heated with carbon monoxide or hydrocarbon. This hydrocarbon gets decomposed at carburising temperature, which diffuses carbon in steel. A carrier gas, which is obtained from endothermic generator, is used in industry.

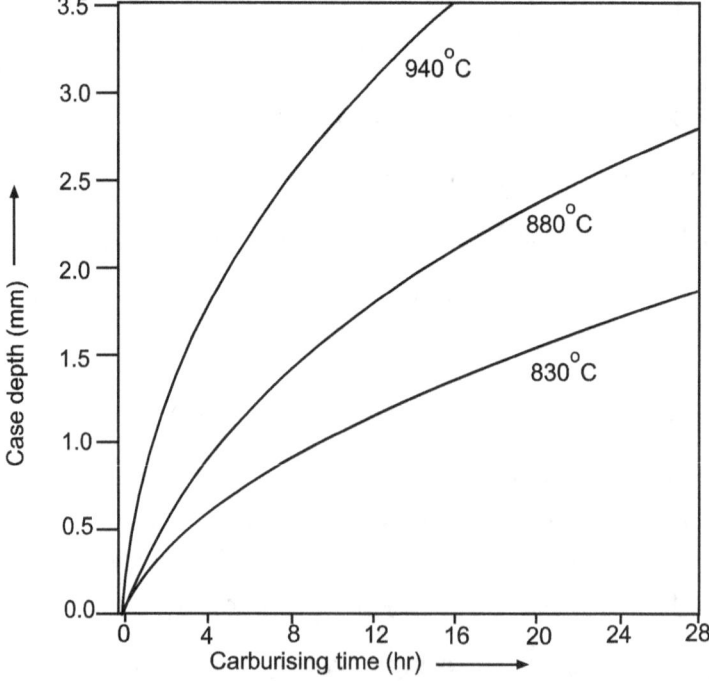

Fig. 3.31: Increase in case depth with time at various temperatures for gas carburising

The part to be carburised is introduced with a fixture in a furnace. Then the carburising gas is purged. The carburising temperature and holding time depends on required case depth. Case depth between 0.2 and 0.5 mm can be obtained in 1 to 2 hours with carburising temperature around 950°C (Fig. 3.31).

Gas carburising overcomes the limitations of pack carburising. The process is advantageous in view of the following:

- Direct quenching is possible,

- Low cost and clean working conditions,

- Close quality control as uniform case depth,

- Greater flexibility in the process and

- The process can be automated.

Very big lots of small components can be used in this process.

3.21.4 Selective Carburising

This method is used for carburising only a part of the component, so that the remaining surface area remains non-hardenable and can be easily machined.

This is carried out by covering the area of steel by a thin layer (0.04 mm) of copper by electroplating. An anticarburising or no-carb paste called linite (talc and white clay mixed in water glass) is also used. But during process, the paste may crack and does not provide the required protection. Copper plating is better for selective carburising.

3.22 HEAT TREATMENT AFTER CARBURISING

(May 06, 09; Dec. 05, 07)

Only increase in surface carbon after carburising does not increase the surface hardness of low carbon steel component. Therefore, carburising must be followed by hardening heat treatment. Heat treatment after carburising is designed, depending on the various factors such as:

- Carburising medium (liquid, gas, solid)
- Composition of steel (plain/alloy)
- Grain size (fine/coarse)
- And finally the requirement of properties (hardness and toughness of case and core).

As the steel is carburised at austenitising temperature, direct quenching hardens both case and core.

Following are the various heat treatments used (Fig. 3.32):

1. Case refining
2. Core refining
3. Partial refining of case and core
4. Double quenching
5. Direct quenching
6. Direct quenching and case refining
7. Interrupted quenching.

These are shown schematically in Fig. 3.32. Consider the carburising of 0.20% carbon steel.

For case refining heat treatment, the carburised steel is slowly cooled from carburising temperature to room temperature. It is reheated slightly above critical temperature of case. Then it is quenched to room temperature. This gives tough ferrite at core and fine martensite at surface. This does not dissolve excess carbides. The method is best suited for fine grained steels [Fig. 3.32 (A)].

For core refining heat treatment, the carburised steel is slowly cooled to room temperature. It is reheated slightly above critical temperature of core and then quenched. This imparts maximum core strength and hardness. But, this coarsens the case structure. In highly alloyed steel, the amount of retained austenite is increased. The core properties are improved due to fine ferrite. This method is useful for fine grained steels [Fig. 3.32 (B)]

The carburised steel is slowly cooled to room temperature and reheated to reach the temperature intermediate to the critical temperature of case and core. Partially refined structure is then observed [Fig. 3.32 (C)].

For coarse grained steels, double quenching is preferred. The carburised steel is slowly cooled to room temperature. It is reheated at a temperature above the critical temperature of core and quenched. Again it is heated above the critical temperature of the case and quenched. This favours solution of excess carbides. The retained austenite is minimum. The case and core get refined. Soft, machinable core with maximum toughness and resistance to impact is observed. This heat treatment gives optimum results to any type of steel [Fig. 3.32 (D)].

In direct quench method, the components are directly quenched in water or oil. Due to very fast cooling, fine ferrite is obtained at core. The size of martensite depends on the initial size of austenite prior to quenching. The amount of retained austenite in this case is more. This treatment is suitable for fine grained steels and alloy steels, which are not coarsened at carburising temperature. It gives unrefined and hardened core and case unrefined with dissolution of excess carbides [Fig. 3.32 (E)].

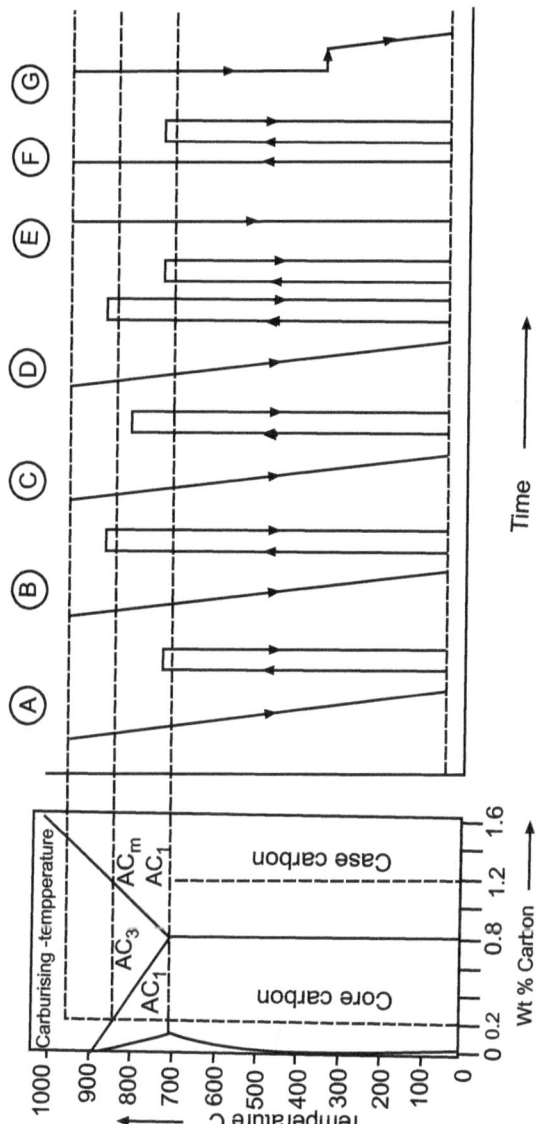

Fig. 3.32: Part of iron-carbon diagram and heat treatment cycles after carburising

Direct quenching from carburising temperature and reheating above critical temperature of case with quenching offers a different structure. It gives a core unrefined with fair toughness. The case gets refined with dissolution of excess carbides. The amount of retained austenite is less compared to that retained in the above treatments. This is adapted to fine grained steels only [Fig. 3.32 (F)].

If the carburised steels are interrupt quenched similar to martempering, a fully hardened structure is obtained. It gives unrefined case with dissolution of excess carbides. Some amount of austenite is retained. Due to holding above M_s temperature, the temperature of case and core gets equalized. This minimizes the distortion and gives steel higher hardness. The hardness of steel increases, if the initial carbon content is high [Fig. 3.32 (G)].

3.23 NITRIDING   (May06, 08, 09; Dec. 09, 10, 13)

This process is similar to carburising, with the difference that instead of carbon, nitrogen content at the surface of steel is increased.

In this process, the steel is heated in an atmosphere consisting of a mixture of ammonia gas and dissociated ammonia. The active nitrogen gets absorbed by the ferrite phase of iron and alloying elements. Nitriding is carried out at a temperature, of about 550°C to 600°C. At this temperature, the maximum solubility of nitrogen in ferrite is 0.6 per cent.

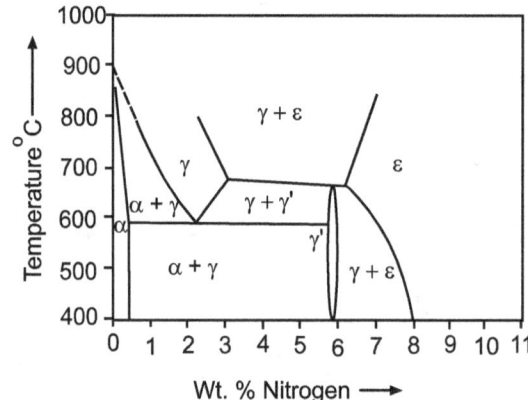

Fig. 3.33: Iron-Nitrogen equilibrium phase diagram

Iron, aluminium, chromium etc. form their respective nitrides. Nitriding increases the hardness, red hardness, wear resistance, fatigue limit etc. All steels are suitable for nitriding, but the steels containing major nitride forming elements give higher hardness. The nitrogen should be in the atomic or nascent form and not in molecular form for nitriding.

The components to be nitrided are kept in an air-tight container through which the nitriding atmosphere is continuously supplied. At the nitriding temperature, ammonia gas is dissociated as follows:

$$2 NH_3 \rightarrow 2N + 3H_2$$

The atomic nitrogen, thus formed diffuses into the iron and forms iron nitrides.

Depending upon the type of medium used, nitriding may be

(a) Gas nitriding or

(b) Liquid nitriding.

In gas nitriding, nitrogen is produced by dissociation of ammonia gas, while liquid nitriding uses a molten cyanide bath. A liquid nitriding bath contains,

(1) NaCN (96.5 %), Na_2CO_3 (2.5 %) and NaCNO (0.5 %) OR

(2) KCN (96 %), K_2CO_3 (0.6 %), KCNO (0.75 %) and KCl (0.5 %)

Liquid nitriding is used, when less case depth is required. Nitriding is a slow process. It may take several hours. The case depth depends on this time (Fig. 3.34)

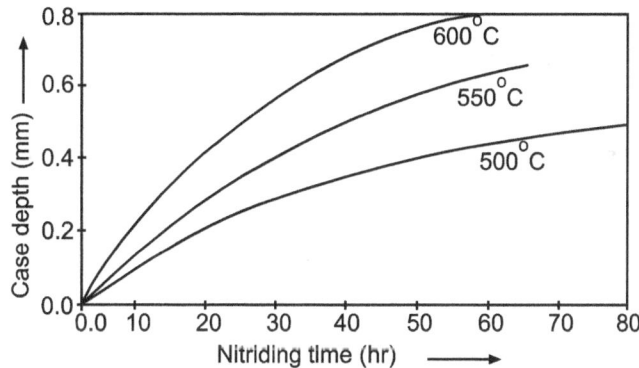

Fig. 3.34: Increase in nitrided case depth with time at various temperatures

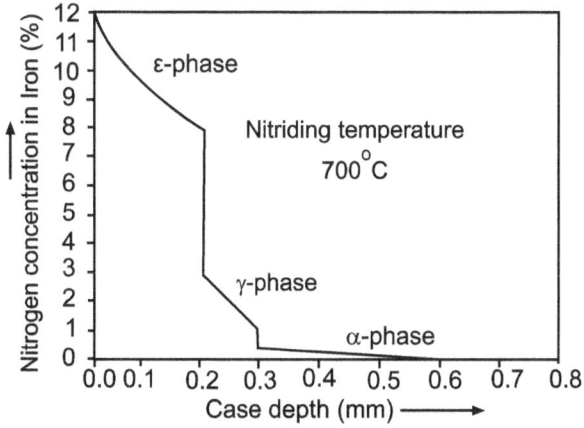

Fig. 3.35: Appearance of different phases in nitrided case

A nitrided case consists of two zones: (Fig. 3.35)

(A) The outer zone consists of nitrides of iron and alloy elements.

(B) The inner zone has only alloy nitrides.

The outer zone is known as *white layer* because of its appearance after etching with nital.

The white layer is not desirable. It is brittle and tends to chip out from the surface.   It is not harmful, if its thickness is less than 0.01 mm. Grinding or lapping may be used, if the white layer is thick.

Nitralloys: Medium carbon steels used for nitriding, containing aluminium, chromium and molybdenum are known as *Nitralloys*.

Aluminium is a strong nitride former. It produces a nitrided case with very high hardness and wear resistance.

Chromium forms hard and stable nitrides. Molybdenum is also a nitride former. It reduces embrittlement of steel during nitriding.

Nitriding of stainless steel gives high hardness and excellent abrasion resistance at the surface.

Nitriding steels should be hardened and tempered before nitriding. This gives maximum toughness to core.

Advantages of Nitriding:
- Nitriding is carried out at a low temperature (around 550°C) and quenching is not required. This reduces distortion of steel component.
- The parts may be machined very close to final dimensions before nitriding, which is not possible in carburising.
- Complex shaped parts can be case hardened easily by nitriding.
- It gives excellent wear resistance.
- The hardness of nitrided case (1000 VPN) does not get affected by heating to temperatures below the nitriding temperature.
- Nitrided steels show better fatigue properties.
- If white layer is not removed, nitriding improves corrosion resistance.
- Nitrided surface shows excellent bearing properties.
- Post nitriding heat treatment is not required.

Disadvantages:

- Long time cycles are required.

- To obtain maximum hardness, special alloy steels should be used.

- The nitrided case is usually brittle.

- Ammonia atmosphere is costly.

- Nitrided cases are very thin (less than 0.5 mm).

- Proper control on white layer is a must because white layer is not desirable.

- Machining and such other operations are not possible after nitriding due to its hard case.

Nitriding is used widely for engine parts such as cams, cylinder liners, valve stems, shafts and piston rods.

3.24 CARBONITRIDING AND CYANIDING   (May 09, 12; Dec. 09)

In this heat treatment, carbon as well as nitrogen are diffused on the surface of steel. It is carried out by following processes:

(a) **Cyaniding:** Carbon and nitrogen are enriched on surface of steel by using liquid salt bath.

(b) **Carbonitriding:** In this process, gas atmosphere is used to add carbon and nitrogen to the steel surface.

The Process:

The temperature used is usually less than that in carburising. The treatments are carried out at a temperature 750 – 850°C. At this temperature, ferrite and austenite phases are present. Nitrogen diffuses in ferrite, while carbon in austenite. At lower temperatures, nitrogen diffuses more and process tends to nitriding, while at high temperatures, carbon diffusion is promoted and process tends to carburising. So, by proper selection of temperature, optimum combination of carburising and nitriding properties occur.

After heat treatment, components are quenched to obtain desired hardness.

In cyaniding, the results of process depend on bath composition and its temperature.

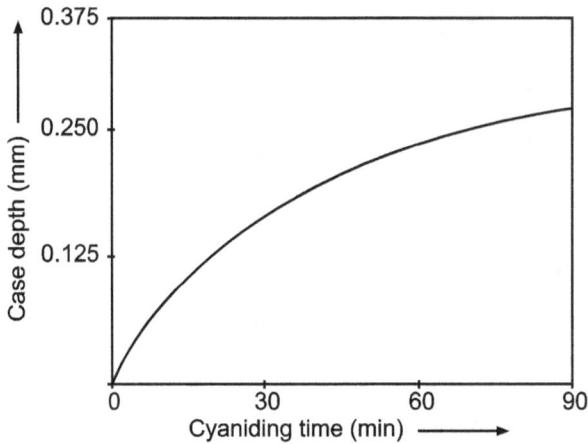

Fig. 3.36: Increase in case depth with time at 830°C in cyaniding

A typical bath composition includes –

$$NaCN = 30 \text{ per cent}$$
$$Na_2CO_3 = 40 \text{ per cent}$$
$$NaCl = 30 \text{ per cent}$$

Molten cyanide decomposes in the presence of air and produces sodium cyanate (NaCNO), which decomposes to active nitrogen as follows:

$$2 NaCN + O_2 \rightarrow 2 NaNCO$$
$$4 NaNCO \rightarrow Na_2CO_3 + 2NaCN + CO + 2N$$

The carbon content in the case increases with increase in cyanide concentration. Cyanide produces very thin cases (less than 0.25 mm thickness). It is used for screws, small gears, nuts, bolts etc.

Carbonitriding uses gas atmosphere to increase carbon and nitrogen on surface of steel. It is not the modification of nitriding. It is a modified carburising. It is also known as dry cyaniding, gas cyaniding and nicarbing. For carbonitriding, (a) carrier gas, (b) enriching gas and (c) ammonia are used.

The carrier gas is a mixture of nitrogen, hydrogen and carbon monoxide. It is purged in the furnace under positive pressure to prevent air infiltration. The enriching gas is usually propane or natural gas. It is the principal source for carbon. Ammonia dissociates at carbonitriding temperature and gives nitrogen. Carbonitriding is followed by quenching either direct from the furnace or after precooling to 800°C. The final tempering treatment is given at 160 – 180°C.

Carbonitriding offers better results with nitro alloys. Increase in case depth with time at various temperatures in carbonitriding is shown in Fig. 3.37.

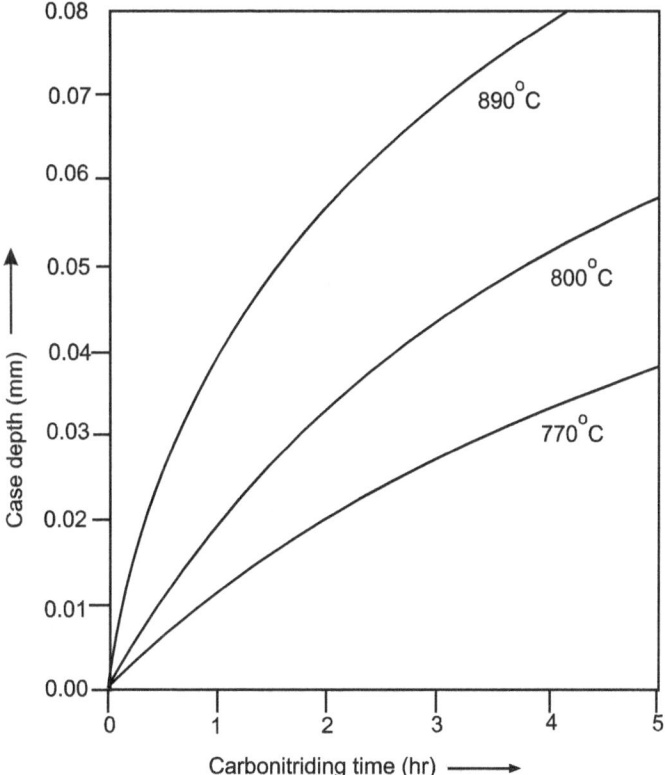

Fig. 3.37: Increase in case depth with time at various temperatures in carbonitriding

Compared to carburising, carbonitriding gives the following advantages:

- Low temperature treatment.

- Slower cooling rates during hardening.

- Reduced distortion due to oil quenching instead of water.

- Nitrogen increases hardenability, so the carbonitriding of less expensive carbon steels give equivalent properties obtained in gas carburising and

- It offers resistance to softening during tempering.

Carbonitriding is used for components requiring hard and long period wear resisting surface as shafts and transmission gears.

3.25 FLAME HARDENING   (May 10, May 11)

This does not change the chemical composition of the steel at surface. This is called as *shallow hardening* method. In this process (Fig. 3.38), selected areas are heated to austenitising temperature and then quenched. This forms martensite similar to conventional hardening, but at surface only. The steel being hardened by this method, should be in the range of 0.3 to 0.6 per cent carbon as these steels exhibit better hardenability.

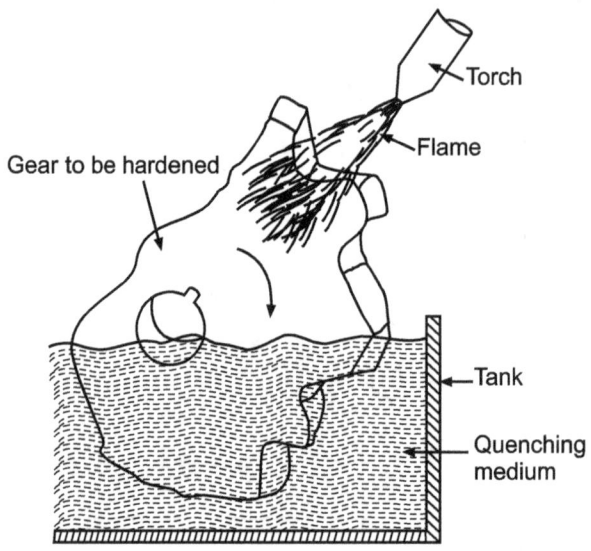

Flg. 3.38: Flame hardening of a large gear teeth

In flame hardening, high temperature is produced by oxyacetylene flame. It generates temperature upto 3000°C. Commercially, process consists of using a machine which automatically heats, quenches and indexes parts.

The depth of hardening depends upon:

    (a)   Flame intensity   (c)   Heating time and

    (b)   Gas flow   (d)   Travelling speed of flame

Due to higher temperature of flame, overheating may occur. This results in cracking after quenching and grain growth below the hardened zone.

Following methods are used for flame hardening:

    (a)   Stationary   (c)   Spinning

    (b)   Progressive   (d)   Progressive and spinning

Stationary method is used for spot or local hardening. In this method, the torch and the component are stationary.

In progressive method, the workpiece is stationary and the torch moves over it. This method is suitable for hardening of large parts, such as guide way of lathe, teeth of large gears etc.

The torch is stationary and the component rotates in spinning method. This method is best suited for hardening parts of circular cross-section such as precision gears, pulleys, wheels etc.

The combination of the above two methods (i.e. progressive-spinning) utilizes rotating component over which a torch moves. This is used for hardening of long circular parts as rolls.

After hardening, quenching is carried out by,

- Air cooling,

- Water spraying,

- Immersing in oil or water.

After quenching, stress relieving and air cooling may be used.

Flame hardening produces much deeper hardened zone ranging from 3 to 6 mm.

Advantages:

- Portable machines may be used.

- Large parts, which cannot be accommodated in furnace, can be hardened.

- Quick, selective hardening process and

- Surface finished components may be hardened as less scaling, distortion is observed.

Disadvantages:

- Possibility of overheating and grain coarsening and

- Case depths, less than 1 mm are difficult to be produced.

3.26 INDUCTION HARDENING   (Dec. 09, 10; May 11)

This method also does not change the chemical composition of surface. This is a selective and shallow hardening method.

In this method, the heat is produced by currents induced in the metal placed in a rapidly changing magnetic field. It consists of an induction coil made up of several turns of copper tubing. This is the primary coil. The part to be hardened is made secondary. (Fig. 3.39).

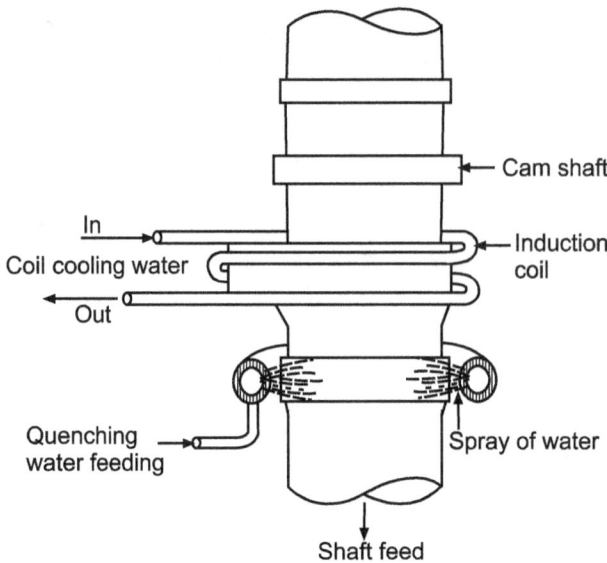

Fig. 3.39: Induction heating and subsequent quenching of a camshaft for induction hardening

Typical coil e.g. round, flat, spot etc. are designed and used as per requirement.

Principle of Induction Hardening:

High frequency alternating current is passed through the water cooled coil, which is placed near the surface of steel. A high frequency magnetic field is set up, which induces high frequency eddy currents and hysteresis currents at the metal surface. Due to resistance of metal to these currents, heat is produced at the surface only.

The high frequency induced currents tend to travel at the surface of the metal. This is known as *skin effect*. This effect increases with increase in the frequency of induction heating. Therefore, it is possible to heat a shallow layer of the steel without heating core. The heat is transferred towards the centre only by conduction.

The depth of the heated layer is inversely proportional to the square root of the frequency (Table 3.3). Normally, 500,000 Hz frequency is used. At the same frequency, greater case depth may be obtained by increasing heating time.

Plain carbon steels with medium carbon content are normally used for induction hardening.

Table 3.3: Effect of frequency on case depth

Frequency (Hz)	Case depth (mm)
1000	4.5 to 8.5
3000	3.5 to 5.0
10,000	2.5 to 3.5
1,20,000	1.5 to 2.0
5,00,000	1.0 to 2.0

Low alloy steels can be readily induction hardened, but highly alloyed steels are more sluggish and may require higher temperature.

Induction hardened part shows less distortion. Induction hardening becomes advantageous as the equipment can be fitted directly into production line. However, the process becomes limited due to its high cost and is uneconomical for irregular shaped parts.

Piston rods, pump shafts, spur gears, rocker levers, crank shaft, camshaft and cams are induction hardened.

3.27 STRENGTHENING MECHANISMS

Due to presence of free moving dislocations the actual strength of metals decreases. The yield strength reduces if these dislocations move freely inside metal lattice. But if the motion of these dislocations is obstructed by some means or by creating some obstacles then the metal will not yield at a lower stress and the metal is strengthened. The strengthening mechanisms based on the principle of retarding the motion of dislocation are

- Solid solution strengthening
- Strain hardening (or) work hardening
- Dispersion strengthening
- Strengthening by grain refinement
- Precipitation hardening

3.27.1 Solid Solution Strengthening

Since solvent and solute atoms differ in size, lattice distortion will take place in the lattice. If the solute atom is larger than the solvent atoms, the compressive strain will set up. And if the solute atom is smaller than the solvent atoms, thereby lattice distortion will occur and the tensile strain will setup. However, in both the cases, the stress fields of the moving dislocation will interact with the stress field of the solute atom, thereby increasing the stress required to move the dislocation through the crystal. In other words, this apposes the motion of dislocations thereby strengthening the solid solution alloy. This is called as solid solution strengthening.

The solid solution strengthening depends upon:

(i) **Quantity of solute:** If the quantity of solute atoms is more, the lattice distortions will be more and more will be the obstacles to the moving dislocations. And higher will be the strength and hardness.

(ii) **Atomic size difference:** As the atomic size difference between the solute and the solvent atoms increases, the intensity of the stress field increases. This impedes the dislocation motion thereby increasing the strength and hardness.

(iii) **Nature of distortion:** The non-regular shape distortion produced by substitution solute atoms is more effective than the spherical distortion produced by interstitial solute atoms.

(iv) **Type of solid solution:** Ordered solid solutions are more stronger and harder than disordered solid solutions since the movement of dislocations is more disturbed in ordered solid solutions.

3.27.2 Strain Hardening (or) Work Hardening

It is defined as a phenomenon by which a ductile metal becomes hard and strong as it is plastically deformed.

For example, if a copper bar is bent (at the centre) at an angle, say 45° and again made straight and the process is repeated for a number of times, more and more force is required for next bending. The bar fails finally at the centre. This is due to increased hardness of bar due to continuous plastic deformation. Most metals strain harder at the room temperature.

3.27.3 Dispersion Strengthening

In dispersion strengthening, the fine hard particles are used to strengthen the metal matrix by impeding the motion of dislocations. And the strengthening depends upon the amount, size, shape and distribution of second phase particles. More the amount of second phase particles, more will be the strength and hardness for the alloy. Very find or too coarse particles have better strengthening effect. The usual dispersed particles are oxides, carbides, borides etc. The dispersion hardened materials are generally manufactured by powder metallurgy.

3.27.4 Strengthening by Grain Refinement

The strength of structure depends upon the shape and size of grains. A fine grained metal or alloy is more harder and stronger than the coarse grained metal or alloy. This is because finer the grain size more is the number of grain boundaries. The grain boundaries acts as obstacless to the motion of dislocation. Hence, smaller the grain size more is the number of grain boundaries and hence more obstacles for the movement of dislocations. This causes the strengthening effect in fine grained structure metals and alloys. This is the principle involved in strengthening mechanism by grain refinement.

The grain refinement

- does not decrease ductility
- lowers the ductile-brittle transition temperature of steels and makes the steels more tough over a wide range of temperatures.
- improve fatigue resistance.

Hence, grain refinement is the most desirable method for strengthening metals and alloys.

3.27.5 Precipitation Hardening or Age Hardenings

For its motion, a dislocation must either cut through or bend and move between the precipitate particles dispersed from a super saturated solid solution. Hence, the stress required to move the dislocation will increase thereby increasing the strength of the alloy. this is the principle involved in the strengthening mechanism of the alloys with precipitation hardening.

Alloys that can be hardened by precipitation treatment are aluminum-copper, aluminum-silicon, copper-tin, magnesium-aluminum etc.

For the precipitation hardening, alloys should

- have decreasing the solubility of second phase with decreasing temperature so that a super saturated solid solution may be obtained.
- with age, the precipitate particles that separate out from the matrix should be coherent since the coherent precipitate particles form powerful obstacles to the motion of dislocations.

The precipitation hardening procedure involves the following three steps:

- Solution treatment
- Quenching
- Ageing

(a) Solution treatment and **(b) Quenching :** The alloy is heated to a particular temperature and held at that temperature for sufficient time so that he alloying elements go into solid solution and form a single phase solid solution. After this the alloy is rapidly cooled to room temperature by quenching in cold water or warm water to obtain a super saturated solid solution.

(c) Ageing: With the passage of time (Ageing) in the cold state, the solute precipitates out of the solid solution gradually. This precipitate is in the form of fine particles which hardens the alloy. This phenomenon is known as precipitation hardening or age hardening or simply ageing.

Precipitation with time at room temperature is called natural ageing where as precipitation at higher temperature (120°C to 200°C) is called as artificial ageing.

The strength of the alloy increases with ageing time as these coherent precipitates grow in size. But after some time, the strength reduces. This reduction in strength with increasing time period is known as over ageing.

MULTIPLE CHOICE QUESTIONS (MCQ's)

1. Isothermal decomposition of austenite gives –
    (a) pearlite   (b) bainite
    (c) cementite   (d) ledeburite

2. Transformation of austenite into pearlite starts with –
    (a) nucleation of ferrite   (b) nucleation of cementite
    (c) formation of ferrite   (d) nucleation of bainite

3. Pearlite is –
    (a) laminar mixture of ferrite and cementite
    (b) fine mixture of ferrite and cementite
    (c) laminar mixture of ledeburite and cementite
    (d) fine mixture of ledeburite and cementite

4. Transformation of austenite into pearlite starts with –
    (a) nucleation of ferrite at grain boundary
    (b) nucleation of cemerite at grain boundary
    (c) nucleation of ferrite inside grain
    (d) nucleation of cemerite inside grain

5.   .... pearlite is formed at lower transformation temperature.
        (a) Granual   (b) Coarse
        (c) Fine   (d) Horizontal

6.   Coarse pearlite is formed with .... transformation temperature ..... cooling rate.
        (a) lower, lower   (b) lower, higher
        (c) higher, higher   (d) higher, lower

7.   When rate of nucleation is more, pearlite obtained is –
        (a) grannual   (b) coarse
        (c) fine   (d) feathery

8.   Find pearlite has .... hardness and .... strength as compared to coarse pearlite.
        (a) more, less   (b) less, more
        (c) less, less   (d) more, more

9.   In which product, cementite plates appear to be embedded in ferrite matrix ?
        (a) Pearlite   (b) Bainite
        (c) Martensite   (d) Austenite

10.   The transformation of austenite into bainite starts with –
        (a) nucleation of cementite   (b) nucleation of ferrite
        (c) formation of cementite   (d) formation of ferrite

11.   A fine mixture of ferrite and cementite is called as –
        (a) pearlite   (b) martensite
        (c) bainite   (d) austenite

12.   Which of the following requires resolution at high magnification for its observations.
        (a) Pearlite   (b) Martensite
        (c) Upper martensite   (d) Bainite

13.   Which has feathery appearance ?
        (a) Upper bainite   (b) Lower bainite
        (c) Pearlite   (d) Martensite

14.   Upper bainite is formed at relatively .... temperature and .... cooling rate.
        (a) higher, higher   (b) higher, lower
        (c) lower, lower   (d) lower, higher

15.   Accicular bainite is formed at .... temperature and .... cooling rate.
        (a) higher, higher   (b) higher, lower
        (c) lower, lower   (d) lower, higher

16. Accicular bainite looks like –
    (a) fine pearlite   (b) coarse pearlite
    (c) martensite   (d) austenite

17. feathery bainite has appearance like –
    (a) martesnite   (b) ledeburite
    (c) austenite   (d) parlite

18. Hardness of upper bainite as compared to lower bainite is –
    (a) higher   (b) lower
    (c) same   (d) cannot compare

19. If spacing of carbide plates decreases, the hardness of austenitic transformation product –
    (a) increases   (b) decreases
    (c) remains same   (d) sometimes increases sometimes decreases

20. If cooling rate increases, the hardness of austenitic transformation product –
    (a) decreases   (b) increases
    (c) remains same   (d) sometimes increases sometimes decreases

21. As the transformation temperature increases, hardness of austenitic transformation product –
    (a) decreases   (b) increases
    (c) remains some   (d) does not depend upon temperature

22. Transformation of austenite into bainite takes place if ausetnite is –
    (a) cooled slowly upto 727°C and then rapidly upto room temperature
    (b) cooled rapidly upto 727°C and then held isothermally
    (c) cooled rapidly upto 550°C and then held isothermally
    (d) cooled slowly upto 550°C and then rapidly upto room temperature

23. If carbon atoms have sufficient time to diffuse out of austenite structure, the transformation product of austenite will be –
    (a) pearlite   (b) bainite
    (c) martesnsite   (d) either pearlite or bainite

24. The structure obtained due to entrapping of carbon atoms in solid solution is –
    (a) pearlite   (b) bainite
    (c) martensite   (d) ledeburite

25. A supersaturated solid solution of carbon in α-iron with B.L.T. structure is –
    (a) pearlite   (b) bainite
    (c) martensite   (d) ledeburite

26. The transformation product of austenite that is obtained without diffusion is –
    (a) pearlite   (b) bainite
    (c) both pearlite and bainite   (d) martensite

27. The transformation product of austenite which is obtained with diffusion –
    (a) pearlite   (b) bainite
    (c) martensite   (d) both pearlite and bainite

28. As carbon content in martensite increases, the axial ratio of B.L.T. structure –
    (a) increases   (b) decreases
    (c) remains same   (d) firstly increase then decrease

29. The transformation in which chemical composition does not change is –
    (a) pearlitic   (b) martensitic
    (c) bainitic   (d) austenitic

30. Martensitic transformation is temperature .... and time ....
    (a) dependant, dependant   (b) dependant, independant
    (c) independant, dependant   (d) independant, independant

31. As carbon percentage increases, the hardness of martensite obtained –
    (a) increases
    (b) decreases
    (c) remains same
    (d) increases upto certain carbon percentage and then decreases

32. As carbon percentage increases, the temperature at which martensitic transformation begins –
    (a) increases   (b) decreases
    (c) remains same   (d) increases initially and then decreases

33. As carbon percentage increases, the temperature at which transformation of austenite into martensite completes –
    (a) increases   (b) decreases
    (c) remains same   (d) initially increases then decreases

34. The martensitic transformation is completed practically at temperature –
    (a) higher than critical temperature (b) room temperature
    (c) lower than critical temperature   (d) practically it is never completed

35. The transformation at which chemical composition of phases change –
     (a) pearlite   (b) bainite
     (c) martensite   (d) both pearlite and bainite

36. Lamellar and Lath are the principle morphological type of –
     (a) pearlite   (b) bainite
     (c) martensite   (d) ledeburite

37. Which morphological type of martensite is desirable in steels ?
     (a) lamellar   (b) lath
     (c) both lamellar and lath   (d) both are undesirable

38. As carbon percentage increases, amount of retained austenite –
     (a) increases   (b) decreases
     (c) remains same   (d) no relation between two

39. If austenitic transformation products are arranged in increasing order of their hardness, the correct sequence will be –
     (a) pearlite, bainite, martensite   (b) pearlite, martensite, bainite
     (c) bainite, pearlite, martens   (d) bainite, martensite, pearlite

40. If austenic transformation are arranged according to increasing order of their transformation temperature, the correct sequence is –
     (a) bainite, pearlite, cementite   (b) cementite, bainite, parlite
     (c) bainite, cementite, pearlite   (d) pearlite, bainite, cmentite

41. Transformation products of austenite can be arranged in increasing order of the temperature at which they are obtained, as –
     (a) upper binite, lower bainite, fine pearlite, coarse pearlite
     (b) lower bainite, upper bainite, fine pearlite, coarse pearlite
     (c) lower bainite, upper bainite, coarse pearlite, fine pearlite
     (d) upper bainite, lower bainite, coarse pearlite, fine pearlite

42. Transformation products of austenite can be arranged in increasing order of cooling rates by which they are obtained as –
     (a) upper bainite, lower bainite, fine, pearlite, coarse pearlite
     (b) lower bainite, upper bainite, coarse, pearlite, fine pearlite
     (c) coarse pearlite, fine pearlite, upper bainite, lower bainite
     (d) coarse pearlite, finite pearlite , lower bainite, upper bainte

43. Transformation products of austenite can be arranged in increasing order of the temperature at which they are obtained, as –
     (a) lath martensite, lamellar martensite, feathery bainite, accicular bainite
     (b) lamellar martensite, lath martensite, feathery bainite, accicular bainite

(c) lamellar martensite, lath martensite, accicular bainite, feathery bainite

(d) lath martesnite, lamellar martensite, accicular bainite, feathery bainite

44. If austenitic transformation products are arranged in increasing order of their hardness, the correct sequence will be –

(a) fine pearlite, coarse pearlite, feathery bainite, accicular bainite

(b) fine pearlite, coarse pearlite, accicular bainite, feathery bainite

(c) coarse pearlite, fine pearlite, accicular bainite, feathery bainite

(d) coarse pearlite, fine pearlite, feathery bainite, accicular bainite

45. Austenite transformations are –

(a) only time dependent

(b) temperature dependent

(c) both time and temperature dependant

(d) neither time nor temperature dependent

46. Interrupted cooling of austenite gives –

(a) pearlite   (b) martensite

(c) bainite   (d) ledeburite

47. T-T-T curves are drawn from the data obtained when temperature is –

(a) increasing   (b) decreasing

(c) oscillating   (d) remaining constant

48. As carbon percentage in steels decreases, the nose of T-T-T curves shifts towards –

(a) left   (b) right

(c) up   (d) down

49.

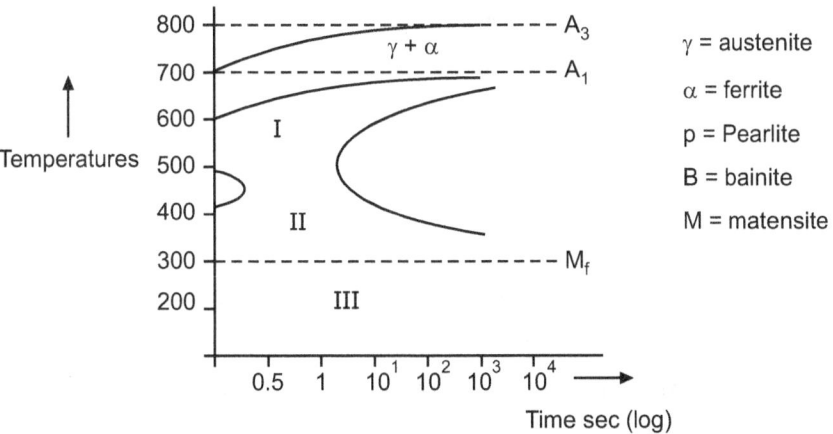

Fig.: 3.40

The above figure shows T-T-T- curve for .... steel.

(a) hypereutectoid   (b) hypoeutectoid

(c) eutectoid   (d) stainless

50. In above diagram phases observed in the region. I -

(a) $\alpha + \gamma + P$ (b) $\alpha + \gamma + B$

(c) $\alpha + \gamma + M$ (d) $\alpha + \gamma + P - M$

51. In above diagram phases observed in the region II –

(a) $\alpha + \gamma + P$ (b) $\alpha + \gamma + B$

(c) $\alpha + \gamma + M$ (d) $\alpha + \gamma + P + M$

52. In above diagram phases observed in the region III are –

(a) $\alpha + \gamma + P$ (b) $\alpha + P + B$

(c) $P + B + M$ (d) $\alpha + P + M$

53. A T-T-T diagram for a hypoeutectoid steel can be identified from –

(a) pearlite   (b) proeutectoid ferrite

(c) proeutectoid cementite   (d) only γ

54. For martesnite transformation, eutectoid steels require cooling rate –

(a) lower than hypereutectoid but more than hypoeutectoid steels

(b) more than hypereutectoid but less than hypoeutectoid steels

(c) more than hypereutectoid as well as hypoeutectoid steels

(d) less than hypereutectoid as well as hypoeutectoid steels

55. Which of the following statement is not correct for a cooling system ?

(a) During solidification of pure metal temperature remains constant

(b) During solidification of alloy metal temperature remains constant

(c) During solidification of pure metal temperature remains decreases

(d) During solidification of pure metal temperature remains varies

56. If nose of T-T-T- shifts towards right, its meaning is –

(a) formation of martensite is possible with lower cooling rates

(b) formation of martensite is possible with higher cooling rates

(c) formation of bainite is possible with lower cooling rates

(d) formation of bainite is possible with lower cooling rates

57. If grain size of austenite increases, nose of T-T-T curves shifts to –

(a) left   (b) right

(c) centre   (d) up

58. Critical cooling rate is .... cooling rate at which .... structure is formed.
    (a) maximum, full martesnite   (b) minimum, full bainite
    (c) maximum, full bainite   (d) minimum full martensite

59. If nose is shifted towards right then CCR is –
    (a) low   (b) high
    (c) zero   (d) infinity

60. If CCR is low then hardenability of steel is –
    (a) high   (b) low
    (c) cannot predict   (d) no relation between two

61.

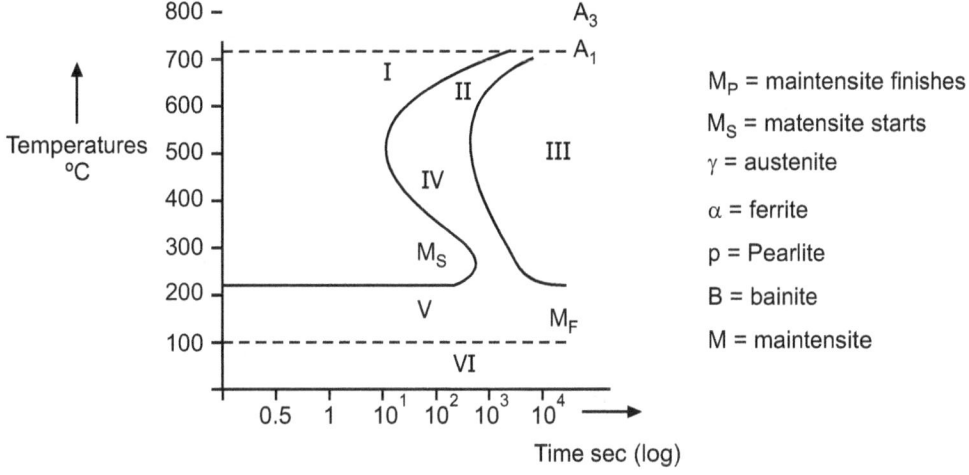

Fig. : 3.41

    Above diagram shows T-T-T- curve for .... steels.
    (a) hypoeutectoid   (b) eutectoid
    (c) hypereutectoid   (d) stainless

62. The phase observed in region I is –
    (a) α   (b) B
    (c) γ   (d) M

63. The phase observed at II is –
    (a) α + B   (b) α + γ
    (c) γ + B   (d) γ + P

64. The phase observed at III is –
    (a) P   (b) γ
    (c) P + α   (d) P + B

65.   The phase observed at IV is –

    (a) γ + P   (b) γ + B

    (c) P + B   (d) γ + P + B

66.   The phase observed in the region V is –

    (a) γ + P   (b) γ + B

    (c) γ + M   (d) P + B + M

67.   The phase observed in the region VI is –

    (a) γ + P + M   (b) γ + P + B + M

    (c) M + retained γ   (d) retained γ

68.

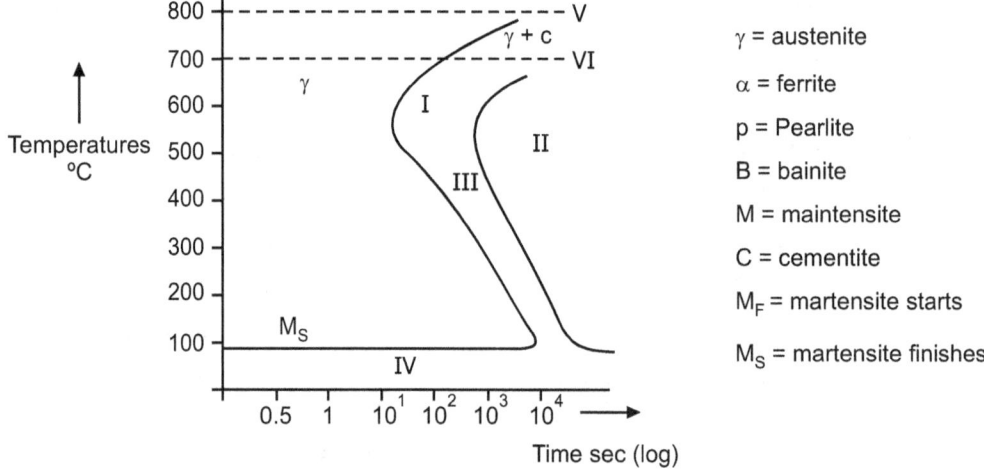

    γ = austenite
    α = ferrite
    p = Pearlite
    B = bainite
    M = maintensite
    C = cementite
    M_F = martensite starts
    M_S = martensite finishes

Fig. 3.42

The above figure shows T-T-T- curve for .... steels.

    (a) hypoeutectoid   (b) eutectoid

    (c) hypereutectoid   (d) mild

69.   The T-T-T- curve for hpereutectoid steels can be identified by –

    (a) proeutectoid cementite   (b) proeutectoid ferrite

    (c) γ   (d) martensite

70.   In the figure, the phase observed at region I is –

    (a) γ + P   (b) γ + C

    (c) P + C   (d) γ + P + C

71.   In the above figure the phase at II is –

    (a) P   (b) P + C

    (c) γ   (d) γ + C

72. In the above figure the phase in the region III is –
    (a) γ + B
    (b) γ + C
    (c) B + C
    (d) γ + B + C

73. In above figure the phase observed in the region IV is –
    (a) M
    (b) γ + M
    (c) P + M
    (d) C + M

74. In the above figure, temperature shown by line V is denoted by –
    (a) A_{cm}
    (b) A_1
    (c) A_2
    (d) A_3

75. In above figure the temperature shown by line VI is denoted as –
    (a) A_{cm}
    (b) A
    (c) A_2
    (d) A_3

76. The nose of T-T-T diagram towards right indicate –
    (a) formation of martensite at higher cooling rate
    (b) formation of martensite at lower cooling rate
    (c) formation of austenite at lower cooling rate
    (d) formation of austenite at higher cooling rate

77. As cooling rate increases hardness of steel –
    (a) increases
    (b) decreases
    (c) remains same
    (d) becomes unpredictable

78.

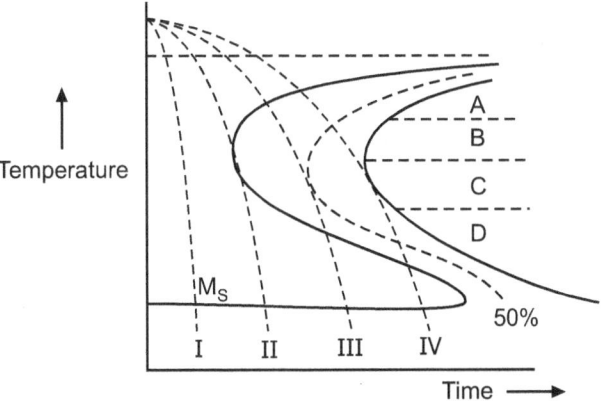

Fig. 3.43

In the above figure, critical cooling rate is shown by –
    (a) curve I
    (b) curve II
    (c) curve III
    (d) curve IV

79. The structure obtained in region A is –
    (a) coarse pearlite   (b) fine pearlite
    (c) upper bainite   (d) lower bainite

80. The structure obtained in the region B is –
    (a) coarse pearlite   (b) finite pearlite
    (c) feathery bainite   (d) lower bainite

81. The transformation structure observed in the region C is –
    (a) coarse pearlite   (b) fine pearlite
    (c) accicular bainite   (d) feathery bainite

82. The transformation structure observed in the region D is –
    (a) coarse pearlite   (b) fine pearlite
    (c) accicular bainite   (d) feathery bainite

83. If steels are cooled continuously at constant cooling rate, then T-T-T curves shift to –
    (a) right and down   (b) left and down
    (c) right and up   (d) left and up

84. Annealing of hypoeutectoid steels is carried out at temperature of about –
    (a) $A_{C1} + 50°C$ (b) $A_{C1} – 50°C$
    (c) $A_{C3} + 50°C$ (d) $A_{C3} – 50°C$

85. Annealing of hypereutectoid steels is done at temperature of –
    (a) $A_{C1} + 50°C$ (b) $A_{cm} + 50°C$
    (c) $A_{C3} + 50°C$ (d) $A_3 + 50°C$

86. If holding time in annealing is increased the hardness is –
    (a) increased   (b) reduced
    (c) initial increased then decreased   (d) not affected

87. The heat treatment done in order to reduce strain hardening due to cold working is –
    (a) hardening   (b) normalizing
    (c) tempering   (d) annealing

88. Which of the following is not an effect of annealing ?
    (a) increase in machinability   (b) reduction in internal stresses
    (c) improvement in homogeneity   (d) increase in hardness

89. Annealing process involves –
    (a) hearting steel to austenite region and then slow cooling
    (b) hearting steel to austenite region and then air cooling

(c) hearting steel to austenite region and then quenching

(d) hearting steel to austenite region and then working

90. Normalizing process involves –

(a) heating the steel to austenite region and then slow cooling

(b) heating the steel to austenite region and then air cooling

(c) heating the steel to austenite region and then cold working

(d) heating the steel to austenite region and then hot working

91. Which of the following is not an effect of normalizing ?

(a) elimination of coarse grained structure

(b) to reduce segregation

(c) to reduce strain hardening effect

(d) to improve machinability

92. Normalizing of hypoeutectoid steel is done at temperature –

(a) AC_3 (b) $AC_3 + 50°C$

(c) AC_1 (d) $AC_1 + 50°$

93. Normalizing temperature for hypereutectoid steel is –

(a) AC_1 (b) $AC_1 + 50°C$

(c) A_{cm} (d) $A_{cm} + 50°C$

94. Which characteristics are different in normalizing and annealing processes of hypoeutectoid steels ?

(a) process temperature only   (b) cooling rate only

(c) both temperature and cooling rate (d) either temperature and cooling rate

95. Which characteristics are different in normalizing and annealing processes of hypereutectoid steels –

(a) temperature   (b) cooling rate

(c) both temperature and cooling rate (d) both are same

96. Hardening process involves –

(a) heating of steel to austenite regions and then slow cooling

(b) heating of steel to austenite regions and then air cooling

(c) heating of steel to austenite regions and then quenching

(d) heating of steel to austenite regions and then cold working

97. Hardening is done in order to get –

(a) fine pearlite   (b) coarse pearlite

(c) bainite   (d) martensite

98. After annealing, microstructure obtained is –
     (a) fine pearlite   (b) coarse pearlite
     (c) bainite   (d) martensite

99. After normalizing, microstructure obtained is –
     (a) fine pearlite   (b) coarse pearlite
     (c) bainite   (d) martensite

100. For hypoeutectoid steels, hardening temperature is –
     (a) A_{C1} (b) $A_{C1} + 50°C$
     (c) A_{C3} (d) $A_{C3} + 50°C$

101. For hypereutectoid steels, hardening is done at a temperature of –
     (a) A_{C1} (b) $A_{C1} + 50°C$
     (c) A_{cm} (d) $A_{cm} + 50°$

102. During hardening what happen to ferrite phase present in proeutectoid austenite ?
     (a) transforms into martensite   (b) transforms into pearlite
     (c) transforms into cementite   (d) remains unchanged

103. During hardening what happens to cementile present in proeutectoid austenite
     (a) transforms into martensite   (b) transforms into pearlite
     (c) transforms into ferrite   (d) remains unchanged

104. After hardening of hypoeutectoid steels, microstructure shows –
     (a) only martesnite   (b) only ferrite
     (c) only cementite   (d) martesniet and ferrite

105. After hardening of hypereutectoid steels, microstructure shows –
     (a) martensite + pearlite   (b) martensite ferrite
     (c) martesnsite + cementite   (d) martensite + austenite

106. Hardening at lower austenitic temperature will give –
     (a) less hardness   (b) higher hardness
     (c) sensitisation   (d) weld decay

107. As autenite temperature for hardening of steel increases, it gives –
     (a) less hardness and coarse grains   (b) more hardness and coarse grains
     (c) less hardness and fine grains   (d) more hardness and fine grains

108. During quenching in steel hardening process, heat removal rate should be –
     (a) high upto nose and then slow   (b) high from start to end
     (c) slow upto nose and then high   (d) slow from start to end

109. Hypereutectoid steels, if annealed from above A_{cm} line will not result in –
    (a) fine grains
    (b) oxidation and decarburization
    (c) coarse grains
    (d) undesirable microstructure

110. Normalizing carried out with higher cooling rate will give –
    (a) fine pearlite
    (b) coarse pearlite
    (c) fine martensite
    (d) coarse martensite

111. If the cooling media is to be arranged in increasing order of cooling rate, then correct order will be –
    (a) furnace, oil, air, brine
    (b) furnace, air, oil, brine
    (c) brine, oil, air, furnace
    (d) furnace, air, brine, oil

112. During hardening of steels, higher cooling rates after passing noise of TTT diagram will result in –
    (a) more cracking and distortion
    (b) more cracking but less distortion
    (c) less cracking and distortion
    (d) less cracking but more distortion

113. In Jominy test, hardenibility is measured in terms of –
    (a) cooling rate
    (b) hardness
    (c) distance
    (d) hardness/cooling rate

114. Hardenability is defined as –
    (a) depth from surface upto which 100% martensite is observed
    (b) depth from surface upto which 90% martensite is observed
    (c) depth from surface upto which 50% martensite is observed
    (d) depth from surface upto which 50% martensite is observed

115. Hardenability of steel can be defined as –
    (a) depth, from surface, upto which hardness 100 BHN is observed
    (b) depth, from surface, upto which hardness 50 BHN is observed
    (c) depth, from surface, upto which hardness 100 RC is observed
    (d) depth, from surface, upto which hardness 50 RC is observed

116. Hardenability gives information about –
    (a) required cooling rate
    (b) maximum hardness
    (c) stress level on surface
    (d) all of these

117. When steel is hardened, the hardness –
    (a) decreases from surface to core
    (b) remains same everywhere
    (c) decreases from core to surface
    (d) depends upon roughness

118. In Jominy test specimen is cooled by –
    (a) water   (b) water from bottom and air from sides
    (c) air   (d) air from bottom and water from sides

119. In Jominy test, hardenability is measured in terms of distance from –
    (a) surface   (b) bottom end
    (c) top end   (d) centre

120.

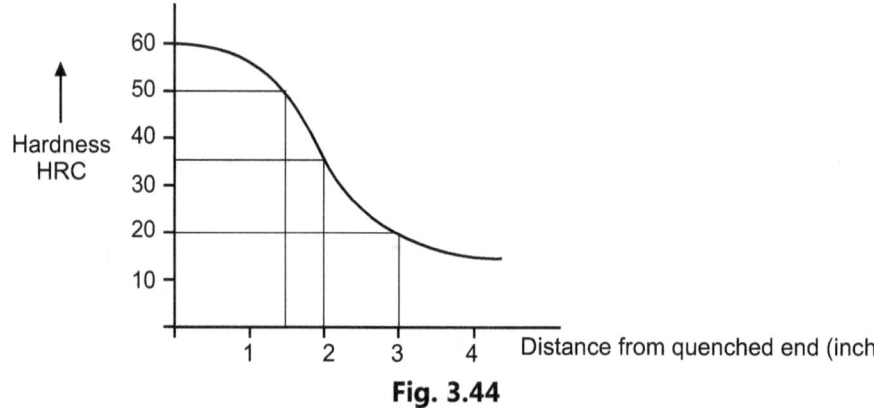

Fig. 3.44

From above hardenability curve, hardenability of given specimen is –
    (a) 3"   (b) 2"
    (c) 1.5"   (d) 60 RC

121.

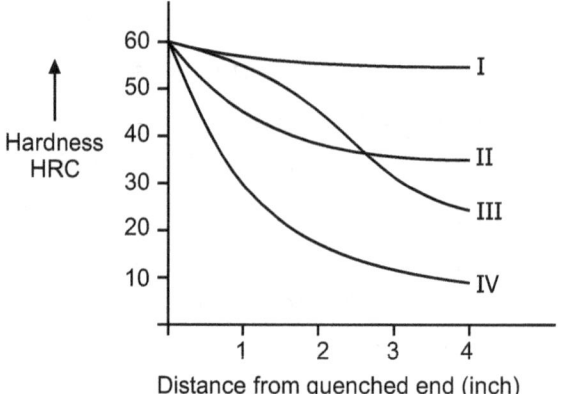

Fig. 3.45

From above diagram, hardenability is maximum for steel with curve –
    (a) I   (b) II
    (c) III   (d) IV

122. From above diagram, the curve for through or totally hardenable steel is –
    (a) I   (b) II
    (c) III   (d) IV
123. From above diagram, the curve for deep hardenable steel is –
    (a) I   (b) II
    (c) III   (d) IV
124. From above diagram, arrange the steels as per increasing order of hardenability –
    (a) I, II, III, IV   (b) IV, III, II, I
    (c) IV, II, III, I   (d) I, III, II, IV
125. From above diagram, the curve for shallow hardenable steels are –
    (a) III and IV   (b) II and IV
    (c) II and III   (d) I and II
126. In Grossman's method, hardenability is measured in terms of –
    (a) distance from surface upto 50% martensite is observed
    (b) distance from surface upto 100% martensite is observed
    (c) maximum diameter of sample which shows 50% martensite at centre
    (d) maximum diameter of sample which shows 100% martensite at centre
127. Hardenability of steel increases with decrease in –
    (a) carbon content   (b) grain size
    (c) alloying element   (d) non-metallic inclusion
127. Due to undissolved carbides in austenite –
    (a) hardness and hardenability both increases
    (b) hardness increases but hardenability decreases
    (c) hardness and hardenability both decrease
    (d) hardness decreases but hardenability increases
129.

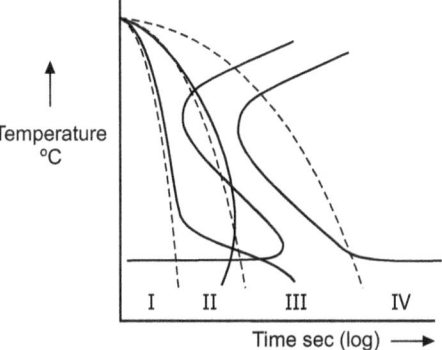

Fig. 3.46

In above diagram, the two media quenching is shown in curve –

(a) I   (b) II

(c) III   (d) IV

130. To get martesnite structure without distortion which cooling is suitable –

(a) I   (b) II

(c) III   (d) IV

131. Two media quenching is suitable for hardening of steels which have critical cooling rates –

(a) low   (b) high

(c) changing   (d) constant

132. Martempering is done on steels to –

(a) reduce internal stresses produced during hardening

(b) reduce retained austenite

(c) improve ductility and toughness

(d) improve hardness

133. Marquenching is not done to –

(a) reduce wraping and distortion

(b) reduce temperature gradient from core to surface

(c) reduce quenching cracks

(d) reduce retained austenite

134. After martempering, the microstructure shows –

(a) austenite   (b) martesnite

(c) pearlite   (d) bainite

135. Purpose of austemperng is to get microstructure of –

(a) austenite   (b) martesnite

(c) pearlite   (d) bainite

136. Suitability of martempering and austempering is for steels having .... and .... hardenability respectively.

(a) high, low   (b) low, high

(c) high, high   (d) low, low

137. Which is not true for austempering ?

(a) It gives bainite structure

(b) It gives high impact strength and notch toughness

(c) It is a type of tempering process

(d) It reduces danger of quench cracks

138. For wire drawing the most suitable heat treatment is –

(a) austempering   (b) patenting

(c) marquenching   (d) ausforming

139. The structure obtained by patenting is –

(a) lower bainite   (b) fine pearlite

(c) coase pearlite   (d) martensite

140. For highly stressed parts of aircrafts, heat treatment suitable is –

(a) patenting   (b) ausforming

(c) austempering   (d) martempering

141. The microstructure after isoforming shows –

(a) austenite   (b) fine pearlite

(c) fine martensing   (d) upper bainite

142.

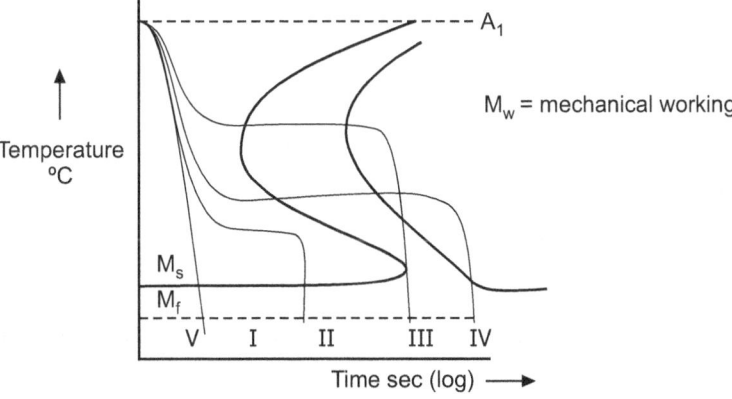

Fig. 3.47

In above diagram, process shown by curve I is –

(a) martempering   (b) ausforming

(c) patenting   (d) austempering

143. In above diagrams, process shown in curve II is –

(a) austempering   (b) ausforming

(c) martempering   (d) patenting

144. In above diagram, process shown by curve III is –

(a) austempering   (b) ausforming

(c) martempering   (d) patenting

145. In above diagram, process shown by curve IV is –
    (a) ausforming   (b) austempering
    (c) martempering   (d) patenting

146. In above diagram, process shown by curve V is –
    (a) ausforming   (b) austempering
    (c) martempering   (d) hardening

147. Which of the following is not an effect of retained austenite in steels ?
    (a) reduces tendency to crack   (b) reduces hardness
    (c) reduces cold workability   (d) reduce dimensional stability

148. The amount of retained austenite in a steel component –
    (a) increases from core to surface   (b) remains same everywhere
    (c) increases from surface to core   (d) is zero at the centre

149. Which of the following method will not reduce retained austenite in steels ?
    (a) mechanical working just above M_s (b) tempering
    (c) increasing quenching temperature   (d) subzero treatments

150. Heating of hardened steel to a temperature below A, and then cooling in air. This process is called as –
    (a) annealing   (b) normalizing
    (c) austempering   (d) tempering

151. Which of the following is not a purpose of tempering ?
    (a) to increase hardness   (b) to reduce retained austenite
    (c) to increase machinability   (d) to increase ductility and toughness

152. Secondary hardness means –
    (a) hardness obtained during annealing
    (b) hardness obtained during tempering
    (c) hardness obtained during subzero treatment
    (d) hardness obtained during cold working

153. Secondary hardness is primarily due to –
    (a) higher carbon %
    (b) lower carbon %
    (c) lower % of alloys forming complex carbides
    (d) higher % of alloys forming complex carbides

154.

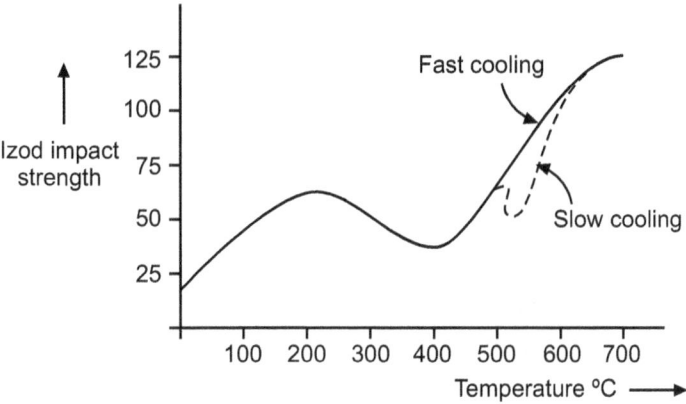

Fig. 3.48

The difference in curves of slow cooling and fast cooling at higher temperatures is due to –

(a) secondary hardening   (b) temper embrittlement

(c) retained austenite   (d) ferrite

155. A coarse grain steel as compared to a fine grained steel will have –

(a) more distortion and wraping   (b) less retained austenite

(c) more toughness   (d) less hardenability

156. Which of the following is not a method of surface hardening ?

(a) 2-media quenching   (b) carburizing

(c) induction hardening   (d) cyaniding

157. In carburizing process –

(a) carbon content at the surface of steel is increased

(b) carbon content at the core surface of steel is increased

(c) carbon content at the total component of steel is increased

(d) carbon content at the core of steel is increased

158. Quenching is not required in –

(a) carburizing   (b) nitriding

(c) carbonitriding   (d) hardening

159. The process that is done at minimum temperature is –

(a) carburizing   (b) nitriding

(c) carbonitriding   (d) hardening

160. In nitriding process, nitrogen diffuses in –
    (a) austenite   (b) ferrite
    (c) cementite   (d) pearlite

161. In carburizing process, carbon diffuses in –
    (a) austenite   (b) ferrite
    (c) cementite   (d) pearlite

162. Choose the correct statement –
    (a) in carbonitriding steel is enriched with carbon and in cyaniding with nitrogen
    (b) in carbonitriding steel is enriched with carbon + nitrogen and in cyaniding with nitrogen
    (c) in carbonitriding steel is enriched with carbon + nitrogen and in cyaniding with carbon
    (d) both, steel is enriched with carbon as well as nitrogen

163. In carbonitriding diffusion of carbon and nitrogen takes place respectively in –
    (a) ferrite and austenite   (b) austenite and ferrite
    (c) ferrite and cementite   (d) austenite and cementite

164. Cyaniding and carbonitriding are done respectively in –
    (a) liquid slat both and gas atmosphere   (b) both in liquid salt bot
    (c) both in gas atmosphere   (d) gas atmosphere and liquid salt path

165. Which of the following is not true about carbinitriding as compared to carburizing ?
    (a) high temperature treatment
    (b) slower cooling rates during hardening
    (c) offer resistance to softening during tempering
    (d) reduced distortion

166. In progressive method of flame hardening –
    (a) workpiece is stationary and torch moves
    (b) workpiece and torch are moving
    (c) workpiece is moving and rorch stationary
    (d) workpiece and torch are moving stationary

167. In induction hardening, the skin effect increases with –
    (a) increase in frequency   (b) increase in voltage
    (c) decrease in frequency   (d) decrease in voltage

168. Due to presence of dislocation, strength of metals –
    (a) increases
    (b) decreases
    (c) remains same
    (d) sometimes increases sometimes decreases

169. Which of these will not obstruct motion of dislocation ?
    (a) addition for foreign atoms
    (b) grain coarsening
    (c) strain hardening
    (d) age hardening

170. Which of the following is not an effect of grain refinement ?
    (a) more obstruction to movement of dislocation
    (b) decrease in ductility
    (c) increase in strength
    (d) increase in fatigue resistance

171. If strength of structure is more, then efforts required to move the dislocations will be –
    (a) more
    (b) less
    (c) cannot predict
    (d) no relation with each other

172. In precipitation hardening, solubility of second phase should ..... with decrease in temperature.
    (a) remain same
    (b) increase
    (c) decrease
    (d) firstly decrease then increase

173. The reduction in strength with increasing strength is called as –
    (a) aging
    (b) age hardening
    (c) precipitation hardening
    (d) over aging

174. Powder metallurgy is most suitable method for .... hardened materials.
    (a) dispersion
    (b) age
    (c) strain
    (d) precipitation

Answer Key

1. (a)	2. (b)	3. (a)	4. (b)	5. (c)	6. (d)
7. (c)	8. (d)	9. (a)	10. (b)	11. (c)	12. (d)
13. (a)	14. (b)	15. (c)	16. (c)	17. (d)	18. (b)
19. (a)	20. (b)	21. (a)	22. (d)	23. (d)	24. (c)
25. (c)	26. (d)	27. (d)	28. (a)	29. (b)	30. (b)
31. (d)	32. (b)	33. (b)	34. (d)	35. (d)	36. (c)

37. (a)	38. (a)	39. (a)	40. (b)	41. (b)	42. (c)
43. (c)	44. (d)	45. (c)	46. (c)	47. (d)	48. (a)
49. (b)	50. (a)	51. (b)	52. (d)	53. (b)	54. (d)
55. (b)	56. (a)	57. (b)	58. (d)	59. (a)	60. (a)
61. (b)	62. (c)	63. (d)	64. (a)	65. (b)	66. (c)
67. (c)	68. (c)	69. (a)	70. (d)	71. (b)	72. (d)
73. (b)	74. (a)	75. (b)	76. (b)	77. (a)	78. (b)
79. (a)	80. (b)	81. (d)	82. (c)	83. (a)	84. (c)
85. (a)	86. (b)	87. (d)	88. (d)	89. (a)	90. (b)
91. (c)	92. (b)	93. (d)	94. (b)	95. (c)	96. (c)
97. (d)	98. (b)	99. (a)	100. d()	101. (b)	102. (d)
103. (d)	104. (d)	105. (c)	106. (a)	107. (b)	108. (a)
109. (a)	110. (a)	111. (b)	112. (a)	113. (c)	114. (c)
115. (d)	116. (d)	117. (c)	118. (b)	119. (b)	120. (c)
121. (a)	122. (a)	123. (c)	124. (c)	125. (b)	126. (c)
127. (d)	128. (b)	129. (c)	130. (c)	131. (b)	132. (d)
133. (d)	134. (b)	135. (d)	136. (c)	137. (c)	138. (b)
139. (b)	140. (b)	141. (c)	142. (b)	143. (c)	144. (d)
145. (b)	146. (d)	147. (c)	148. (c)	149. (c)	150. (d)
151. (a)	152. (b)	153. (d)	154. (b)	155. (a)	156. (a)
157. (a)	158. (b)	159. (b)	160. (b)	161. (a)	162. (d)
163. (b)	164. (a)	165. (a)	166. (a)	167. (a)	168. (b)
169. (b)	170. (b)	171. (a)	172. (c)	173. (d)	174. (a)

QUESTIONS

HEAT TREATMENT OF STEELS

1. State whether the following statements are True or False and justify your answers.

   (i)   Slow cooling of steel from austenitic region forms pearlite.

   (ii) Bainite forms on continuous cooling.

   (iii) Martensite has a BCT structure.

   (iv) The shifting of nose of a T-T-T curve to the right is beneficial in hardening.

(v)   Very low carbon steels are called as non-hardenable steels.

(vi) Annealing of steel results in fine grain size.

(vii) The inter-lamellar distance in pearlite after normalizing is less than in annealing.

(viii) Hypoeutectoid steels are not hardened from $AC_1 + 50°C$.

(ix) Hardenability increases with increase in austenite grain size.

(x)   Martempering is a type of tempering.

(xi) Ausforming is used for highly stressed parts.

(xii) Retained austenite and the austenite, which occurs at high temperature are same.

(xiii) Retained austenite is a useful phase.

(xiv) High temperature tempering improves machinability.

Ans.:

(i) True   (ii) False (iii) True   (iv) True   (v) True   (vi) False   (vii) True

(viii) True   (ix) True   (x) False   (xi) True   (xii) False   (xiii) False   (xiv) True

2. State the properties that can be altered by heat treatment.

3. Classify various heat treatments and give purpose in one sentence each.

4. In what respect, martensite differs from pearlite ?

5. What is the significance of CCR ?

6. What are the various heating and cooling medias used in heat treatment ?

7. Explain the importance of the annealing process.

8. Annealing is not recommended as final heat treatment for hypereutectoid steel. Explain with reasons.

9. Draw the temperature bands for –

    (1) Annealing and its type, (2) Normalizing and (3) Hardening.

10. Explain the various factors affecting hardening.

11. Explain the mechanism of heat removal during quenching for -

    (a) Metal strip and

    (b) Steel casting.

12. Does carbon content affect the hardenability of steel ? What is the importance of chemical composition of steel with respect to hardenability ?

13. Explain the formation of quench cracks.

14. Write short notes on:

    (a) Spheroidizing annealing.

    (b) Quenching medium.

    (c) Measurement of hardenability.

    (d) Secondary hardening.

    (e) Grain size in steel.

15. Draw self explanatory sketches for:

    (a) Superimposition of cooling curve on T–T–T curve.

    (b) CCT curve.

    (c) Formation of BCT structure.

    (d) T–T–T curve showing hardening, austempering and ausforming.

SURFACE HARDENING TREATMENTS OF STEELS

1. State True or False with justification.

    (i) Carburizing is not possible in low carbon steels.

    (ii) Pack carburizing is carried out in inert atmosphere.

    (iii) Heat treatment is necessary after carburising.

    (iv) For nitriding heat treatment, higher temperature such as 900° C is required.

    (v) Carbonitriding is carried out in cyanide salt bath.

    (vi) Carbonitriding is advantageous over carburising.

    (vii) Flame hardening alters the chemical composition of surface of steel components.

    (viii) Thin case depth cannot be obtained in flame hardening.

    (ix) Highly electrical conductive materials are usually induction hardened.

Ans.:

    (i) False   (ii) False   (iii) True   (iv) False   (v) False

    (vi) True   (vii) False   (viii) True   (ix) False

2. What is the principle used for carburising ?

3. Compare pack, liquid and gas carburising.

4. Give the typical mediums used for carburising.

5. Explain in detail, heat treatment used after carburising.

6. "Alloy steels are nitrided effectively". Explain.

UNIVERSITY QUESTIONS

HEAT TREATMENT OF STEELS

1. State whether the following statements are True or False and justify your answers.

    (i)   Carbon content of steel does not affect the hardness of martensite.   **(May 08)**

    (ii) Hypereutectoid steels are hardened from above A_{cm}.   **(May 09)**

    (iii) Annealed steels are hardened than normalised steel.   **(May 09)**

    (iv) Hardness increases during tempering .   **(May 09)**

2. Explain the following transformations in details: **(Dec. 08, May 11)**

    (a)   Austenite to Pearlite,   (b) Austenite to Bainite and

    (c)   Austenite to Martensite.

3. Explain the procedure followed for plotting a T-T-T curve.   **(May 08, Dec. 08)**

4. What is principle difference in a T-T-T and CCT curve ?   **(May 08, May 09, 11)**

5. What are the factors that affect the position of a T-T-T curve ?   **(May 11)**

6. Is there any significance of selecting annealing temperatures ?
    Differentiate between Annealing and Normalizing.   **(May 11)**

7. What is the importance of hardenability term ?   **(May 10, 11)**

8. Write short notes on:

    (i)   Stress relivening   **(May 10)**

    (ii) Martempering   **(May 10)**

    (iii) Retained austenite   **(May 10)**

    (iv) Tempering methods   **(May 09)**

    (v)   Jominy test.   **(Dec. 09)**

9. Differentiate between hardness and hardenability. Explain one method of measuring hardenability and factors influencing hardenability.   **(May 11)**

10. What are similarity between annealing and normalizing ?   **(May 11)**

11. What are advantages of surface hardening treatments over through hardening treatments. Compare liquid carbuising and gas carburising.   **(May 11)**

12. Draw standard Jominey hardenability test set up.   **(Nov. 10)**

SURFACE HARDENING

1. State true or false with justification:

   'Plain carbon steels cannot be nitrided effectively'.   **(May 09)**

   Ans. True

2. Why surface hardening treatments are necessary for certain components ? **(May 11)**

3. Explain the factors on which the results of flame hardening depend.

   (Dec. 08, May 11)

4. What is the principle of induction hardening ?   **(Dec. 08; May 10, 11)**

5. Write short notes on:

   (a) Carbonitriding   **(May 09)**

   (b) Cyaniding   **(Dec. 09)**

   (c) Sursulf process   **(Dec. 09)**

   (d) Carburising   **(May 09)**

   (e) Nitriding   **(Dec. 09; Nov. 10)**

   (f) Flame hardening   **(May 10, 11)**

6. How nitriding differs from other H.T. ?   **(May 08, Dec. 08)**

   ❑❑❑

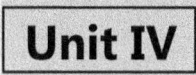

Unit IV

Chapter 4

CORROSION AND ITS PREVENTION

4.1 INTRODUCTION

Metallic materials were much frequently used for various engineering and technological applications. All the metals and their alloys except noble metals occur in nature as a chemical compound viz. oxides, sulphates, halides, etc. Pure elemental metals are obtained from naturally available minerals and then metal can be used for various applications. When a metallic material is exposed to the environment enriched with moisture and gases or immersed in liquid like acids or alkalies, it will undergo disintegration and lead to the formation of its chemical compound. This process will reduce the service life period of the metallic component or damage the equipment.

Now-a-days, it is a very severe problem and the destruction of metals due to environment has lead to form a separate study matter under the name, 'corrosion science.'

Definition :

- *Corrosion is defined as unintentional destruction of solid body due to direct chemical or electro-chemical reactions starting from the surface.*

- *"Corrosion is defined as destruction or deterioration and consequent loss of a solid metallic materials, starting at its surface, due to an unintentional chemical or electro-chemical attack, by their environment."*

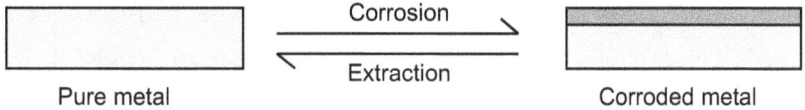

Fig. 4.1 : Corrosion versus extraction

Thermodynamically, the compounds of metals are more stable (hence less energetic) as compared to the pure metals. i.e. if a pure metal is obtained after metallurgy, then slowly they get converted to their combined form (or compounds) naturally.

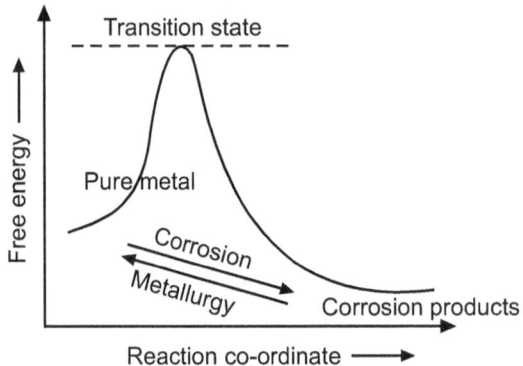

Fig 4.2: Free energy change during corrosion

4.2 CAUSE OF CORROSION

Except noble metals (gold, silver, etc) all other metals exist in nature in the combined forms such as oxides, hydroxides, carbonates, sulphides, sulphates, etc. The extraction of metals from their ores requires a considerable energy to be supplied to the process.

Therefore, the isolated pure metals can be considered as being in a much higher energy state than in the corresponding ores and hence, they exhibit a natural tendency to return back to their lower energy state (i.e. combined state or compound form). Thus corrosion can be regarded as the tendency of the metals to revert back to their more stable chemical forms such as oxides, sulphide, etc. in which they occur in nature.

4.3 ECONOMIC IMPORTANCE

Everyday corrosion of many metallic items of common use is taking place all around. Corrosion is a serious problem because the life of the plant or equipment is very much reduced due to corrosion. An engineer whether dealing with design or process operation, or may be a mechanical, chemical or civil engineer has to face this serious problem of corrosion. For example, chemical industries face many corrosion problems, some of which are so serious as to cause shut down of plants and collapse of structures involving hazards to human life. It is very difficult to assess the exact loss caused due to corrosion. This changes from process to process and from locality to locality.

In tropical countries, like India, the corrosion problem is more serious than in cold countries. In India the direct loss due to corrosion per annum is estimated to about Rs. 200 crores and annual expenditure in controlling corrosion is to the order of Rs. 50 crores. Thus corrosion is a matter of grave concern due to the enormous cost involved in the replacement and maintenance of metallic parts in all kinds of applications.

However, in order to be able to make rational decisions regarding (i) avoiding severely corrosive conditions or (ii) providing efficient protection against corrosion, it is necessary to have a basic understanding of corrosion behaviour.

4.4 CLASSIFICATION (TYPES OF CORROSION)

The corrosion of metals and alloys is due to either chemical or electro-chemical reactions between a metal surface and the medium or environment.

Although corrosion occurs in many ways depending upon the corrosive environment, these may be broadly classified into (i) Dry corrosion or Direct chemical corrosion and (ii) Wet corrosion or Electro-chemical or immersed corrosion.

Dry corrosion occurs at a gas-metal interface and the reaction is a chemical combination between the metal and an oxidising component of its environment.

The wet corrosion occurs at solution - metal interface and is the result of electro-chemical reaction between a metal and its surroundings.

In both cases, the reactions take place at the interfaces of metal and surrounding; and the rate of reaction is modified by the properties of the corrosion products i.e. metallic compounds that are formed as a result of corrosion. The formation, destruction or removal and reformation of naturally occurring film on the surface of metals at the site of corrosion reaction largely affects the rate of corrosion and corrosion control.

4.5 DRY OR DIRECT CHEMICAL CORROSION

In this type of corrosion, the metal is surrounded by gases such as oxygen, halogen, sulphur dioxide, hydrogen sulphide, etc. in the surrounding environment and as a result, corrosion occurs mainly through the direct chemical action of environment or atmospheric gases with the metal surfaces in immediate proximity.

"Dry corrosion is a phenomenon involving direct chemical reactions between metal and a gas or liquid, which is not an electrolyte."

This type of corrosion produces two important effects on the metal (a) metal is consumed and (b) the properties of the metal are changed.

The extent of dry corrosion depends upon the following factors :

- Chemical affinity between the corrosive environment and solid metals.
- Capacity or ability of reaction products to form a protective film on the metal surface.

There are three types of dry corrosions depending on the corrosive environment : (a) Oxidation corrosion, (b) Corrosion by other gases and (c) High temperature corrosion.

4.6 OXIDATION CORROSION

It is brought about by the direct action of oxygen at allow or high temperatures on metals, usually, in the *absence of moisture*. At ordinary temperatures metals, in general, are very slightly attacked. However, alkali metals (Li, Na, K etc.) and alkaline earths (Be, Mg, Ca, Sr etc.) are even rapidly *oxidised at low temperatures*. At high temperatures, almost all metals (except noble metals viz. Ag, Pt, Au) are oxidised.

Mechanism of Oxidation :

The reactions in the oxidation corrosion are :

$$2\,M \longrightarrow 2\,M^{n+} + 2\,ne^- \qquad\qquad \text{[Oxidation or loss of electron]}$$
$$\text{(Metal ion)}$$

$$2\,ne^- + O_2 \longrightarrow nO^{2-} \qquad\qquad \text{[Reduction or gain of electron]}$$
$$\text{Oxide ion}$$

$$\text{Overall :} \quad 2\,M + O_2 \longrightarrow 2\,M^{n+} + nO^{2-}$$
$$\text{[Metal oxide]}$$

The oxidation occurs first at the surface of the metal and the resulting metal oxide layer forms a barrier that tends to restrict further oxidation. The gas molecules are *adsorbed* rapidly by the surface of the metal as molecules, atoms or ions and then diffusion of gas in metal takes place. The gas molecules are held by the molecules of the metal through the residual valency of surface molecules. This layer of adsorbed gas is only one molecule thick.

When the temperature rises, the *adsorption*, which is a purely physical phenomenon, turns into *chemisorption* and the gas molecules dissociate into atoms and a solid or liquid reaction product is formed on the surface. The reaction continues as these freshly formed atoms or ions diffuse into the metal lattice at isolated points and form oxide lattice. In the case of oxygen, oxide film is formed, in the case of H_2S, sulphide is formed.

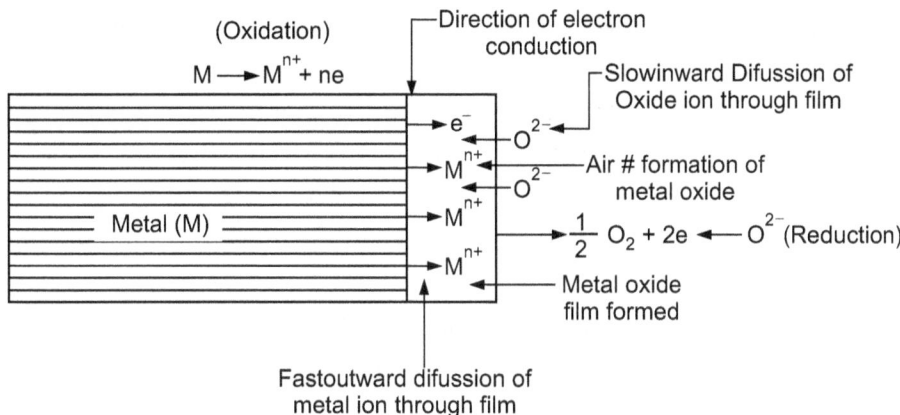

Fig. 4.3 : Mechanism of oxidation

For oxidation to continue, either the metal must diffuse outwards through the film to the surface or the oxygen must diffuse inwards through the film to the underlying metal. The metal cations are appreciably smaller than the oxygen ions (anions) and therefore, cations have much higher mobility. Thus the outward diffusion of metal is generally much more rapid than the inward diffusion of oxygen.

The nature of the oxide formed plays an important role in oxidation corrosion process –

Metal + Oxygen $\longrightarrow$ Metal oxide (corrosion product)

When oxidation starts, a thin layer of oxide is formed on the metal surface, and the nature of this layer of film decides the further action. (A layer is called film, when its thickness is less than 300 A and it is called scale, if its thickness exceeds 300 A). (1 A $= 10^{-8}$ cm)

4.7 NATURE OF FILMS

The film formed may be unstable, volatile or stable.

Unstable : The oxide film may be *unstable*, which decomposes back into the metal and oxygen.

Metal oxide $\rightleftharpoons$ Metal + Oxygen

Therefore, oxidation corrosion is not possible in such cases. e.g. silver, platinum, gold etc. do not undergo oxidation corrosion. In the case of noble metals, e.g. platinum oxide formed is unstable and so there will be no corrosion.

Volatile : The oxide film volatilizes as soon as it is formed; thereby leaving the underlying metallic surface exposed for further attack. This causes rapid and continuous corrosion, leading to excessive corrosion. e.g. molybdenum oxide (MoO_3) is volatile.

Stable : A stable layer, fine grained in structure which can get adhered tightly to the metal surface. Such type of layer or film may cut off the penetration or diffusion of oxygen into the underlying metal and seals the metal surface from any further attack of atmospheric oxygen. Such a protective film act as a shield for metal surface and prevents futher oxidation corrosion. The oxide films formed on the surface of most of the metals like Al, Pb, Cu, Sn etc., are stable and protective, adhering and impervious in nature and consequently prevent further oxidation corrosion.

The stable films formed on metallic surfaces may be further divided into three types (a) stable but porous, (b) stable, non-porous and tenacious, (c) stable, non-porous but brittle.

(a) Stable but porous : The film of the product formed, which cannot completely cover the metallic surface forms a porous film. Therefore, the atmospheric oxygen has an access through the pores to diffuse into the underlying surface of metal. This causes serious corrosion.

According to *Pilling-bedworth rule*, "an oxide is *protective* or *non-porous*, if the volume of the product (oxide in this case) is at least equal in volume to that of the metal from which it is formed." On the other hand, "If the volume of the product is less than the volume of the metal from which it is formed then the layer or film formed is *porous* (i.e. non-continuous) and hence *non-protective*; because it cannot prevent the access of oxidising substance (oxygen in this case) to the fresh metallic surface below."

$$\text{Pilling-Bedworth ratio} = \frac{\text{Volume of oxide}}{\text{Volume of metal forming the oxide}}$$

$$= \frac{\text{Mole weight of oxide/density of oxide}}{\text{Mole weight of metal/density of metal}}$$

If P.B. ratio > 1, film is stable and protective

If P.B. ratio > 1, film is unstable and non-protective

If P.B. ratio > 2, again unstable due to compressive stresses.

Alkali metals (such as Li, Na, K etc.) and alkaline earth metals (such as Be, Mg, Ca etc.) form oxides which have smaller volumes than the metals from which they are formed. Hence the oxide formed on the surface is porous in nature and this porosity of oxide films does not offer any resistance to oxygen of the surroundings and easily allows the oxygen to diffuse into the metal. In general, oxides which are porous in nature and occupy less volume than the metal itself offer no protection to the surface of the metal and the metal is, therefore, easily corroded even at low temperatures.

(b) Stable, non-porous and tenacious : The film of the product may be non-porous and tenacious which built upto certain thickness. In such cases, the rate of corrosion decreases with time. This type of corrosion is common in most of the metals.

Metals like aluminium forms oxide whose volume is greater than the volume of metal (Al) and an extremely tightly-adhering non-porous layer is formed. Due to the absence of any pores or cracks in the oxide film, it forms a barrier for further action and hence, the rate of oxidation is rapidly decreased to zero.

(c) Stable, non-porous but brittle : In some cases, non-porous product i.e. film may be brittle and may crack after sometime. Hence deeper corrosion may take place in such cases.

Heavy metals form an oxide film which is continuous and does not allow the atmospheric oxygen to diffuse into the metal so easily. These oxide films, therefore, offer resistance to process of oxidation and protect the metal from corrosion. The rate of thickening of these oxide films follows a decreasing parabolic growth law, but the film of oxide is under great lateral compression, as a result of which these oxide films have a tendency to crack. This tendency of cracking increases with increase in thickness, especially at high temperatures. Hence when there are fluctuations in temperature, the film may crack and the oxidation which has stopped because of thickness of oxide layer, may once again increase. This goes on intermittently.

If the temperature is very high, the oxygen diffuses into the metal through the intervening layer of oxide and the metal also diffuses outwards through the oxide film. Thus diffusion occurs both ways. The composition of the scale varies in composition from layer to layer. Iron and iron-rich alloys provides example of this type.

4.8 CORROSION BY OTHER GASES

Whether corrosion of a metallic surface by other gases such as SO_2, CO_2, Cl_2 etc. will take place or not, depends on their chemical affinity for the metal under consideration and the intensity of attack depends on the nature of the film formed on the metallic surface, i.e. protective or non-protective. e.g. AgCl film formed due to the attack of chlorine on silver is protective i.e. non-porous which decreases the intensity of attack. While when chlorine acts on tin surface the $SnCl_4$ formed being volatile leaves and the metal surface is exposed for further attack. This results in gradual but complete destruction of the tin metal.

Hydrogen embrittlement is the action of atomic hydrogen formed as a result of chemical or electrolytic action, occurring at metal surfaces under specific environments. For example, in petroleum industry, the presence of aqueous solutions of H_2S in the system causes evolution of atomic hydrogen at the steel surface and forming a troublesome FeS scale at ordinary temperature.

$$Fe + H_2S \longrightarrow FeS + 2H$$

The evolved atomic hydrogen readily diffuses and collects in the voids or larger faults in the metal. In these voids, the atomic hydrogen recombines to form entrapped molecular hydrogen.

$$H + H \longrightarrow H_2$$

As this diffusion and accumulation of molecular hydrogen continues, a high pressure is built up. If this pressure exceeds the yield strength of the metal then blistering and fissures occur which results in lowering the strength and ductility of the metal. At times, this may result in embitterment of the metal.

At high temperatures, the atomic hydrogen is formed by the thermal dissociation of molecular hydrogen. This atomic hydrogen which is chemically very active at high temperature readily combines with C, S, O and N (which are normally present in small quantity in metals). When it reacts with carbon of steel, methane (CH_4) gas is formed which develops intergranular cracking, blistering etc. This is called *'decarburization.'* Decarburization causes brittleness and reduction in strength of the steel.

4.9 HIGH TEMPERATURE CORROSION

The scaling of metals which takes place at elevated temperatures under dry conditions is known as high temperature corrosion.

At ordinary temperatures, the stable state of most metals is in the form of an oxide. This can be seen from Table 4.1, which lists the free energy of formation of one mole of different oxides at 25 C.

Table 4.1 : Free energy of formation of metal oxides (kJ mol^{-1})

Metal oxide	Free energy of formation	Metal oxide	Free energy of formation
Al_2O_3	− 1576	NiO	− 217
Cr_2O_3	− 1045	Cu_2O	− 145
TiO_2	− 853	Ag_2O	− 13
Fe_2O_3	− 740	Au_2O_3	+ 163

Except in the case of gold, the free energy change is negative, indicating that the stable form is the oxide. Only gold occurs in the metallic form in nature. All other metals are to be reduced to the metallic state by an extraction process. While using most metals in the metastable state, we depend on the fact that the thermal energy at the service temperature will be small enough to keep the oxidation rate within the desired limits. As the service temperature increases, the oxidation becomes a serious problem.

The rate of oxidation of a metal at an elevated temperature depends on the nature of the oxide layer that forms on the metal surface. For good oxidation resistance *the oxide layer should be adherent to the surface.* The adherence of an oxide film is dependent on the ratio of the volume of oxide formed to that of metal consumed during oxidation. This ratio is known as the Pilling - Bedworth ratio. If the ratio is less than unity, tensile stresses will be set up in the oxide layer. The oxide being brittle cannot withstand tensile stresses, therefore, it cracks and does not remain protective against further oxidation. While if the ratio is more than unity, the oxide layer will be in compression and will cover the metal surface uniformly and becomes protective. If the ratio is much greater than unity, there is a risk of too much compressive stresses being set up and again cracking the layer.

Table 4.2 : Pilling - Bedworth ratio for some oxides

Metal oxide	Ratio	Metal oxide	Ratio
Fe_2O_3	2.16	Al_2O_3	1.38
Cr_2O_3	2.03	MgO	0.79
Cu_2O	1.71	Na_2O	0.58
NiO	1.60	K_2O	0.41

When a metal is subjected to alternate heating and cooling cycles in service, the relative thermal expansion of the oxide and the metal also determines the stability of the protective layer. Thermal shock caused by rapid heating or cooling may cause the layer to crack. If the oxide layer is volatile as is the case with molybdenum and tungsten oxides at high temperatures, there can be no protection.

When the oxide layer is adherent to the metal surface, further oxidation can take place only by means of *diffusion through the oxide layer* of the oxygen anions or the metal cations. When the diffusion of the oxygen anions controls the oxidation rate then oxidation takes place at the metal-oxide interface. If the metal cations diffuse through the oxide layer in the opposite direction then oxidation takes place at the oxide-oxygen interface. As the oxide layer increases in thickness, the diffusion distance through the layer also increases.

The thickness of the layer increases as the square root of time at constant temperature.

$$x = \sqrt{Dt}$$

where x = increase in thickness

D = Diffusion coefficient

t = time

This is called the parabolic law of oxidation. Many metals obey the parabolic law at some temperature range of oxidation. The square of the layer thickness is proportional to the diffusion coefficient. The diffusion coefficient increases with temperature in an exponential manner. Correspondingly, the oxidation rate also increases exponentially with temperature. According to Arrhenius equation as -

$$k = A\, e^{-(E/RT)}$$

where k = rate of corrosion, A = frequency factor

E = activation energy, R = gas constant

T = absolute temperature.

Hence as the temperature increases, problem of metal protection also aggravates rapidly. The activation energy for oxidation is the same as the activation energy for diffusion through the oxide layer.

If the Pilling - Bedworth ratio is much greater than unity, the oxide layer tends to crack on reaching a critical thickness. This mainly happens when the oxidation process occurs at the metal - oxide interface, where the expansion cannot be accommodated as easily as at the oxide - gas interface. When the excess layer beyond the critical thickness peels off, the oxidation rate becomes constant indicating a constant critical oxide thickness at the metal surface.

The oxidation resistance of a metal can be improved by the addition of suitable alloying elements to the base metal. The alloying element must be present in sufficient concentration to produce the desired oxide layer. The most common alloying elements *added to iron* for this purpose are Cr, Al and Ni. The oxidation rate of iron as a function of chromium content is shown in Fig. 4.4. The rate decreases with increasing chromium content. The addition of chromium enables the formation of a thin protective layer of Cr_2O_3 on the surface of iron.

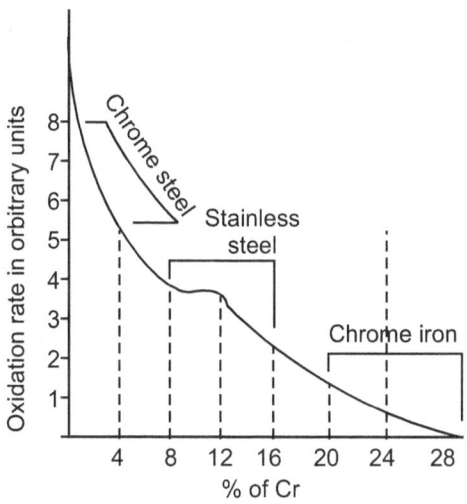

Fig. 4.4 : Oxidation rate of Fe as a function of % Cr

For oil refinery components upto 10 % Cr is alloyed with iron. Alloys with greater than 12 % Cr are called stainless steels which are used for turbine blades, furnace parts and valves of I.C. engines 12% Cr in steel gives excellent corrosion resistance upto 1000°C ; while for resistance above 1000° C, 17 % Cr is used, 18 - 8 stainless steel containing 18 % Cr and 8 % Ni is best commercially available oxidation - resistant alloys. *Kanthal* with 24 % Cr; 5.5 % Al and 2 % Co added to Iron is used for furnace windings upto 1300 C. *Inconel* with 76 % Ni; 16 % Cr and 7 % Fe has excellent oxidation resistance and good mechanical properties *Chromel*, (10 % Cr alloyed with Ni) and *alumel*, (2 % Al; 2 % Mn; 1 % Si alloyed with Ni) are used upto 1100 C as heat resistant thermocouple wires.

Another form of high-temperature corrosion occurs when liquid metals flow past other metals. This type of corrosion occurs in soaking pits for molten metals, reheating furnaces and heat-exchangers carrying liquid metal coolants used in nuclear power systems. The corrosion reaction in this case is essentially a process of mass transfer and is not dependent upon local cell potentials for its driving force. Actually, the corrosion is due to the tendency of the solid to dissolve in the liquid metal upto the solubility limit at the given temperature.

The liquid - metal attack may either form a simple solution of the solid metal, a chemical compound or be the selective extraction of one of the component metals in a solid alloy. This occurs when there is a temperature or concentration gradient within the solid - liquid system. Serious damage by liquid-metal attack is observed in heat exchangers carrying (Bi and Na) liquid coolants. As the solid container usually copper tubing, approaches equilibrium with the liquid - metal coolant in the hot zone of the heat exchanger, a portion of solid container dissolves in liquid-metal coolant. When this coolant liquid-metal moves towards the cooler parts of the heat-exchanger, the solubility limit decreases and therefore, some of the dissolved solid metal is thrown out, which deposits on the inner walls at cooler end. Thus because of temperature gradient within the solid-liquid system, the exchanger tube at the hot zone gets corroded and the cold end gets plugged with the corrosion product. This may result in shut down of liquid-metal heat-exchangers if proper precaution is not taken.

The life of heat exchangers can be prolonged by the addition of certain inhibitors to the liquid alloy coolant to form protective films to prevent high temperature corrosion.

4.10 WET OR ELECTRO-CHEMICAL CORROSION

Though electro-chemical mechanism is followed during corrosion still it is customary to classify the different corrosion reactions into a few general types depending on the special situations in which these occur. e.g. (1) Immersed corrosion, (2) Galvanic corrosion, (3) Concentration cell corrosion, (4) Pitting corrosion, (5) Intergranular corrosion, (6) Water line corrosion, (7) Stress corrosion, (8) Soil corrosion etc.

In all these cases to follow the electro-chemical mechanism, the following factors are essential :

- Formation of anodic and cathodic areas separated by finite distance.
- A conducting medium called electrolyte to maintain good electrical contact between anodic and cathodic areas.
- A potential difference between anodic and cathodic areas (These may be two dissimilar metals or two different areas on the surface of the same metal or alloy) to maintain a constant flow of electric current.

Anodic and cathodic areas are developed on the metal surfaces due to the structural and chemical inhomogeneity existing in metals and environments.

Anode or anodic area is that portion of the metal surface which is corroded (i.e. oxidised or loses electrons) and dissolves as ions. From anode current (electrons) leaves the metal and enters the electrolyte.

Cathode or cathodic area is that portion of the metal surface from where the electron current leaves the electrolyte and enters or returns to the metal. Here the metal is not affected as reduction takes place.

As both anodic and cathodic areas are immersed in the electrolyte hence electrical balance of the system is restored by the reaction between electrons and the positive ions in the electrolyte.

On prolonged corrosion, the metal would deteriorate over the complete surface as the anodic and cathodic areas interchange during the actual corrosion.

4.10.1 Basic Principles

(a) Electrochemical cells :

An electrochemical cells is one in which channel reactions generate electricity. The essential components of an electro-chemical cell are electrolyte (ionic conductor), anode, cathode and external circuit (electronic conductor). In electro-chemical cells at cathode reduction reaction occurs while oxidation reaction occurs at anode.

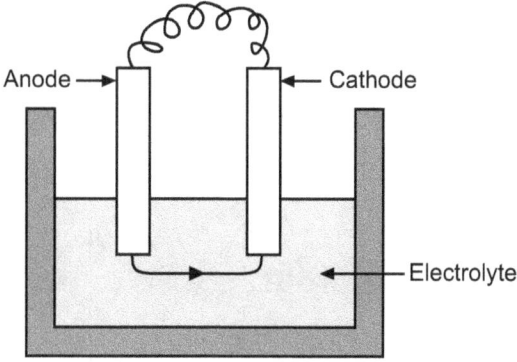

Fig. 4.5 : Electro-chemical cell

(b) Electrode potential :

If an electrode is immersed in an electrolyte contained its own ions, two types of reactions (1) oxidation i.e., dissolution of metal electrode ($M \rightarrow M^{n+} + ne$) and (2) reduction i.e., deposition of metal ion at the electrode ($M^{n+} + ne \rightarrow M$) occur. Due to these reactions the electrodes acquires a charge i.e., it will acquire a negative charge (anode) when metal dissolution reaction occurs at its surface and acquire a positive charge (cathode) when metal deposition reaction occurs. These reactions continue till equilibrium is established between the electrode surface and electrolyte. This difference of electrical potential between electrode and electrolyte is termed as single electrode potential or half cell potential.

To measure a single electrode potential, it is connected by another half cell, so that potential difference between the two electrodes can be measured. Thus, relative value of single electrode potential with respect to another electrode which is called reference electrode can be measured. This reference electrode is a standard hydrogen electrode whose potential is taken to be zero.

The standard electrode potentials at 25°C for various metals with reference to hydrogen are listed in Table 4.3.

Table 4.3: The e.m.f. or galvanic series

Elements	Elecctrode potential at 25°C (volts) anode	
Li	+ 3.02	Anode
K	+ 2.92	(Active)
Na	+ 2.72	
Mg	+ 2.34	
Al	+ 1.67	↑
Zn	+ 0.76	Chemical
Cr	+ 0.56	activity
Fe	+ 0.44	increases
Pb	+ 0.12	
H_2	0.00 (Reference)	
Cu	− 0.34	
Ag	− 0.80	Cathode
Au	− − 1.70	(noble)

Gold is the most noble metal and will not dissolve easily and hence has outstanding corrosion resistance. Lithium at the top of the list is the most active metal and hence exhibit poor corrosion resistance.

If two different metals are coupled together in the same electrolyte, the metal with the more positive potential will suffer corrosion.

(c) Galvanic cells :

A galvanic cells is formed. When two dissimilar metals are in electrical contact with each other and are dipped in an electrolyte. Fig. 4.6 shows a galvanic cell in which zinc and iron electrodes are dipped in an electrolyte solution ($FeCl_2$) and are electrically connected.

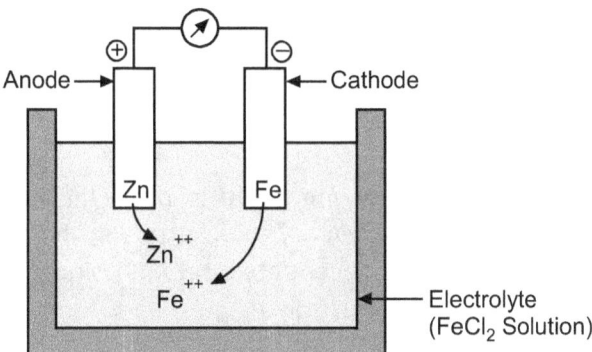

Fig. 4.6 : Galvanic cell

When two dissimilar metals are electrically connected, the metal higher in the electromotive series (Table 4.2) corrodes and becomes anode. The metal which is lower in the series becomes cathode. In this case zinc electrode, acts as anode and iron electrode acts as cathode. The dissolution of zinc (anode) takes place as per the reaction

$$Zn \rightarrow Zn^{++} + 2e$$

These electrons move through the electrolyte to the iron electrode (cathode). Hence, zinc dissolves and iron is protected.

The potential difference between the electrodes and the ratio of the areas of cathode to the anode controls the rate of galvanic corrosion. Corrosion rate will be very high if the difference in potential and/or the ratio of cathode to anode areas, is more.

Types of galvanic cells :

There are three types of galvanic cells :

    (i) Composition cells.

    (ii) Concentration cells.

    (iii) Stress cells.

(i) Composition cells :

The best examples of composition cell is galvanized steel i.e. coating of zinc on steel. The zinc coating which is less noble than iron serves as anode and iron serves as cathode. Hence, iron is protected even if it is exposed to atmosphere whereas the zinc coating is peeled off.

Other examples of composition cells are :

•   Steel screws in brass.

- Steel shaft in bronze bearings.

- Lead-tin solder around the wire.

(ii) Concentration cells :

When two electrodes of same metal are immersed in the same electrolyte with different concentrations, a concentration cell is formed. The electrode in the dilute solution is anodic with respect to the electrode in the concentrated solution since the electrode potential depends upon the concentration of the electrolyte.

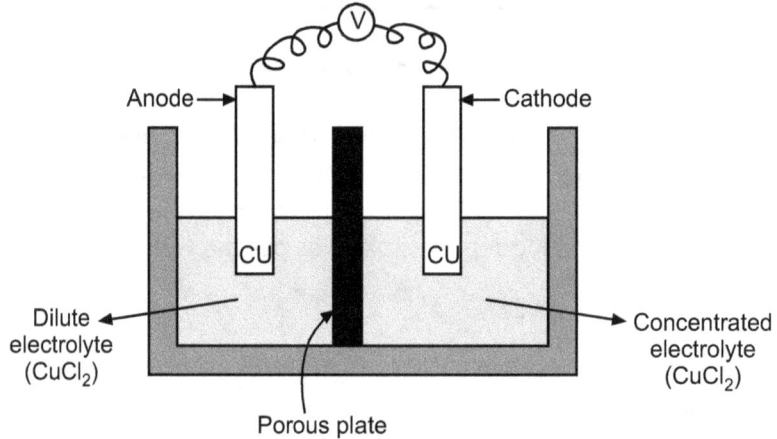

Fig. 4.7 : Concentration cell

(iii) Stress cells :

Stress cells are formed due to residual stresses which are induced during cold working of metals. The over-stressed region is more active and becomes anode with respect to a stress free region.

In polycrystalline materials, stress cells are also formed because the atoms at the grain boundaries will have a different electrode potential than the interior atoms. Usually the grain boundaries are anodic to the interior of the grains.

4.11 MECHANISM OF WET OR ELECTRO-CHEMICAL CORROSION

Corrosion of metallic surfaces in aqueous solutions or moist conditions is electro-chemical phenomenon associated with electron flow (electric current) between anodic and cathodic areas. *Reaction at anode* is the dissolution of metal and formation of corresponding ions, while *at cathode* either hydrogen gas is evolved or oxygen is absorbed depending on the nature of corrosive environment.

Depending on the nature of metallic component and the surrounding medium, the wet corrosion takes place by either of the following two ways :

1. By Hydrogen evolution mechanism or

2. By Oxygen absorption mechanism.

4.11.1 Hydrogen Evolution Mechanism

Corrosion by hydrogen evolution mechanism takes place in acidic environments (pH $\leq$ 4) such as acid industrial waters, solutions of non-oxidising acids (HCl), and where the concentration of dissolved oxygen is low.

Here, simply the displacement of hydrogen ions from the solution by metal ions takes place. Therefore, all metals which are above hydrogen in the electrochemical series will have a tendency to corrode in acid solution by this mechanism. The anode areas, in this type of attack, are very large areas while the cathode areas are small areas or points.

This is due to the fact that iron surface is covered with oxide film which causes difference in hydrogen overpotential at few points. Therefore, some areas act as cathode and some as anode.

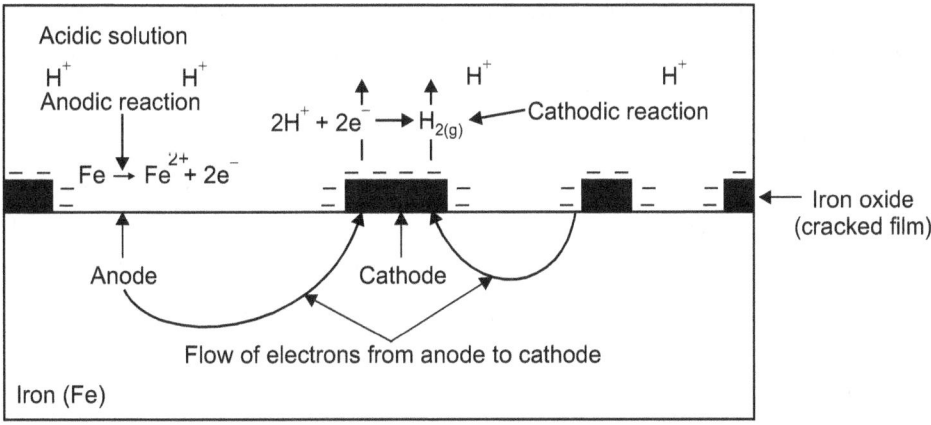

Fig. 4.8 : Hydrogen evolution mechanism

The reactions taking place at anode and cathode areas are as below.

At anode, metal goes into the solution as ions :

$$M \longrightarrow M^{+n} + ne^-$$

At cathode, elimination of hydrogen takes place :

$$2\,H^+ + 2e^- \longrightarrow H_2 \uparrow$$

The overall reaction can be written as :

$$M + 2nH^+ \longrightarrow M^{+n} + nH_2 \uparrow$$

Thus flow of electrons takes place from large anodic areas to small cathodic areas where hydrogen gas is evolved.

For example, a steel tank, containing acid industrial waste and small piece of copper scrap in contact with the steel, will undergo corrosion by hydrogen evolution mechanism. The portion of the steel tank in contact with copper is corroded most. The reactions are :

$$Fe \rightarrow Fe^{++} + 2\,e^- \text{ (At anode)}$$

$$H^+ + e^- \rightarrow H \text{ (At cathode)}$$

$$H + H \rightarrow H_2 \uparrow \text{ (At cathode)}$$

Overall reaction : $\quad Fe + 2\,H^+ \rightarrow Fe^{2+} + H_2 \uparrow$

The concentration of Fe^{2+} ions increases at anode and hydrogen overpotential at cathode which reduces the potential difference and the rate of corrosion. Hence severity of such type of corrosion is less.

4.11.2 Oxygen Absorption Mechanism

Corrosion by this mechanism proceeds in mild acidic; alkaline or neutral environment (pH > 4) and when the dissolved oxygen is present in electrolyte. For example, iron and steel plate is corroded in neutral aqueous solutions of electrolytes (NaCl solution) in the presence of atmospheric oxygen.

Consider a steel plate lying on the ground exposed to moist atmosphere. An oxide layer is formed on the surface of steel in due course of time, and drops of water may collect over the small cracks in the oxide film. Thus water acts as electrolyte, the cracks in oxide film as anode and the oxide-coated steel as cathode. The anodic area is restricted to small area of the crack while cathodic area is mostly the entire surface of the steel plate. Hence the total corrosion current is restricted to small area leading to a very strong localised attack on the exposed steel surface. The reactions at anode and cathode are as below :

At anode (crack) : (not covered with oxide film)

$$Fe \rightarrow Fe^{++} + 2\,e^-$$

$$Fe^{2+} + 2\,Cl^- \rightarrow FeCl_2$$

At large cathode (covered with oxide film) : The electrons flow from anode which are intercepted by oxygen atoms of atmosphere. These in presence of water drop form hydroxyl ions as below :

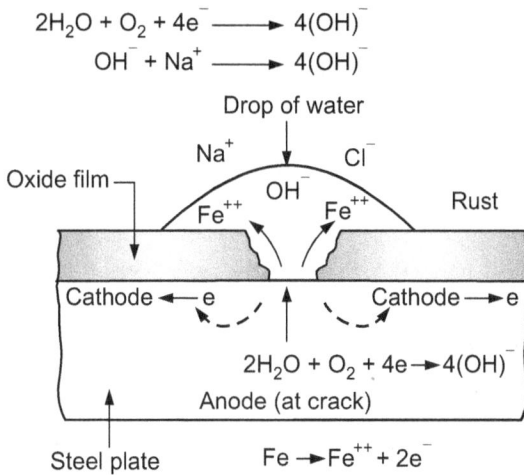

Fig. 4.9 : Oxygen absorption mechanism

Both anodic and cathodic products are water soluble and they diffuse towards each other. When they meet, $Fe(OH)_2$ (Brown) is formed; Fe^{2+} + 2 $(OH)^-$ $(\varnothing$ $Fe(OH)_2$; which in the presence of enough oxygen is converted to $Fe(OH)_3$ (Hard rust) which deposits as rust because it is less soluble.

If the supply of oxygen is not sufficient then the corrosion product is black anhydrous magnetite Fe_3O_4.

If anodic area is less then anodic current density is very high and under such conditions the process of corrosion is very rapid. If anodic area is covered by deposited rust, the process becomes slow or it stops due to repairing of film caused by deposition of rust.

4.12 FACTORS INFLUENCING THE RATE OF WET CORROSION

The rate of electrochemical corrosion is directly proportional to the electron flow from anodic area to cathodic area and this is further influenced by various factors as below :

4.12.1 Factors Related to the Metallic Surface : The Factors Depending on the Nature of the Metal or an Alloy are :

(a) Position of corroding metal in electrochemical series :

In the electrochemical series alkali metals or more active metals are at the top while the noble metals or less active metals are at the bottom. When two metals or alloys are in electrical contact in presence of an electrolyte (i.e. conducting medium), the more active metal (i.e. higher up in the series) suffers corrosion. However metals occupying bottom (i.e. having less tendency to lose electrons and form cations) possess little tendency to be oxidised to positive ions and hence, they are not easily corroded. The rate and severity of corrosion depends upon the difference in their positions and greater is the difference, faster is the corrosion of the anodic metal or alloy.

(b) Hydrogen over-voltage :

When two dissimilar metals are in electrical contact, certain extra voltage is needed to evolve hydrogen at a particular metallic cathode than that is needed to evolve hydrogen at platinum cathode. Depending upon the nature of cathodic metal, evolution of hydrogen is either slow or brisk. This evolved hydrogen forms a film around cathodic metal thereby developing back potential. The extra voltage is required to overcome this effect of back potential and is known as *"hydrogen overvoltage."*

If the metal has impurities having high value of hydrogen overvoltage, a back potential will be set up and corrosion will diminish or even stop. For example, iron containing impurities like lead or tin corrodes much slowly as compared to iron having impurities like copper or platinum.

Thus, *the presence of impurities with low hydrogen over-voltage increases the rate of corrosion while presence of impurities with high over-voltage decreases the rate of corrosion of a metal.*

(c) Relative areas of anodic and cathodic parts :

When two dissimilar metals or alloys are in electrical contact, the corrosion of the anodic part is directly proporitional to the ratio of areas of cathodic and anodic parts. Corrosion is more rapid, severe and localized, if the anodic area is smaller because in such case the current density is much greater. Larger cathodic area demands great number of electrons which can be met by smaller anode area only by undergoing fast corrosion. Thus anodic metal changes into metal ions more briskly, e.g. corrosion protective coating of Sn, Ni or Cr on Iron breaks even at few points, then the corrosion at these points is quite intense.

(d) Purity of metal :

Impurities when present in a metal generally cause 'heterogeneity' thereby forming tiny electro-chemical cells (at the exposed parts). e.g. zinc metal with lead or iron as impurity undergoes corrosion of zinc around the impurity. The rate and extent of corrosion increases as the exposure and percentage of impurities increase. Hence corrosion resistance of a metal can be increased or improved by increasing the purity of the metal.

(e) Physical state of metal :

The rate of corrosion is influenced by the physical state of a metal (such as grain size, uneven surface, stress etc.) The smaller the grain size of a metal or alloy, the greater will be its solubility and therefore, greater will be corrosion. This is called *grain boundary corrosion.*

Presence of uneven surface increases the corrosion rate. In such cases, the crests having more contact with air behaves as anode while the troughs or crevices having comparatively less contact with air behaves as cathode. This creates a potential difference between crests or peaks and troughs or crevices resulting in corrosion at anode i.e. crests. This type of corrosion is called *crevice corrosion* e.g. at rivetted joints, irregularities at the two metal joint gets corroded.

Similarly, the electrode potential of a strained metal is higher than that of annealed metal and hence, more strained (i.e. bent portion etc.) portion gets corroded.

(f) Nature of surface film :

In aerated atmosphere practically all metals get covered with a thin surface film (few angustrom thick) of metal oxide the thickness of which varies with the nature of the metal and environmental temperature. Metals such as Ca, Ba, Mg, Li, Na, K etc., form oxide films whose specific volume is less than that of the metal atom; hence the film formed will be porous.

$$2\,M \quad + \quad nO_2 \;\rightarrow\; 2\,M_2O_n$$

(More volume)   (Less volume)

———————— Contraction ————→

While metals like Al, Ni, W, Cr etc., form oxides whose specific volume is greater than the parent metal atom;

$$4\,M \quad + \quad nO_2 \;-\!\!\rightarrow\downarrow\; 2\,M_2O_n$$

(Less volume)   (More volume)

———————— Expansion ————→

hence the resulting oxide film formed is impervious (i.e. non-porous). Such a film protects the metal from further corrosion (i.e. oxidation).

Some metals like Al, Cr, Co, Mg, Ni, Ti etc., are passive metals. These metals exhibit high corrosion resistance than expected from their positions in electrochemical series or galvanic series. This is because of the formation of highly protective but very thin film (about $4 \infty 10^{-4}$ i.e. 0.0004 mm thick) of oxide on the surface of an alloy or metal. Further, the film is of self-healing nature (i.e. film if broken will repair or replenish itself) on re-exposure to oxidising conditions. The corrosion resistance of stainless steel is due to the passivating character of chromium present in stainless steel.

(g) Nature of corrosion product :

During corrosion of a metal or an alloy, films of corrosion products (e.g. oxides, carbonates, hydroxides of metals) are formed on the metallic surface. If the corrosion product is soluble in the corroding medium, it will be easily removed from the surface exposing the bare and fresh metallic surface for renewed attack by environment and this will increase corrosion. Whereas if the corrosion product is insoluble or sparingly soluble it can adhere to the metal surface thereby restricting further corrosion. Similarly, if the corrosion product formed interacts with the medium to form another insoluble product (e.g. $PbSO_4$ formation in case of Pb in H_2SO_4 solution) then the corrosion product will function as physical barrier thereby suppressing further corrosion.

4.12.2 Factors Related to the Environment

These are as follows.

(a) pH of the solution i.e. electrolyte :

If the solution or electrolyte is neutral (pH = 7) or alkaline (pH more than 7) then the rate of corrosion is retarded and in acidic solution
(pH less than 7) the rate of corrosion increases.

For example : The corrosion rate of iron in oxygen-free water is slow, until the pH is below 5. The corresponding corrosion rate in the presence of oxygen is much higher.
At pH = 4 the corrosion rate is enhanced due to oxidation of ferrous (Fe^{2+}) ions to ferric [Fe^{3+}] ions by the dissolved oxygen at the anodic area. Consequently, corrosivity of materials which are readily attacked by acids can be reduced by increasing the pH of the solution. Thus, Zn suffers minimum corrosion at pH = 11. Al has minimum corrosion rate around pH = 5.5.

(b) Temperature of electrolyte :

Ionisation and fluidity of the solution increases with rising temperature thereby increasing the corrosion rate e.g. caustic embrittlement takes place only at high temperatures in high pressure boilers.

(c) Humidity :

Humidity in air is also responsible for atmospheric corrosion. For example : Iron does not rust when exposed to dry air or moisture free air, but when exposed to humid or moist air iron undergoes rusting in a short time. The critical humidity
(i.e. the relative humidity above which the atmospheric corrosion rate of metal increases rapidly) depends upon the physical characteristics of the metal and the nature of corrosion products. The corrosion of the metallic surface is rapid in humid atmosphere because atmospheric gases such as CO_2, O_2, H_2O (vapour) etc. get dissolved in water and produce an electrolyte which sets up an electrochemical corrosion cell.

Further, the oxide film on the surface of a metal absorbs moisture though it is a solid body. In the presence of absorbed moisture on the surface, electrochemical corrosion is bound to occur. Rain water supplies moisture for electrochemical attack and at the same time washes away a part of the oxide film from the metallic surface causing enhanced atmospheric attack. Thus nature of source of mositure also plays an important part in electro-chemical corrosion.

(d) Presence of impurities in atmosphere :

The atmosphere in industrial area is contaminated with corrosive gases such as CO_2, H_2S, HCl, Cl_2, H_2SO_4 fumes etc. These gases increase the acidity of the liquid adjacent to the metallic surfaces so also electrical conductivity is increased. This increases the corrosion current flowing in the localized electrochemical cells on the exposed metallic surfaces. Similar in marine atmosphere, chlorides of sodium and other metal present in sea water increases the electrical conductivity of liquid layer in contact with the metallic surface; which results in increased and excessive corrosion of metallic surface.

(e) Presence of suspended particles in atmosphere :

Solid particles suspended in air are also responsible for corrosion. For example, chemically active particles such as NaCl, Na_2SO_4, $(NH_4)_2SO_4$ etc., are capable of absorbing moisture and thus, act as strong electrolytes which lead to enhanced corrosion. Similarly, chemically inactive particles such as charcoal particles which absorb moisture as well as gases like SO_2, SO_3 etc., and thus slowly enhance the rate of corrosion.

(f) Formation of oxygen concentration cell :

Differential aeration occurs when one part of the metal is exposed to a different air concentration than the other. The region where the oxygen concentration is smaller (e.g. oxide-coated part or less exposed part) becomes anodic; while more oxygen concentration regions [i.e. parts which are more exposed to air or oxygen] becomes cathodic. The more oxygenated and less oxygenated parts of metallic surface form "oxygen-concentration cell" in which the anodic part (less exposed) gets corroded. In other words, corrosion occurs where access to oxygen is least. This is known as "Differential aeration principle" given by Evans.

Some examples of corrosion by differential aeration are :

• When a pipe-line layed under ground passes through dry soil as well as moist soil, that part of pipe line passing through moist soil has restricted access to oxygen or air and thus, behaves as anodic while that part passing through dry soil has more access to air or oxygen and thus, becomes cathodic. This results in corrosion of pipe passing through moist soil.

• Water line corrosion is common in case of ships, water storage steel tanks, etc., where a portion of a metallic surface is below water and remaining portion is above water. The metallic portion at the water surface is in contact with more-oxygenated water while the metallic portion which is well below the water surface is in contact with less-oxygenated water. This results in the formation of cell where metallic portion well below water is anodic while the metal surface in contact at water level is cathodic. Thus corrosion of metallic surface just below the water level takes place.

• Oil-pipe lines are corroded at the joints if these are leaking. The oil film at the joint restricts the access for oxygen to the inner part and thus, corrosion starts just below the oil film.

• When rivets or bolts used for fixing plates of a metal are not sufficiently tight, a film of moisture may spread under these. Due to restricted access for air under the bolts or rivets severe corrosion starts below the rivets or bolts.

• Iron corrodes under drops of water or a salt solution. Areas covered with drops have less access for oxygen and therefore, become anodic with respect to the other areas which are freely exposed to air or oxygen. Thus the portion of iron which is covered by water drops corrodes.

Table 4.4 : Comparison between Dry and Wet corrosion :

Dry corrosion	**Wet corrosion**
1. This is due to direct chemical reaction.	1. This is due to electrochemical reaction.
2. It takes place in presence of atmospheric gases.	2. It takes place in presence of acidic, alkaline or neutral electrolyte.
3. Rate of corrosion is slow.	3. Rate of corrosion is high.
4. Product of corrosion is oxide, chloride, sulphide etc.	4. Product of corrosion depends on electrolyte and dissolved salts.
5. Anodic and cathodic areas not formed.	5. There is formation of anodic and cathodic areas.

4.13 ATMOSPHERIC CORROSION

The heaviest toll of corrosion of most metals and alloys in service is due to the atmospheric corrosion. The atmospheric corrosion is primarily due to the combined effect of (1) the oxide film formation, and (2) film breakdown.

Thus in atmospheric corrosion two types of reactions take place (a) Metal-gas type, and (b) Metal-liquid type.

The film formation is due to the oxidising action of air on the metal surface and if the oxide formed is continuous and protective the further attack is reduced. This follows the course of dry corrosion (oxidation corrosion).

The film break-down is due to electro-chemical action in presence of moisture or electrolyte on the metal surface. Cracks and discontinuities in the film produced will expose the fresh metal surface to the action of humid atmosphere. This will form localised corrosion cells. Then further corrosion will take place according to "Oxygen absorption mechanism" of wet corrosion.

The factors which decide the nature and extent of the atmospheric corrosion and corrosion products are as follows :

- The chemical affinity between the metallic surface and the corrosive environment.
- The nature of the film or scale formed on the metallic surface.
- Critical humidity value of the metal.
- Suspended particles (solid or liquid) in the atmosphere.
- Atmospheric impurities (industrial waste gases e.g. SO_2, H_2S etc.)

The first two factors are already discussed under "Dry corrosion."

Critical humidity value :

For breaking the film formed and electro-chemical corrosion to start, it is not necessary that dew point should reach. The reaction can occur far below the dew point, provided the critical humidity value is exceeded.

"The critical humidity for a metal is defined as the relative humidity above which rate of atmospheric corrosion of a metal sharply increases." This critical humidity value depends upon the physical characteristics of the metal as well as its corrosion products.

For example : Below 50 to 60 % relative humidity primary film of oxide gets formed on the iron surface. When relative humidity exceeds 60 % the primary oxide film on iron breaks and corrosion continues until a fine film of rust is formed on the surface of iron. This film is potentially active and therefore, if the relative humidity goes beyond 80 % there is a sudden increase in corrosion rate with the formation of usual red rust.

Suspended particles : There are three types of suspended particles :

- Essentially active (dissociating mineral salts) e.g. ammonium sulphate near towns and sodium chloride near sea.
- Essentially neutral but capable of absorbing active gases from the atmosphere such as various allotropes of carbon.
- **Neutral particles such as crystalline silica :** These have very little effect on corrosion because of their negligible capacity of absorption.

Industrial waste gases :

SO_2 is the most active and affects the atmospheric corrosion to large extent.

It has a tarnishing effect on copper and silver articles. Nickel articles are fogged in presence of SO_2 of atmosphere if the critical humidity value for nickel exceeds. Due to fogging a creamy white film is formed on nickel surface.

SO_2 combines with the essentially active suspended particles (if present in atmosphere) which get settled on the metal surface. Thus, SO_2 can start the corrosion of iron at the second critical humidity value (i.e. 80 %).

Similarly, if second type of suspended particles are present in atmosphere, these absorb sulphur dioxide thereby increasing its local concentration on the metal surface.
e.g., charcoal particles adsorb traces of sulphur dioxide and greatly increase the corrosion rate of iron articles.

4.14 IMMERSED CORROSION

When the metallic surfaces are dipped or immersed or put under the solution or electrolyte, the corrosion that takes place is called *immersed corrosion*. It takes the course of electro-chemical mechanism and corrosion rate is proportional to the electron flow. Thus electro-chemical cell is set up and anodic and cathodic areas are caused due to

- Physical difference which might have developed during fabrication.

- More than one phase if present in the metal.

- Due to differential aeration.

- Surface discontinuities due to crystal junctions etc.

Even very slight differences in the different parts of metal surface can start the electro-chemical corrosion.

The factors which influence the corrosion rate are as below :

(a) Metallic factors :

- Electrode potential

- Ease of hydrogen evolution

- Presence of different phases in the metallic surface.

(b) Environmental factors :

- Temperature

- Rate of supply of oxygen

- pH of solution

- Metal-ion concentration

- Conductivity of solution

- Nature and distribution of corrosion products

- Relative movement of metal and environment.

The mechanism of immersed corrosion is mostly hydrogen evolution at cathode.

4.15 PITTING CORROSION

When the corrosion is concentrated at some specific spots on the metal surface leaving the surrounding area practically unaffected, it is called *pitting corrosion*. It is called pitting because at the spots of attack pits, pin-holes or cavities are formed.

Pitting corrosion frequently ruins the tubes, pipes, vessels of various types.

It is due to the break-down of protective film on the metallic surfaces at some points. This forms a small anode and a large cathode and therefore, will follow the oxygen absorption mechanism. The protective film may break due to any of the following
reasons :

- Surface roughness,

- Scratches or cut-edges,

- Local straining,

- Sliding under load,

- Particular type of chemical attack,

- Presence of impurities such as sand, dust, scale etc. embedded on the metal surface.

Stainless steel and aluminium show pitting corrosion in chloride solutions.

Pitting tendency of stainless steel is decreased by the addition of 2 to 4 % of molybdenum.

4.16 UNIFORM CORROSION

In this type of corrosion a uniform decrease in volume of a metal takes place at a result of chemical action and soluble corrosion products are formed. In this type of corrosion, metal gets converted into soluble corrosion products at a constant rate which can be controlled to some extent. Under these conditions the useful life of a given material can be easily estimated and unexpected failure need not be feared. Uniform corrosive attack is rare, in practice. It is observed in metals like zinc, lead and aluminium.

4.17 GALVANIC CORROSION

When two dissimilar metals such as zinc and copper are electrically connected and exposed to electrolyte, the metal higher in the electrochemical series, i.e. zinc in the present case, undergoes corrosion and this type of corrosion is called *galvanic corrosion*. Zinc is higher in electrochemical series, hence forms anode and undergoes corrosion while copper, which is lower than zinc in electrochemical series, acts as cathode. The type of cathodic reactions depend on the nature of corrosive environment. The flow of electron current takes place from anodic zinc (undergoing corrosion) to the cathodic copper (remains unaffected).

At anode, $\qquad$ $Zn \rightarrow Zn^{++} + 2e^-$ (Oxidation)

At cathode, $\qquad$ $Cu^{++} + 2e^- \rightarrow Cu$ (Reduction)

Net cell reaction $\quad Zn + Cu^{++} \rightarrow Zn^{++} + Cu$

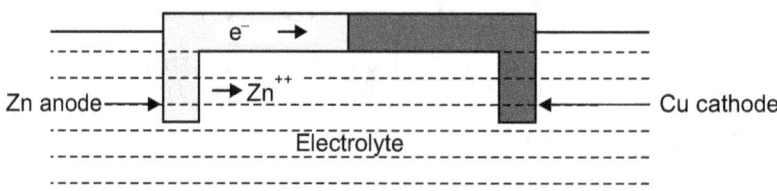

Fig. 4.10 : Galvanic corrosion

Steel screws in brass marine hardware, a steel propeller shaft in bronze bearing and lead-antimony solder around copper wire are some well known examples of galvanic corrosion.

4.18 SOIL CORROSION

Corrosion by soils is very important in case of water mains, electric cables and other underground structures, which are embedded in the soil. The corrosiveness of the soil depends upon the following factors : (i) its acidity, (ii) degree of aeration, (iii) electrical conductivity, (iv) content of moisture and salt, (v) texture of soil, (vi) presence of bacteria and micro-organisms.

- The corrosion in soil depends upon the content of oxygen, moisture and soluble matter. The greater the contents, greater is the corrosion.

- Corrosion increases with increase in the concentration of H^+ ions.

- Greater the electerical conductivity, greater is the corrosion.

- Certain types of bacterias in the soil are responsible for the oxidation of organic matter and other oxidisable matter and produce gases which may cause corrosion.

- Presence of strong currents may also stimulate electrolytic corrosion.

- Soil corrosion is purely electro-chemical in nature. The texture of soil is determined by the percentage of particles of various sizes. When the particle size is small, the corrosion is more.

The mechanism of soil corrosion is similar to hydrogen evolution corrosion, if the solids are acidic in nature. The rate of corrosion in acidic soils, depends upon the pH or acidity of the soil, the presence of salts and the content of oxygen etc.

If air pockets are present in the soil, differential aeration corrosion may take place in different parts of the pipeline buried underground.

4.19 INTERGRANULAR CORROSION   (Dec. 2012)

This type of corrosion takes place because of loss of coherence between the grains. It occurs along grain boundaries and only where the material is highly sensitive to corrosive attack. When the grain boundaries contain material which has more solution potential than the grain centre, in the particular environment, the intergranular attack takes place and produces serious damage only at the grain boundaries and leaves the grain interiors unattacked or only very slightly attacked. Intergranular corrosion may be regarded as localised corrosion and depends upon the metallic structure as well as on the conditions that exist at grain boundaries, and other internal discontinuities such as slip planes.

Intergranular corrosion follows the path of grain boundaries and takes place on microscopic scale without any evidence of intensive attack. Because of this, failures due to such corrosion occur without indicating any warning (due to loss of cohesion between grains). This type of corrosion causes brittleness or weakness in the underlying metal and is generally encountered in alloys.

Such corrosion is observed in defective welding and heat treatment of stainless steels; copper and aluminium alloys. Microscopic examination can show intergranular corrosion. It also has adverse effects on the mechanical properties of alloys.

4.20 WATERLINE CORROSION

This type of corrosion is also called as differential oxygen-concentration corrosion. It is generally observed that maximum corrosion takes place in a steel tank containing water along a line just below the level of water because access of oxygen is much less there. The area above the water line is highly oxygenated and hence acts as cathodic area. Consequently it is not corroded. However, little corrosion takes place when the water is relatively free from acidity. Waterline corrosion is also caused in marine ships and is accelerated by marine plants which are attached to the sides of ships. This type of corrosion can be prevented to a great extent by painting the sides of a ship by special anti-fouling paints.

At anode, $Fe \rightarrow Fe^{++} + 2e^-$

$$Fe^{++} + 2Cl^- \rightarrow FeCl_2$$

At cathode, $4e^- + O_2 + 2H_2O \rightarrow 4OH^-$

$$OH^- + Na^+ \rightarrow NaOH$$

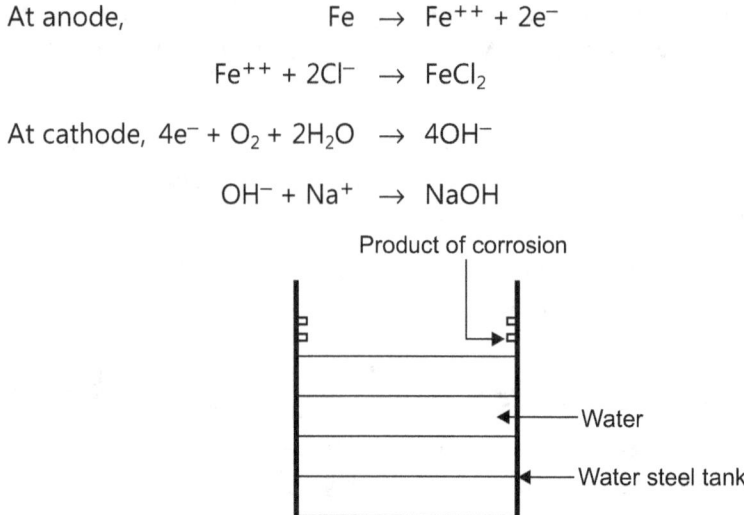

Fig. 4.11 : Water line corrosion

4.21 CREVICE CORROSION

It is a local corrosion usually created by dirt deposits, corrosion products, cracks in paint coatings etc. This is commonly observed near the gaskets, bolts, rivets, lap joints etc. Crevice corrosion is usually due to changes in acidity in the crevice, lack of oxygen in the crevice and concentration of detrimental ionic species in the crevice. Selection of resistant materials, proper design to minimize crevices and maintaining the surfaces clean are some of the control measures that can be taken to control crevice corrosion.

4.22 MICROBIOLOGICAL CORROSION

This type of corrosion is caused by metabolic activities of various micro-organisms and hence it is known as *microbiological corrosion*. The micro-organisms are either aerobic or anaerobic which develop in an environment with or without oxygen. The various micro-organisms responsible for corrosion failures due to their activities are sulphate reducing micro-organism or bacteria, sulphur bacteria, iron and manganese micro-organisms, film forming micro-organisms etc.

Sulphate reducing bacteria such as sporovobrio desulphuricous causes anaerobic corrosion of iron and steel as these bacterias grow in anaerobic conditions. They need oxygen as well as sufficient amount of sulphates for their growth. Their growth is maximum between pH 5 to 9 and temperatures of 20-30°C. The microbiological corrosion of iron under anaerobic conditions probably take the following course of reactions.

$$8\,H_2O \rightleftharpoons 8\,H^+ + 8\,(OH^-) \left.\vphantom{\begin{array}{c}1\\2\\3\end{array}}\right\}$$ (Anodic solution of iron)

$$4\,Fe + 8\,H^+ \rightleftharpoons 4\,Fe^{2+} + 8\,H$$

$$H_2SO_4 + 8\,H \rightleftharpoons H_2S + 4\,H_2O$$ (Depolarisation due to bacteria)

$$Fe^{2+} + H_2S \rightleftharpoons FeS + 2\,H^+ \left.\vphantom{\begin{array}{c}1\\2\\3\end{array}}\right\}$$ (Corrosion products)

$$3\,Fe^{2+} + 6\,(OH^-) \rightleftharpoons 3\,Fe(OH_2)$$

This corrosion is localised as well as rapid and the main corrosion products are FeS (Black) and ferrous hydroxide, $Fe(OH)_2$.

Iron and manganese micro-organisms are also aerobic in nature. They grow in running water as well as in stagnant water at temperatures between 5 to 35°C and pH ranging from 4 to 10 under aerobic (in presence of dissolved oxygen) conditions. They digest iron and manganese ions into their cells in presence of oxygen (aerobic) and form insoluble hydrates of iron and manganese dioxide (MnO_2). These products are thrown out of their bodies later on; which form a layer of corrosion product.

4.23 STRESS CORROSION

This type of corrosion is produced by the combined effect of mechanical stress and a corrosive environment on a metal. This is also known as a stress cracking.

Stress corrosion or stress cracking is common in fabricated articles of some alloys such as high zinc brasses and nickel brasses. It is due to the presence of stresses caused by heavy working like rolling, drawing or insufficient annealing. Stress corrosion is highly localized and the attack takes place when the overall corrosion is almost negligible.

The corrosion agents are highly specific and selective in case of stress corrosion. For example, mild steel is stress corroded by caustic alkalies and nitrate solutions while brass is stress corroded by traces of ammonia. Stainless steel is stress corroded by chloride solutions.

Stress corrosion is probably due to localised electro-chemical reactions, occurring along narrow paths forming local anodic and cathodic areas on the metal surface. Presence of stress gives rise to strain, which develops small localised zones of higher electrode potential. These zones become very reactive chemically and can be attacked even by traces of corrosive environment, resulting in the formation of cracks.

The most important factors involved in stress corrosion are :

1. Magnitude and direction of stress.

2. Specific environment and

3. Structure and composition of alloy.

The *magnitude* required for this type of corrosion is about 50% of the yield strength. The stress may be applied externally or it may be residual stress resulting from cold working, unequal cooling, or volume changes accompanied by internal structural arrangement.

For stress corrosion, different environments are required for different alloys. For example, season cracking of brass takes place only in the presence of traces of ammonia or amines.

Season cracking due to stress corrosion generally takes place in copper alloys such as brass. Pure copper does not undergo stress corrosion, but presence of small amounts of alloying elements such as zinc, aluminium, arsenic, phosphorus, antimony etc. make the copper susceptible to stress corrosion.

4.24 VELOCITY RELATED CORROSION

4.24.1 Impingement Corrosion or Erosion Corrosion

Erosion or impingement corrosion is due to the combined effect of corrosion and erosion i.e. abrasion produced by the impingement or strike of entrapped air bubbles, abrasive particles suspended in the liquid or turbulent flow of liquids. Impingement corrosion usually occurs in systems where fluid moves with high velocities. Failure of part in service may occur with faulty design and poor selection of construction materials.

Due to the impingement of fluid with very high velocity on the metal surface local breakdown of the protective oxide film takes place. This makes the contact point (from where the protective film has been broken) anodic with respect to the unbroken protective oxide film which acts as cathode. The rate of impingement corrosion is usually very high since the fast moving fluid stream causes depolarization of local anodes (corroding areas) by sweeping away corrosion product and depolarization of the local cathodes (non-corroding areas) y brining a plentiful supply of dissolved oxygen to them. This makes the bare metal to be more anodic and increases the impingement corrosion.

A few examples where impingement corrosion are corrosion in pumps, valves, turbine blades and tubes carrying sea water.

4.24.2 Cavitation Corrosion

It occurs due to the formation and collapse of vapour bubbles or cavities on or near the metal surface. Cavitation corrosion occurs in systems which are subjected to rapidly changing pressures because liquid bubbles will form and collapse during low and high pressure cycles respectively. High impact stress will be produced due to the collapse of the liquid bubble on or near the metal surface. And this stress is responsible for cavitation damage because when corrosive liquid (electrolyte) comes in contact with these pits, the corrosion effect is further accelerated. The mechanism of cavitation corrosion is shown in stepwise in Fig. 4.12.

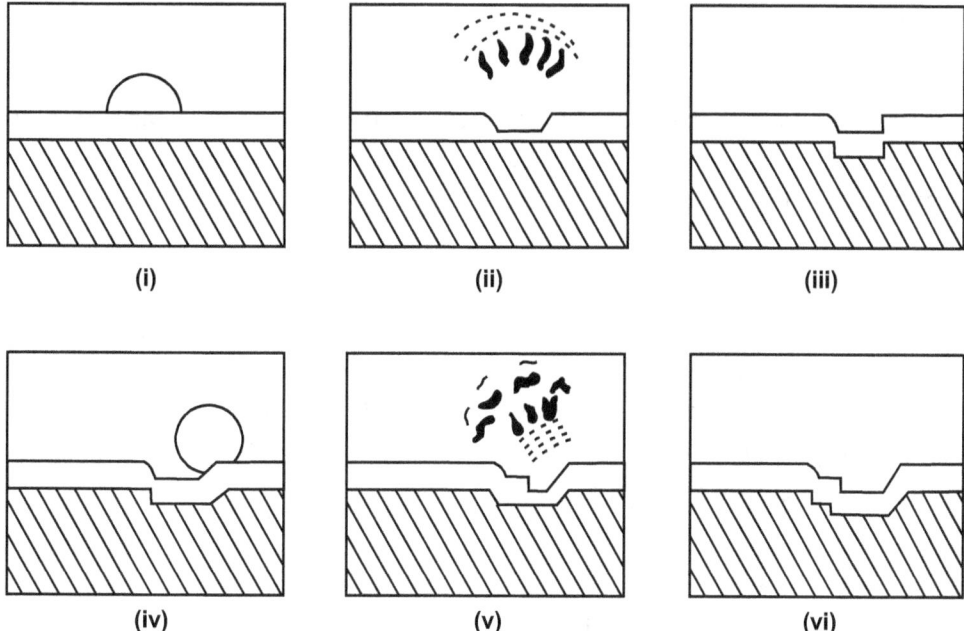

Fig. 4.12 : Mechanism of cavitation corrosion

Fig. 4.12 (i) - the formation of bubble on protective oxide film.

Fig. 4.12 (ii) – the collapse of the bubble which destroys the film.

Fig. 4.12 (iii) – the corrosion of newly exposed metal surface and the film reformation.

Fig. 4.12 (iv) – the formation of a new cavitation bubble at the same spot.

Fig. 4.12 (v) – the collapse of new bubble and the destruction of protective film.

Fig. 4.12 (vi) – the corrosion of newly exposed areas and the reformation of oxide film.

A few examples of cavitation corrosion re corrosion in marine propellars, hydraulic turbines, pump impellars and diesel engine cylinder.

4.24.3 Fretting Corrosion

This occurs at contact areas between two surfaces of materials which are subjected to vibration stresses. It is common at surfaces of clamped or press fits, keyways, engine bearings and bolted and rivetted joints.

Metal surfaces are usually protected from atmospheric oxidation by the formation of thin protective oxide layer. When two metals parts are placed ion contact under load and subjected to relative motion, the protective oxide film breaks at high stress points causing the surface to expose to the atmosphere. The exposed metal surface, under the action of vibrational stresses and corrosive atmosphere, tends to oxidize which results in fretting corrosion. In the case of steel, patches of finely divided ferric oxide appears as a result of fretting corrosion. Soft materials are usually more susceptible to fretting corrosion than hard materials.

Fretting corrosion destroys the dimensional accuracy of closely fitted parts, increases the susceptibility of fatigue of dynamically loaded machine parts and deteriorates the bearings surfaces, particularly the surface of ball roller bearing.

4.24.4 Corrosion Fatigue

Corrosion fatigue is due to the combined effect of fatigue stress and corrosive environment. The fatigue of the metal occurs well below the normal fatigue limit. Due to corrosion fatigue cracks in groups appear on the surface of the metal. Corrosive environment reduces the fatigue life to a large extent. The environments which produce pitting attack on the surface of the material cause corrosion fatigue.

A mechanism for corrosion fatigue takes places in two steps. In the first step due to corrosion, the pits of various depth are formed on the surface of metal. In the second stage, the cracks appear on the surface and further development of these cracks take place. This is due to the formation of concentration cell between the bottom of pits and the surface of the metal. Once a crack has been formed, it will spread rapidly due to the combined action of corrosion and alternate stress. Due to the applied alternate stress, the electrode potential of pit becomes more anodic than the electrode potential of the surface. And it is assumed that as the cracks increase in depth, the e.m.f. produced by the stress cells increases and the net result is the failure of metal by corrosion fatigue.

Damage ratio (D.R.) :

It gives the effect of corrosion of fatigue strength

$$\text{D.R.} = \frac{\text{Fatigue strength after corrosion}}{\text{Fatigue strength without corrosion}}$$

D.R. = 0.2 for carbon steels with salt water as corrosive medium

= 0.5 for stainless steels with salt water as corrosive medium

= 0.4 for aluminium alloys with slat water as corrosive medium

For examples, where failure occurs due to corrosion fatigue are marine propellar shaft, super heater tubes, rock drill in mines and turbines.

The most important protective measure against corrosion fatigue is treatment of the corroding medium and surface protection of the metal such as carburizing steel.

4.25 TESTING AND MEASUREMENT OF CORROSION

Measurement of corrosion is usually done for (1) Monitoring the corrosion process taking place, (2) Evaluating the quality of the material being used, or (3) For studying the mechanism of corrosion.

But one of the most difficult aspects of corrosion studies is the development of a means by which the relative resistance of different metallic surfaces to certain corroding media and conditions, can be evaluated. Since many variables are involved in the process of corrosion, it becomes practically impossible to devise a single test that will give results which are commensurable with service conditions.

The different methods generally used for the measurement of corrosion are :

(1) Weight-Loss Method :

Often a test is set up in the laboratory to show relative corrosion resistance of material as measured by loss of weight. In this test, a clean metallic standard test piece is measured, weighed and exposed to corroding media for a known time. Then the piece is taken out, cleaned to remove the corrosion products and reweighed. The rate of corrosion, of the material piece is calculated by using the equation,

$$R = \frac{K \cdot W}{D \cdot A \cdot T}$$ where K = constant, W = loss in weight in milligrams, D = density of the

material in g/cm^3, A = surface area of test piece in sq. cm., T = time of exposure nearest to 1/100th of an hour. The results are generally expressed in millimeters per year [MPY] or milligrams per square decimeter per day [$mg \cdot dm^{-2} \cdot d^{-1}$]. Assuming that the surface corrosion was uniform, these units can be converted to depth of corrosion.

(2) Electrical Resistance Method :

This method is employed for materials to be used in the form of thin wire or strip and the property used is 'Electrical resistance increases as the corrosion decreases the cross-section of metallic material.' Hence, periodic or continuous measurement of the resistance between the ends of a specimen can be used to monitor the corrosion. The electrical resistance measurement has nothing to do with the electro-chemistry of corrosion reaction. Here, only the bulk property is measured which depends on the cross-sectional area of the material.

(3) Corrosometer Method :

Corrosometer measures the change in resistance of a standard probe as corrosion converts the metal to a corrosion product. A second reference probe covered with a highly corrosion-resistant coating is connected to a bridge arrangement. The ratio of the resistance of corroding test piece to the resistance of its non-corroding counterpart (reference probe) is directly related to the extent of corrosion.

By this method, corrosion rates can be measured, without removing the metallic material from its position and without interrupting the process. Hence changes due to corrosion can be detected early and remedial measures can be initiated.

4.26 PROTECTION FROM CORROSION

Because of enormous quantities of iron and steel rendered unserviceable by corrosion every year, the problem of preventing corrosion is important to metallurgists and engineers.

Certain metals such as aluminium and magnesium withstand atmospheric corrosion well because of the formation of an impervious layer on the surface of the metal which prevents further corrosion. Iron rust, on the other hand, is a porous, loosely adherent mass which not only permits the corrosive attack to continue but also accelerates it by holding the additional electrolyte in its pores.

Cold working accelerates corrosion. Surface of a drawn wire rusts quickly. If a metal contains punched rivet holes it corrodes rapidly near the holes because of the potential difference between the cold worked metal and the adjoining metal which has not been worked. Rivets should have the same composition as the metal or the contact will corrode rapidly.

Considering all these aspects, one can conclude that the types of corrosion are numerous and the conditions under which corrosion takes place are also extremely varied. Hence diverse methods are to be used to deal with different types of corrosion phenomena.

4.27 METHODS FOR PREVENTION OF CORROSION

The different methods used for the preservation of metal and their alloys from the corrosive attacks of the environments can be considered under following general headings :

- Proper design and material selection.
- Improving the characteristics of metal :

    (a) Purification, (b) Alloying.

- Cathodic protection :

  (a) Sacrificial anode method, (b) Impressed current method.

- Anodic protection :

  (a) Potentiostat, (b) Anodizing.

- Modifying the environment :

  (a) Deactivation, (b) Dehumidification, (c) Alkaline neutralization,

  (d) By using inhibitors.

- Application of protective coatings :

  (a) Chemical conversion coatings, (b) Organic coatings, (c) Organic linings,

  (d) Ceramic protectives, (e) Metallic coatings.

4.28 IMPROVEMENT/CHANGES IN DESIGN

A *proper design* is capable of preventing the occurrences of inhomogeneities in the metal and also in the corrosive environment. Such a proper design should avoid the presence of crevices between adjacent parts of the structure; even if the metals are same, because concentration differences are created due to crevices. Bolts and rivets are, therefore, to be replaced by butt-weld. If it is not possible to avoid crevices in a given design, efforts should be made to minimize the effects due to crevices. The accumulation of dirt or deposits of various kinds cause localized corrosion. Hence the design should allow adequate cleaning and flushing of those parts which are susceptible to deposits, dirt etc.

Sharp corners as well as recessess should also be avoided as these permit the formation of stagnant areas and accumulation of solids. The equipment when supported on legs will permit free access of air and prevent the formation of stagnant pools or damp areas.

While dealing with corrosive liquids, the design should permit uniform flow, because stagnant area on one hand and highly turbulent flow may result in accelerated corrosion.

Similarly, a design should prevent conditions which may subject some areas of structure to stress (e.g. cold working). If possible such equipments may be annealed in order to minimize residual stress to the lowest practical value.

The important cares taken during design are :

- Contact of dissimilar metals should be avoided in the presence of corroding solution. If this care is not taken then active metal undergoes corrosion more rapidly.

- If two dissimilar metals are in contact, then the anodic metal must have large surface area with respect to the cathodic metal. Small anodic area corrodes rapidly due to large corrosion current product from cathodic area.

- If two dissimilar metals are to be used then these must be close to each other in electrochemical series.

- An insulating fitting is placed during joining of two dissimilar metals.

- Any surface coating should be avoided for anodic metal.

- Texture of metal should be coarse grained.

- Metallic surfaces must possess smooth finish.

- Metals at anodic end in galvanic series will undergo corrosion rapidly.

4.28.1 Selection of Material

Selection of the right type of materials is the main factor in controlling corrosion. The choice of the material should be made not only on the cost and structure but also its chemical properties and the environment should also be considered. The metallic materials should be used in their purest form as far as possible.

Corrosion resistance as well as strength of many metals can be improved by alloying. e.g. (i) stainless steels containing chromium produce an exceptionally coherent oxide film which protects the steel from corrosive attack. (ii) Highly stressed 'Nimonic' alloys (i.e. Ni-Cr-Mo alloys) that are used in gas turbines are quite resistant to hot gases. (iii) Cupro-nickel [Cu : Ni :: 70 : 30] alloys containing just 0.2 % of iron are extensively used for condenser tubes and bubble trays of fractionating columns in oil refineries.

If two metallic materials have to be in contact then they should be so selected that their oxidation potentials are as near as possible. Further, the area of inactive metal i.e. more noble should be smaller than that of active or anodic metal.

Wherever practicable, the metallic parts during storage should not come in contact with moisture. Therefore, while packing, the metal parts should be sealed in a low permeability plastic in presence of activated silica or alumina gel.

Corrosion can be controlled by suitably adjusting the acidity or alkalinity i.e. pH of the environment. Every metallic surface has minimum corrosion at a specific pH. When control of pH is not practicable, corrosion can be reduced by using inert coatings or inactive metals.

When contact of dissimilar metals is unavoidable, suitable insulators should be inserted between them to reduce current flow and attack on the anode.

4.29 IMPROVING THE CHARACTERISTICS OF METAL

(a) Purification of metal :

Impurities in metal make it heterogeneous thereby decreasing the corrosion resistance. Pure metals possess higher electro-chemical corrosion resistance e.g., Super purity Al (higher than 99.99 %) and chemical lead
(99.998 %) are used in specific conditions. But in many cases this is not practicable because of the cost considerations and decrease in certain mechanical properties such as strength.

(b) Alloying :

If metals are suitably alloyed both strength and corrosion resistance of most commercial metals can be increased. For maximum corrosion resistance to develop, the alloy should be completely homogeneous. In case of metals such as iron, nickel, copper, etc., the corrosion can be controlled by alloying because of their large capacity of solid solution.

Metals which are susceptible to corrosion can be made passive (Passivity is the lack of activity under conditions where normally a metal is expected to react readily) by alloying with one or more metals which are passive e.g. iron can be made passive by alloying it with the transition metal such as chromium, molybdenum, nickel etc.

4.30 CATHODIC AND ANODIC PROTECTION

If it is impracticable to change the nature of the corrosion medium then corrosion control may be achieved by cathodic protection or anodic protection.

4.31 CATHODIC PROTECTION

The principle involved in this method is to force the metal to behave like cathode. Since there will not be any anodic area, the corrosion of the metal does not take place. The principle can be explained by considering the corrosion of a typical metal say 'M' in an acidic medium. The electrochemical reactions taking place in such a system are the dissolution of the metal and the evolution of hydrogen gas according to the following equation :

$$M \longrightarrow M^{n+} + ne^-$$

$$2 H^+ + 2 e^- \longrightarrow H_2$$

Cathodic protection can be achieved by supplying electrons to the metallic structure which is to be protected.

There are two ways of cathodic protection :

- By using galvanic or sacrificial anode i.e. galvanic protection.
- By using impressed current called as impressed current cathodic protection.

(a) Sacrificial Anode Method :

The metallic structure to be protected is connected by a wire to a more anodic metal. This results in concentrated corrosion at the more anodic (more active) metal; and this more active metal gets corroded slowly. The original metallic structure now behaves as cathodic and therefore is protected. The more active metal used for this purpose is known as sacrificial anode, which when gets consumed i.e. completely corroded is replaced by a new one. Mg, Zn, Al and their alloys are generally used as sacrificial anode. This method is used to protect buried pipelines, water tanks, underground cables, ship hulls etc.

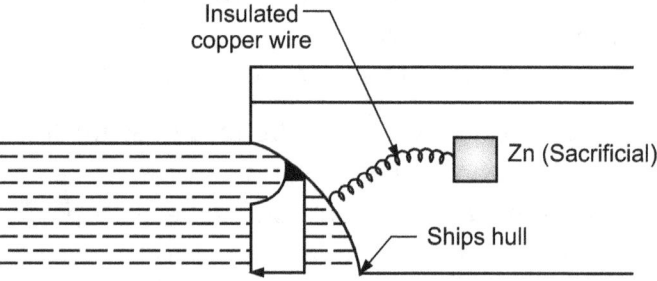

Fig. 4.13 : Sacrificial anode

(b) Impressed (external) Current Method :

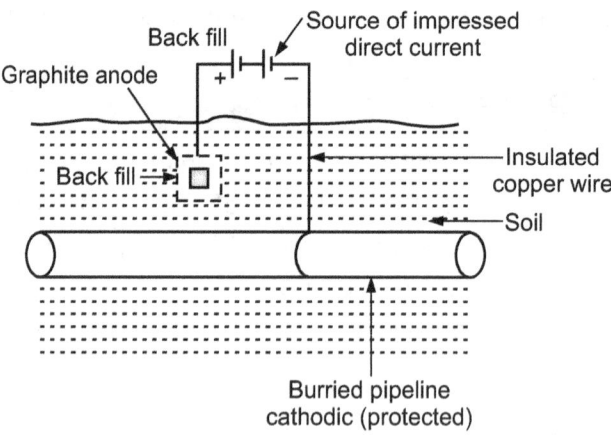

Fig. 4.14 : Impressed current protection

In this method, an impressed current is applied in the opposite direction to counter-balance or nullify the corrosion current. The corroding metallic surface is thus converted (under the situation) from anode to cathode and thus protected. Generally, the impressed current is taken from a battery or rectifier using an insoluble anode such as platinum, graphite, stainless steel etc. This type of cathodic protection is useful in protecting box water coolers, water tanks, underground oil or water pipeline, transmission line towers etc.

Limitations of cathodic protection :

- Capital investment and maintenance cost is high.

- Cathodic protection system which is protecting one pipeline may increase the corrosion of another adjacent pipeline or some metallic structure in the vicinity due to stray currents. This may lead to technical and legal problems.

- If the cathodic reaction produces hydrogen it may produce blisters on the protected metal itself. If a metallic surface (protected) is having a coating (protective) over it, then this coating may get peeled off i.e. will be removed.

- If a sacrificial anode metal is too active relative to the protected metallic surface or a too high potential as compared to open-circuit voltage for the metal/metal ion cell is used then problems associated with the evolution of H_2 or formation and accumulation of OH^- ions will be more.

Table 4.5 : Comparison of Sacrificial anode and Impressed current methods

Sacrificial anode	Impressed current
1. They are independent of any source of electrical power.	1. Requires mains supply or other source of electric power.
2. Their usefulness is generally restricted to the protection of well coated structures.	2. Can be applied to a wide range of structures including large uncoated structures.
3. They are relatively simple to install, additions may be made until the desired effect is obtained.	3. Needs careful design but it is easy to adjust the output.
4. They may be required at a large number of positions.	4. Small total number of anodes are required.
5. They are less likely to affect any nearby structures as the output is low.	5. Effects on nearby structures are required to be assessed.
6. Their output cannot be controlled but by selecting a proper material electrode, potential can be kept well below the damage point.	6. Controls are simple and even can be made automatic to maintain potential well below the damage point.

7. Their connections are protected cathodically.	7. Requires high insulation on connections to the positive side.
8. They cannot be misconnected so that polarity is reversed.	8. Requires polarity to be checked during commissioning because mis-connections may reverse the polarity and accelerate corrosion.

4.32 ANODIC PROTECTION

In this method, a metal is passivated by applying current in a direction that will render the metal more anodic. Anodic protection is based on the formation of a protective film on metals by externally applied anodic currents. For metals with active-passive transitions e.g. iron, nickel, chromium, titanium and their alloys, if a carefully controlled anodic currents are applied they are passivated and the rate of metal dissolution is decreased. To protect a structure anodically, a device called 'Potentiostat' is used.

(a)   Potentiostat is an electronic device which maintains a metallic surface (to be protected) at a constant potential with respect to a reference electrode. Potentiostat has three terminals. Terminal 1 is connected to the structure to be protected. Terminal 2 is connected to auxilliary cathode usually of Pt or Platinum clad electrode. Terminal 3 is connected to reference (calomel) electrode.

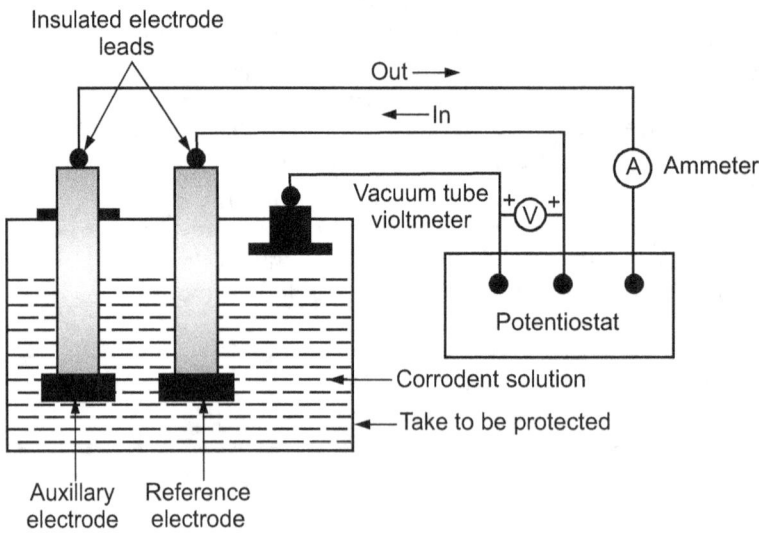

Fig. 4.15 : Anodic protection

The optimum potential required for protecting a metallic surface is previously determined by electro-chemical measurements. The main conditions in anodic protection are

(1) Potential range over which the metal is passive should be wider i.e. a range of about 50 mV. (2) The current density required to start the protection should be as low as possible. (3) Lower the passive current needed for maintaining the protection, lesser will be the operating cost of the device.

Advantages :

- Low operating cost.
- Applicable to wide range of corrodents.
- Ability to protect complex structures.
- Few auxilliary electrodes are necessary.
- Feasibility of the process can be predicted in the laboratory by simulation.
- Protection current gives an indication of corrosion rate.

Limitations :

- It is suitable for metal-corrodent systems which show active-passive behaviour.
- It has high cost of installation.
- If the system goes out of control, then there is a risk of high corrosion rate.

(b) Anodizing :

Metals like Al, Ti, etc. and their alloys form a thin oxide film on their surface when exposed to air. The oxide film for above metals is non-porous, adhesive and uniform in nature thereby providing better corrosion resistance to the base metal. However, the thickness of naturally formed oxide layer is very small and it does not protect the base metal properly. To overcome this problem, the thickness of existing oxide film is increased by electrolysis. The process is known as anodizing.

Besides improving corrosion resistance, the anodized layer (oxide layer) also improves hardness, wear resistance, electrical insulation etc.

In anodizing, the component to be protected is connected as anode in electrolytic cell, containing strong electrolyte such as conc. H_2SO_4. A small amount of current is passed which oxidizes the anode. The thickness of the oxide film is controlled by time and current density. The oxide layer formed is porous in nature which are then sealed by immersing the article in a bath of oil, wax, dye or boiling water etc. Then the anodized article can be put to actual use.

Anodic oxidation of aluminium :

When exposed to air, aluminium forms an oxide film of 0.01 μ to 0.1 μ thickness on its surface. If aluminium is made an anode in an acid electrolyte (H_2SO_4 ; oxalic acid or chromic acid etc.) the thickness of the oxide film increases to 10 to 20 μ. This increase in thickness is due to the formation of microscopic pores in the oxide film. The pores allow the electrolyte to penetrate deeper and form thicker film. The film so formed by anodic oxidation has open pores in the beginning, but these open pores are sealed immersion in boiling water. As a result of which, the oxide film gets converted into $Al_2O_3 \cdot H_2O$ (hydrated form) which occupies more volume thereby the pores are sealed. Alternatively, sealing can be done by immersing the component in boiling dilute sodium dichromate solution.

Table 4.6 : Comparison of Anodic and Cathodic protection :

Anodic protection	Cathodic protection
1. Applicable to metals showing active-passive transition only.	1. Applicable to all metals.
2. More aggressive corrodents can be handled.	2. Used where no source of power is available by employing sacrificial anodes.
3. Though installation cost is high, operating cost is lower.	3. Lower installation cost.
4. Few electrodes are needed for replacement because of better throwing power.	4. Standard and well established method.
5. Feasibility can be predicted in laboratory and hence designing becomes easier.	5. Feasibility cannot be predicted in laboratory.

4.33 MODIFYING THE ENVIRONMENT

The corrosive effect of the environment can be reduced either by removing the harmful constituents or adding some such substances which will neutralize the corrosive effect of the harmful constituents of the environment.

(a) Deactivation : Quantity of dissolved oxygen in the environment decides whether oxygen concentration type of corrosion will proceed or not. By adjusting the temperature along with proper mechanical agitation the dissolved oxygen can be expelled from the environment. As the rate of corrosion decreases exponentially with the decrease of temperature, hence slight decrease in temperature would cause a pronounced decrease in the amount of corrosion product. This is known as deaeration. In deactivation method either sodium sulphite (Na_2SO_3) or hydrazine hydrate ($N_2H_4 \cdot H_2O$) is added to the liquid medium. Both the chemicals react with the dissolved oxygen readily, thus removing the oxygen from the site of corrosion and hence prevent corrosive action.

$$2\,Na_2SO_3 \ + \ O_2 \ \longrightarrow \ 2\,Na_2SO_4$$

$$N_2H_4 \ + \ O_2 \ \longrightarrow \ N_2 \ + \ 2\,H_2O$$

(b) Dehumidification : This involves reducing the moisture content of air well below the critical humidity limit for the metal so that the amount of water condensed on the metallic surface will not be sufficient to cause corrosion. For this purpose substances such as alumina, silica gel etc., are used. These substances can adsorb moisture preferentially on their surface. This is applicable on economic considerations to closed areas such as air-conditioned places where steel articles are prepared.

(c) Alkaline neutralisation : In this method the acidic nature of the corrosive environment is neutralized by using alkaline substances such as NH_3, NaOH, lime, sodium salts of petroleum phenols etc. These alkaline substances are injected in vapour or liquid form to the corroding environment (H_2S, HCl, SO_2 etc.) or its part. This method is used in refinery to control corrosion of equipment.

(d) By using inhibitors : A small quantity of some substances when added to corrosive environment effectively decrease the rate of corrosion of metal. Such substances are called *inhibitors*. These are either organic or inorganic substances. These dissolve in the corrosive medium and form protective layer either on anodic or cathodic area. Those which cover anodic areas are chromates, phosphates, tungstates of transition elements, while those cover the cathodic area are amines, mercaptans, substituted ureas, etc.

They are divided into cathodic and anodic inhibitors on the basis of whether they inhibit anodic or cathodic reaction.

(i) Anodic and Cathodic inhibitors :

As corrosion is electrochemical in nature, the inhibitive action of any substance is the result of control of anodic and cathodic reactions.

Anodic inhibitors form soluble compounds with dissolved metal ions, which deposit on metal surface to form a protective film, which reduces corrosion of anode. They are oxidising agents like chromates, nitrates and ferric salts.

In an acidic environment, evolution of hydrogen gas takes place at the cathode. Corrosion can be reduced by slowing diffusion of hydrated hydrogen ions to the cathode or by increasing the overpotential of hydrogen evolution. Antimony and arsenic ions deposit metallic film on the cathode and retard hydrogen-evolution reaction. In a neutral environment, cathodic reaction is the result of oxygen absorption and formation of hydroxyl ions. Sodium sulphite or hydrazine are used to remove oxygen from the solution.

$$2\,Na_2S_2O_3 \;+\; O_2 \;\rightarrow\; 2\,Na_2SO_4$$

$$N_2H_4 \;+\; O_2 \;\rightarrow\; N_2 \uparrow +\; 2\,H_2O$$

Cathodic inorganic inhibitors like magnesium, zinc or nickel salts are effective in neutral and alkaline environment. They react with hydroxyl ions at cathode and form insoluble hydroxides. These get deposited on the cathode. Above inhibitors can also be classified as :

(ii) Inorganic inhibitors and organic inhibitors :

In neutral and alkaline solutions, chromates and nitrites act as anodic inhibitors. They are the most efficient inhibitors for controlling the corrosion of iron and steel in neutral and alkaline waters. Alkali inhibitors like sodium hydroxide, sodium carbonates and bicarbonates form metal hydroxides which serve as protective deposits. They are anodic inhibitors. Inorganic inhibitors do not give any protection in presence of acids and reducing conditions. For such conditions, polar organic compounds and colloidal organic materials are used as inhibitors. Their inhibitive action is because of physical and chemical adsorption of molecules on metal surface. They act as anodic, cathodic or mixed inhibitors. Due to physical adsorption of inhibitor, resistance to current flow at cathodic area increases. Due to chemisorption, co-ordinate covalent bond is formed between inhibitor and metal, so anodic polarisation takes place. Amines, heterocyclic nitrogen compounds, substituted urea and thiourea and metal soaps are used as organic inhibitors.

Vapour-phase inhibitors are used to inhibit atmospheric corrosion of metals without placing it in direct contact of metal's surface. They possess high vapour pressure and are effective if used in close spaces like inside of packages. Some heterocyclic nitro-compounds, esters of carboxylic acid can be used as vapour-phase inhibitors.

4.34 PROTECTIVE COATINGS

Application of protective coatings is one of the oldest way to protect underlying material. A coated component is protected due to isolation of the component from the corroding environment. Depending on the type of metal, application, cost, etc. specific surface coating may be selected.

Whatever may be substance used for giving a coating on metallic surface for protecting it from corrosion, it must function as below :

- It should physically isolate the underlying metal from the corroding environment.
- Under service conditions of temperature and pressure, the coating should be chemically inert to the environment.

- It should prevent the penetration of the environment to the material which it protects.

Some protective coatings in addition to above functions, impart certain specific mechanical and physical properties such as wear resistance, hardness, oxidation resistance, electrical and thermal insulating properties.

4.35 DIFFERENT WAYS OF SURFACE COATING

(a) Chemical conversion coatings :

These are inorganic surface barriers produced by chemical or electro-chemical reaction taking place at the base metal. These are used for increasing the corrosion resistance as well as decorative effect of the base metal. However, these are mainly used as base for paints, lacquers etc. The following are important conversion coatings :

Phosphate coatings which are produced by the chemical reaction of the base metal with aqueous solution of phosphoric acid and iron, manganese or zinc phosphate along with accelerators such as copper salts.

Phosphate coatings are grey but can be turned into black by using Bonderising as dye.

Chromate coatings are used for zinc, cadmium-plated parts, aluminium and magnesium. These are produced by dipping the article first in acid potassium chromate and then in neutral chromate solution.

Chemical oxide coatings are produced by treating the base metal with alkaline oxidizing solution or gases.

Anodized coatings which are generally produced on Al, Zn, Mg and their alloys by electrolytic process in which base metal is made anode. Anodized coatings possess improved corrosion resistance as well as resistance to mechanical injury.

(b) Organic coatings :

These are inert organic barriers such as paints, varnishes, lacquers and enamels which are applied on the metallic surface. The protective value of these coatings depends on (i) Its chemical inertness to the corrosive medium, (ii) Surface adhesion, (iii) Impermeability, and (iv) Proper method of application.

These are mainly used when corrosion rate of an unprotected metal is less than 1.25 mm per year.

The main drawback is that there is always a possibility of an abrasive and erosive action, which can easily destroy the continuity of a thin film thereby exposing the underlying metal to the corrosive action of the environment.

(c) Organic linings :

Rubber and plastics are often used to protect the underlying metal from corrosion under highly corrosive conditions. The thickness of these linings varies from 3 mm to 6 mm depending on the requirements.

The most widely used plastic for sheet lining is polyvinyl chloride. It has high chemical resistance and can be cemented rather easily to the metal surface.

(d) Ceramic protectives :

These possess high resistance against oxidation even at high temperatures. They possess high chemical inertness to all corrosive environments except alkalis and HF. These are of two types, vitreous enamels and ceramic coatings.

Vitreous enamels are glass-like materials which are fixed on the metal to provide the required protection. These are usually applied to cast iron and steel equipments such as tanks, kettles, pipings, etc.

Ceramic coatings are similar to vitreous enamels but they possess higher refractoriness and hence are useful for metal protection against erosion, oxidation and intergranular corrosion at high temperature. These are applied to nozzle, motor tube lining, vanes and blades in gas turbines, tail pipe linings in ram jets, inner combustion chamber lining, burner parts, thermocouple tubes etc.

(e) Metallic coatings :

Nearly all metals can be applied as protective coatings to the base constructional metal. These are divided into (i) Anodic coatings and (ii) Cathodic coatings.

1) Anodic coatings :

For this purpose, the coating metal should have higher electrode potential i.e., anodic than the base metal (i.e., the metal on which coating is to be obtained). For example, more active metals such as Zn, Al and Cd are used as coating metals for steel as base metal. Zn, Al and Cd are anodic because their electrode potentials are higher than that of iron, the base metal. If at all pores, breaks occur in these anodic coatings, the underlying metal iron remains protected. Due to crack, a galvanic cell between Zn (if it is coating metal) and the exposed iron (i.e., exposed part of base metal) is formed. Zinc is anodic to iron therefore, zinc will dissolve anodically while iron being cathodic will be protected. Hence until all the zinc near the exposed iron is not consumed by anodic corrosion, iron will not be attacked by the environment. Thus, zinc coating protects iron sacrificially.

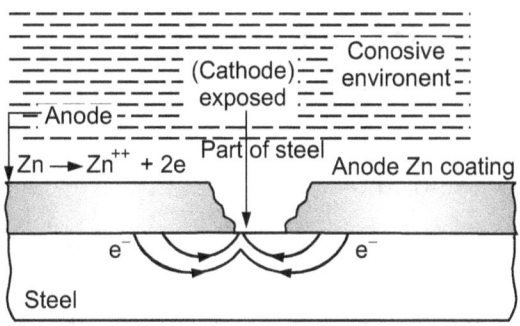

Fig. 4.16 : Functioning of anodic coating

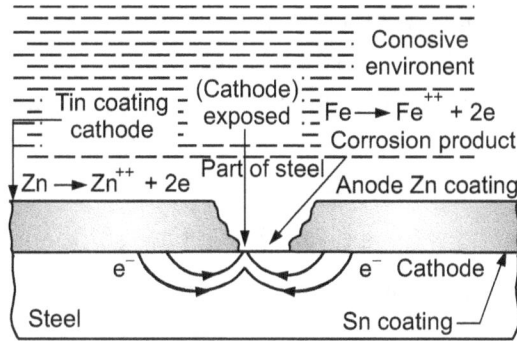

Fig. 4.17 : Functioning of cathodic coating

2) Cathodic coatings :

This is obtained by coating more noble or less active metal (i.e. having lower electrode potential) than the base metal. Because of their higher corrosion resistance they protect the base metal. For the effectiveness of cathodic coatings, they should be completely continuous, free from breaks, pores or discontinuities. If such coating gets damaged or punctured, the base metal gets corroded to a large extent. The extent of corrosion in this case of the base metal, is much more than if it were not coated. For example, tin coating on iron sheet can provide protection only till the time the coating is continuous and intact. However, if the coating breaks, tin (being lower in electro-chemical series than iron) becomes cathode, while the exposed iron acts as anode. A galvanic cell is developed and extensive localized attack at the small exposed part takes place, thus causing severe pitting. At times the base metal, iron, will be perforated.

4.36 METHODS OF APPLYING METAL COATINGS

Before applying a protective coating on to a base metal, the selection of a proper coating metal and coating process is most important, so that effective protection will be obtained.

4.36.1 Selection of Proper Coating Metal

A proper coating metal is selected on the basis of following points :

(1) Relative position of the base metal and the coating metal in the electro-chemical series or Galvanic series is to be studied carefully.

   If the metal of which coating is desired is active metal than the base metal then essentially the coating metal should be higher (more anodic) in the electrochemical series than the base metal. In such combination, the base metal is protected electrolytically from corrosion. Such coating should be completely non-porous.

   While the cathodic (i.e. noble or less active) coating will form a barrier between the base metal and the environment and thus preserves it from the attack. The surface of such cathodic coatings should be essentially continuous because it is cathodic in nature and therefore, in the event of rupture of the film, instead of sacrificing for the base metal, it accelerates the attack on the exposed areas of the base metal.

(2) The metal of which coating is to be given should have sufficient resistance to corrosion.

(3) The coating should be sufficiently ductile and hard.

4.36.2 Selection of Proper Coating Process

A proper coating process should be adopted to meet the requirements of the job as well as it should be suitable for the coating and base metals. For this following points are to be considered :

- Suitability for coating and base metals.
- Size and shape of the article to be coated.
- Optimum temperature suitable for coating metal and base metal.
- Physical properties required of coating for quality such as (a) Average thickness of coating, (b) Porosity or continuity, (c) Uniformity of coating, (d) Adherence, (e) Flexibility.

The different methods used for applying the protective metallic coatings are :

- Hot dipping : (i) Galvanising, (ii) Tinning.
- Metal cladding.
- Cementation : (i) Sherardizing, (ii) Chromizing, (iii) Colourizing
- Metal spraying
- Electro-plating.

4.36.3 Preparation of Metal Surface for Coating

Whatever may be type of coating required to be given on to the surface of a base metal, it has to be prepared in a proper way so that the coating will have good adhesion. The preparation of the surface involves three steps :

(1) The removal of grease and other surface contamination either by solvent degreasing, making the parts to be cleaned cathodic in alkaline solution at current density 1.0 amp. per sq. dm. etc.

(2) The removal of oxide scale and corrosion product either by abrasion or by acid pickling.

(3) Finally an etching treatment to secure adhesion or a buffing and polishing to improve the appearance of the applied coating.

4.37 HOT DIPPING PROCESS

In this process, the article to be coated is dipped in a bath of either molten metal or alloy of which coating is desired. After a sufficient time the article is removed with the adhering film of coating. The metal to be coated should have relatively low melting point [e.g. Zn (m.p. 419°C) and Sn (m.p. 232° C)] because high temperatures can cause following troubles :

(1) Alter the mechanical properties of the base metal.

(2) Undue contamination of the bath by solution of the base metal.

(3) Too extensive penetration and alloying of the coating with the underlying metal.

For promoting adherence, some alloy formation at the interface between the base metal and the coating is desirable. The hot-dipping process is widely used for applying coatings of low-melting metals and alloys such as zinc (Galvanizing), Tin (Tinning), lead, terneplate (lead-tin alloy) etc.

4.37.1 Galvanizing

Zinc coatings by hot dipping i.e., galvanizing is applied to base metals especially iron and steel when these are to be exposed to the atmosphere or soil. 'Sacrificial' electro-chemical protection to the base metal offered by zinc coating may extend for distance of 0.5 cm or more if the aqueous environment is fairly conductive.

Nature of Galvanized Coating :

Galvanized coating if properly applied consists of inner zones of iron-zinc alloy and an outer layer of almost pure zinc. The composition of iron-zinc alloy changes from outer layer to the surface of iron. The zinc content in alloy goes on decreasing as we go from outer layer to the base metal. Next to base metal, iron, there is a hard layer of $FeZn_3$ followed by $FeZn_7$, a layer responsible for adherence of zinc coating to iron. Next outer coating is $FeZn_{13}$ which limits the diffusion rate of zinc thereby controlling the rate of formation of zinc coating. Outermost layer is of pure zinc.

The protective action of zinc coatings is best effective in the pH range 6.0 to 12.5. If the galvanized articles are subjected to corrosive environments within the above mentioned pH range then it can serve the purpose for many years.

Process :

Galvanizing is carried out in the following stages :

(1) Preparation of surface :

Surface contaminations are removed in the following manner :

(a) *Pickling treatment :* The iron or steel article is pickled for 15 to 20 minutes in a pickling solution consisting of 7 % sulphuric acid at 60° C to 80°C.

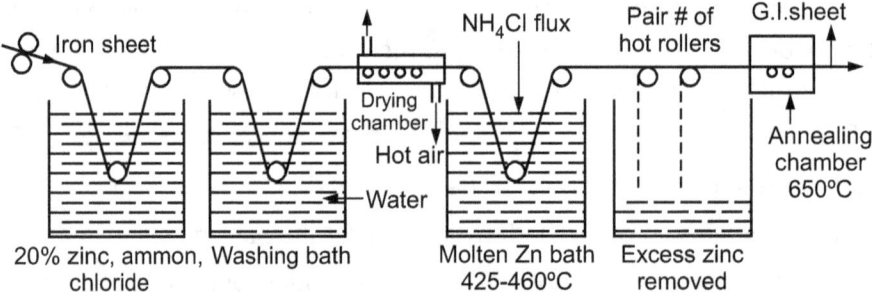

Fig. 4.18 : Galvanizing of steel sheet

(b) *Preliminary treatment :* The pickled article is treated with 5 % hydrofluoric acid to dissolve sand grains etc. if present on the surface of article. It is then stored under water to prevent oxidation.

(c) *Cleaning solution :* Finally, before the article is treated in zinc bath, it is passed through about 20 % zinc ammonium chloride solution so as to clean any superficial oxide if formed during storage.

(2) Zinc bath treatment :

The article is then washed, dried and then dipped in a bath of molten zinc, maintained between 425 C to 460 C. During this zinc bath is kept covered with a flux such as ammonium chloride so as to avoid oxide formation. The article coated with zinc layer is then passed through a pair of hot rollers to remove excess of zinc and to produce uniform layer on the article.

(3) Finally the article is annealed at a temperature of 650° C and then slowly cooled.

Protective action of zinc [Galvanization] :

Thin coating of zinc in galvanized iron does not allow iron to come in contact with air and moisture, and hence protects it from rusting. Even when the protective zinc coating is broken, iron remains protected because standard reduction potential (S.R.P.) of Zn^{2+}/Zn electrode (– 0.76 V) is less than S. R. P. of Fe^{2+}/Fe electrode (–0.44 V). Hence the oxidation reaction $Zn \rightarrow Zn^{2+} + 2\ e^-$ (with lower S.R.P.) occurs preferentially. As such, it is zinc which tends to lose electrons, and not iron. Thus the reaction $Fe \rightarrow Fe^{2+} + 2\ e^-$ necessary for rusting does not take place.

Zinc loses electrons and passes into the solution as Zn^{2+} ions at the anodic area. Hydrogen is discharged from the surface of iron in the cathodic area. Zinc is thus sacrificed in protecting iron. At areas where the surface coating is undamaged, zinc is protected from corrosion by firmly adhering layer of zinc oxide.

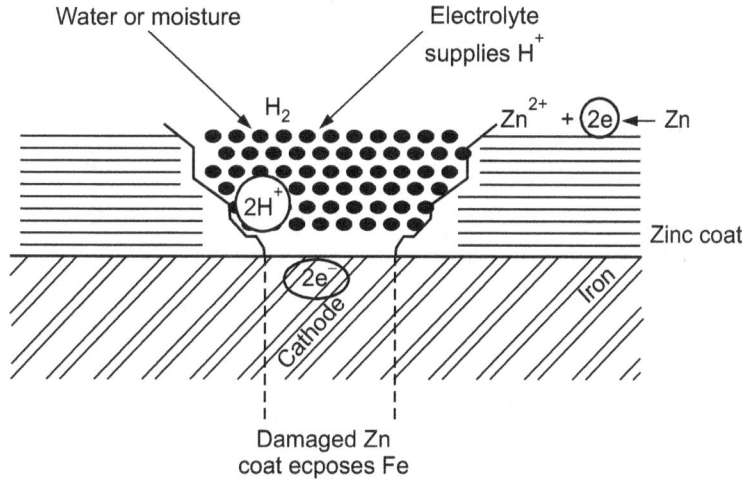

Fig. 4.19 : Protective action of Zn in GI sheet

Galvanized iron containers cannot be used for the purpose of canning food because zinc will pass into solution forming poisonous zinc salts which will poison the contents.

Applications :

The articles such as roofing sheets, pipes, wires, wire cloth, nails, pipe fittings etc. are protected from corrosion by them.

Galvanized (zinc-coated) articles should not be used for preparing food, especially if acidic in nature.

Zinc coatings are also effective on iron and steel articles exposed to sea water and other solutions high in chlorides.

4.37.2 Tinning

Tinning is similar to galvanizing. The essential differences are :

(1) Zinc coating in galvanizing and tin coating in tinning are used.

(2) In galvanizing, the iron sheet after passing through molten zinc, directly comes out and then annealed while in tinning the iron sheet after passing through molten metal, passes through palm oil before it comes out.

Process :

First the steel sheet is pickled in dil. H_2SO_4 (4 to 8 %) at about 75°C for 3 to 5 minutes before tinning to remove the oxide film.

After pickling, the steel sheets are made to pass by feed rollers in turn through the flux (a molten layer of zinc chloride, through the first compartment of molten tin at $300° - 340°$C). Then the sheets pass through second compartment of molten tin at $238°$ to $243°$ C. The sheet coming out of second compartment passes through a series of rollers in palm oil bath. The palm oil keeps the tin molten as well as a thin layer of palm oil adhering to the tin layer protects it from oxidizing during solidification of tin in air.

The palm oil is removed by saw dust or other similar material when the sheet comes out of palm oil. Then saw dust is removed and sheet is polished by dry flannel rollers.

This process produces a thin film of thickness 0.003 to 0.005 mm on the steel sheets.

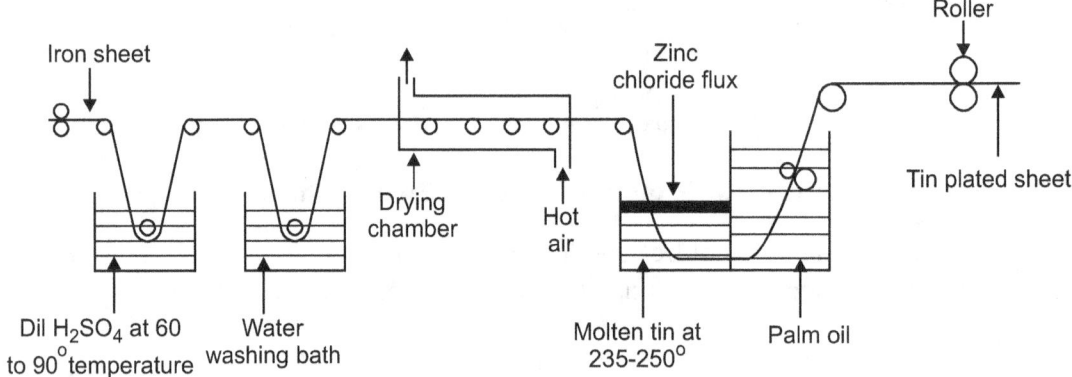

Fig. 4.20 : Tinning of steel sheet

Protective action of Tin [Sn] :

Tin is resistant to corrosion, hence a thin coating of tin over iron protects it from rusting. Tin coating, however, is not so durable as that of zinc in G. I. sheets. Moreover, when the layer of tin is broken and some iron surface is exposed, rusting is more rapid compared to unprotected iron piece. This is because S.R.P. of Fe^{2+}/Fe (– 0.44 V) is lower than S.R.P. of

Sn^{2+}/Sn (– 0.14 V). Therefore, the oxidation reaction Fe $\rightarrow$ Fe^{2+} + 2 e^- (with lower S.R.P.) is driven to the right. Thus, rusting is facilitated.

[However, S.R.P. of Sn^{2+}/Sn electrode (– 0.14 V) is less than S.R.P. of Cu^{2+}/Cu electrode (+ 0.34 V). Hence Sn can protect copper as Zn protects iron.]

In this case, hydrogen ions [H^+], originating from the solution of electrolyte, are discharged at the tin coating adjacent to exposed iron surface where dissolved oxygen acts as depolarizer. Electrons pass from iron (anodic area) to tin (cathodic area). Thus at the exposed iron surface (anodic area), ferrous ions pass into solution. These Fe^{2+} ions are oxidised to Fe^{3+} ions (ferric) by dissolving oxygen and produce rust.

Tin plated containers are used in canning food. As long as the coating is not damaged, tin being more resistant to corrosion withstands the action of acids present in food. However, when the plated surface gets damaged, iron passes into solution but no poisonous tin compounds pass into the solution.

Applications :

- Because of its non-toxicity, tinning is widely used for coating steel, copper, and brass sheets used for food containers.

- Copper wires are tinned to facilitate soldering.

- Tinned cans used for packing meat and some vegetables get blackened; while certain highly coloured fruits get bleached. To prevent this blackening or bleaching, the tinned cans should be lacquered or enameled on the inside.

4.38 METAL CLADDING

"Metal cladding involves bonding firmly and permanently, a dense, homogeneous layer of a coating metal to the base metal on one or both sides."

The thickness of the cladding metal usually ranges from 5 to 20 % of the composite plate. The cladding is accomplished for the following reasons :

- To develop surface properties in steel sheets of more expensive, corrosion-resistant and high melting metals or alloys such as monel, stainless steel, copper etc.

- For combining the strength of steel wire with the high electrical conductivity of copper.

- For providing anodic protection to aluminium alloys.

The choice of cladding material will therefore, depend upon the specific surface property that is to be developed or enhanced.

One method of cladding consists of casting a duplex ingot with the coating material on the outside and subsequently rolling the ingot into sheet, bar or plate or drawing it into wire.

In another method of cladding, the base metal sheet is sandwitched between two thin sheets of the coating material, which are then passed through rollers under the action of heat and pressure. This method is widely used in aircraft industry for manufacturing 'Alclad' sheets. Alclad is obtained by sandwitching Duralumin plate between two layers of 99.5 % pure aluminium.

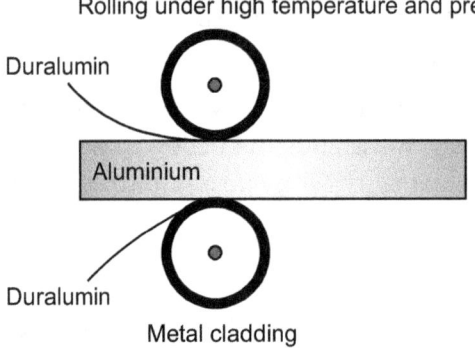

Fig. 4.21 : Metal cladding

Generally metals such as nickel, copper, silver, platinum, etc., and alloys such as stainless steel nickel alloys, copper alloy etc., are used as cladding material while mild steel, aluminium, copper, nickel and their alloys are used as base metals.

Application :

In air craft industries for manufacturing of Alclad, it is obtained by sandwitching Duralumin between two layers of 99.5% Al.

4.39 CEMENTATION

Cementation or diffusion coatings are obtained by heating the base metal in intimate contact with a powder of the coating metal. Diffusion of coating metal into the base metal takes place forming the layers of alloy of varying composition.

This process is suitable for coating small articles of uneven surfaces and intricate shapes such as bolts, screws, threaded parts, valves and gauge tools, because the coatings obtained by cementation are uniform in thickness irrespective of the geometry of the treated surface.

In cementation process, the base metal is usually iron or steel and the coating metals used are those which can alloy with iron e.g. Zinc, chromium and aluminium. The cementation processes are known as Sherardizing, Chromizing and Colourizing when the coating metals used are zinc, chromium and aluminium respectively.

(1) Sherardizing :

Sherardizing is cementation with zinc powder. First the article to be impregnated is cleaned and then packed with zinc dust in a light drum (to minimize the oxidation of zinc). The drum is then rotated slowly while it is being heated by gas or electricity. The temperature of the drum is kept between 350°C to 370°C. (Higher temperature leads to coarse crystalline coating of high iron content while lower temperature results in porous coating). The thickness of the coating can be controlled by changing the duration of treatment from 3 to 12 hours. At the end of the process, a minutely thin film of zinc alloy is obtained on the base metal. To get the best results, the purity of zinc dust used should be near 90 %.

Sherardized coatings consist of one structural layer of $FeZn_7$ only. These coatings generally possess minute cracks because the coefficients of expansion of base metal and the coating i.e zinc-iron alloy are different. But these cracks do not affect the protective property of the coating as sherardized coating produces sacrificial electrolytic protection.

As due to sherardizing very little change in dimension takes place therefore, it is used for protecting small steel parts such as nuts, bolts, washer etc. against atmospheric corrosion.

(2) Chromizing :

The base metal should be either low carbon steels (Carbon content 0.1 to 0.2 %) or carburized high carbon steels. Chromizing is carried out by packing the article to be chromized in a barrel along with a mixture of well-powdered chromium (55 %) and alumina (45 %) and is heated in an inert atmosphere at about 1300° – 1400°C for 3 to 4 hours. Alumina prevents the coalescence of chromium particles.

The corrosion resistance of chromized coatings is comparable to that of ferrite stainless steels. Chromium forms solid solutions with iron with chromium content from 10 to 20 % depending upon the time and temperature of treatment.

It is mainly used for gas turbine blades.

(3) Colourizing :

Colourized coatings are very much useful for protecting metals against high temperature oxidation.

First the article is sand blasted and then heated in a tightly-packed drum alongwith a mixture of powdered aluminium, aluminium oxide and a small quantity (1 to 5 %) of ammonium chloride (acts as flux). The drum is heated to about 840° to 930°C for 4 to 6 hours while it is being slowly rotated. The thickness of iron-aluminium alloy (Al_3Fe) produced is 0.025 to 0.15 mm thick.

To increase the penetration of aluminium by diffusion, the above treated article is held at 820° to 980° C for 12 to 48 hours in open. This reduces the aluminium content of the surface to 25 % as against 60 % in the above case, and the thickness of the alloy layer increases to 0.6 to 1.0 mm.

Colourizing is applied to various surface parts, tubes of air heaters, radiant steam superheaters, pyrometric equipment etc.

4.40 METAL SPRAYING

This is a process of obtaining a coating on the base metal by spraying the molten metal of which coating is desired, by means of a portable spraying apparatus.

Process :

First the surface of the base metal is prepared by sharp sand blasting for 1 to 3 hours so that a clean, fresh surface but highly roughened is obtained.

Then the coating metal is sprayed on the prepared surface of the article either by Wiregun method or Powder metal method.

Wire gun method, which is widely used for common metals uses a light weight 'pistol' which can be held in hand so as to direct the stream of metal at will. It consists of coaxial barrels. Through central barrel the coating metal is fed in the form of wire. The gaseous mixture acetylene and oxygen is supplied through the tube surrounding the wire barrel. The gas mixture is allowed to burn at the mouth of the barrel. This oxy-acetylene flame melts the protruding part of the wire. Through an outermost tube, surrounding the gas inlet, compressed air is admitted which atomizes the molten metal as well as projects it against the surface to be coated.

In powder metal method, finely divided powder of a metal is sucked from the coating powder chamber into a blow pipe using either aspirator or suction pump. As this powder passes through the flame of a blow pipe it gets disintegrated into a cloud of molten globules. These are projected against the base metal and are absorbed on the surface of base metal. By this method, coatings of relatively low-melting metals like Zn, Sn can be obtained.

Nature of Coating :

Molten metal particles after stricking the surface of base-metal, flatten into flakes and interlock with the surface irregularities. Sprayed coatings are continuous but porous to some extent.

Advantages :

- Greater speed of working.
- Metal film is applied to the finished article or structure in place.
- Metal film can be applied to any desired spot.

- No further deformation of film as it is applied in situ.
- Particles of the sprayed coated metal form a work hard surface due to impact.

Disadvantages :

- Adhesive strength of coating is comparatively low (as compared with hot-dipping or electro plated).
- Coatings are rather porous and hence have a tendency to catch soot and other forms of contaminations.

Applications :

- Sprayed coatings can be applied even to non-metallic surface such as wood, plastic etc.
- Metal spraying is used for reclaiming the worn out machine parts.
- To protect the equipment in chemical industry.
- Coating by metal spraying can be used for giving the coatings of aluminium, brass, cadmium, copper, lead, monel metal, nickel, tin, zinc etc. on many articles.

4.41 ELECTROPLATING

In principle, electroplating is the reverse of corrosion. In electroplating, metal is deposited from the solution while in corrosion, metal is dissolved in solution. When metals are electroplated for the purpose of protection against corrosion, care should be taken to verify the relative positions of the coating metal and the base metal in Galvanic series. A galvanic cell formed by the coating metal with the base metal should not increase the corrosion of the base metal. Hence the coating metal should be more anodic than the base metal.

For protecting steel articles from corrosion, the coating metals used are zinc, nickel, chromium, tin and copper. At times alloys such as lead-tin, tin-copper, tin-zinc, and tin-nickel are also used.

Nickel alone if used as a coating metal for steel, then sufficient thickness of the coating should be obtained because nickel is cathodic to iron. Thin coatings of nickel can serve the purpose for indoor atmosphere, while for outdoor atmosphere, first a thin copper coating and on that a nickel coating of sufficient thickness is obtained.

Chromium coatings are used in automobile industry. Chromium coatings are generally thin and contain number of pores. As the thickness of coating increases so also the number of pores and the coating tends to crack. In commercial practice, 4 different coats are given on steel to safeguard it from corrosive attack, immediately above steel article surface is nickel - 0.005 mm, then copper - 0.013 mm, then nickel - 0.02 mm and finally chromium 0.003 mm, while on brass articles only two layers i.e. under coat of nickel - 0.03 mm and final coating of chromium - 0.003 mm is used. Chromium electroplated coatings possess very high corrosion resistance.

In internal combustion engines, to increase wear resistance as well as running performance, electroplated chromium layer is used for certain parts which possess the required mechanical properties for their function but is readily corroded when subjected to working atmosphere.

Electroplating is also used for temporary purpose in metal treatment. e.g. Steel parts are copper plated before carburizing so that undesired parts will not be carburized.

In the process of hardening, portions of steel are protected from nitriding by electro-plating tin, or copper-tin alloys on such portions.

The setup of electrolysis is as shown in Fig. 4.22. In electrolysis, article which is coated is connected to cathode and electrolyte consist metal to be coated on article surface. Here electrolyte undergoes ionization to produce metal ions. They are attracted towards surface of cathode, where it accepts electrons and deposits on cathodic surface. As the process of electrolysis goes on, the concentration of metal ion in an electrolyte decreases. To form uniform coating, it is necessary to add electrolyte or anode is made of coating metal. Therefore, it undergoes process of ionization and supplies metal ions continuously required for electrolysis. e.g. In electroplating of Cu, electrolyte used is $CuSO_4$ and anode is Cu metal. Following reactions take place.

At anode, $Cu \rightarrow Cu^{++} + 2e^-$ (Oxidation reaction)

At cathode, Cu^{++} (from electrolyte) $+ 2e^- \rightarrow Cu$ (Reduction reaction)

Application :

Electroplating in automobile industry, Electrodeposition in thin film formation.

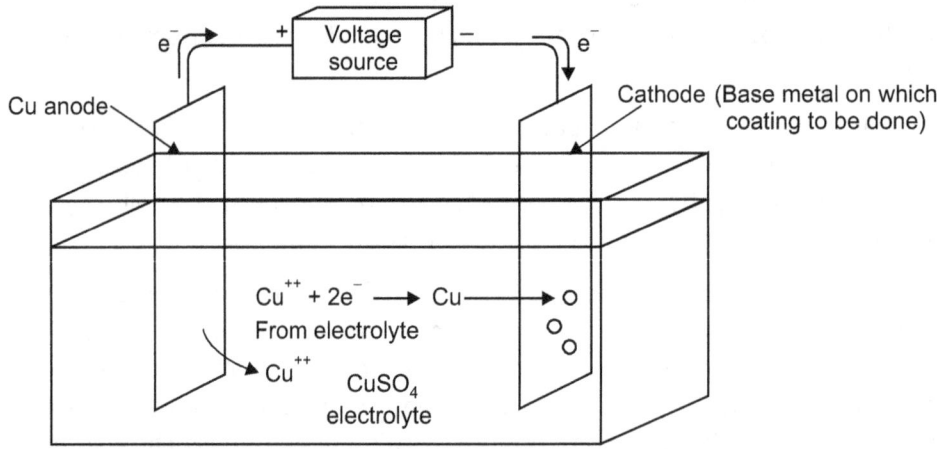

Fig. 4.22 : Electrolyte bath in which deposition of Cu on cathodic surface going on

4.42 PAINTS AND VARNISHES

Organic coatings which are inert organic barriers such as paints, varnishes, lacquers, enamels etc. find wide applications under conditions where the corrosion rate of the unprotected metal does not exceed 1.25 mm per year. The coatings of paints and varnishes are applied on metallic surfaces and other constructional materials for corrosion protection as well as decoration.

The protective value of these coatings depend on :

- their chemical inertness to the corrosive environment,
- their good surface adhesion,
- the impermeability to water, salts and gases and most important is
- the proper method of application.

(a) Paints :

Paint is mechanical dispersion mixture of two or more pigments in a vehicle. The vehicle is a liquid, consisting of non-volatile, film forming material like drying oil and a highly volatile solvent called thinner. When paint is applied to a metal surface (usually by brushing or spraying), the thinner evaporates while the drying oil slowly oxidizes forming a dry pigmented film.

Characteristics of good paints :

- It should be fluid enough to be spread easily over the surface.
- It should possess high hiding and covering power.
- It should form a quite tough, uniform and adhesive film.
- The film should not crack on drying.
- It should protect the painted surface from corrosiont.
- It should form film, the colour of which is quite stable to the effect of atmosphere and other agencies.
- Film should be glossy and stable.
- It can be easily applicable with brush or spraying device and that it yields a smooth and uniform surface.
- It should possess high adhesion capacity to the material over which it is intended to be used.

Constituents of paints :

1. **Pigment :** It gives colour to the paint e.g. White (Zn oxide), Red (Ferric oxide), Blue (Prussian blue).

2. **Vehicle or drying oil :** It is film forming constituent of paint e.g. Glyceryl esters of high molecular weight fatty acids.

3. **Thinners :** It reduces viscosity of the paint to suitable consistency e.g. Turpentine, mineral spirit, benzene.

4. **Driers :** These are oxygen carrier catalysts. Oxidise oil rapidly. e.g. resonates, linoleates, tungstates etc.

5. **Extenders or fillers :** It reduces cost of product, increases covering power, help to reduce cracking etc. e.g. barite, talc, asbestos.

6. **Plasticizers :** It provides elasticity to paint, minimizes cracking e.g. Tricresyl phosphate, triphenyl phosphate etc.

(b) Varnishes :

It is a homogeneous colloidal dispersion solution of natural or synthetic resins in oil or thinners or both. There are two types of varnish :

1. **Oil varnish :** It is a homogeneous solution of one or more natural or synthetic resins in a drying oil and a volatile solvent. This type of varnish dries up by evaporation of volatile solvent, followed by oxidation and polymerization. It takes comparatively more time for drying, but film produced is hard, lustrous and durable e.g. Copal varnish. They are used for exterior and interior work.

2. **Spirit varnish :** It contains a resin dissolved in a completely volatile solvent. Such varnish dries by the evaporation of the solvent. Spirit varnish dries rapidly, leaves behind film, which is brittle and so it has a tendency to crack or peel off. Moreover, the film is easily affected by weathering. e.g. spirit varnish is used for polishing wooden furniture.

Characteristics of good varnish :

1. It must form glossy, shiny and transparent film.
2. Film must dry quickly.
3. Film must be soft.
4. It must resist wear and tear.
5. Film must not shrink or crack on drying.

Constituents of varnish :

1. **Resin :** Natural resins like shellacs, kauri, rosin, copal etc. and synthetic resins like phenol aldehyde, alkyds, urea formaldehyde etc. it provides an element of hardening, resistance to weathering, durability etc.

2. **Solvents or Thinners :** e.g. Turpentine, petroleum spirit, kerosene etc. usually employed. It increases fluidity.

3. **Driers :** It accelerates drying rate of oil e.g. resonates, naphthalene derivatives of Pb, Co, Mn etc.

4. **Anti-skimming agent :** Like tert-amyl phenol, glycol etc. gives resistance to peeling of film.

MULTIPLE CHOICE QUESTIONS (MCQ's)

1. Corrosion process is more similar to –
   - (a) oxidation
   - (b) reduction
   - (c) purification
   - (d) concentration

2. In electrochemical cells –
   - (a) electricity generates chemical reactions
   - (b) chemical reactions generate electricity
   - (c) electrolyte generates electricity
   - (d) electrolyte causes chemical reaction

3. Consider following two statements –
   - (i) Metal dissolution reaction takes place at anode.
   - (ii) Anode has negative charge of these statements –
   - (a) both are correct
   - (b) only it is correct
   - (c) both are incorrect
   - (d) only (ii) is correct

4. In electrochemical cell, reactions start at any electrode due to –
   - (a) joining to second electrode internally
   - (b) joining to electrodes externally
   - (c) contact with electrolyte
   - (d) supplying electricity

5. In electrochemical cell, the condition required to create potential difference is –
   - (a) joining of two electrodes, through electrolyte
   - (b) joining of two electrodes by electrodes by electric wire
   - (c) non-equilibrium between electrolyte and electrode
   - (d) non-equilibrium between electrolyte and external circuit

6.   Which of the following statements is not true about electrode potential ?

(a) It is difference of electric potentials between electrolyte and electrode.

(b) It is also called as half cell potential.

(c) Its absolute value cannot be measured.

(d) Its value is measure with reference to potential of Cu electrode.

Consider the following electrode potentials value and answer the questions :

Element	Electrode potentials (volts)
Na	2.92
Mg	2.34
Al	1.67
Zn	0.76
Cr	0.56
Fe	0.44
Pb	0.12
H_2	0.00
Cu	– 0.34
Ag	– 0.8
Au	– 1.7

7.   If above metals are arranged in ascending order of their chemical activity, correct sequence will be –

(a) H_2, Pb, Cu, Fe   (b) H_2, Cu, Ag, Au

(c) H_2, Pb, Fe, Cr   (d) Cr, Fe, Pb, H_2

8.   From above table, Na is .... active and will act as .... when used with other element in table.

(a) most, anode   (b) most, cathode

(c) least, anode   (d) least, cathode

9.   From above table, least active elements is –

(a) Na   (b) H_2

(c) Au   (d) cannot be determined

10.   From above table, the element with least corrosion resistance is –

(a) Na   (b) H_2

(c) Au   (d) cannot be determined

11.   From above table, element with highest corrosion resistance is –

(a) Na   (b) H_2

(c) Au   (d) Cu

12. From above table, oxidation of which element will take place at the earliest ?
    (a) Na   (b) H₂
    (c) Au   (d) Fe

13. Considering galvanic series only, iron components can be protected by applying layers of .... on it.
    (a) Pb, Cu   (b) Ag, H₂
    (c) Zn, Cu   (d) Zn, Al

14. Considering galvanic series only, iron components cannot be protected by coatings of –
    (a) Al   (b) Pb
    (c) Zn   (d) Mg

15. Metal with lesser value of electrode potential will corrode ...... and become ..... in a galvanic cell.
    (a) lesser, anode   (b) lesser, cathode
    (c) more, anode   (d) more, cathode

16. More corrosion of Al electrode will take place if other electrode is –
    (a) Na   (b) Mg
    (c) H₂   (d) Cu

17. Which of the following pairs of electrodes will show maximum rate of oxidation ?
    (a) Na, H₂   (b) Na, Au
    (c) H₂, Au   (d) it depends upon nature of electrolyte

18. Which of the following pair of electrodes will show minimum of corrosion reaction ?
    (a) H₂, Pb   (b) H₂, Cu
    (c) Cu, Ag   (d) Cu, Pb

19. Which of the following is not an example of composition cell ?
    (a) steel screw in brass   (b) grain boundaries and grains of steel
    (c) galvanised steel   (d) lead-tin solder around wire

20. In polycrystalline materials, the electrochemical cells formed are –
    (a) composition cells   (b) concentration cells
    (c) stress cells   (d) Daniel cells

21. During cold working of metals .... cells are formed.
    (a) composition   (b) stress
    (c) concentration   (d) dry

22. In cold worked component, over stressed regions are .... active as compared to stress free region and hence becomes .....
    (a) more, cathode   (b) more, anode
    (c) less cathode   (d) less anode

23. In polycrystalline materials, grain boundaries are .... stressed as compared to grain interiors and hence act as .... of galvanic cell.
    (a) less, cathode   (b) less, anode
    (c) more cathode   (d) more anode

24. Which of the following is not true about concentration cells ?
    (a) Use of one electrode.
    (b) Use of same electrolyte.
    (c) Use of two electrode with same material.
    (d) Use of different concentrations of same electrolyte.

25. Which of the following statements is incorrect ?
    (a) In dry corrosion, direct chemical reaction between metal and gas takes place.
    (b) An electrolyte is required in wet corrosion.
    (c) Dry corrosion may take place in the presence of liquid.
    (d) Dry corrosion takes place due to potential difference.

26. In oxidation corrosion, rate of diffusion oxygen ions is .... as compared to metal ions because the size of oxygen ions is ......
    (a) more, more   (b) less, less
    (c) more, less   (d) less, more

27. In oxidation corrosion rate of diffusion of cations is .... than anions because their size is ....
    (a) more, more   (b) more, less
    (c) less, less   (d) less, more

28. During oxidation corrosion, mobility of ions in .... direction is more.
    (a) outward   (b) inward
    (c) opposite   (d) parallel

29. During oxidation corrosion, metal ions move in .... direction.
    (a) outward   (b) inward
    (c) opposite   (d) parallel

30. During oxidation corrosion, anions move in .... direction.
    (a) outward   (b) inward
    (c) opposite   (d) parallel

31. The oxide film that pro ides minimum corrosions is –
    (a) stable and porous   (b) unstable
    (c) volatile   (d) porous

32. The oxide film that provides maximum corrosion is –
    (a) stable   (b) unstable
    (c) volatile   (d) non-porous

33. The oxide film produced by noble metals, due to corrosion is –
    (a) stable   (b) unstable
    (c) volatile   (d) porous

34. When metal oxide decomposes back in to metal and oxygen, such film produced is –
    (a) stable   (b) unstable
    (c) volatile   (d) porous

35. The oxidation corrosion is not possible if the oxide film is –
    (a) stable and porous   (b) unstable
    (c) volatile   (d) porous

36. If volume of corrosion product is less than volume of metal then film obtained is –
    (a) unstable   (b) volatile
    (c) porous   (d) non-porous

37. Pilling Bedworth ratio can be given as –
    (a) mass of oxide/mass of metal   (b) volume of oxide/volume of metal
    (c) mass of metal/mass of oxide   (d) volume of metal/volume of oxide

38. Pilling Bedworth ratio for various metals is given below :

Metal	Fe	Al	Mo	Na	Mg	W
PB ratio	1.77	1.38	3.4	0.58	0.79	3.4

    From above table, the metal that provide stable and non-porous films are –
    (a) Mo and W   (b) Na and Mg
    (c) Fe and Al   (d) none of above

39. From above table, metal film that will generate severe compressive stress –
    (a) Fe   (b) Al
    (c) Mg   (d) W

40. From above table, the volume of metal is greater than volume of its oxide, is far
    (a) Fe   (b) Al
    (c) Mg   (d) W

41. The nature of the oxide film formed due to corrosion of metal does not depend upon –
    (a) Pilling-Bedworth ratio   (b) temperature
    (c) electro-chemical potential   (d) nature of metals

42. The stability of film formed due to corrosion of metal does not depend upon –
    (a) thickness of film   (b) exposed temperature
    (c) Pilling-Bedworth ratio   (d) valency of metal

43.   For formation of oxide free energy of formation of oxide of a metal should be –
      (a) positive   (b) zero
      (c) negative   (d) infinity

44.   Free energy of formation of Au_2O_3 from Au is + 163 kJ/mol. Therefore this metal will occur in nature in the form of –
      (a) Au_2D_3 (b) AuO
      (c) Au   (d) $Au_2O_3 + H_2O$

45.   Cr is added to steel in order to prevent –
      (a) dry corrosion   (b) wet corrosion
      (c) galvanic corrosion   (d) stress corrosion

46.   Which of the following statements is not true ?
      (a) Hydrogen embrittlement increases brittleness.
      (b) Hydrogen embrittlement reduces strength.
      (c) Hydrogen embrittlement is due to evolution of hydrogen.
      (d) Hydrogen embrittlement is called as decarburization.

47.   When surface is rough, the crests act as .... and corrodes .... as compared to troughs.
      (a) cathode, less   (b) anode, less
      (c) cathode, more   (d) anode, more

48.   Corrosion is more severe is –
      (a) anode area is less
      (b) both anodic and cathodic areas are equal
      (c) anode area is more
      (d) no relation between corrosion and electrode area

49.   If hydrogen over voltage is more corrosion rate will be
      (a) less   (b) more
      (c) continuous   (d) increase

50.   Dry corrosion does not depend upon –
      (a) chemical affinity between corrosive environment and metal
      (b) ability of corrosion products to form protective film on metal surface
      (c) temperature
      (d) hydrogen-over voltage

51.   Which of the following factor affecting wet corrosion, does not depend upon environment ?
      (a) pH of electrolyte   (b) humidity
      (c) hydrogen-over voltage   (d) temperature

52. Which of the following factors affecting wet corrosion, depends upon environment ?
    (a) Purity of metal   (b) Humidity
    (c) Hydrogen-over voltage   (d) Nature of film

53. The rate of corrosion is more if product of corrosion .... environment.
    (a) is soluble in
    (b) in insoluble in
    (c) sparingly soluble in
    (d) forms another insoluble product by interacting with

54. An iron part is half dipped in water (H_2O) and half open in air corrosion of .... will take place rapidly as it has .... concentration of oxygen.
    (a) outer, more   (b) inner, less
    (c) outer, less   (d) inner, more

55. The critical humidity for a metal is –
    (a) same as relative humidity
    (b) the relative humidity above rate of atmospheric corrosion increases
    (c) the relative humidity above rate of atmospheric corrosion decrease
    (d) the relative humidity above rate of atmospheric remains constant

56. Corrosion at the leakage joints of oil-pipe lines is due to –
    (a) activeness of oil   (b) action of oil and atmosphere
    (c) concentration difference   (d) surface protection

57. If joints of oil-pipe line are leaking, corrosion will start at –
    (a) at area uncovered away from leak   (b) area covered by oil film
    (c) uncovered area near the oil film   (d) depending upon nature of oil

58. Which of the following factor will not decide nature of corrosion and corrosion products ?
    (a) critical humidity of metal
    (b) chemical affinity between surface and environment
    (c) atmospheric impurities
    (d) density of metal

59. Which of the following is not a cause of formation of an electro-chemical cell ?
    (a) Presence more than one place
    (b) Differential areation.
    (c) Surface discontinuities
    (d) Chemical affinity between surface and environment

60. Which of the following is not true about uniform corrosion ?
    (a) Insoluble products are formed   (b) Takes place at constant rate
    (c) Failure can be estimated easily (d) It is rare type of corrosion.

61. Soil corrosion is more if its oxygen content is .... and moisture is ....
    (a) more, less   (b) less, less
    (c) more, more   (d) less, more

62. Soil corrosion is more if its electrical conductivity is .... and particle size is ....
    (a) more, large   (b) less, large
    (c) more, small   (d) less, small

63. Which of the following is not true about intergranular corrosion ?
    (a) It is localized effect
    (b) It take place following some warning
    (c) It increases brittleness
    (d) It takes place on microscopic way

64. The most common type of corrosion observed in fabricated parts of steels is –
    (a) crevice corrosion   (b) dry corrosion
    (c) stress corrosion   (d) waterline corrosion

65. Corrosion observed in the welded parts of steel is generally –
    (a) intergranular corrosion   (b) stress corrosion
    (c) crevice corrosion   (d) dry corrosion

66. Corrosion observed near dirt deposits is called as –
    (a) intergranular corrosion   (b) crevice corrosion
    (c) microbiological corrosion   (d) stress corrosion

67. The corrosion commonly observed near gaskets is –
    (a) microbiological corrosion   (b) crevice corrosion
    (c) intergranular corrosion   (d) stress corrosion

68. Season cracking is nothing but a type of .... corrosion.
    (a) soil   (b) intergranular
    (c) dry   (d) stress

69. Season cracking is most common in –
    (a) pure copper   (b) pure iron
    (c) brass   (d) steel

70. In stainless steels, corrosion due to heat treatment is –
    (a) weld decay   (b) crevice corrosion
    (c) stress corrosion   (d) dry

71. Which type of corrosion takes place due to relative motion between metal surface and its environment?
    (a) Pitting   (b) Crevice
    (c) Frosion   (d) Intergranular

72. Corrosion that takes place due to fluctuating pressure of liquid flowing over metal surface is ----
    (a) Pitting   (b) Crevice
    (c) Intergranular   (d) Cavitation

73. Fatigue strength due to corrosion is ---- normal fatigue strength without corrosion.
    (a) Less than   (b) Greater than
    (c) Equal to   (d) Not related to

74. Cavitation corrosion depends upon
    (a) Flow, pressure   (b) Pressure fluataions in flow
    (c) Flow velocity   (d) Suspended particles in flow

75. The corrosion taking place at turbine blades is ----
    (a) Cavitation corrosion   (b) Erosion corrosion
    (c) Crevice corrosion   (d) Pitting corrosion

76. The corrosion taking place a pump impeller surface is ---- corrosion
    (a) Cavitation   (b) Impingment
    (c) Erosion   (d) Crevice

77. Corrosion taking place between vibrating parts is called as ---- corrosion.
    (a) Crevice   (b) Erosion
    (c) Cavitation   (d) Fretting

78. The surface of ball or roller bearing commonly gets damaged due to ----- corrosion.
    (a) Crevice   (b) Erosion
    (c) Fretting   (d) Cavitation

79. The dimensional accuracy of closely fitted parts is endangered due to ---- corrosion.
    (a) Crevice   (b) Erosion
    (c) Fretting   (d) Cavitation

80. The failure of marine propeller shaft generally take place due to -----
    (a) Crevice corrosion   (b) Corrosion fatigue
    (c) Fretting corrosion   (d) Cavitation corrosion

81. Impingement corrosion does not depend upon ----
    (a) Flow velocity   (b) Nature of suspended particles
    (c) Fluid density   (d) Quantity of suspended particles

ANSWER KEY

1. (a)	2. (b)	3. (a)	4. (c)	5. (c)	6. (d)
7. (c)	8. (a)	9. (c)	10. (a)	11. (c)	12. (a)
13. (d)	14. (c)	15. (b)	16. (d)	17. (b)	18. (a)
19. (b)	20. (c)	21. (b)	22. (b)	23. (d)	24. (a)
25. (d)	26. (d)	27. (b)	28. (a)	29. (a)	30. (a)
31. (b)	32. (c)	33. (b)	34. (b)	35. (b)	36. (c)
37. (b)	38. (c)	39. (d)	40. (c)	41. (c)	42. (d)
43. (c)	44. (c)	45. (a)	46. (d)	47. (d)	48. (a)
49. (a)	50. (d)	51. (c)	52. (b)	53. (a)	54. (b)
55. (b)	56. (d)	57. (b)	58. (d)	59. (d)	60. (a)
61. (c)	62. (d)	63. (b)	64. (c)	65. (a)	66. (b)
67. (b)	68. (d)	69. (c)	70. (a)	71. (c)	72. (d)
73. (a)	74. (b)	75. (b)	76. (a)	77. (d)	78. (c)
79. (c)	80. (b)	81. (c)			

UNIVERSITY QUESTIONS

1. (a) What is corrosion ?

    (b) State the factors that influence the rate of electro-chemical corrosion.

2. (a) What is atmospheric corrosion ? Explain any two factors that cause the atmospheric corrosion.

    (b) Give a brief account of galvanic corrosion of metals.

3. (a) What are the pre-requisites of electro-chemical corrosion to take place and how are these satisfied in atmospheric corrosion of metals ?

    (b) Define immersed corrosion. Explain the mechanism of immersed corrosion.

4. What is chemical corrosion ? Describe its mechanism.   **(Dec. 97, May 2000)**

5. What is electro-chemical corrosion ? Explain its mechanism.

    (May 97, 99, 2000, 2001, Jan. 2001, Dec. 98)

6. In practice, what factors lead to electro-chemical corrosion and how can you minimize the corrosion in each case ?

7. Explain what happens and why ?

    (a) If one surface of the metal is exposed to atmosphere while other is protected.

    (b) If two plates of the same metal are connected and dipped in neutral electrolyte while the other plate is exposed to oxygen.

    (c) When only one part of the metal is under stress and strain.

    (d) If iron, copper and zinc plates are placed in the moist atmosphere separately.

8. (a) Explain why corrosion occurs under a rivet ?

    (b) Discuss the factors affecting the rate of corrosion.

(Dec. 97, 98, 99, May 2000, 2001)

    (c) Describe the galvanising and tinning processes.

9. Describe 'wet' corrosion.

10. Explain the formation and growth of the oxide film on the surface of the metal by chemical attack of oxygen.

11. (a) What is the cause of corrosion of metals ?

    (b) Explain the economic importance of corrosion.

12. Explain the mechanism of hydrogen evolution and oxygen absorption in electrochemical corrosion. Give figures.   **(Dec. 96, 99, Jan 03, May 03)**

13. Give the experimental determination of rate of corrosion.   **(May 97)**

14. What is corrosion ? What are different types of corrosion ? Explain the mechanism of oxidation corrosion.

15. Explain the effects of nature of film formation on oxidation corrosion.

16. Give an account of different methods used for the measurement of corrosion.

17. Write note on diffferential aeration corrosin.   **(May 99, 2000)**

18. Write notes on (any four) :

    (a) Galvanic corrosion, (b) Soil corrosion, (c) Waterline corrosion, (d) Crevice corrosion, (e) Microbiological corrosion, (f) Stress corrosion, (g) Factors influencing rate of corrosion.

19. Tin and zinc platings are used for prevention of corrosion. Which one is better and why ?

20. Write a note on cementation of metal surface with special reference to shearardizing.

21. Describe the hot dipping process of metal coating by either galvanizing or tinning.

22. What is the function of 'Cathodic protection' in corrosion control ?

23. Discuss the importance of design in corrosion control.

24. Write notes on :

    (a) Cathodic protection   **(Dec. 96, May 97)**

    (b) Protective coatings   **(May 97, Dec. 97)**

25. Give two methods of cathodic protection of metals.

    (Dec. 97, 98, 99, May 99, 2000, 2001, Jan. 2001)

26. Explain the importance of design and material selection in controlling corrosion of metallic materials.

27. Explain the following methods used for corrosion control (a) Sacrificial anode method,
    (b) Anodizing.

28. Distinguish between anodic protection and cathodic protection.

29. Give an account of different ways of surface coatings.

30. While applying a metal coating for corrosion protection, explain the importance of selection of (a) proper coating metal, and (b) proper coating process.

31. Give an account of hot dipping processes.

32. Explain the process of galvanizing with schematic diagram.

33. Explain the process of tinning with schematic diagram.

34. Give an account of cementation processes.

35. Give an account of metal spraying and state its advantages and disadvantages.

36. Write notes on :

    (a) Protection of metals by tinning   **(Jan. 03)**

    (b) Metal cladding   **(Jan. 03)**

    (c) Anodic protection.   **(Jan. 03)**

    (d) Protection of corrosion by spraying   **(May 03)**

    (e) Electroplating   **(May 99, 2003, Jan. 2001)**

❑❑❑

Chapter 5

CAST IRONS

5.1 INTRODUCTION

Cast irons are distinguished from steels by higher carbon content, good castability and less ductility under normal conditions. The carbon content of cast iron varies between 2.00 to 6.67%. However, commercial cast irons contain 2.3 to 3.8% carbon with sulphur, phosphorus, manganese and silicon. They cannot be forged, rolled, drawn or pressed into required shape. Due to their low melting temperature, better fluidity and good castability, cast irons are usually cast. The casting may be in sand mould or metal mould. Casting process consists of melting a metal and solidifying it directly to the desired shape in a mould.

Cast iron shows the following advantages and properties over steels:

- It is the least expensive ferrous material for casting.

- Cast irons show lower melting points (1140 to 120°C) than steels (1300 - 1500°C).

- They possess better wear and abrasion resistance.

- Good damping capacity (Fig. 5.1) and high compressive strength are the unique properties of cast irons in ferrous alloys.

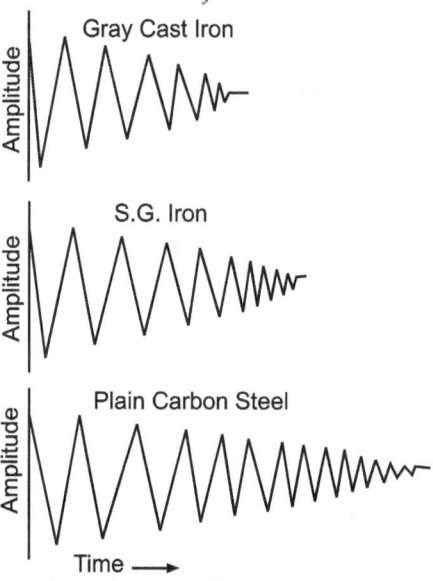

Fig. 5.1: Curves illustrating damping of vibrations in various engineering materials

- Cast irons can provide a wide range of metallic properties by altering chemical compositions and heat treatments.
- They exhibit high casting qualities as higher fluidity, less shrinkage, casting soundness, high yield.
- Various machining operations are possible.
- Certain applications require typical properties, which only cast iron can offer among the range of ferrous metals and alloys.
- In general, compared to steels, cast irons show very less ductility, tensile properties, toughness etc.

Typical properties of various cast irons are given in Table 5.1.

Table 5.1: Typical properties of various cast irons

Type	UTS (MPa)	% Elongation	Hardness, BHN
White C.I.	250 to 450	Nil	400
150 grade Gray C.I.	150	–	160 to 200
400 grade Gray C.I.	400	–	160 to 200
Black heart malleable	300 to 350	6 to 12	150
White heart malleable	340 to 480	3 to 15	230 max
Pearlitic malleable	450 to 700	3 to 6	150 to 290
Ferritic S.G. Iron	350 to 420	12 to 22	160 to 210
Pearlitic S.G. Iron	700 to 800	2	230 to 350

5.2 EFFECT OF VARIOUS ELEMENTS ON CAST IRON

(Dec. 10, 11, May 12)

(a) Carbon: (Dec. 09, 10)

This is a principal alloying element. Less carbon percentage gives fully cementite structure. Graphite formation starts with increasing carbon. With higher carbon percentage, the cementite gets decomposed into iron and graphite and matrix becomes ferrite. The hardness also decreases with increase in carbon.

(b) Silicon: (Dec. 09, 10, 11)

It promotes decomposition of cementite. It is said to be graphitizer. The silicon percentage decides the amount of graphitization. The percentage of Si is in the range of 0.5 to 3.0. A balance of silicon and carbon gives optimum strength. With lower silicon content and higher cooling rate, white cast iron is produced, while more silicon and slow cooling rate favours formation of gray cast iron.

(c) Sulphur:

Sulphur content in cast iron varies between 0.06 and 0.12%. Sulphur reacts with iron to form iron sulphide. This is a low melting compound. It melts at elevated temperature and gives possibility of cracking called as **hot shortness**. This can be reduced by addition of manganese, as sulphur has more affinity towards manganese than towards iron. This MnS is of round shape and well distributed, showing no adverse effect on the properties of cast iron. When sulphur content is more, the combined carbon is also more, which makes the cast iron hard and brittle. Higher sulphur tends to reduce fluidity; which is responsible for the blowhole defect in casting.

(d) Phosphorus: `(Dec. 10)`

The cast irons contain phosphorus between 0.10 and 0.90% which is from iron ore. Phosphorus reacts with iron to form iron phosphide (Fe_3P). This iron phosphide forms a ternary eutectic with cementite and austenite. The ternary eutectic is known as steadite (Fig. 5.2).

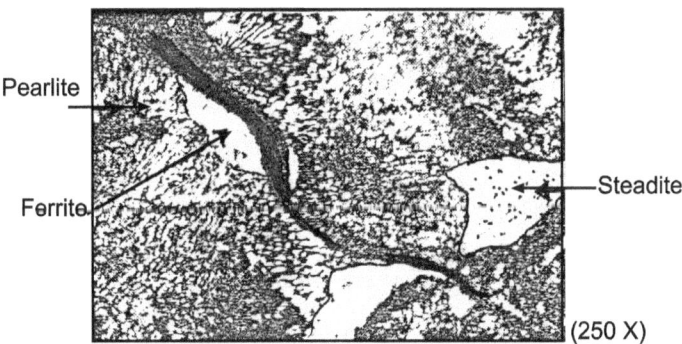

Fig. 5.2: Microstructure of gray cost iron showing steadite

Steadite is brittle. A network along austenite dendrite is observed with high phosphorus content. So, the brittleness of cast iron increases. Apart from this, phosphorus increases fluidity and thereby, very thin castings can be produced.

Increasing silicon and phosphorus have similar effect as increasing carbon.

(e) Manganese:

(0.1 to 1.0%). This small amount of manganese exercises practically no effect on microstructure. The important function of manganese is to avoid harmful effect of sulphur. It is a carbide stabilizer.

5.3 EFFECT OF COOLING RATE ON MICROSTRUCTURE OF CAST IRON

The cooling rate has a considerable effect on microstructure of cast irons. As the mechanical and structural properties of cast irons are governed by microstructure, cooling rates should be studied.

Fast cooling rates tend to form cementite as less time is available for graphitization. So, it results in white cast irons. Similarly, a very slow cooling rate promotes graphitization. The decomposition of Fe_3C occurs as,

$$Fe_3C \longrightarrow 3\,Fe + C_{(graphite)}$$

Intermediate cooling rate gives a combination of white cast iron at surface and gray cast iron in core. This becomes the best combination of hardness and toughness.

5.4 CLASSIFICATION OF CAST IRONS

Cast irons are classified as:

1. Plain cast irons and
2. Alloy cast irons.

The plain cast irons are further classified on the basis of their microstructures and fracture appearance as follows:

- White cast irons,
- Gray cast irons,
- Malleable cast irons,
- Nodular cast irons and
- Chilled cast irons.

Typical compositions of various cast irons are given in Table 5.2.

Table 5.2: Typical compositions of some cast irons

Type of cast iron	% C	% Si	% S	% P	% Mn	Other
White cast iron	2.5 to 4.5	8.8 max	0.08 max	0.1 max	0.4	–
Malleable cast iron	2.5 to 4.5	0.8 max	0.8 max	0.1 max	0.4	–
Gray cast iron	3.0 to 4.0	1.5 to 3.0	0.1 to 0.2	0.15 to 0.8	0.5 to 0.8	–
Ductile iron	3.0 to 3.5	0.2 to 3.0	0.02 max	0.15	0.5 to 0.8	0.2% Mg

Table 5.3: Typical compositions and properties of some alloy cast irons

Type	% C	% Si	% Mn	% S	% P	% Ni	% Cr	Other	UTS (MPa)	Hardness BHN
Ni-Hard	2.8	1.3	–	–	–	21.0	2.0	–	–	600
Ni-Resist	2.9	2.1	1.0	0.05 max	0.1 max	15.0	2.0	6% Cu	215	130
Silal	2.5	5.0	–	–	–	–	–	–	215	–

The alloy cast irons are further classified as:

- Ni-hard cast irons,
- Ni-resist cast irons and
- Meehanite.

A wide range of cast irons may be obtained by: (May 10)

- Controlling cooling rate,
- Carbon content,
- Nature of impurities
- Alloy additions and
- Heat treatment.

In any type of cast iron, carbon exists either in combined form or free form. The combined carbon is called as cementite (Fe_3C), while free carbon is called as graphite. The cementite may be distinguished from graphite by its higher hardness and excellent wear resistance. The size, shape, form and distribution of carbon greatly affect its mechanical properties.

White cast iron is an iron-carbon alloy containing total carbon as cementite. Gray cast iron consists of carbon in free form, i.e. graphite. Malleable cast irons are obtained from white cast iron by heat treatment. Nodular cast irons are produced by inoculation in molten gray cast iron. Chilled and mottled cast irons are those types, which are produced by controlling cooling rates. Alloy cast irons depend on the type and percentage of alloy addition.

5.5 WHITE CAST IRON   (May 09)

The total carbon present in white cast iron is in the combined form i.e. cementite.

The white cast irons are further divided as:

- Hypoeutectic (2 to 4.3% C),
- Eutectic (4.3% C) and
- Hypereutectic cast irons (> 4.3% C).

Because of free cementite in microstructure, such cast irons appear white; when fractured. The microstructural changes during solidification of white cast iron can be well explained by iron-iron carbide diagram.

The graphitization is suppressed by,

- Controlling chemical composition and

- Fast cooling.

Most of the commercially used white cast irons are from hypoeutectic grades.

The slow cooling of white cast irons can be discussed as follows

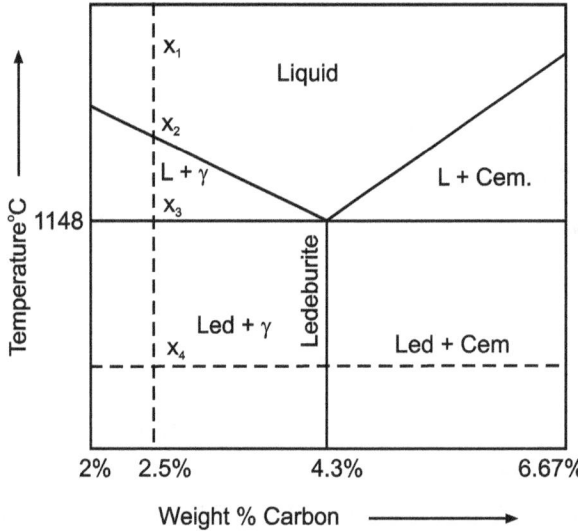

Fig. 5.3: Slow cooling of white cast irons

(A) Cooling of Hypoeutectic Cast Iron:

Consider the cooling of 2.5% carbon alloy. The alloy at x_1 in Fig. 5.3 exists as a uniform liquid solution of carbon dissolved in liquid iron. It remains in molten condition from the temperature x_1 to x_2. As the cooling crosses x_2 stage, solidification of alloy starts. It begins by formation of austenite crystals (dendrites). These are called as primary dendrites. As the temperature falls, primary or proeutectic austenite continues to solidify. Its composition moves along the solidus line. This continues upto x_3. According to lever rule, the amount of austenite just above x_3 will be,

$$\text{Amount of austenite} = \frac{4.3 - 2.5}{4.3 - 2.0} \times 100$$

$$= 78\%$$

The remaining 22% of the alloy still exists in a molten state with 4.3% carbon.

At x_3, the remaining liquid of eutectic composition solidifies at the constant temperature (1148°C). This forms an eutectic mixture of austenite and cementite called *Ledeburite*. Since, the reaction takes place at the higher temperature, ledeburite appears to be coarse rather than fine mixture typical of many eutectics.

As temperature falls between x_3 and x_4, the solubility of carbon in austenite decreases as per AC_m. This causes precipitation of proeutectoid cementite. It gets deposited on the cementite already present.

Just above x_4, the amount of austenite can be calculated by using a lever rule.

$$\text{Amount of austenite} \quad = \quad \frac{6.67 - 2.5}{6.67 - 0.8} \times 100 = 71\%$$

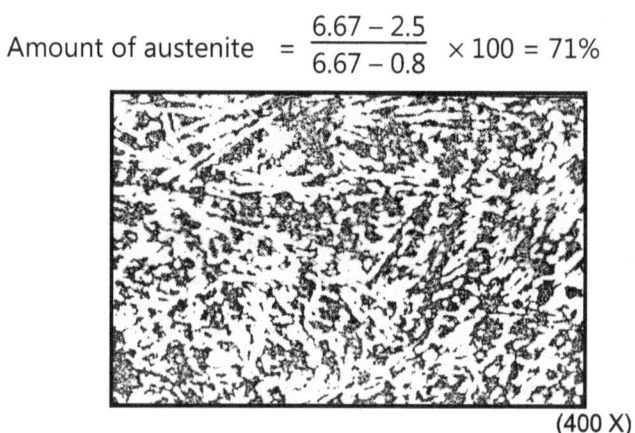

(400 X)

Fig. 5.4: A typical dendritic microstructure of white cast iron

This austenite undergoes eutectoid transformation at constant temperature x_4 (727°C). Austenite transforms to Pearlite.

Cooling to the room temperature, the structure remains unchanged. So finally, the typical microstructure of white cast iron consists of dentrites of transformed austenite (pearlite) in a white interdendritic network of cementite (Fig. 5.4). Higher magnification reveals dark areas of pearlite.

(B) Cooling of Eutectic Cast Iron:

This is an alloy of iron and carbon (5.4%). This alloy solidifies at 1148°C. An eutectic transformation takes place and gives a mixture of austenite and cementite i.e. Ledeburite.

Further cooling from eutectic to eutectoid temperature (i.e. 1148 to 727°C) does not bring any appreciable change in the microstructure. Only the amount of cementite increases.

At eutectoid temperature (727°C), the austenite gets transformed to pearlite.

At room temperature, the microstructure consists of cementite and pearlite (i.e. transformed ledeburite).

(C) Cooling of Hypereutectic White Cast Iron:

The phase changes of hypereutectic white cast iron are similar to those of hypoeutectic type. Only difference being the formation of cementite instead of austenite.

The primary proeutectic cementite separates as dendrites upto eutectic temperature. At this temperature, the remaining liquid gets transformed into eutectic mixture of cementite and austenite.

Below the temperature of eutectoid reaction, again a combination of pearlite and cementite is observed.

At the room temperature, the microstructure consists of dendrites of primary cementite in the matrix phase of transformed ledeburite.

The cementite is a hard and brittle compound. Since, white cast iron contains a large amount of cementite as a continuous interdendritic network, it makes cast iron hard, wear resistant, but extremely brittle and difficult to machine. Due to this, the applications of white cast irons are limited.

White cast irons are used in following applications:

    (a)   Liners for cement mixers, ball mill,

    (b)   Drawing dies and extrusion nozzles,

    (c)   Raw material for malleable cast iron,

    (d)   Friction plates, and

    (e)   Road roller surface.

White cast iron is used for the above parts, where hardness and wear resistance is of prime importance. Some of the typical properties of white cast iron are given in Table 5.1.

5.6 MALLEABLE CAST IRON   (May 08, Dec. 09, 13)

It is discussed earlier that white cast iron has cementite structure, which is very hard and brittle. So, annealing heat treatment is used to make the white cast iron soft i.e. malleable. Cementite is a metastable phase, which decomposes into iron and carbon.

A very long time heat treatment at higher temperature is called as *malleabilizing treatment*. The malleabilizing treatment converts cementite of white cast iron into irregular nodules of temper carbon (i.e. graphite) and ferrite.

The malleable cast irons are produced from white cast irons having the following chemical composition:

Carbon   2 to 2.5%

Silicon   0.8 to 1.35%

Manganese   0.20 to 0.50%

Phosphorus   < 0.17%

Sulphur   0.05%

A typical malleabilizing treatment (Fig. 5.5) consists of heating white cast iron at a temperature around 900°C for a long time. The process is carried out in two stages. **(May 10)**

    (a)   first stage annealing and

    (b)   second stage annealing.

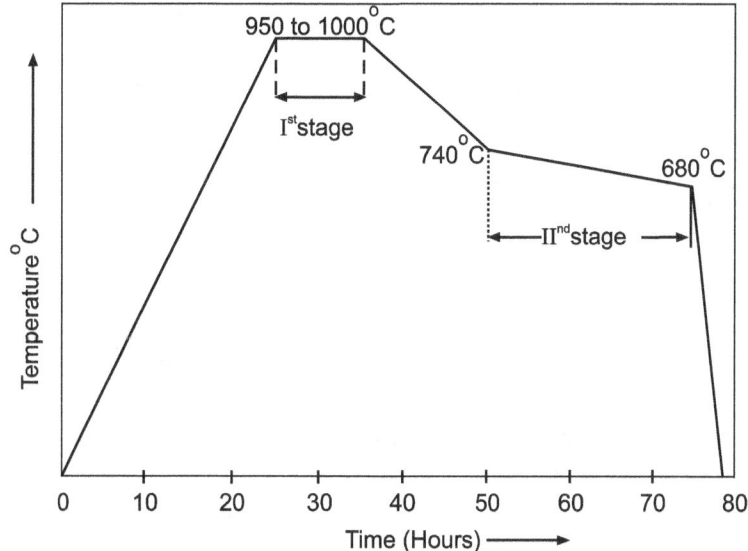

Fig. 5.5 : Malleabilizing heat treatment

(a) First Stage:

In the first stage annealing, the white cast iron is slowly heated to a temperature of 900°C. During heating, the pearlite is converted to austenite at the lower critical line. This austenite dissolves some additional cementite as it is heated to annealing temperature. The graphitization starts by precipitation of a graphite nucleus, which grows in all directions giving irregular nodule or spheroidal shape usually called as temper carbon.

This process may require 24 hours to 48 hours. Temper carbon is formed at the interface area between primary carbides and saturated austenite. Nucleation and graphitization can be accelerated by addition of sub-microscopic particles in iron during melting.

The rate of graphitization depends upon:

    (a)   Chemical composition,

    (b)   Nucleation tendency and

    (c)   Temperature of annealing.

Increasing annealing temperature, increases the rate of decomposition of primary carbide and produces more graphite particles per unit area. This first stage annealing is continued until all massive carbides are decomposed.

The soaking time (holding time at desired temperature) depends upon the size of casting. After completion of the first stage annealing, the microstructure consists of temper carbon nodules distributed throughout the matrix of saturated austenite.

After first stage annealing, the castings are rapidly cooled to about 750°C within 6 to 10 hours.

(b) Second Stage:

During the second stage annealing, the castings are slowly cooled through the critical range at which eutectoid reaction would take place. During this cooling, the carbon from austenite is converted into graphite, which deposits on the existing temper carbon particles. The remaining low carbon austenite transforms to ferrite. After completion of graphitization, no further structural changes take place during cooling upto the room temperature. At this stage, the microstructure remains constant i.e. temper carbon nodules in ferrite matrix. This is called as Ferrite malleable cast iron. (Fig. 5.6).

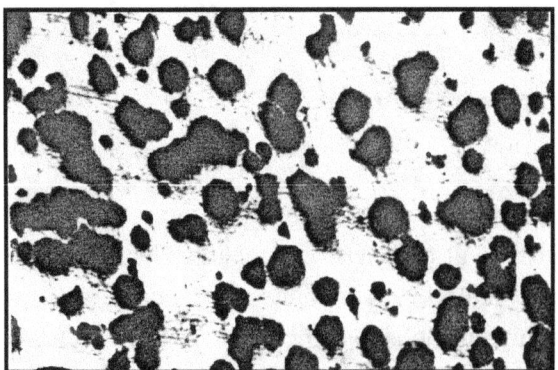 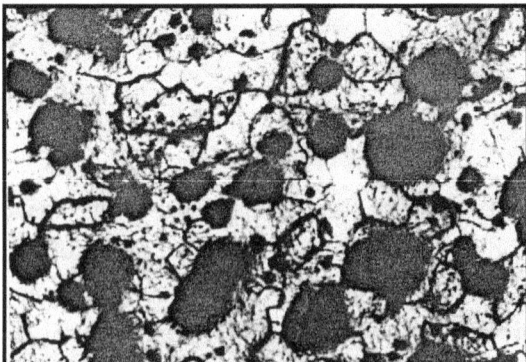

Fig. 5.6: Typical microstructure of ferritic malleable cast iron

Due to nodular shape of temper carbon, the ferrite matrix remains continuous. This gives better toughness.

The graphite nodule also serves as a lubricating phase for cutting tools. This offers a very high machinability to malleable cast irons.

(a) Copper - alloyed malleable iron,

(b) Copper - molybdenum malleable iron.

Applications of Ferrite Malleable Iron:

- Automotive components

- Agricultural field

- Rail road equipments

- Expansion joints and railing castings on bridges

- Chain hoist assemblies

- Pipe fittings.

Pearlitic Malleable Cast Iron: (May 10)

If a very small percentage of iron carbide is present in the microstructure, the mechanical properties drastically change. First stage graphitization is a stage must for malleable cast iron, whether it is pearlitic or ferritic type. The combined carbon can be retained in matrix by:

- Addition of manganese or

- Avoiding second stage annealing by fast cooling.

The amount of pearlite depends upon the rate of cooling and the temperature from which fast cooling starts. This cooling rate should be fast enough throughout the eutectoid temperature range or the matrix will be fully pearlitic. This results in strong and hard cast iron. These cast irons are also alloyed to improve corrosion resistance, hardenability and strength.

Applications of Pearlitic Malleable Cast Irons:

- Axles, housings, camshaft, crankshaft in automobiles,

- Gears, chain links, sprockets and elevator brackets in conveyor equipment,

- Rolls, pump parts, nozzle, cams, rocker arms as machine parts,

- Gun mounts, tank parts and pistol parts in ammunition,

- In tools as wrenches, hammers, clamps and shears.

Black Heart Malleable Iron:

This cast iron is produced by heating white cast iron in the air-tight boxes, but in contact with air at 850°C to 950°C. The cementite decomposes into small rosette of graphite. It is called as black heart due to its dark appearance, when fractured. It is because of formation of graphite.

White Heart Malleable Iron:

In this process, the castings are packed in the air-tight boxes with iron oxide. They are heated to about 1000°C. The ore oxidises and carbon in the castings draws it out. It gives ferritic structure near the surface and a pearlitic structure near the centre of casting. This cast iron behaves similar to mild steel castings, but with the advantages of very much lower melting point and higher fluidity.

Bull's-eye Structure:

This is obtained, when the cooling rate through the critical range is not fast enough to retain all combined carbon. Then the areas surrounding temper carbon nodules will be completely graphitized. The areas at the greater distance from nodules will be pearlitic. Such a structure is referred as a bull's eye structure.

Welding of pearlitic malleable cast iron is rarely recommended. It forms a brittle and low strength white iron layer under weld bead. This is because of melting and rapid freezing of malleable cast iron. Also, some of the temper carbon gets dissolved. This alters the pearlitic structure adjacent to white iron in the welding zone.

5.7 GRAY CAST IRON   (Dec. 09)

The fractured surface of these cast iron is always observed as of gray colour and hence, it is called gray cast iron. This is one of the most widely used types of cast iron. It contains the total carbon in free form i.e. graphite, which is of flake shape. In the production of gray cast iron, the alloy composition and cooling rates are adjusted to favour transformation of cementite into:

- Graphite and
- Austenite or Ferrite.

Mainly, hypoeutectic cast irons (2.5 to 4 per cent carbon) are used commercially.

In malleable cast iron, the graphite is formed during heat treatment, while in gray cast iron, it is formed during solidification. Due to flake shaped graphite, the continuity of matrix breaks and it shows less strength.

The solidification of these alloy starts by formation of primary austenite. Due to eutectic reaction, the carbon initially appears in cementite form. The graphitization processes may be accelerated by,

- High carbon content,
- High temperature and
- Proper percentage of graphitizing element e.g. silicon.

If the above factors are properly controlled, the alloy will follow a stable iron-graphite equilibrium diagram as shown in Fig. 5.7. At eutectic temperature, austenite and graphite are formed. The cementite gets rapidly graphitized. The appearance of graphite is like irregular, elongated and curved plates.

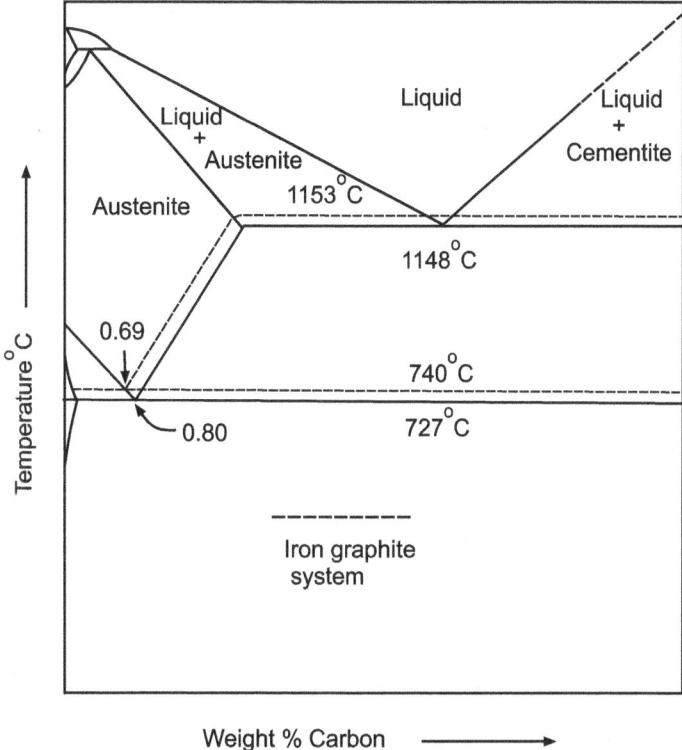

Fig. 5.7: Iron-graphite system superimposed on iron-iron carbide system

The solubility of carbon in austenite decreases with cooling. This favours additional precipitation of carbon. This precipitated carbon is graphite.

If the graphitization of eutectoid cementite occurs entirely, then ferrite matrix is formed. On the other hand, if the graphitization of eutectoid cementite is prevented, the matrix will be fully pearlitic. So, the matrix is determined by condition of eutectoid cementite. The matrix in which graphite is embedded, decides the strength of gray cast iron. A combination of ferrite and pearlite with graphite flake can also be obtained.

Silicon in Cast Iron:

Silicon is a very important element in the metallurgy of gray cast iron. It has following effects, when added in cast iron:

- increases fluidity,
- controls solidification,
- shifts eutectic composition to left,
- decreases austenite area,
- acts as a graphitizer and
- favours solidification as per iron-graphite system.

The relation of carbon and silicon content on the microstructure of thin sections of cast iron is shown in Fig. 5.8.

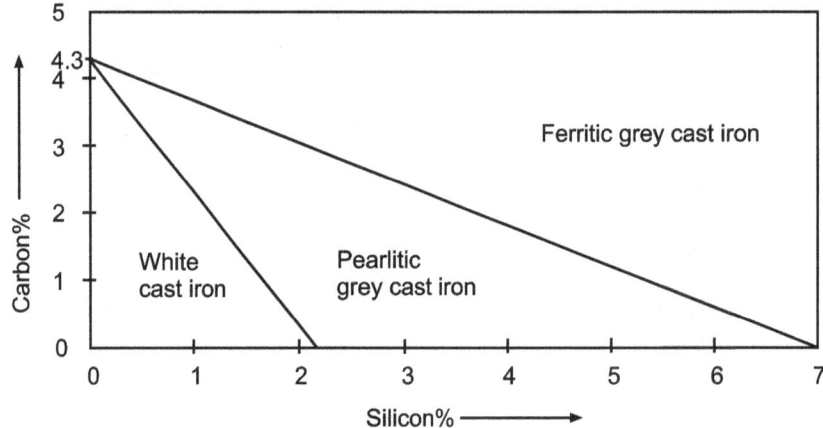

Fig. 5.8: Relation of microstructure with carbon and silicon content of cast iron

The effects of other elements are already discussed.

A typical microstructure of gray cast iron is shown in Fig. 5.9.

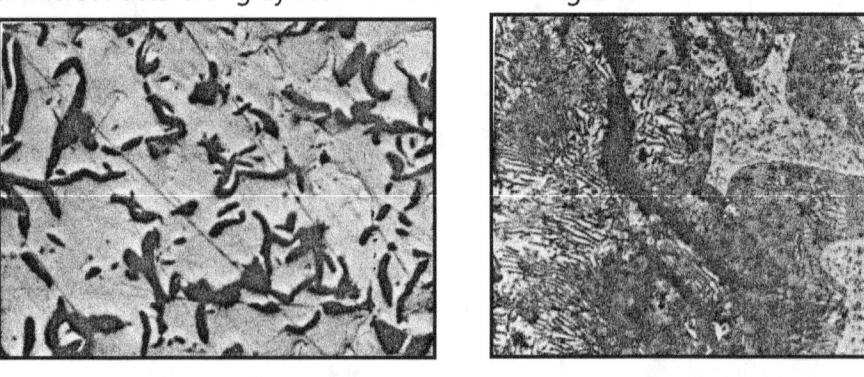

| (a) Unetched (100 X) | (b) Etched (200 X) |

Fig. 5.9: Typical microstructures of gray cast iron

5.8 SIZE AND DISTRIBUTION OF GRAPHITE FLAKES

Gray Cast Iron microstructure consists of graphite flakes and ferrite or pearlite matrix.

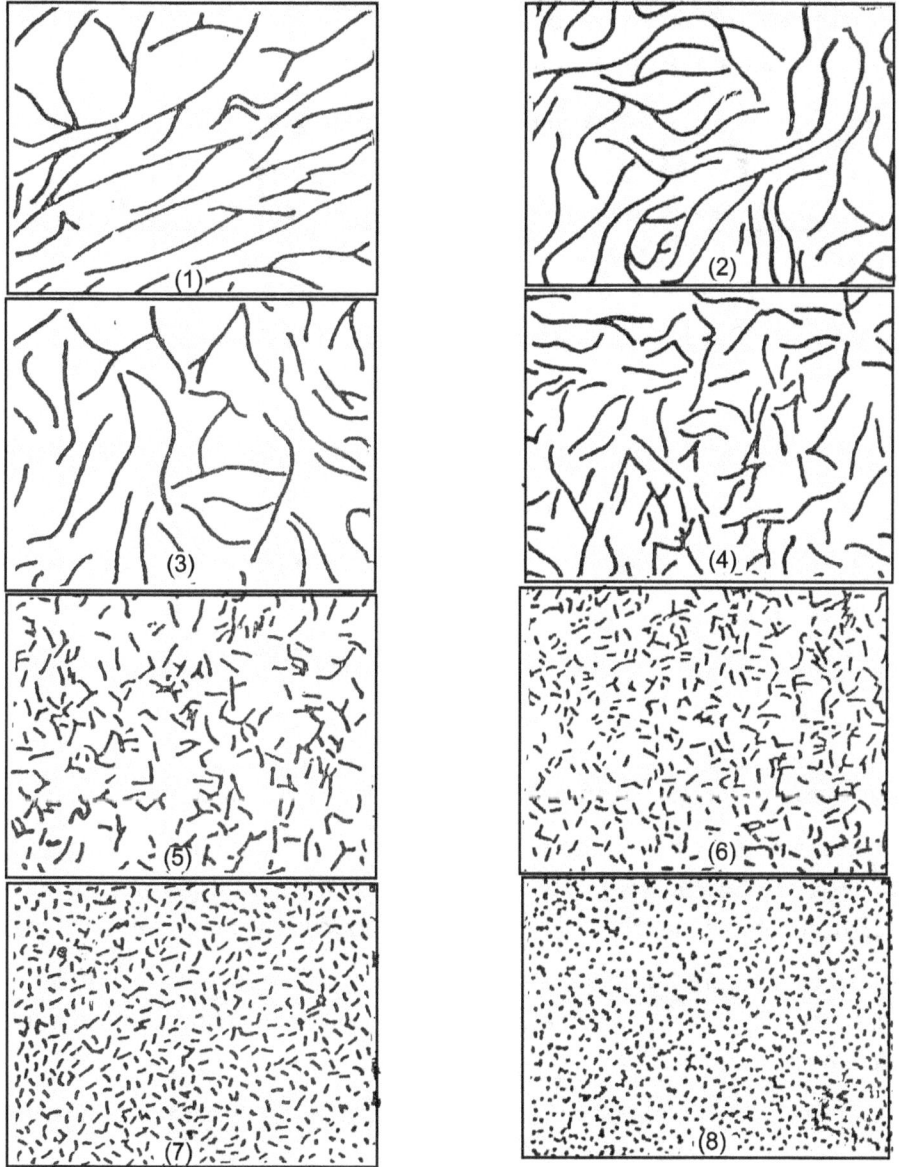

Fig. 5.10: Graphite size rating chart

The pearlitic matrix improves strength and ductility of cast iron. The large sized graphite flakes interrupt the continuity of pearlite matrix and lower the mechanical properties of cast iron. So, small graphite flakes are preferred.

The determination of graphite flake size is usually done by comparison method. The standard charts are made by the AFS (American Foundrymen's Society) and ASTM (American Society for Testing Materials). The samples can be compared in unetched condition at 100X. The largest graphite flake should be compared.

The numbers are represented as given in Table 5.4.

Table 5.4: Graphite flake sizes

AFS – ASTM Flake size No.	Length of longest flake at 100X (inch)
1	4 or more
2	2 to 4
3	1 to 2
4	$\frac{1}{2}$ to 1
5	$\frac{1}{4}$ to $\frac{1}{2}$
6	$\frac{1}{8}$ to $\frac{1}{4}$
7	$\frac{1}{16}$ to $\frac{1}{8}$
8	$\frac{1}{16}$ or less

The flake size comparison chart is shown in Fig. 5.10.

Coarse and less amount of graphite is formed due to slow cooling of hypoeutectic iron because of large crystals of primary austenite. Amount of graphite may be increased by increasing carbon percentage. The flake size can be reduced by increasing silicon content.

Addition of small amount of materials called inoculant, reduce flake size and improve distribution. Inoculating agents are metallic calcium, aluminium, titanium, zirconium, silicon carbide, calcium silicide etc.

The gray cast irons are also characterized and classified as per type of graphite distribution. Following are various graphite flake types:

- Type A
- Type B
- Type C
- Type D
- Type E

These are shown in Fig. 5.11.

 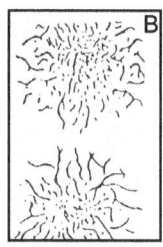 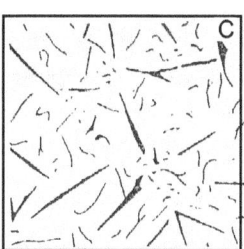

Uniform distribution,   Rosette grouping,   Superimposed flake size,
random orientation   random orientation   random orientation

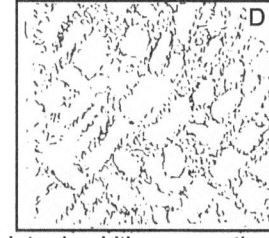 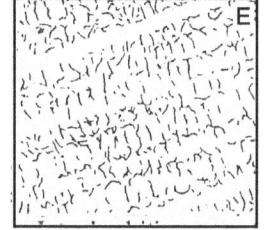

Interdendritic segregation,   Interdendritic segregation,
random orientation   preferred orientation

Fig. 5.11: Types of graphite flakes in gray iron

- The most desirable flake pattern in gray cast iron is uniform distribution and random orientation of type A. This is observed in a eutectic alloy.

- The type B shows a rosette pattern. This is observed in mottled cast iron, which consists of mixture of white and gray iron. The cooling in this region is optimum.

- Type C shows a large and straight flakes with random orientation. The flake sizes are superimposed (mixed). This results from hypereutectic irons. To avoid this type, carbon content should be reduced.

- Type D shows interdendritic segregation and random orientation, while type E shows interdendritic segregation with preferred orientation. Both result from the graphitization of a normal eutectic structure. These types occur in high purity and in rapidly cooled irons. The interdendritic pattern and high graphite content weaken the iron. These types can be avoided by slow cooling rates and addition of grain refiners i.e. inoculants.

5.9 PROPERTIES OF GRAY CAST IRON   (May 10, Dec. 08, 09)

Gray cast iron castings are specified in seven classes as Nos. 20, 25, 30, 35 40, 50, 60. It gives minimum tensile strength of test bars in thousands of pounds per square inch.

e.g. Class 20 - 20000 psi   Minimum tensile strength
      Class 40 - 40000 psi

Typical Mechanical Properties of Gray Cast Iron:

Most of the gray cast iron shows higher compressive and torsional shear strength. They possess low notch sensitivity. The damping property is a unique property of this cast iron.

Applications of Gray Cast Irons: (Dec. 2009)

Following are some typical examples of gray cast irons.

    (a)   Counter weights for elevators and industrial furnace doors.

    (b)   Guards and frames around hazardous machinery.

    (c)   Many types of gear housings.

    (d)   Enclosures of electrical equipments.

    (e)   Pump and steam turbine housing.

    (f)   Lathe bed.

    (g)   Motor frames.

    (h)   Base for heavy machinery.

5.10 CHILLED CAST IRON   (Dec. 2013)

This is a combination of two types of cast irons namely white cast iron and gray cast iron. These are produced by casting the molten metal with a metal chiller. This results in very fast cooling rates at the surface, which is in contact of metal chiller. It gives hard, abrasion resistance white iron structure backed up by soft and tough gray iron core. So, a combination of the properties of white cast iron and gray cast iron occurs.

The intermediate portion between white and gray cast iron gives a mixture of cementite and graphite flakes called mottled cast iron.

Thickness of white layer is called as depth of the chill. The depth of chill decreases with increasing carbon content, addition of manganese, phosphorus, nickel and thickness of chilling plate.

Applications of Chilled Cast Iron:
- Railway car wheels,
- Crushing rolls,
- Stamp shoes and dies,
- Sprockets, ploughshares and other heavy duty machinery parts.

5.11 NODULAR CAST IRON

This is also known as ductile iron and spheroidal iron.

In this type of cast iron, graphite is present in the form of tiny balls or spheroids. These compact spheroids interrupt the continuity of matrix much less than graphite flakes. This results in higher strength and toughness. The spheroids are more round than the irregular aggregates of graphite found in malleable iron.

The graphite gains spheroidal shape because of addition of a small amount of alloy elements as magnesium or cerium. These additions are made to the laddle just before casting. Desulphurization is necessary before laddle addition as Mg has a strong affinity towards sulphur. By adjusting the rate of cooling and the composition, the matrix can be ferritic or pearlite. The ferritic matrix gives maximum ductility, toughness and machinability. The nodulizing elements have a low density, hence, they are always added in the form of master alloys.

Some of the mechanical properties of nodular iron are given in Table 5.1.

Fig. 5.12 shows typical microstructure of nodular cast iron.

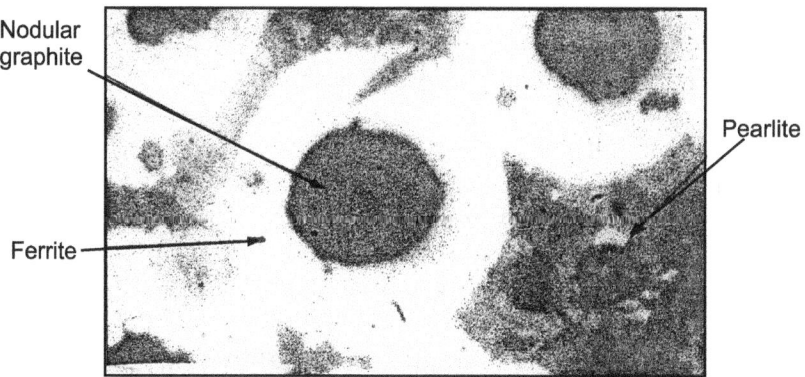

**Fig. 5.12: A typical microstructure of nodular cast iron
Etched (Bull's eye structure)**

Applications:

- In agriculture - tractor and implement parts.
- In automotive - crankshaft, piston and cylinder heads.
- Electrical fittings, switch boxes, motor frames, circuit breaker parts.
- In mining - hoist drums, drive pulleys, flywheels, elevator buckets.
- Steel mill - work rolls, furnace doors, table rolls and bearings.

- Tool and die - wrenches, levers, handles, chuck bodies and dies for shaping non-ferrous metal and alloys.

5.12 ALLOY CAST IRONS

These are the cast irons, in which the alloying elements are intentionally added to modify properties. The effect of alloying elements may be explained as follows:

(1) Chromium:

It tends to increase the combined carbon. It forms complex iron- chromium carbides. It increases strength, hardness and resistance to wear and heat. The machinability gets decreased. The effect of Cr is discussed as follows:

% of Chromium	Its effect on the structure
0.0	Ferrite and coarse graphite
0.6	Fine graphite and pearlite
1.0	Fine graphite, pearlite and small carbides
3.0	Graphite disappears
5.0	Massive carbides
10 - 30	Very fine carbides

Upto 35% Cr may be added to improve resistance.

(2) Copper:

It acts as a graphitizer. It is added in the range of 0.25 to 2.5%. Copper breaks the massive cementite, which increases its strength.

(3) Molybdenum:

It acts as a mild stabilizer for carbides. It is added in the quantities from 0.25 to 1.25%. It improves fatigue strength, tensile strength, transverse strength and hardness.

(4) Vanadium:

It is a powerful carbide former. It stabilizes cementite by reducing graphitization. It is added between 0.10 and 0.25%. It increases tensile strength, transverse strength and hardness.

(5) Nickel:

It also acts as a graphitizer (0.5 to 0.6%). It controls the structure by retarding austenite transformation and stabilizing pearlite. It maintains the cementite at eutectoid quantity. For excellent abrasion resistance, about 4% Nickel with 1.5% Chromium.

The composition and mechanical properties of some low alloy cast irons are given in table 4.11.

TYPES OF ALLOY CAST IRON

5.13 NI-HARD

This is a modification of white cast iron. By addition of chromium and nickel, the hardness and wear resistance of white cast iron is improved. During solidification, the austenite transforms to martensite because of increased hardenability. As the M_f i.e. temperature of martensite finish transformation is below the room temperature, this structure shows austenite. The microstructure at the room temperature consists of

(a)   austenite matrix,   (b)   martensite needles and

(c)   massive alloy carbides.

Nickel may act as graphitizer, if added alone; hence, chromium is added with nickel. These cast irons contain -

Nickel 3 to 5%.

Chromium 1 to 3%.

Ni-hard cast iron has a continuous network of carbides, which reduces a fatigue and impact strength. So, 4 to 8% Ni and upto 13% Cr is added to break the network. This is called as modified Ni-hard cast iron. Due to higher nickel and chromium percentage, untransformed austenite in cast condition increases. After heat treatment, this untransformed austenite changes to bainite or martensite.

5.14 NI-RESIST

This is a modification of gray cast iron. It can be obtained by adding a large amount of nickel. Nickel increases stability of austenite and the matrix becomes austenitic. Sometimes, they are also called as austenitic cast irons.

Ni-resist iron contains:

Nickel   -   15 to 35%

Chromium   -   upto 5%

Copper   -   5 to 8% *

Magnesium   -   0.08% *

(* Found in certain grades only)

The microstructure shows graphite nodules and alloy carbides in austenitic matrix.

These are characterized by,

(a) Higher corrosion resistance,

(b) Erosion resistance,

(c) Scaling resistance.

These are used in,

- Generator and motor covers,
- Pump bodies and impellers,
- Exhaust manifolds,
- Sewage pipelines etc.

5.15 SILAL AND NICHROSILAL

The oxidation resistance of cast iron can be improved by adding silicon upto 7%. The microstructure shows fine graphite in ferritic matrix. This is called as Silal. It is hard and brittle.

Nichrosilal contains nickel (about 20%) and chromium (about 4%). It reduces brittleness of silal cast iron by changing ferrite matrix to austenite.

These are used in,

- High temperature moulds,
- Steam/gas turbine parts,
- Melting crucibles etc.

5.16 MEEHANITE

It is also called as high duty cast iron. It is produced by adding calcium silicide to gray cast iron. It gives a fine and uniform size and distribution of graphite flakes. This gives better mechanical properties.

QUESTIONS

1. State whether the following statements are *True* or *False* and justify your answers.

   (i)   Malleabilizing is an annealing treatment given to white cast irons.

   (ii) Cast irons are superior to steels.

   (iii) The properties of cast iron can be altered by cooling rate.

   (iv) White cast iron is used as liners for ball mill.

(v)   Welding of pearlitic malleable cast iron is rarely recommended.

(vi) High carbon content in cast iron favours graphitization.

(vii) Type A graphite is desired for engineering applications.

(viii) Gray cast iron is used in crushing rolls.

(ix) Chilled cast iron is used in crushing rolls.

(x)   The nodular shape of graphite is preferred to flake shape.

(xi) Alloy cast irons are superior than plain cast irons.

Ans.:

(i)   True   (ii) False   (iii) True   (iv) True   (v) True   (vi) True

(vii) True   (viii) True   (ix) True   (x) True   (xi) True

2. Discuss the applications of various cast irons.

3. Why are the alloys of iron and carbon with carbon percentage 2 to 6.67 called as cast iron ?

4. Write a short note on alloy cast iron.

5. Suggest a suitable cast iron for following applications –

    (i)   Flywheels,

    (ii) Crusher jaws,

    (iii) Automotive shafts.

6. Why is the iron-iron carbide diagram not referred for the study of cast irons ?

UNIVERSITY QUESTIONS

1. Compare the microstructures of white cast iron, gray cast iron, nodular cast iron and malleable cast iron.   **(Dec. 08)**

2. Differentiate between pearlitic and feritic malleable cast iron ?   **(Dec. 08)**

3. How S.G. iron is produced.   **(Dec. 08)**

4. Explain the effect of various elements on the microstructure of cast iron. **(Dec. 09)**

5. What are the advantages of cast iron over steels ? Differentiate.   **(May 09)**

6. Suggest a suitable cast iron for cylinder head.   **(May 09)**

7. Compare SG iron and malleable iron with respect to microstructure, production, composition and application. **(May 09, 10)**

8. White cast iron finds limited application in engineering in industry. Do you agree/disagree ? Justify. **(May 09)**

9. Explain the meaning of ductile and malleable cast irons in terms of ductility and malleability. **(Dec. 09)**

❏❏❏

Chapter 6

NON-FERROUS ALLOYS

6.1 INTRODUCTION

Non-ferrous metals and alloys do not contain iron as a major element. They exhibit different properties compared to ferrous metals and alloys. Hence, their applications also differ from ferrous metals. Copper, aluminium and their alloys are the principal non-ferrous groups. In this chapter, the following major non-ferrous alloys are discussed.

1. Copper and its alloys,
2. Aluminium and its alloys,
3. Nickel and its alloys,
4. Lead and its alloys,
5. Tin and its alloys,
6. Titanium and its alloys,
7. Zinc and its alloys,
8. Bearing metals and
9. Noble metals.

6.2 COPPER AND ITS ALLOYS   (Dec. 2009, 2013; May 2010, 11)

Copper is extracted from its ore, called copper sulphide. Pure copper possesses the following properties:

* Higher electrical and thermal conductivity.
* Good corrosion resistance.
* Better machinability and ease of fabrication.
* Good ductility and malleability etc.
* Melting point 1083°C.
* Density.

Copper is mostly used for electrical applications. It is also used for other applications, which include automobile radiator, water heaters, refrigerators, heat exchangers, distillery equipments etc.

Copper is usually alloyed to improve its properties. Addition of even a very small quantity of other element improves the properties of copper. For example,

(a) **Arsenical copper:** Arsenic, when added upto 0.3%, improves corrosion resistance of copper. This is used in condenser applications.

(b) **Free-cutting copper:** Tellurium, when added upto 0.6%, improves machinability of copper. This is used in small sized electrical instruments.

(c) **Silver-bearing copper:** Silver, when added upto 0.1%, prevents softening of copper during soldering purposes.

(d) **Phosphorised copper:** Phosphorus, when added upto 0.02%, controls the electrical conductivity of copper.

Important copper alloys are as follows:

- Brasses,
- Bronzes,
- Cupronickels and
- Nickel silvers.

6.2.1 Brasses   (May 2013)

Brass is an alloy of copper and zinc. Addition of zinc in varying percentage results in improving colour, strength, machinability, hardness etc. of the alloy.

A typical copper zinc equilibrium diagram is as shown in Fig. 6.1.

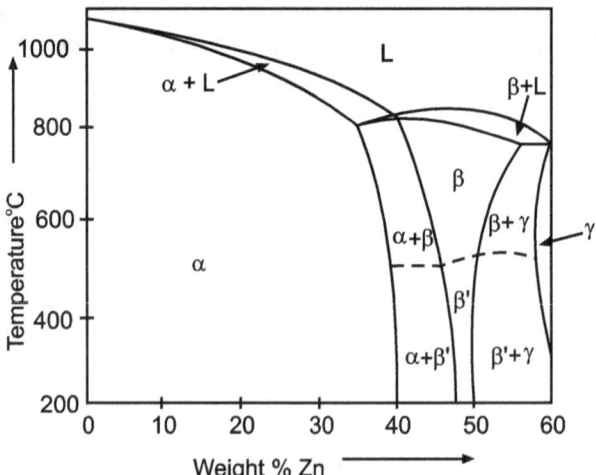

Fig. 6.1: The copper rich portion of copper-zinc equilibrium diagram

The solubility of zinc in copper varies with temperature.

Two phases are observed in copper-zinc system. The α phase is a solid solution of zinc in face centred cubic copper. The solubility of zinc in α solid solution is 32.5 per cent at 903°C. It increases upto 39 per cent at 456°C. Further addition of zinc results in the formation of an intermediate solid solution called Beta (β) phase. It has a body centred cubic structure.

Beta (β) phase shows random dispersion of copper and zinc atoms at higher temperatures. This structure is called as disordered solid solution. With decrease in temperature, copper atoms get arranged at the corners and zinc atoms at the centers of the cube. Due to this definite position in the BCC lattice, the resulting phase is called as 'ordered solid solution'. This is shown as β' phase. This disorder to order transformation takes place at 456°C with brasses having more than 39 per cent zinc.

Copper-zinc alloys have one more solid solution called gamma (γ) phase. It is observed in brasses having more than 55% zinc. Gamma phase is very brittle and hard. So these brasses are not used commercially.

Due to these two distinct phases, the brasses are classified as alpha (α) brasses and alpha plus beta (α + β) brasses.

A] Alpha Brasses: (May 2011, Dec. 2011)

These are the alloys of copper and zinc having zinc percentage upto 36. However, optimum properties of strength, ductility and hardness are observed in brasses having 30 per cent zinc. Therefore, alpha brasses are usually termed as 70: 30 brasses (70% Cu and 30% Zn). These are called as alpha brasses as they essentially contain a single phase i.e. alpha (α). In general, these brasses show higher ductility and corrosion resistance. α brasses are usually classified by their colour.

   (1) Red brasses,   (2) Yellow brasses.

(1) Red brass:

These are the brasses having zinc percentage upto 20. These brasses do not show the problem of dezincification or season cracking. These brasses have a better corrosion resistance. Following are the important red brasses.

(a) **Gilding metal:** (95% Cu, 5% Zn). These alloys are having zinc around 5 per cent. Addition of zinc improves strength of copper. This alloy shows good ductility and better pressing ability. This is used for fuse caps of detonators, medals, coins, tokens, emblems and dress jewellery. This alloy can be gold plated to improve aesthetic look.

(b) Red brass: (85% Cu, 15% Zn). This alloy shows improved corrosion resistance. This is used for hardware purposes such as screws, sockets and for condenser and heat exchanger tubes.

(2) Yellow brass:

These brasses are having 20 to 36 per cent zinc. Due to higher zinc percentage, these brasses are susceptible to stress corrosion cracking (i.e. season cracking) and dezincification (These are explained in detail in the book 'Engineering Metallurgy – I chapter No. 8 corrosion and its prevention). Following are important brasses from this group.

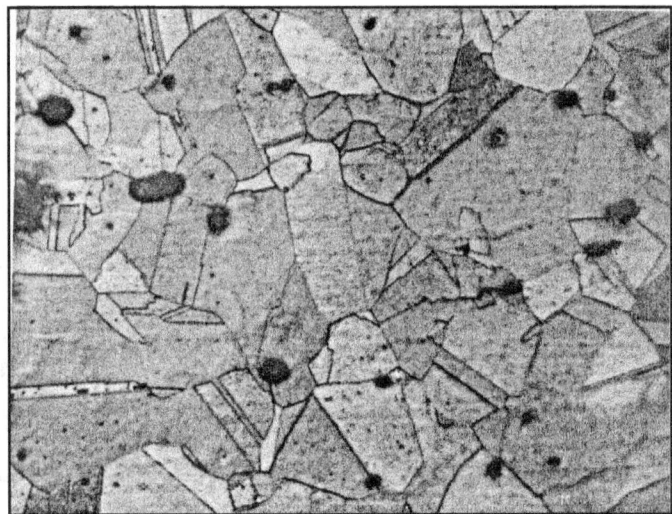

Fig. 6.2: Microstructure of cartridge brass (200 X)

(a) Cartridge brass: (70% Cu, 30% Zn). This is a typical single phase brass. This shows higher ductility and malleability. It can be easily cold worked due to its single phase structure. It shows an excellent deep drawing property. These brasses are usually cold worked and annealed. They show a typical equiaxed grain structure and twins in annealed condition (Fig. 6.2). As the name itself implies, the cartridge brass is mainly used for making cartridge cases in ammunition. Other applications of cartridge brass include radiator cores, headlight reflectors, hardwares, plumbing accessories etc.

(b) Admiralty brass: (71% Cu, 28% Zn, 1% Sn). Addition of tin improves strength and corrosion resistance of brass. This brass retains its strength even at a higher temperature and hence. it is used for condensers and heat exchanger tubes in steam power plants.

B] Alpha plus Beta Brasses: (Dec. 2012)

These contain 38 to 45 per cent zinc. Referring to Cu-Zn binary diagram, it would be clear that these brasses show two phase structure. Among these two phases, the β phase is more hard and brittle. This phase becomes ductile at a higher temperature. Therefore, alpha plus beta brasses are never cold worked. However, they can be hot worked effectively. Following are the important α + β brasses:

(1) Muntz metal: (May 2012)

(60% Cu, 40% Zn). This is the most widely used α + β brass. This shows excellent hot working properties. A typical microstructure of muntz metal is shown in Fig. 6.3. In the sheet form, this alloy is used for ship sheathing, perforated metal and decoration. It is also used in pump parts as valve, condenser tubes, brazing rods and utensils.

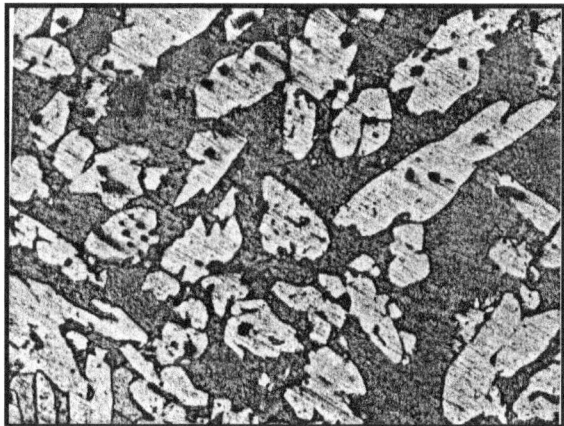

Fig. 6.3: Microstructure of Muntz Metal (200 X)

The machinability of muntz metal is improved by addition of 0.4 to 0.8 per cent lead. This is also called as leaded brass.

(2) Free cutting brass:

(61.5% Cu, 35.5% Zn, 3% Pb). The addition of lead in higher percentage improves machinability and corrosion resistance. Lead does not get dissolved in brass and hence, it appears in the form of globules. It is used for machine parts and also for hardwares.

(3) Naval brass: (Dec. 2008)

(60% Cu, 39.25% Zn and 0.75% Sn). Tin increases corrosion resistance of brass. The name Naval brass is due to its higher salt water corrosion resistance, which makes it useful in naval (marine) applications. Naval brass is used for condenser plates, propeller shafts, piston rods and other marine hardwares.

Naval brass is also called as Tobin bronze.

(4) Forging brass:

(60% Cu, 38% Zn, 2% Pb). As these brasses show excellent hot working properties, they are used for hot forgings.

(5) Manganese bronze:

(58.5% Cu, 39% Zn, 1.4% Fe, 1% Sn, 0.1% Mn). This is a type of brass and not bronze. Due to its higher strength and wear resistance, it is used for clutch disks. It is also used for extrusion, pump rods, shafts etc. Manganese bronze is one of the high tensile brasses.

(6) Brazing brass:

A brazing brass has a typical composition as follows:

Copper – 50%

Zinc – 50%

This brass has lower melting point. It is used for joining of brasses.

C] Cast Brasses:

Generally, plain brasses are used for mechanical workings, while alloy brasses are used for casting purposes. Cast brasses contain higher amounts of lead, tin etc.

A typical example of cast brass is leaded red brass. Its chemical composition is as follows:

Copper - 85%

Tin   - 5%

Lead   - 5%

Zinc   - 5%

It is also called as leaded gun metal or ounce metal. This brass shows a good castability and machining property. It is used in low pressure valves, pipe fittings and small pump castings.

6.2.2 Bronzes

If an alloy of copper contains any alloying elements other than zinc, it is called as bronze e.g. Copper and aluminium alloy is called as aluminium bronze. Following are some of the important bronzes:

(A) Tin bronze,

(B) Silicon bronze,

(C) Beryllium bronze and

(D) Aluminium bronze.

(A) Tin Bronzes:

These are the alloys of copper and tin. Copper-tin equilibrium diagram is shown in Fig. 6.4. The solubility of tin in copper varies with temperature. The higher solubility of tin in copper observed during the temperature range of 520°C - 586°C is 15.8 per cent. Above 586°C, the solubility of tin decreases. At 798°C, tin shows 13.5 per cent solubility in copper. Below 520°C, again the solubility of tin in copper decreases upto room temperature.

The following transformations are observed in Cu - Sn equilibrium diagrams.

    (1) Peritectic transformation at 798°C. α + L → β

    (2) Eutectoid transformation of β at 586°C. β → α + γ

    (3) Eutectoid transformation of δ at 350°C. δ → α + ∈

The transformations below 586°C are very slow. Therefore, practically the dotted vertical line gives solubility limit. For this reason, slow cooled tin bronzes (less than 7% Sn) show only single phase (i.e. α).

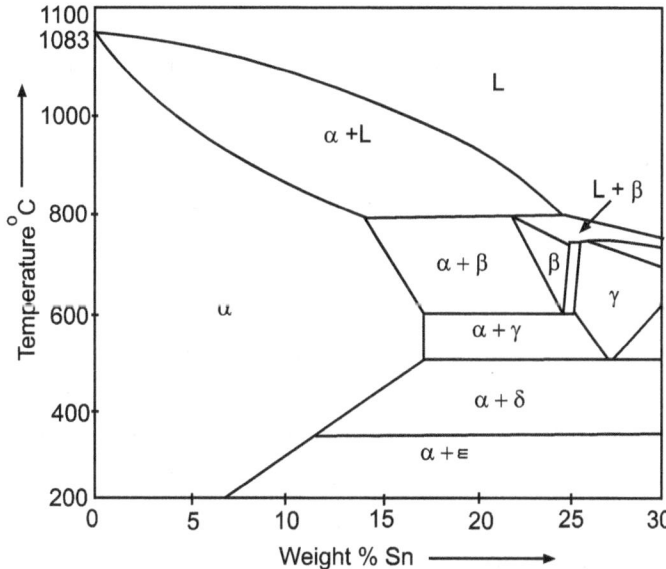

Fig. 6.4: Copper-rich portion of copper-tin equilibrium diagram

The copper-tin equilibrium diagram shows a wide separation of liquids line from solidus line. This results in coring. Therefore, coring is always observed in cast tin bronzes.

Tin oxide is formed during casting of tin bronzes. These are hard and brittle oxide particles. Tin oxide reduces mechanical properties. Hence, deoxidisers are often added during melting. Phosphorus is a strong deoxidiser for tin bronze.

Following are the applications of tin bronzes with varying tin percentages:

Table 6.1: Applications of tin bronzes

1.	Upto 8% Sn	Sheet, wires, coins, electric sockets, snap switches.
2.	8 – 12% Sn	Machine and marine components.
3.	12 – 20% Sn	Bearings, bushings.
4.	20 – 25% Sn	Bells

Following are some of the typical types of tin bronzes.

(1) Low tin bronze:

It contains 0.1 to 0.25% lead, 3.75 to 3.9% tin and balance copper. This alloy is hardened by cold working. It has good elastic properties, corrosion resistance, fatigue resistance etc. It is used for springs, contact blades etc.

(2) Gun metal: **(May 08, 09, 11, 12)**

It contains 88% copper, 10% tin and 2% zinc. Similar to phosphorus, zinc also acts as a deoxidiser. Gun metal shows excellent fluidity and corrosion resistance. It is used for making gun barrels and other ordance components.

Leaded gun metal also shows better castability. It has a typical composition as 85% Cu, 5% Sn, 5% Pb and 5% Zn. Due to lead, this alloy shows good machinability.

It is used in low pressure valves, pipe fittings, marine castings etc.

(3) Phosphor bronze:

In tin bronzes, phosphorus is added for deoxidising purpose. Cast phosphor bronzes contain 0.03 to 0.25% phosphorus, 10% tin and balance copper. It shows excellent casting properties. It is used for making bearings and bushes due to its antifriction properties. Wrought phosphorus bronzes contain 0.1 to 0.5% phosphorus, 5 to 6% tin and balance copper. These alloys are cold worked to improve strength and hardness. These are used for electrical contacts, springs etc.

(4) Leaded bronze or Plastic bronze:

It contains lead in the range of 5 to 24%, tin around 2% and balance copper. It shows the highest bearing properties and is used for bearing applications.

(B) Silicon Bronze:

Silicon bronzes are the alloys of copper and silicon. A copper rich portion of copper-silicon equilibrium diagram is shown in Fig. 6.5.

The maximum solubility of silicon is 5.3 per cent at 853°C. It decreases with decrease in temperature. Silicon shows less than 4.0 per cent solubility in copper at room temperature. These alloys are not heat treated to improve their hardness. They are cold worked to achieve the desired strength.

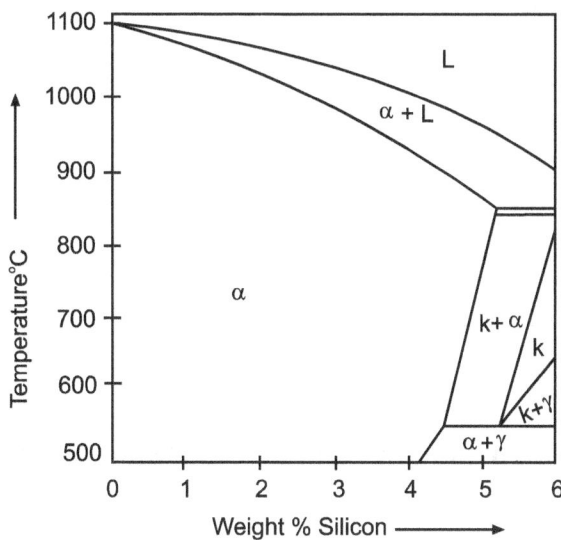

Fig. 6.5: Copper-rich portion of copper-silicon equilibrium diagram

Silicon bronzes (3 to 5% Si) exhibit excellent corrosion resistance, good castability and higher strength. These alloys are used for pressure vessels, marine containers, marine hardwares, electrical fittings etc.

(C) Beryllium Bronzes:

Beryllium bronzes are the alloys of copper and beryllium. The copper rich portion of Cu-Be equilibrium diagram is shown in Fig. 6.6. It would be clear from this diagram that beryllium shows about 2.1 per cent solubility in copper at 864°C. It is less than 0.25 per cent at room temperature. This drastic change in solubility gives rise to precipitation hardening property.

The optimum properties are obtained in 2.0 per cent alloys. The precipitation hardening cycle includes heating of alloy at 800°C and quenching in water. This is followed by reheating upto 300°C for a couple of hours to accelerate aging.

Beryllium bronzes show a combination of excellent formability with high yield strength, better fatigue strength, high resilience and non-sparking properties.

These bronzes are used in diaphragms, contact bridges, bolts, screws, springs etc., in electrical applications. They are also used as non-sparking tools.

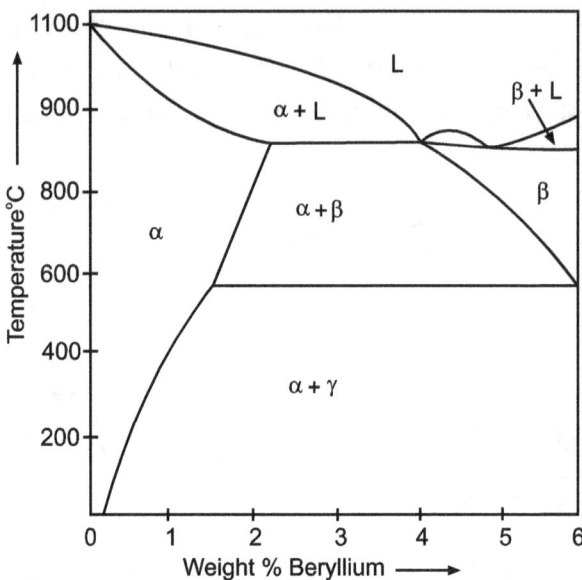

Fig. 6.6: Copper rich portion of copper-beryllium equilibrium diagram

(D) Aluminium Bronzes:

These are the alloys of copper and aluminium. Fig. 6.7 shows copper-aluminium equilibrium diagram. The solubility of aluminium in copper at 1040°C is 7.4 per cent. The solubility increases with decreasing temperature. The maximum solubility of aluminium is 9.4 per cent at 565°C.

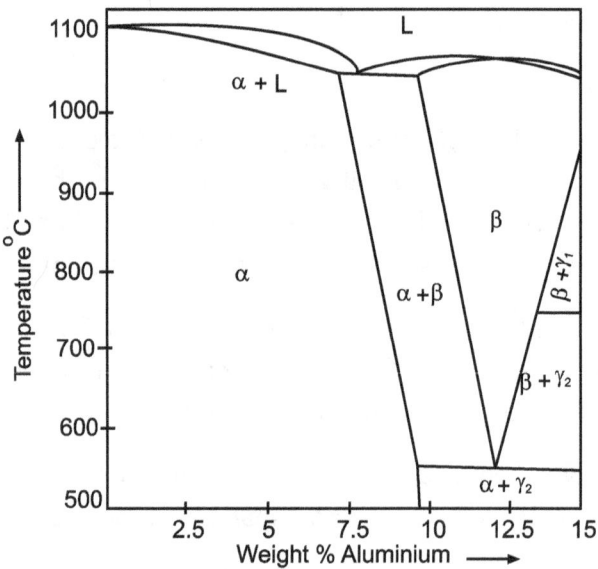

Fig. 6.7: Copper rich portion of the copper-aluminium alloy system

Aluminium bronzes with 11.8 per cent aluminium undergo eutectoid transformation at 565°C as $\beta \rightarrow \alpha + \gamma_2$.

Similar to steels, aluminium bronzes can also be heat treated, e.g. quenching this alloy (with 11.8% Al) from 900°C produces a structure which consists entirely of the β phase. This is analogous with martensite in steel. Therefore, it is stated that aluminium bronzes show martensitic transformation. Aluminium bronzes show excellent high temperature corrosion resistance. This is because of the formation of a protective self healing film of Al_2O_3. They show a good combination of ductility and strength.

Aluminium bronzes are called as imitation gold due to their colour and high degree polishing.

Following are the two types of aluminium bronzes:

(1) Single phase aluminium bronzes:

These alloys contain 4 to 7.5 per cent Al. Due to single phase structure, they can be cold worked. They show an excellent ductility and malleability. The corrosion resistance of these alloys is better for atmospheric and water environment. They are used for condenser tubes, corrosion resistant vessels, marine sheathing etc.

(2) Two phase aluminium bronzes:

They contain 7.5 to 11 per cent Al. These can be heat treated. They are hot worked effectively. They are used for gears, pump parts, non-sparking tools, drawing and forming dies, bearing bushings etc.

6.2.3 Copper-Nickel Alloys

These are the alloys of copper and nickel. Upto 60 per cent nickel is used with copper. These are relatively expensive copper-base alloys. Copper and nickel are completely soluble in each other in liquid as well as solid state. Following transformation is observed in all copper-nickel alloys. $L \rightarrow \alpha + L \rightarrow \alpha$.

Therefore, all copper-nickel alloys show a single phase (i.e. α) at room temperature. Due to complete solubility, these alloys cannot be heat treated. Their properties can be altered only by cold working. The mechanical properties such as strength, hardness are improved with the addition to nickel upto 65 per cent. Following are the important types of copper-nickel alloys.

(a) Cupronickels: These alloys contain nickel upto 30 per cent. The cupronickel alloys have a higher resistance to corrosion, fatigue and erosion corrosion. They are used for condensers, heat exchanger tubes, distillators etc.

(b) Constantan: This is the alloy containing about 45 per cent nickel. This alloy has a very high electrical resistivity. Its electrical resistivity is almost constant over a temperature range. Constantan is used in the form of wires for making resistors and thermocouples.

6.2.4 Nickel–Silvers

These are the alloys of copper, nickel and zinc. A typical composition contains 50 to 70 per cent Cu, 5 to 30 per cent Ni, 4 to 30 per cent Zn. The addition of nickel to copper zinc alloy gives it a silver-blue-white colour. They are also called as *German silver*. They show a higher corrosion resistance and better cold working properties. Silver, chromium etc. can be effectively plated on these alloys. They are used for rivets, screws, jewellery etc. and domestic table cutlery as an alternative to stainless steel.

Two phase ($\alpha + \beta$) nickel-silvers are observed with 50 to 60 per cent copper. They show high modulus of elasticity and are used for springs and electrical contacts in telecommunication system.

Some of the typical copper alloys are tabulated with their compositions, properties and applications in Table 6.2.

Table 6.2: Typical compositions, properties and applications of some copper base alloys

(May 08, 09, 10; Dec. 08, 09, 10)

	Alloy	Compositions	Properties	Applications
1.	Gilding metal	95% Cu, 5% Zn	Better ductility and formability.	Fuse caps of detonator, coins and emblems.
2.	Red brass	85% Cu, 15% Zn	Better corrosion resistance.	Condenser and heat exchanger tubes.
3.	Cartridge brass	70% Cu, 30% Zn	Higher ductility and malleability.	Cartridge cases in ammunition, headlight reflector.

... Contd.

4.	Admiralty brass	71% Cu, 28% Zn, 1% Sn	Improved strength and corrosion.	Condenser and heat exchanger tubes in steam power plants.
5.	Aluminium brass	76% Cu, 22% Zn, 2% Al	Higher corrosion resistance.	Marine applications.
6.	Muntz metal	60% Cu, 40% Zn	Excellent hot working properties.	Pump parts, brazing rods and utensils.
7.	Free cutting brass	61.5% Cu, 35.5% Zn, 3% Pb	Higher machinability and corrosion resistance.	Machine parts and hardwares.
8.	Naval brass or Tobin bronze	60% Cu, 39.25% Zn, 0.75% Sn	Increased corrosion resistance to salt water.	Propeller shaft, piston rod and marine hardware.
9.	Forging brass	60% Cu, 38% Zn, 2% Pb	Good hot working properties.	Hot forgings.
10.	Manganese bronze	58.4% Cu, 39% Zn, 1.4% Fe, 1% Sn, 0.1% Mn	Higher strength and wear resistance.	High tensile bolts, clutch disc etc.
11.	Brazing bars	50% Cu, 50% Zn	Low melting point.	Brazing rods.
12.	Leaded red brass or leaded gun metal or ounce metal	85% Cu, 5% Sn, 5% Pb, 5% Zn	Good castability and machinability.	Low pressure valves, pipe fittings and pump castings.
13.	Low tin bronze	0.1 to 0.25% Pb, 3.75 to 3.95% Sn, balance Cu.	Good elastic properties, corrosion resistance and fatigue resistance.	Springs, contact blades.
14.	Phosphor bronze	0.03 to 0.25% P, 10% Sn, balance Cu.	Excellent casting and antifriction properties.	Bearing and bushes.
15.	Leaded bronze or plastic bronze	5 to 24% Pb, 2% Sn, balance Cu.	Highest antifriction properties.	Bearings.
16.	Silicon bronze	4 to 5% Si, balance Cu.	Good corrosion resistance, strength and castability.	Pressure vessels, marine containers.
17.	Beryllium bronzes	2% Be, balance Cu	Excellent formability, fatigue strength and non-sparking properties.	Diaphragms, contact bridges in electrical application and non-sparking tools.

18. Aluminium bronzes			
(a) Single phase	4 to 7.5% Al, Cu balance	Excellent ductility, malleability and corrosion resistance.	Condenser tubes, marine sheathing.
(b) Two phase	Cu 7.5 to 11% Al, balance Cu	Good hot working properties.	Gears, dies, non-sparking tools.
19. Cupronickel	Maximum 30% Ni, balance Cu	Higher resistance to corrosion, fatigue and erosion.	Condensers, distillators.
20. Constantan	Maximum 45% Ni, balance Cu	High electrical resistivitty.	Resistors and thermocouple wires.
21. Nickel silver or german silver	50 to 70% Cu, 5 to 30% Ni, 4 to 30% Zn	Good cold working property and high corrosion resistance.	Domestic table cutlery as an alternative to stainless steel.

6.23 ALUMINIUM AND ITS ALLOYS

Aluminium: (May 10)

It is the second most used non-ferrous metal. It is alloyed with silicon, copper and magnesium to improve its properties. Some of the important properties of aluminium are as follows:

- Aluminium is light in weight. It has low density (2.7 gm/cm^3), which is almost one-third that of iron (7.8 gm/cm^3).
- It has low melting point (660°C).
- It shows higher ductility and malleability.
- It shows better corrosion resistance because of formation of self-healing oxide film.
- It has a good heat and electrical conductivity.
- It can be cold or hot worked.
- Its strength can be increased by cold working.
- It has a good machinability.
- It is non-magnetic and non-sparking.
- It is a strong deoxidiser and grain refiner for steel.

Considering the above properties, aluminium is used for electrical conductors, cooking utensils, food containers, transportation industries, chemical storage equipment, structural frames for light loads etc.

Aluminium Alloys: (May 10, Dec. 09, 10, 11)

These are designated by LM (i.e. Light Metal) series. Aluminium alloys are classified as follows:

(A) Wrought aluminium alloys and (B) Cast aluminium alloys

OR (A) Heat-treatable aluminium alloys and (B) Non-heat treatable aluminium alloys.

Following are the important aluminium alloys:

- Aluminium-Copper alloys.
- Aluminium-Silicon alloys.
- Aluminium-Manganese alloys.
- Aluminium-Magnesium alloys.
- Aluminium-Silicon-Magnesium alloys.
- Aluminium-Zinc alloys.

(a) Aluminium-copper alloys:

Aluminium-copper equilibrium diagram with aluminium rich portion is shown in Fig. 6.8.

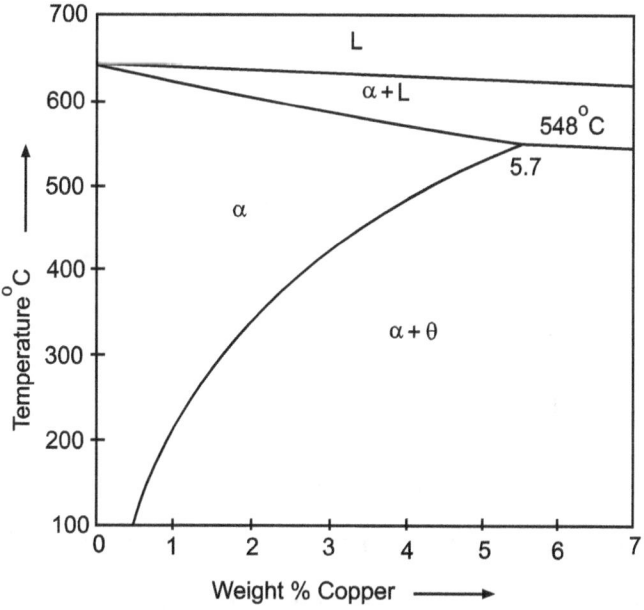

Fig. 6.8: Aluminium rich portion of the aluminium-copper equilibrium diagram

The maximum solubility of copper in aluminium is 5.7 per cent at 548°C and the solubility decreases to 0.5 per cent at the room temperature. Due to this, Al-Cu alloys (with 2.5 to 5% Cu) can be heat treated by precipitation hardening. Copper forms an intermediate theta (θ) phase as $CuAl_2$. The alloy is heated to single phase region followed by rapid cooling. This prevents precipitation of θ phase. The alloys remain in super-saturated condition. Natural or artificial aging allows slow precipitation of θ phase. This imparts hardness in alloy.

A typical precipitation hardenable alloy is duralumin (with 4% Cu). It shows good hardness, strength and forming properties. It is used in aircraft applications. Al-Cu alloy with 4.4 per cent copper, 0.8 per cent Mn and 0.8 per cent Si shows a high tensile strength and is used for aircraft fittings.

Al-Cu casting alloys contain 8 per cent copper, with 0.8 per cent silicon. They are used for flywheel, rear axle housing, bus wheels, crank cases etc.

(b) Aluminium-Silicon Alloys:

These are the alloys of aluminium and silicon containing silicon upto 12 per cent. Al-Si alloys are also called as *Silumin alloys*.

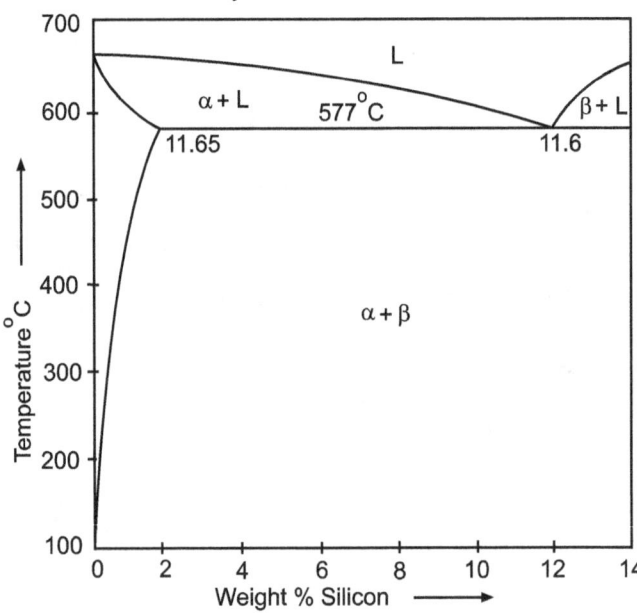

Fig. 6.9: Aluminium rich portion of aluminium-silicon equilibrium diagram

Fig. 6.9 shows aluminium-silicon equilibrium diagram with aluminium rich portion. The maximum solubility of silicon in α solid solution is 1.65 per cent at 577°C. An eutectic reaction is observed at 577°C with 11.6 per cent silicon. With increasing silicon, mechanical and casting properties are improved. In hypereutectic Al-Si alloys, a coarser eutectic is observed, which reduces its mechanical properties. The structure refinement is carried out by addition of modifying agents as metallic sodium in melt.

Following are some of the typical Al-Si alloys:

(1) **LM - 6:** It contains around 12 per cent Si. Due to its higher corrosion resistance and fluidity, it is used as castings in automobiles. It is used in water cooled manifolds for pump parts, intricate castings etc.

(2) **LM - 13:** It contains silicon upto 12.5%, 2.5% Ni, 1% Cu, 1.2% Mg. It shows good forgeability and low coefficient of thermal expansion. It is used for forged automobile pistons.

(c) Aluminium-Manganese Alloys:

Because of limited solubility (1.82%), manganese is not used as a major alloying element. With 1.2% Mn and 0.6% Si, Al-Mn alloys show good formability, resistance to corrosion and good weldability. It is used for food and chemical handling equipments.

(d) Aluminium-Magnesium Alloys:

Most of the Al-Mg alloys containing about 5% Mg (LM 5) are characterized by good weldability, corrosion resistance and strength. It is used for cable sheathing and other marine applications.

Al-Mg alloys with 3.5 to 8.0% Mg are used in dairy and food handling equipments due to their improved corrosion resistance.

Al-Mg alloy with 10.0% Mg (LM 10) is age hardenable. It shows the highest mechanical properties. It shows poor casting properties. It is used for aircrafts and automobile components.

Al-Mg alloy with 4% Cu, 2% Ni and 1.5% Mg is used for pistons and cylinder heads of internal combustion engine. It is called as Y-alloy or LM 14.

(e) Aluminium-Silicon-Magnesium Alloys:

These alloys have excellent corrosion resistance. They can be worked easily. They contain upto 0.6% Si and 1.0% Mg. They are used in aircraft landing mats, furniture, vacuum cleaner components etc.

(f) Aluminium-Zinc Alloys:

A typical wrought Al-Zn alloy contains 5.5% Zn, 2.5% Mg and 1.5% Cu. It has the highest tensile strength among all aluminium alloys. It is used in aircraft structural parts.

Some of the aluminium alloys with their compositions, properties and applications are tabulated in Table 6.3.

Table 6.3: Typical compositions, properties and applications of some aluminium alloys

(May 08, 09, 10; Dec. 08, 09, 10

	Alloys	Compositions	Properties	Applications
1.	Duralumin	4% Cu, balance Al	Good hardness, strength and age hardenable.	Aircraft industry.
2.	LM - 6	12% Si, balance Al	High corrosion resistance of fluidity.	Intricate castings for automobile and pump parts.
3.	LM - 13	12.5% Si, 2.5% Ni, 1% Cu, 1.2% Mg, balance Al	Good forgeability and low coefficient of thermal expansion.	Forged automobile pistons.
4.	LM - 5	5% Si, balance Al	Good weldability and corrosion resistance.	Cable sheathing and marine applications.
5.	LM - 10	10% Mg, balance Al	Properties-age hardenable and poor castability.	Aircraft and automobile component.
6.	Y-alloy	4% Cu, 2% Ni, 1.5% Mg, balance Al	Low thermal expansion.	Pistons and cylinder leads of I.C. engines.

6.4 NICKEL AND ITS ALLOYS   (May 08, 09)

Nickel shows good corrosion and oxidation resistance. It offers better formability. Nickel is used mainly for production of stainless steel. It is also used for electroplating. Due to its chemical inertness, it is also used for crucibles used in chemical laboratories. Nickel finds a unique application as screens in centrifuges used in sugar factories.

Following are the important nickel alloys:

(1) Dura nickel:

It can be mechanically worked and age hardened. It is a nickel aluminium alloy. It contains 93.90% Ni, 0.15% C, 0.25% Mn, 0.55% Si and 4.50% Al and Fe, S, Cu and Ti. It shows higher corrosion resistance and strength. It is used for diaphragms, bellows, snap-switch blades, fish hooks and parts of fishing tackle.

(2) Permanickel:

It contains higher nickel percentage (about 98.65%). It also contains other elements such as C, Mn, Fe, S, Si, Cu, Ti, Mg etc. It can be age hardened. It shows almost similar properties that of duranickel. It is used in preference to duranickel, where higher electrical conductivity and magnetic properties are required.

(3) Grade nickel:

Nickel is also available in the following grades with small additions of alloying elements:

(a) **A nickel:** 99% Ni (+ Cobalt) with Silicon, Fe, C, Mn.

- Used for vessels and evaporators in chemical industries.

(b) **D Nickel:** 95% Ni (+ Co), 4.75% Mn, Fe, C, Si, Cu.

- Used for spark plug wires and contact wires in furnace.

(4) Monel:

It is a nickel-copper alloy.

A wrought monel alloy contains 66% Ni (+ Co), 30% Cu with Fe and Mn. While a cast monel contains 64% Ni (+ Co), 30% Cu, 2% Si and other elements. Silicon improves fluidity.

Monel has a high corrosion resistance to acids and alkalies. It shows improved properties over copper alloys. Following are the types of Monel:

(a) **R Monel (with sulphur):** Used for automatic screw machine work.

(b) **K Monel (with 3% Al):** Used for marine pump parts, aircraft instruments.

(c) **H Monel (with 3% Si):** Used for valve seats.

(d) **S Monel (with 4% Si):** Pump liners etc.

(5) Electrical-Resistance Alloys (Nichrome):

Following are the important nickel alloys used as electrical resistant alloys:

(a) **80% Ni, 20% Cr:** Used as electrical heating elements for domestic ovens and industrial furnaces.

(b) **60% Ni, 16% Cr, 24% Fe:** Used as electrical heating elements for toasters, irons, heater pads etc.

(c) **35% Ni, 20% Cr, 45% Fe:** Used for heavy duty rheostats.

(6) Inconel:

It contains 76% Ni, 16% Cr, 8% Fe. It has good corrosion resistance, strength and toughness. It shows high temperature oxidation resistance. It is used in heaters, regenerators and dairy equipments. It is also used for retorts, containers and muffle used in furnace.

(7) Inconel X:

It contains 2.50% Ti and about 1% Al with usual Inconel. It is age hardenable Inconel. It shows high temperature strength. It is used in gas turbine supercharger and jet propulsion parts.

(8) Hastelloy:

These are nickel, chromium, molybdenum and iron based alloys. Following are the types of hastelloy and their uses:

(a) Hastelloy A: Used in chemical industry as containers (60% Ni, 20% Mo, 20% Fe).

(b) Hastelloy B: Used as above (62% Ni, 28% Mo, 5% Fe).

(c) Hastelloy C: Used for pump and valve parts, spray nozzles etc. (54% Ni, 17% Mo, 15% Cr, 5% Fe, 4% W).

(d) Hastelloy X: Used for aircraft parts as jet engine tail pipes (47% Ni, 9% Mo, 22% Cr, 18% Fe).

(9) Invar:

It is Nickel-iron alloy with 35% nickel. Invar means invariable. It does not show changes in dimensions with a change in temperature. It has a very low coefficient of thermal expansion.

It is used for measuring instruments like scales, verniers etc.

(10) Kovar:

It contains 28% Ni, 18% Co, 54% Fe. It has a coefficient of expansion similar to glass. It is used in the production of glass to metal seals.

(11) Elinvar:

It contains 36% Ni and 12% Cr with balance iron. It has almost negligible elastic changes with changes in temperature. It is used in watches for making hair springs and balance wheels.

(12) Permalloy:

It is also nickel and iron alloy. It contains around 7.8% nickel. It has a higher magnetic permeability (ten times that of iron). It possesses lower electric resistivity. It is used in apparatus operating in weak magnetic fields as radio and telecommunications. It is mainly used as magnetic soft material.

(13) Perminvars:

It contains 45% Ni, 25% Co, balance Fe. It has a constant magnetic permeability, which does not vary with variations in the magnetic field. It is used in various electrical coils, instruments and communication systems.

(14) Alnico:

It contains 8 to 10% Al, 15 to 30% Ni, 5 to 30% Co with Fe. It has high magnetic properties. It is used to make powerful magnets.

Permanent magnets are made by powder metallurgy method using Al, Ni and Fe.

It finds applications in motors, generators, microphones, speakers etc.

(15) Superalloys:

The nickel-base superalloys contain cobalt, iron, molybdenum, chromium, tungsten and aluminium. They exhibit higher strength and hardness at elevated temperatures and hence, they are used in gas and jet turbines, turbochargers and other power generating systems.

One of the typical examples of super alloys is 'TD-Nickel'. It contains 2% ThO_2 (Thoria) uniformly dispersed in a matrix of 98% Ni.

Some of the nickel alloys with their compositions, properties and applications are tabulated in Table 6.4.

Table 6.4: Typical compositions, properties and applications of some nickel alloys

	Alloys	Compositions	Properties	Applications
1.	Duranickel	93.9% Ni, 0.15% C, 0.25% Mn, 0.55% Si, 4.5% Al with Fe, S, Cu, Ti.	High corrosion resistance and age hardenable.	Diaphragms, snap switch blades, fish hooks.
2.	Permanickel	98.65% Ni, with C, Mn, Fe, S, Si, Cu, Ti, Mg.	Age hardenable.	Used instead of duranickel, where higher electrical conductivity and magnetic properties are required.

... Contd.

3.	Monel	66% Ni (+ Co), 30% Cu, with Fe and Mn.	High corrosion resistance and strength.	Marine pump parts, aircraft instruments.
4.	Electrical resistant alloys	80% Ni, 20% Cr.	Higher electrical resistivity.	Heating elements for domestic ovens and industrial furnaces.
5.	Inconel	76% Ni, 16% Cr, 8% Fe.	Good corrosion resistance, oxidation resistance and strength.	Retorts, containers and muffles for furnace.
6.	Inconel - X	2.5% Ti, 1% Al with Inconel.	Age hardenable and good high temperature strength.	Gas turbine, supercharger and jet propulsion parts.
7.	Hastelloy - A	50% Ni, 20% Mo, 20% Fe.	High corrosion resistance.	Containers in chemical industries.
8.	Invar	35% Ni, balance Fe.	Dimensional stability at different temperatures, low coefficient of thermal expansion.	Measuring instruments as verniers, scales etc.
9.	Covar	28% Ni, 18% Co, 54% Fe.	Coefficient of expansion similar to glass.	Glass to metal seals.
10.	Elinvar	36% Ni, 12% Cr, balance Fe.	Constant elasticity with temperature changes.	Hair springs and balance wheels in watches.
11.	Premalloy	78% Ni, balance Fe.	High magnetic permeability, low electric resistivity.	Radio and telecommunication as magnetic soft material.
12.	Perminvars	45% Ni, 25% Co, balance Fe.	Constant magnetic permeability with varying magnetic field.	Electrical coils and communication instruments.
13.	Alnico	8 to 10% Al, 15 to 30% Ni, 5 to 30% Co, balance Fe.	Good magnetic properties.	As permanent magnets in microphones, speakers and motors.
14.	Superalloys	Co, Fe, Mo, Cr, W, Al, with Fe.	Hot strength and red hardness.	Gas and jet turbines, turbocharger.

6.5 LEAD AND ITS ALLOYS

Lead:

Lead is also one of the metals widely used in engineering applications.

Lead exhibits following properties:

- It is a heavy weight metal. Its specific gravity is 11.34 gm/cm^3.
- It has a low melting point (327°C).
- It is very soft, ductile and malleable.
- It has high corrosion resistance, low electrical conductivity and high coefficient of expansion.
- It's radiation absorbing power is very high.
- It cannot be strain hardened by cold working at room temperature, since, its recrystallization temperature is below room temperature.
- It shows higher corrosion resistance to chemicals and atmosphere.

Lead is mainly used:

- For radiation shielding.
- For cable sheathing.
- In the manufacture of storage batteries.
- In production of paints.
- For weights in counter balance.
- As drawing lubricants.
- It is also used in copper alloys and steels to improve machinability.
- It finds application as inert anode in electroplating of some metals.

Lead Alloys:

Following are some of the important lead alloys:

(A) Lead – antimony alloys, (B) Lead-tin alloys, (C) Lead, bismuth, tin, antimony and cadmium eutectic alloys and (D) Lead, tin-antimony alloys.

(A) Lead-Antimony Alloys: Antimony is commonly used as an alloying element with lead. The lead-antimony equilibrium diagram is shown in Fig. 6.10. This is a typical eutectic system. The eutectic reaction is observed with 11.2% antimony at 250°C. The recrystallization temperature of lead increases with addition of antimony. The hardness and tensile strength gets increased with antimony. Antimony is added upto 12%. This alloy is used mostly in lead storage batteries. Due to its ductility, it can be coated on cables. It is also used in collapsible tubes.

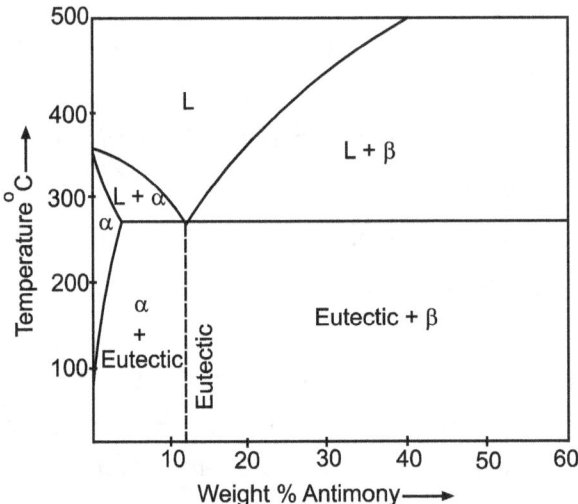

Fig. 6.10: Lead rich portion of lead-antimony equilibrium diagram

(B) Lead-Tin Alloys: Tin is another commonly used alloying element. Fig. 6.11 shows lead-tin equilibrium diagram. This is also an eutectic system. The eutectic reaction occurs at 183°C with 61.9% tin. Tin increases hardness and strength. These alloys are used as solders due to their low temperature melting and flowing properties. Following are the typical solder metals:

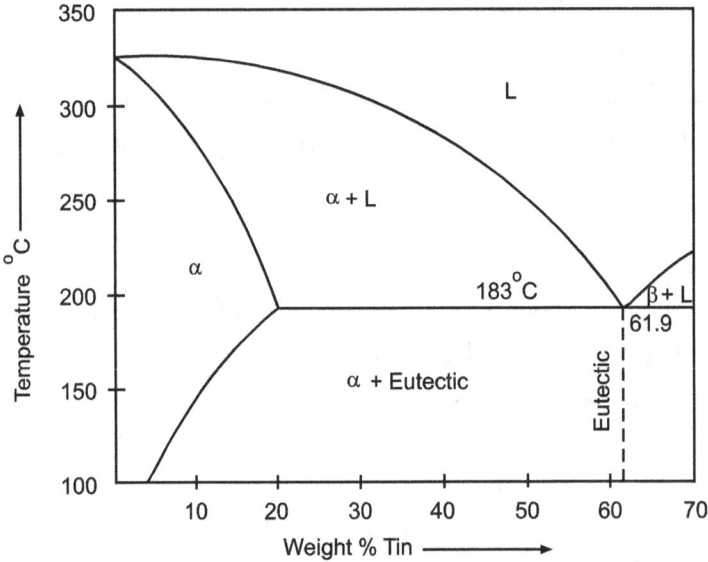

Fig. 6.11: Lead-tin equilibrium diagram

(i) **Tinman's solder:** It contains 62% tin. Due to its eutectic nature, it solidifies at a constant temperature and shows good wettability. Therefore, it is used for soldering electronic components.

(ii) **Plumber's solder:** It contains 20 to 40% tin. As it deviates from eutectic temperature, it does not get solidified at a constant temperature. It remains in a mushy (semi-solid) stage for a long time. This pasty nature of alloy helps a plumber for joining the pipes. Therefore, it is called as Plumber's solder.

(iii) **Terne metal:** It contains 10 to 25% tin. It is used for coating steel sheets in order to improve its corrosion resistance.

(C) Lead, bismuth tin, antimony and cadmium eutectic alloys (Fusible alloys): These are eutectic alloys of lead, bismuth, tin, antimony and cadmium. These alloys usually show very low melting points as low as 60 to 80°C. They are used as safety guards in various equipments and machinery. Their main uses are - electric safety fuses, boiler and pressure cooker plugs. They are also used in fire protection equipments.

One of the commonly used fusible alloy is Wood's alloy. It contains – 50% Bi, 25% Pb, 12.5% Sn and 12.5% Cd.

(D) Lead-Tin-Antimony Alloys: These alloys are called as *Type Metals*. It contains lead 60 to 95%, 2 to 25% Sb and 2 – 7% Sn. It has a low melting point and good fluidity. It expands during solidification and can take all details in die sharply. Therefore, it is used as a type metal. These types are used as letters for printing. After being used for a long time, these types ware out. Due to their low melting point and castability, they can be remelted and reused.

Some of the lead based alloys are tabulated in Table 6.5.

Table 6.5: Typical compositions, properties and applications of some lead alloys

	Alloys	Compositions	Properties	Applications
1.	Tinman's solder	62% Sn, balance Pb.	Eutectic, good wettability, low melting temperature.	As solder in electronic components.
2.	Plumber's solder	20 to 40% Sn, balance Pb.	Remains pasty during solidification.	Plumbing work as joining of pipes.
3.	Terne metal	10 to 25% Sn, balance Pb.	Good corrosion resistance.	For coating steel sheets.
4.	Fusible alloy (Wood's alloy)	50% Bi, 25% Pb, 12.5% Sn, 12.5% Cd.	Low melting point and eutectic.	Safety fuses for boiler and pressure cooker.
5.	Type metal	60 to 95% Pb, 2 to 25% Sb, 2 to 7% Sn.	Low melting point, good fluidity, higher die casting properties.	For types used in letter printing.

6.6 TIN AND ITS ALLOYS

Following are some of the important properties of tin:

- It is a white coloured, soft metal.
- It has good corrosion resistance.
- It's melting point is 232°C.
- It's density is 7.3 gm/cm^3 and
- It undergoes polymorphic transformation from tetragonal to cubic structure. This results in decrease in density from 7.3 to 5.75. Due to this expansion, metallic tin gets disintegrated to coarse powder known as tin pest or tin plauge.

Tin is used in the following applications:

- Pure tin is used in electrotinning and as alloying element.
- Hear tin (with 0.4% Cu) is used for making wrapping foils and collapsible tubes.
- Tin is used with other metals as solder alloys.
- Tin alloy, called 'Pewter' (with 7% Sb, 2% Cu and balance Sn) is used in candlesticks.
- Tin alloys are used for bearings.

6.7 BEARING MATERIALS   (Dec, 07, 08, 13; May 10)

These are antifriction materials used as rotating shaft holders and supporters. These are required in construction of machinery, engines or any rotating and reciprocating parts.

Bearings are classified as:

- Sliding bearing,
- Rolling bearing, and
- Thrust bearing.

Bearing alloys include:

- Babbits,
- Bronzes,
- Silver-lead alloys,
- Aluminium alloys, and
- Cast irons etc.

Requirements for Bearings:

If the rotating parts are properly lubricated, the bearing and shaft can work without any problem. However, if insufficient quantity of lubricant is used, excessive heats is generated and wear of surface occurs due to friction between shaft bearings. Therefore, a bearing material should essentially possess the following properties:

- It should have a higher compressive strength. It should not get deformed under working heavy loads.
- It should be hard enough and wear resistant to provide longer life.
- It should have enough plasticity and deformability to sustain large deflection of shaft.
- It should have high fatigue strength.
- It should exhibit antisiezing properties.
- It should possess better thermal conductivity for heat dissipation.
- It should have enough corrosion resistance.
- It should be able to retain oil on the surface.
- It should have a good machinability.
- Metallurgically, it should have a combination of hard and soft phases.

For bearing material homogeneous material is not suitable. A heterogeneous material, more than one phase, which differs in properties e.g. combination of hard phase in soft matrix, is preferred as bearing material. The soft phase wears out forming a film on the surface. The surface area becomes rough and increases its oil retaining capacity. With increasing working load, the hard phase gets pressed into soft matrix. Here, soft matrix works as cushion. The bearing can sustain more load in this case. Therefore, instead of a homogeneous material, a heterogeneous polyphase material is preferred for bearings.

1. White metal or Babbits: (Dec, 07, 08, May 11, 12)

These are also called as low-melting bearing alloys. Lead based or tin based babbits containing antimony are most popular from this group.

- Lead based: 1 - 10% Sn, 10 - 15% Sb, 1.5 - 3.5% Cu, 1 - 1.7% Cd, 1.0% As and balance Pb.
- Tin based: Upto 10% Pb, 5 - 12% Sb, 3 - 5% Cu, 0.1% As.

Copper is added to babbit, to eliminate the problem of segregation. This problem arises due to difference in the density of the compounds Sn - Sb and Cu_3Sn. The micro-structure (Fig. 6.12) of a typical tin based babbit consists of:

- Cube-shaped particles (cuboids) of Sn - Sb compound,
- Needle shaped particles of Cu - Sn or Cu_6 - Sn_5,
- Star shaped particles of Cu_3 - Sn and
- Ternary eutectic of Cu-Sn - Sb.

If copper is not added, hard Sn - Sb cuboids float on surface during solidification. This creates hard surface and soft-core. With copper addition, Cu - Sn needles form a network, which prevents floating of cuboids.

This fulfils one of the requirements of bearing material, that is a combination of hard phase and soft matrix.

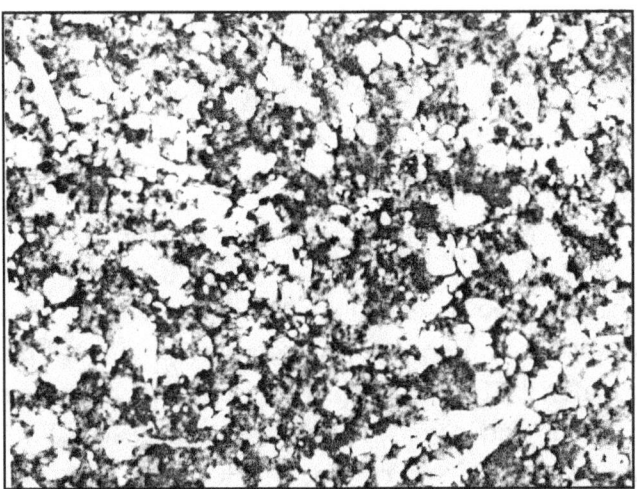

Fig. 6.12: Microstructure of Babbit (200 X)

Babbits containing a large amount of tin are suitable for bearings used in high power machinery such as steam turbines and turbo superchargers.

Lead based babbits consist of crystals of solid solution of Sn in Sb and chemical compound of CuSb. The eutectic Pb-Sb is a soft matrix. It is used in the bearings of I.C. engines, lathe machines, milling and shaping machines, fans, electric motors etc.

Lead based babbits show higher coefficient of expansion. They are not used under high loads as they contain more brittle eutectic.

Lead calcium babbits are the cheapest babbits used in rail road application.

2. Copper lead alloys:

They contain 20 to 40 per cent lead. They are manufactured by powder metallurgy or by casting process. They are used as steel backed bearing produced by casting. They are used in automotive and aircraft applications.

3. Tin bronzes:

These are copper based alloys containing 5 to 20% tin. Due to presence of residual phosphorus, they are also termed as phosphorbronzes. With addition of zinc, it is called as gun metal. All these are bearing metals recommended for heavy loads i.e. preference to babbits.

4. Aluminium alloys:

These alloys exhibit high corrosion resistance, fatigue strength, high compressive strength, good wear resistance and higher thermal conductivity. They contain Ni, Fe, Si and Cu etc. Their microstructure consists of fine particles of tin, $NiAl_3$ and $CuAl_2$ in the matrix of aluminium solid solution. These bearings are suitable for shafts rotating at high speeds and with high loads. They are used for connecting rods and main bearings in engines.

5. Silver bearings:

Steel bearings are plated with silver and then with lead to improve anti-seizing properties. They possess high fatigue strength and corrosion resistance. They are used for heavy loads in aircraft industry.

6. Self-lubricated bearings:

These bearings are manufactured by powder metallurgical methods. Copper-tin or iron-graphite powders are mixed, pressed and sintered. As powder metallurgical parts have a higher porosity, the bearings made by this method possess 40 to 50% porosity. These pores are capable of holding oil. They are impregnated with oil under pressure. They do not require external lubrication. Therefore, they are termed as self-lubricating bearings. The shafts are mounted on such bearings. During rotation of a shaft, oil comes out from pores. Oil forms a film on the surface of bearing. This prevents direct contact of shaft and bearing. When the shaft stops rotating, the oil gets sucked in the pores back. This prevents wastage of lubricating oil. These bearings are widely used, where external lubrication is not possible and permissible, e.g. in food, paper and textile industries.

7. Gray cast iron:

The micro-structure of gray cast iron consists of graphite flakes in ferrite and/or pearlite matrix. The graphite is very soft phase and behaves as a solid lubricant. Phosphatising improves properties of gray cast iron. These bearings are easy to cast, machine and involve low cost. These bearings are used in refrigerators, compressors and railway cars.

8. Non-metallic bearings:

These are also called as dry and anticorrosive bearings. Nylon, teflon, graphite, molybdenum disulphide are non-metallic materials used for bearings. Graphite dispersed aluminium is also used for bearings.

These are used, where external lubrication is not possible and permissible; e.g. food, paper, textile industry.

Table 6.6 gives applications of various bearing materials.

Table 6.6: Applications of various bearing materials

	Bearing material	Applications
(a)	Tin based babbits	Steam turbines turbo-supercharger.
(b)	Lead based babbits	I.C. engine, lathe and milling machines, fans, electric motors.
(c)	Lead calcium babbits	Rail road applications.
(d)	Copper-lead alloys	Automotive and aircraft industry.
(e)	Tin bronzes	Heavy load bearings.
(f)	Aluminium alloys	Connecting rod and main bearings of engine.
(g)	Silver bearings	Heavy load bearings in aircraft industry.
(h)	Self-lubricated bearings	Food, paper and textile industry.
(i)	Gray cast iron	Bearings in refrigeration compressors and railway cars.
(j)	Non-metallic bearings (nylon, teflon and graphite)	Food, paper and textile industry.

Noble Metals:

These metals are placed at extreme cathodic end of galvanic series. These are also called as precious metals. They have a group of eight elements including gold, silver, platinum, palladium, iridium, rhodium, ruthenium and osmium. All of them have some common properties as softness, high electrical conductivity and corrosion resistance. Silver and its alloys are used in photographic application, plating, reflectors, jewellery and dental restoration material. Gold and its alloys are used for coins, jewellery, electroplating, thermal limit fuses etc.

Platinum is used as chemical crucibles, thermocouple, electrical contacts, dental foils and catalyst.

QUESTIONS

1. State whether true or false and justify.

    (a) α-brasses are cold worked, while α + β brasses are hot worked.

    (b) Muntz metal is also called as leaded brass.

    (c) Tin bronzes are often referred as phosphor bronzes.

    (d) Beryllium bronzes cannot be precipitation hardened.

    (e) Aluminium bronzes can be hardened similar to steels.

    (f) Copper-nickel alloy of any composition shows a single phase structure.

    (g) Nickel-silver alloys contain a very small amount of silver.

    (h) Duralumin is used in aircraft fittings.

    (i) Invar is used for making measuring scales.

    (j) Plumber solder and tinmann's solder can be used for soldering purposes.

    (k) A homogeneous material is more suitable for bearing applications rather than a heterogeneous material.

    (l) Teflon is used in food industries as a bearing material.

    Ans.:

(a) True	(b) False	(c) True	(d) False	(e) True	(f) True
(g) False	(h) True	(i) True	(j) False	(k) False	(l) True

2. What is brass ? Explain the difference between alpha and alpha plus beta brass.

3. In which respect are the brasses different from bronzes ?

4. What is plastic bronze ? Where it is used ?

5. How is the strength of silicon bronzes increased ?

6. Explain any two copper-nickel alloys with respect to their compositions, properties and applications.

7. Which is the major area of applications of Nickel alloy ? Why ?

8. What are the important applications of lead ?

9. Why are most of the lead alloys used as solder metal or fusible alloy ? Give a typical example of each.

10. What are the requirements of bearing material ?

11. Draw a microstructure of babbit and explain various phases.

12. Which are the various non-metallic bearings ? What is their unique advantage over other bearings ? Give their applications.

13. Give compositions, properties and typical applications of the following non-ferrous alloys:

(a) Gilding metal	(g) Nickel-Silver
(b) Tobin bronze	(h) Nickel-Superalloys
(c) Manganese bronze	(i) Duralumin
(d) Leaded gun metal	(j) Hastelloy
(e) Silicon bronze	(k) Wood's alloy
(f) Cupro-Nickel	(l) Permalloy
	(m) Type metal

UNIVERSITY QUESTIONS

1. What is bearing material ? How is it classified ?   **(Dec. 08)**

2. Compare the properties of steel and cast iron.   **(Dec. 09)**

3. Write note: Manufacturing of ferritic malleable cast iron from white cast iron.

(Dec. 09)

4. What is effect of C, Si and cooling rate on microstructure and properties of cast iron ? How are they controlled ?   **(May 10)**

5. Classify various Aluminium alloys. What is the effect of alloying element on properties of Aluminium ? What are applications of pure aluminium.   **(May 10)**

6. What is LM series ? Explain LM - 6 and LM - 5.   **(Dec. 09)**

7. Give compositions, properties and typical applications of the following non-ferrous alloys:

    (a) Cartridge brass

    (May 08, 11, Dec. 09)

    (b) Aluminium brass

    (Dec. 08, May 10)

    (c) Muntz metal **(May 10)**

    (d) Beryllium bronze **(May 10)**

    (e) Y-alloy **(Dec. 08)**

    (f) Dura-nickel **(Dec. 09)**

    (g) Monel **(Dec. 09)**

    (h) Elinvar **(Dec. 08)**

    (k) Invar **(Dec. 08)**

    (i) Babbit **(Dec. 08, May 11)**

    (j) Naval brass **(Dec. 08)**

    (l) Turbine blade **(May 08)**

    (m) Admiraly brass **(May 11)**

    (n) Gun metal **(May 11, May 09, Dec. 10, May 10)**

    (o) Cosume jwellery **(May 09)**

    (p) Measuring tape **(May 09)**

    (r) Bell **(May 09)**

    (s) Aircraft component **(May 09)**

    (t) Bearing **(May 09)**

    (u) Non-sparking tool **(May 09)**

8. Differentiate between brass and bronze.   **(Dec. 10, May 11)**

9. Explain Al-Si phase diagram.   **(Dec. 10)**

❑❑❑